S

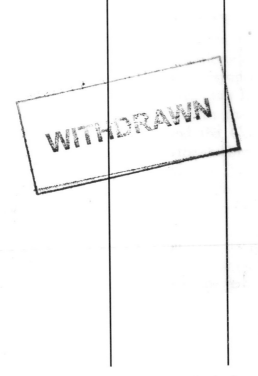

By *Amanda Craig*

A Private Place

A Vicious Circle

In a Dark Wood

Love in Idleness

Hearts and Minds

The Other Side of You

The Lie of the Land

The Golden Rule

FOREIGN BODIES

AMANDA CRAIG

ABACUS

First published in Great Britain in 1990 by Century Hutchinson
This paperback edition published in 2022 by Abacus

1 3 5 7 9 10 8 6 4 2

A CIP catalogue record for this book
is available from the British Library.

ISBN 978-0-349-14504-4

Typeset in Goudy by M Rules
Printed and bound in Great Britain by
Clays Ltd, Elcograf S.p.A.

Papers used by Abacus are from well-managed forests
and other responsible sources.

Abacus
An imprint of
Little, Brown Book Group
Carmelite House
50 Victoria Embankment
London EC4Y 0DZ

An Hachette UK Company
www.hachette.co.uk

www.littlebrown.co.uk

To my mother and father

'Then first did I begin rightly to see the wide
difference that lies between the novelist's and
the poet's ideal *jeune fille* and the said *jeune
fille* as she really is'

CHARLOTTE BRONTË, *Villette*

... 'I am no child, no babe.
Your betters have endured me say my mind,
An' you cannot, best you stop your ears.
My tongue will tell the anger of my heart
Or else my heart, concealing it, will break;
And rather than it shall, I will be free
Even to the uttermost, as I please, in words.'

The Taming of the Shrew
IV. iii

Acknowledgements

I would like to thank Emily Patrick and Susanna Fiennes for their advice as to how a painter might develop, Rod and Conrad Williams for help with story structure, Alice Thomas Ellis, Imogen Parker and Robyn Sisman for believing in difficult women, and my husband Rob for marrying one.

Acknowledgements

Foreword

'I do not write for such dull Elves
As have not a great deal of Ingenuity themselves.'

Jane Austen, 29 January 1813

Foreign Bodies has been out of print for over thirty years, and despite some trepidation I have agreed to have it republished, partly because it is the first in my series of interconnected novels, partly because I have returned to Santorno in my next novel, *The Three Graces*, and partly because I believe that the story of its disastrous publication might be of interest.

To create an unsympathetic or challenging protagonist is a tricky choice at the best of times. I was in my twenties when I wrote and rewrote *Foreign Bodies*. Being the generation below Martin Amis, I thought that writing about a difficult young woman rather than a difficult young man would be fun and original. I named my heroine after two famous literary Emmas, those of Jane Austen and Flaubert; I was thinking of Jane

Austen's disarming warning about her Emma as "a heroine whom nobody but myself will like", but I did not expect this to be so painfully true.

My background is liberal, cosmopolitan and not at all that of my creation. I grew up in Italy, and I know it as a real place. However, by the 1990s, Tuscany had become a kind of upper-middle class Disneyland. John Mortimer had written an amusing comedy, Summer's Lease, set in it, and Merchant Ivory's lush, dreamy films had revived interest in both E. M. Forster's *A Room With a View* and *Where Angels Fear to Tread*. Elizabeth von Arnim's *The Enchanted April*, also about a transformation via "sunshine and wisteria" was being filmed. Once again, the hills were alive with New Romantics trailing through olive groves.

I wanted both to satirise this type but also to depict someone who is, despite her preconceptions, does have an eventual future as a painter. In making Emma quite so opinionated and over-determined (these being typical of someone who is actually quite frightened) I thought I was depicting an interesting and unusual protagonist.

A number of other new women writers were also working on iterations of this kind of heroine. Some, like Jeanette Winterson, Candia McWilliam, Helen Simpson, Linda Grant. Mary Wesley and Helen Dunmore were exploring being ambitious, intellectual, ethnically diverse or sexually adventurous. Despite living through the second wave of feminism, women in the 1990s were still not supposed to behave like this. Ideally, what got rewarded in the literary world was someone who, despite her intelligence, was as meek and miserable as an Anita Brookner heroine. (The bonkbuster minxes of the 1980s were, of course, riotous fun but exacerbated this problem because a literary heroine had to sweep her skirts away from their polluting touch.) Above all, they had to be *nice*.

I wanted to write about a young woman who was in rebellion against conventions. To me, she was a variation on Forster's Lucy Honeychurch in *A Room With a View*, someone who also had an artistic gift (painting rather than music), a contrary temper, a tempting offer (Oxford rather than marriage) and a series of dramatic, life-changing experiences in Italy. I made Emma obnoxious but, I hoped, funny and sympathetic.

Alas, no. Even before publication, Foreign Bodies received a long and hostile review in a Sunday broadsheet that killed it stone dead. It claimed that I had written a novel like that of the appalling Miss Lavish, E. M. Forster's silly romantic novelist in *A Room With a View*. Emma's character was considered violently objectionable, and my deliberate riffs on Forster naively cliched. My novel was derided as "pricelessly funny", its ironies being perceived as inadvertent. Another critic loftily quoted Plato that "the unexamined life is not worth living", as if the whole point of Emma's story were not that she does indeed come to examine her choices as she is propelled towards enlightenment.

A debut novel is unlike any other experience in a writer's life. I did have a couple of good, small reviews including one by the columnist Zoe Heller, and Kate Saunders, (who became a close friend and a prize-winning writer) but they were exceptional. The overwhelming consensus was that it was a bad book because I had created a snotty heroine, and I was probably an appalling person myself for so doing.

The shock of receiving what felt like a deluge of antipathy in the national press may be more familiar today to those who fall foul of social media. I was extremely unhappy for a long time. But I also wrote my second novel *A Private Place* (1991), set in a progressive school very much like the one where I had experienced five years of relentless bullying. It did better; and then I wrote my satire on literary London, *A Vicious Circle*, which was a best-seller.

Half the battle of being a professional writer is just keeping on keeping on. I was lucky enough to eventually find a wonderful new publisher, Richard Beswick at Little, Brown. My novels, though they can each be read on their own, are interconnected with minor characters becoming major ones, and the more people enjoy one the more they tend to relish the rest. But over the years, many devoted readers have complained that the first one was out of print and expensively rare. Because Emma has continued in my imagination all this time, I thought I would write what happened to her, and Andrew Evenlode, and some of the characters in my fictional Tuscan hill-town in the intervening years.

Foreign Bodies is as flawed a work of fiction as you might expect from a young writer, and these days, when explicit sex-scenes and depictions of coercive control are rather more usual in literary fiction, it even may be anodyne. Yet there have always been readers who understand that a novel that begins with its narrator running away from home and slamming the front door on her cloak might just be a comedy, albeit one involving murder and a love story. At any rate, here is Emma Kenward again, sticking out her chin and preparing to confront her future.

Amanda Craig, October 2021

Running away from home, I slammed the front door on my cloak and had to ring the bell to be released.

Perhaps I should have left it there and rushed on into the frozen morning, regardless. Perhaps I should have known that no new stage in one's life is achieved without pain, humiliation and murder of one sort or another. But, in my fury, I did not consider this. That cloak was the first garment I had bought of my own choice, with my own money. It was, I felt, a declaration of independence, a property of the adult I wished to become. It had been the pretext for the most colossal row of all, and I was damned if I was going to leave it. Besides, I was itching for the last word.

'Bloody hell,' I said, and rang the bell again. Every other window of Stanhope Square was curdled with ruched curtains; I had the feeling that a hundred eyes were watching. My mother's heels jabbed across the parquet inside.

'Oh,' she said, sweetly, 'I was hoping it might be the Jehovah's Witnesses.'

'I'm leaving,' I informed her, whisking myself free. 'Really?' She sounded bored. 'Where to?'

'I left a note.'

'Don't tell me – on the mantel?'

'Yes,' I admitted.

'But darling,' said my mother, with a malicious smile, 'I thought you despised conventions.'

This was a palpable hit. 'That's right,' I said. 'Go ahead and sneer. It's your last chance. You may even find you miss me when I've gone.'

'Where did you say you were off too?'

'Guess.'

I wanted to see her squirm, at least in ignorance.

My mother circumflected her eyebrows. I could see she thought I was trying it on. What made me even angrier was that, in the back of my mind, I had been hoping for some sort of last-minute reconciliation or apology so that I wouldn't have to leave, at least not like this.

'Italy,' I told her. 'Tuscany, in fact.'

'My dear, how charming, revisiting our old haunts. If you'd said Balham, or Birmingham, now ...'

'I would still be away from you, you menopausal old bitch.'

We were both taken aback by my venom. My jaw began to ache with the effort not to burst into tears. My mother showed no such sign of weakness; indeed, she was smiling her infuriating, superior little smile. This, I reminded myself, was the woman who gave me a book on Rubens, the painter I most loathe and despise, for Christmas.

'If you're going to go,' she said at last, 'you'd better hurry up. You may have time to lounge around all day, but I have better things to do. I don't suppose there's some chap in tow, is there? No, I thought not. That will relieve your father, even if I'd take it as a welcome sign of normality.'

We had both gone too far now. I stared at the hat stand in the hall, bristling like a domesticated Medusa, and said, 'You can think what you bloody well like, but I'm leaving England, I'm not going to Oxford to be taught by that horrible man, and I never, ever, want to see any of you again.'

I turned, swept up my cloak in one hand, lifted my suitcase in the other, and staggered down the steps. Behind me, the door clicked shut. She had not even bothered to say goodbye.

'Good riddance!' I said loudly, hoping the rest of the Square was listening. There was a faint pattering, as if of applause from a distant audience. It began to rain.

At the Underground I squelched, trembling, to a map on the wall to find Heathrow. Being petrified of public transport and hopeless at understanding diagrams, I either take taxis or walk everywhere. The only places I knew how to get to were the National Gallery, Sloane Square and St Pancras Station; any deviation from these routes I found as frightening as a medieval mariner venturing into dragon-infested waters. It wasn't that I was incurious, quite the contrary, but I found the whole business of dealing with shop assistants, bus conductors, tourists or just casual passers-by so intimidating that even walking to the local newsagents was an ordeal which made the soles of my feet perspire.

To my relief, the tube was, unlike so much else, accessible to logic, and I was able to collapse onto the hideous tartans of the right train. I examined my reflection in the darkened glass of the window opposite, convinced that I must have undergone some physical change as a result of stress. Distorted, I looked, quite literally, beside myself; otherwise, I was disappointed to note, my face appeared much the same.

Would I ever escape plainness? This, the banal preoccupation of most adolescents, as I was all too aware from reading tales of angst and acne in magazines at school, was of particular importance to me. I cannot bear plain people.

I know it's wrong. I know people can't help what they look like (though I'm often tempted to suggest plastic surgery to

3

perfect strangers) and that people's faces do not necessarily reflect their true natures, but I couldn't believe it. It stood to reason that people who habitually wore pleasant expressions would develop different muscles in their faces to those who were unpleasant. People who led dull lives must, I believed, eventually wake up to the sort of faces they deserved, just as people who led a life of passion or intellect would bear definite physical traces of it on their countenance.

It was therefore intensely irritating to me that, instead of the haggard, ascetic face I felt should correspond to the passions that boiled beneath my skull, my own face resembled one drawn on an egg.

I was, I thought despondently, utterly without distinction. No cheekbones had started to emerge from the bland oval of my countenance. My nose, a neat but indistinct blob, denoted nothing but the necessity of breathing; my mouth was neither generously large nor interestingly mean. My eyes are that most dismal and English of colours, grey. Being fair, I gave the impression of lacking both eyebrows and lashes: so far, any attempt to give these definition with the aid of cosmetics had resulted in an appearance so maniacally artificial as to render the exercise pointless. My hair, though long and blonde, looked like a hank of sheep's wool. I had the two things most privileged children acquire: clear skin and good teeth. I also have a chin. My chin is my great consolation. When I am frightened or unhappy, which is often, I am told I raise it as if to meet an invisible fist.

As to the rest of me, I tried to look at it as seldom as possible. Women are continually admonished, in the interests of health and narcissism, to examine every inch, but I found the notion appalling. The last time I had taken a good look at my body, it had been not only lumpy but covered in jagged red weals, as if some monster were trying to claw its way out from inside. The

4

sight had been so shocking that I resolved from that moment on to treat anything below my neck as a kind of parasitical appendage and felt much better for so doing.

The tube emerged into daylight – if you could call a January morning in suburbia that – and I kept my spirits up by imagining I had a laser gun designed to strafe every building erected after 1840. This was so cheering that at the airport I was able to demand a ticket for the next flight to Rome with what I felt was cosmopolitan self-assurance.

My suitcase moved away on the conveyor belt. Along just such a mechanical Styx my grandfather had glided off six months ago into the crematorium flames. He had left me £3,000 in his will, and given me the only piece of advice that I had ever found remotely useful.

'Look for the darkest dark and the lightest light,' he told me. 'Find the extremes in any situation, and hang on to them for dear life. They are the only truths you can be certain of, and once you've found them, everything else becomes relative.'

There had been quarrels over the money, as over everything else. My parents were shocked at his leaving me such a sum – laughably small though it was to them. To me, it seemed a fortune. Perhaps I should explain that my parents, like many wealthy people, do not believe in giving their offspring any allowance that could constitute a degree of independence. This was thought to be 'spoiling', especially where girls were concerned. My clothes were bought for me with and by my mother, who had the absolute power of both choice and veto; out of term, I was equipped with a succession of execrable camel or navy gabardine skirts, court shoes and little blouses with frilly collars beneath which a discreet string of my grandmother's pearls was expected to be worn. I was given a small sum designed to cover medical necessities, and another small sum with which to buy school textbooks. Anything else I was expected to earn in school holidays. My parents, who read nothing but *The Times* and Jeffrey Archer, had acquired the idea that a good upbringing was one in which the tender or temperamental offspring was impressed with the creed that one could not ever expect something for nothing.

This may not sound like hardship, even in Kensington. What made it unbearable for me was not only my fear of strangers, but the fact that my odious younger brother, Justin (whose ambition has always been to become an accountant and retire to the Bahamas at thirty), had presents and allowances showered on him both in school and out of it. So my legacy, which no doubt Pompa had intended to redress the balance, was seen (at least by my mother) as partisanship of an incomprehensible kind.

'He was potty, of course,' said my mother. 'He never recovered from that first stroke.'

My father grunted, and swallowed his whisky.

'It will do very nicely for pin money,' my mother continued. 'Or else in a building society, until you've passed your driving test, Emma.'

'I don't think so,' I said.

'Well, what else are you going to do with it? Fritter it away on bits of tat from the King's Road? Really, you must learn the value of money. The sooner you get a job and get out of the house, the better. You have no concept of the real world.'

'It wasn't on the school curriculum.'

'Well, now's your chance to fill in the gaps,' said my father, with forced heartiness. 'And, talking of gaps, what are you going to do for the remainder of yours?'

'We can't let you go on moping around the house for the next twelve months before you go up to Oxford.' My mother tightened her lips, like someone drawing the string round a bag. 'Most girls would be thanking their lucky stars, and be off somewhere having fun.'

'Or else getting valuable work experience,' said my father.

'Valuable to whom?' I asked, bitterly. 'Besides, where on earth could I find a job that wouldn't send me potty with boredom?'

'Harrods!' exclaimed my father. It was a solution he applied to every problem, indiscriminately, along with writing letters to *The Times*; as a consequence, his desk was full of cheques to one and acknowledgement slips from the other.

'She could get a job in the sales.'

'Or else as an au pair.' This was from Justin.

'I loathe children,' I answered pointedly. 'I abhor machines. I cannot abide shops. I am *not most girls*. When are you going to realize that? I am neither frivolous nor sociable, and looking at you, Mummy dear, I can't see the point in being so.'

Instant eruption. They had all been waiting for something like this. Threats of incarceration in my room, immediate enrolment at Lucie Clayton's, moans from my father about what a sweet little baby I had been, and why had I turned out to be such a monster, etc. I'm sure they'd have roared with laughter if they had seen it in an Alan Ayckbourn play. Justin oiled off to his beloved computer. I told my parents I had never asked to be born. It seemed the right moment to utter banalities of this kind.

'Presumably contraception existed even in the antediluvian days when you had a sex life,' I said. 'Or hadn't they got around to scanning for female embryos in the 1970s?'

'How humourless the young are, Charles!' My mother gave a humourless laugh.

'Your own worst enemy, just like that Oxford chap said. He saw what you were like in a single interview,' my father said, nodding his head.

This monstrous remark, made by a supercilious young don, had been passed on via the usual Establishment network of gossip, and thrown in my face once a week since the summer. It never failed to goad me beyond endurance, not so much the injustice of it, but the irony. How could I be my own worst enemy when I was my only friend? How could any enemy be worse than my parents?

'She'd better do a typing course,' my mother said wearily. 'God knows, with a personality like yours, Emma, you'll end up a graduate dustbin cleaner.'

'If I were slimy little Justin and had got into Oxford, you'd be sending me on a congratulatory world cruise, not discussing my future as a typist,' I croaked, terrified I was about to burst into tears. 'Does it not occur to you that I might want something more interesting out of life than that?'

'There's nothing wrong with hedging one's bets.'

'It might leave one fenced in.'

'To be fenced in is better than never fitting in.'

'That, no doubt, is the principle behind lunatic asylums.'

'There are times when we consider sending you to see a psychiatrist, yes.'

Incredulous, I laughed. 'You actually think anyone who dis-agrees with the way you see the world must be mad?'

'Academically, as you know, you're very bright, but it isn't normal not to have any friends.'

'I do have friends.'

'Oh? Where? Who?' asked my father, gobbling slightly. 'Why do we never meet them?'

'Because you're too boring,' I said.

'I don't believe you,' said my mother. 'Nobody likes a prig. You must try to be less of a bluestocking.'

'Why? So that some fat businessman can unravel me in a typing pool?'

My father, who is fat and a businessman, shouted back, 'Well, if you're not a bluestocking, what are you?'

I stuck my chin out, and said to them, my enemies, what I had not even dared to say to myself.

'An artist.'

Distorted announcements of departures and delays boomed in my ears like recriminations. I walked down concrete ramps to the next flight to Rome. Most of the other passengers were Italian, laden with sale goods and Christmas presents from relatives. Their voices fell on my ear like warm oil. I wanted to laugh as I saw them push and shove to get on to the plane just as I had once seen Michelangelo's souls of the blessed scramble up one wall of the Sistine Chapel to heaven.

'Make a queue, please, sir,' said the bossy British Airways stewardess. 'You'll all get in much faster.'

I snickered as she was overwhelmed by flailing arms and shopping bags.

Soon England was reduced to a puddle of brown and green chunks, flushed away into blankness and replaced by the vaporous continents of the upper air: those dazzling lagoons and icy archipelagos of cloud that give the traveller the illusion of a world elsewhere. Fierce white light suddenly pierced every porthole. It seemed like the first sun for months. I felt I was coming home.

But, when the aeroplane landed in Rome, it was almost as cold and wintry as London. All the way to the railway station, I looked eagerly for familiar landmarks, but recognized nothing apart from the Colosseum. The buildings I remembered as golden looked like rotting bananas in the dull air, and the faces in the streets were sallow and sullen.

Dismayed, I wondered if Italy had changed so much during my five years' absence or, more dreadfully, whether memory had cheated me. Well, I had burnt my boats. And besides, there was

Sylvia. I wrapped my cloak around me like a cocoon, thought of her and Pompa, and tried not to panic.

At Termini, people stood huddled in knots, all dressed in drab, green winter coats. Electric cars, laden with luggage, shepherded them about with officious toots and cries. Every platform reeked of urine. Dun-coloured trains released sudden gushes of water, like mechanical monsters in pens.

I passed men in felt hats smoking out of windows, soldiers who whistled and called out 'Ciao, bella! Sprechen Sie Deutsch?', sad-faced women dreaming of stardom over magazines as shining and deceptive as fairground mirrors. When I lifted my suitcase, my shoulders felt as if they would burst into flame from the strain. Dingy brocade curtains flapped loose, stiff as dead bats on either side of the window. Beneath each luggage rack was a small mirror, flanked by old prints of Tuscan cities: Florence, Siena, Lucca, Arezzo, said the copperplate beneath. I looked carefully at them all, wishing I had looked up Santorno in a Baedeker.

There was a hiss, a jolt, and suddenly the great blocks of black marble supporting the platform roof started to glide away. A sallow matron whose cardigan, peculiarly, was covered in tufted warts similar to those on her face, entered and closed the window with a snap. Her husband followed, and took a Mickey Mouse comic out of his briefcase.

I looked at them with distaste, hardly daring to move. I exist in perpetual extremes of contempt for people patently less intelligent than myself, and the fear that, because of this, they may be altogether better at surviving the real world.

After a number of long, rumbling tunnels, we emerged into countryside. Hills began to flex in the distance. A waiter pushed a thin, tinkling trolley packed with mineral water and rolls, which when bitten into opened like huge prosthetic lips revealing a gullet of Parma ham.

At Orvieto, three young men entered, and tried to talk to me in broken English. I shook my head violently, wondering if it was my clothes or my colouring that instantly gave me away, and took Sylvia's astonishing invitation out of my bag, though I knew its contents by heart. Hers were the only letters I had ever received from someone outside my family. I had spent hours trying to copy the slash and loop of her calligraphy, topped by banners of black ink, and tailed like the haunches of fabulous beasts.

December 3

> *Bar Popolare Santorno*
> *Toscana*

Hi there!
How's life in glum old London? Still pretty bad, I guess, from your letters. Sorry not to have replied before – things haven't been too great here. Basically, Dave and I have decided to split – he says we suffocate each other creatively. Anyway, he's going off to Greece or India and staying with Slim and Izzy, these neighbours, to get his head together, so if you've still got this great yen to see Italy again, why not come and stay a few months? My house is small, not like the luxury you're used to, but it's a dream for painting. Men, who needs them? Look at Camille Claudel. Did you see the French movie about her life? All the other guys are very simpatico.
If the idea grabs you, just turn up. There's no phone, but Santorno is right on the Rome-Urbino railway line. My place is just outside the town, along the parterre beneath the Palazzo Felice.
Ciao and mille baci,
Sylvia

How romantic, how artistic, to write from a bar! I had a vision of Sylvia drinking bright-green absinthe, surrounded by other painters, poets and musicians – desperately poor, but destined to be the creators of masterpieces. I knew that practically every artist save Alma-Tadema and that overstuffed cream puff of a diplomat, Rubens, had lived or died in poverty; I was determined not to be afraid of it either. I imagined a society of men and women in which I would be recognized and accepted as one who lived on a higher spiritual plane. Everyone would speak like Oscar Wilde. We would challenge life instead of accepting it, we would defeat the materialism of the age ...

Cortona and Arezzo went by. The train turned east, towards the Apennines and darkness, decelerating. It had been motionless for a minute or so at a singularly drab station, on the edge of an equally drab town, before I realized that this sprawl of breeze blocks and barbed wire was my destination.

Even in twilight, Santorno had an unappetizing appearance. I could see at least two houses beyond the station entrance that were not only modern but that actually sported plaster gnomes on the gateposts. Rubbish blew about the empty streets like tumbleweed. It did not look like any kind of spiritual home at all, but this was where Sylvia lived. The train gave a melancholy hoot, and I scrambled to collect my things, falling down the carriage steps just as it began to move off.

Later, I learned that every Tuscan town has a dual identity. Santorno is no exception. For each campanile, cobbled street and castellated wall up above, there is a supermarket, car park and apartment block down below. Each half, so different, is dependent on the other, existing in a state of mutual parasitism. There is a curious result to all this. Each by reason of antiquity or modernity, beauty or affluence believes itself to be the real town. In reality, they are no more divisible than body and brain.

I passed from the new to the old in a taxi, my spirits rising with every bend in the road. Droplets of light sprang up like dew on the plains as we climbed, and the smell of green things came through the open window. Cypress trees, dark and slender, posted the road. One had been snapped in two; as we passed it, the headlights outlined the charred wreck of a car on the terrace below.

My driver clicked his tongue. 'They still haven't taken it away! What a disgrace! Are you here on holiday, signorina?'

'More or less,' I said.

'You speak Italian well.'

'Thank you. My parents used to live in Rome, but I haven't been back since I was a child.'

'If I could speak English, I'd emigrate and go to America.'

'Why? It's so beautiful here!' I was determined to find it so, whatever daylight revealed.

'Anywhere is beautiful when you have money,' he told me sourly.

But old Santorno, city of mysteries, as it called itself in a garish roadside advertisement, would live up to my expectations. I could see its profile, inky against an indigo sky, and it was enough to reassure me. By the dim yellow light of a lamp, suspended in the jaws of a wrought-iron dragon rearing out from the city walls, the car turned, and I wrenched my eyes away. Patience, I thought. The pollarded trees along the parterre stretched mutilated hands to the sky, soughing as the taxi passed them.

'You say you want the house at the end?' asked the driver suddenly.

'Yes, please.'

'There is no house at the end.'

'What?' I felt sure he must be lying. 'It must be, it says so in my friend's letter.'

'Only a country lane,' he said, dismissively. 'For that you need a jeep or a Cinquecento. Otherwise, there is the Hotel Max in Santorno, with disco. You like disco?' He turned, leering like a gargoyle.

'No,' I answered, amazed at my calmness. 'My friend is expecting me. I'll walk.'

I paid him, and he shot off in ill humour and a spray of gravel. I began to trudge down the country lane that began where the parterre ended. It was ridged and rutted, and almost liquid with mud; my boots began to leak, and my cloak flapped and wrapped itself around them. By rights, I should now have been a gibbering wreck, but my faith in Sylvia was so absolute that I could have walked across quagmires for her.

Then, to my left, I heard a low growl and the rattle of a chain. An explosion of barking broke out. From some cavernous depth in the hillside, a troglodytic grunting started up, and a line of pale shapes advanced, hissing.

I gave a shriek. A light was switched on and a figure appeared at the top of an outside flight of stairs.

'Who's there?' it called in Italian.

'Sylvia?' I squeaked. 'Is that you?'

'*Che?*'

'I'm looking for an American lady, Sylvia Lurie. She lives near here.'

'Go further on down, about five hundred metres.'

'Thank you.'

The figure disappeared, banging the window ill-temperedly. Navigating past the snarling dog, I shooed the geese away with my suitcase.

I was tired, hungry and dirty, but it no longer mattered. Ahead, I could see the glow of another light. The moon emerged, like a small polished circle in a tarnished sky. Sylvia's

14

house detached itself from the shadows, and the sound of a voice, singing, came to me down the night wind. It called to me, drawing me on and on, until I could bear it no longer. I put down my suitcase and began to run.

2

The ceiling overhead was barred with black beams, like staves of music, from which the solitary semi-quaver of a spider hung, swaying in eddies of cold air. Wind seethed up the hillside, drumming the house, rattling panes of glass in their flaky green frames, and causing unfastened shutters to bang and clap in uneven concert. I sat up.

My room was icy. I had never slept anywhere so underheated. Breath seemed to freeze solid as I yawned, and the windows were white with condensation. The light that came through them was fluorescent with brightness. There was a smell of paraffin from the extinguished portable stove in one corner, mingled with beeswax, dust and turpentine.

Apart from a battered wooden chest, my bed and a chair, the room was empty. The bumpy whitewashed walls, the sloping, rose-red floor, needed no ornament. Two windows at right angles to each other were so deep-set as to form niches in the thick stonemasonry. One held a pewter bucket arranged with dried grasses; the other, a stone basin with a hole half-plugged by a screw of paper through which the wind whistled. The overall shape of the room was triangular, with two of the walls forming an acute angle, like the prow of a boat.

Its bareness was to me perfection. I thought of the room I

had left behind, with its string of plaster sausages round the ceiling, its kidney-shaped dressing table oozing a froth of pink frills, and the nightmare of tasteful beige carpet on which no paint must ever be spilt. Then I rubbed the misted pane of glass beside me and looked out.

Beyond the road I had walked along the night before, the tops of terraced olive trees swayed and tossed, like water roaring down a gigantic waterfall from all directions. Great billows and spumes of silver streamed in the valley below, dashing against lines of dark cypress which appeared and disappeared like half-submerged rock over which the leaves poured in perpetual motion. The hills opposite formed a semi-circle, opening at one end to a wide plain far below, dotted with fields and hamlets.

Above eye level, the impression of verdancy stopped abruptly. Terraced fields and groves were replaced by chalky rocks, the kind that seem artificial in Renaissance paintings. Only the scrub gave any indication that it was still winter, for the terraced trees were evergreen, and the sky a high and lapidary blue.

Greedily, incredulously, I stared. Here was the landscape I had haunted the National Gallery to rediscover, here those hills undulating like the bodies of gigantic deities, those shining little roads and rivers winding away in a haze, the glamour of golden light. It had ruined every country in the world but this for me; it was my promised land.

The cold was beginning to numb my feet. I opened my suitcase and looked at the clothes I had brought. They were few. My cloak had been my sole sartorial extravagance. I had brought only jeans, shorts, a green sprigged Laura Ashley dress, a Liberty silk shirt and, luckily, a few shirts and jumpers. I put on half my entire wardrobe and walked out on to the landing between the two bedrooms. It had a large fireplace

17

supported by a long black beam, and a thick pair of doors to the garden outside.

There was a precipitous wooden stair, almost a ladder, to the ground floor, with a bathroom tucked away beneath it. I performed the usual tedious ablutions, and went on into the kitchen.

Sylvia stood with her back to me. Her long mahogany plait reached her waist, and she wore a black woollen dress that outlined her body before being caught up by a wide leather belt the same purple as her boots. Large silver earrings, shaped like fuchsias, dangled from her ears. Even washing up, she seemed so charged with vitality that the globes of onions looped from rafters above her head shone like strings of artificial lights.

'Hi.'

'Hallo.'

'How'd you sleep?'

'Well, thanks. And you?'

'The fucking wind kept me awake all night.'

She scowled, and I trembled in case I was the real cause of her bad mood.

'I'm sorry,' I said, watching her anxiously, so anxiously that she grinned at me, wickedly, as if she read my thoughts. Walking over, she gave me a hug. I returned her embrace awkwardly.

'It's really good to see you again,' she told me. 'I guess too many things are getting on my nerves. Let's have breakfast. Coffee? Toast? I've got some incredible honey, like toffee, but the bread has gone stale. Maybe if we toast it next door, it won't be so hard.'

'Yes,' I said, gazing at her. 'Anything you like.'

Had Sylvia suggested I cut off my little finger and toast that instead, I would probably have agreed. We had met a year ago,

18

when I was still at school, and ever since I had thought of very little else.

Even my parents had to admit I had been a model pupil.

I did not smoke, drink, take drugs, make up or break down. I passed examinations with relentless success, and I hated everyone and everything there like poison.

'Ugly, ugly, ugly,' I would mutter, looking at the Victorian liver-coloured brick, the faces of staff and pupils, the scummy coastal town on the edge of which the school sprawled in all its neo-Gothic hideosity. It had, according to legend, been built by a biscuit manufacturer after he had seen St Pancras Station – presumably the most beautiful sight that met his eyes as he escaped from the dreary northeast – and he had become bankrupt in pursuit of his dream. The house subsequently became a lunatic asylum, then a well-known girls' boarding school. It was debatable, as I often chose to remark, whether the original owner would have noticed any difference between the two.

It was a completely awful, old-fashioned dump. I nicknamed it St Crumpet's. My mother had been head girl there in her day, and was still remembered with tremulous veneration. Minor female members of the royal family had been through its portals for a specious polish; dim-witted neo-debutantes followed suit. Famous for preserving both the innocence and the ignorance of its pupils, it advertised itself (discreetly, of course) as being 'one big happy family': a description which should have made the most stupid parent think twice.

But mostly, only stupid girls went there. It was neither academic nor artistic. Designed to turn out young ladies whose idea of fulfilment was a brief stint as a secretary, marriage to a banker, a clutch of children and a Volvo, its fortes were tennis and domestic science. The only piece of poetry you could guarantee would be known to every pupil was Betjeman's 'Vers de Societé'. There is no point in describing what I endured. I endured it.

I worked. There was really nothing else for me to do, you could say that much for it, and it had quite a good library, chiefly filled with Victorian novels – some of which, as they were in French and German, escaped the vigilant censorship of the headmistress. I came top of the class with such monotony that teachers made spiteful little jokes about me, toadying to the rest. It was the only revenge possible for them, I suppose. I learned first to cry in complete silence, and then not to cry at all.

There was no privacy, that was the worst thing. To be utterly lonely and never alone is a torture only the English could have thought up.

What made it worse was that, unlike the other pupils, who merely missed their dogs, ponies and families, I retained the memory of another existence. I remembered Italy.

My father had been sent out to run the Italian office of his company when I was seven. We followed him, and for five years lived a life of endless treats. There were large, extravagant parties thrown in the company penthouse of an old palazzo near the Spanish Steps, to which famous people – writers, artists, visiting academics, nothing like the stodge of Kensington – came. We had a roof terrace billowing with poisonous, fondant-coloured oleander blossom, and a local restaurant where children were treated like princes, not unwelcome pieces of baggage.

I had arrived a sickly little English thing, pale, shy, addicted to television and fairy tales. Italy changed that as irrevocably as a dose of radiation. I went to an Italian *liceo*, then to a tiny, wonderful prep school run by two eccentric old Englishwomen and a gentle, effete young man. I became strong, confident, even pretty; and I was not conscious of it, any more than one is conscious of good health, until it is gone.

I was already drawing a good deal. My cats looked like cats, my mats like mats. I could perform minor feats of illusion, making two dimensions three; I had discovered the importance of drawing shadow, not outline. Much of this I learned after copying Renaissance drawings from a book which my grandfather, passing through, gave me for a birthday present.

I saw *La Bohème*. I went round museums. For three glorious months, there was a weekly school trip to the British Council to see Kenneth Clarke's *Civilization*. From then on, my imagination was filled with the heroism of the artist, his struggles, his poverty, his humiliations and his ultimate triumph. It was always a man that I pictured. It never occurred to me that I might one day stumble along these paths myself; the most I hoped for was to be the wife or servant of such a man.

I lived through my eyes, yet I remember little now. Images remain, fragments of beauty as brilliant as the beads in a kaleidoscope: cypress black against a blinding blue sky, the scissoring flight of swallows, crumbling ochre walls.

I drew then for pleasure, not ambition or the desperation to preserve.

My parents were pleased, but no more than mildly interested; they are not the sort who have their darling's every tottering foray into Art framed and preserved for posterity in the drawing room.

'Very nice, dear,' my mother would say, absently.

'Much better than the bricks at the Tate, what?' my father agreed.

Pompa, though, was a different matter.

He was a botanical painter, a modern Redouté, and had spent every penny of quite a large inheritance going off to obscure parts of the world in search of rare plants. He carried a swordstick and possessed only two suits, worn on alternate days and both made in Jermyn Street, which he said saved him money because each one would last him twenty years. He always carried exquisitely laundered handkerchiefs, redolent of Trumper's bay rum. He knew about every subject under the sun, unlike my father, who, I was quickly discovering, knew only about boring things like money. Pompa's shock of white hair seemed to stand out as if electrocuted by pure intellect. I adored him.

Unlike my parents, who were always fussing around Justin, he always seemed more concerned about me than about anyone else. We didn't talk much, but we had an understanding; on my rare visits to his Georgian house in Shropshire, we would listen to his collection of Italian opera or go off on long walks together, during which he would teach me the names of wild flowers. I never told him about school but he must have guessed, because just before his first heart attack, when I was fifteen, there was a colossal row when he told them to send me somewhere else.

'Interfering old monster!' said my mother. 'Imagine, I asked him what was wrong with a place which had produced the happiest days of my life, and he had the insolence to say that's just what he feared!'

'I'm afraid he's very autocratic,' my father said, trumpeting into his handkerchief, as he usually did when nervous.

'I have always thought of your father, striding about the Third World, as the poor man's burden,' said my mother. 'He's squandered your inheritance grubbing around for roots, and now he wants to interfere in Emma's education, when she's quite difficult enough as it is.'

I didn't mind. I was flattered, thrilled, to be the subject, not the object, of so much acrimony, and more so when he told me I should attempt Oxbridge.

'What about art school?' I asked. 'A girl from St Crumpet's went to one, about ten years ago.'

'Don't bother with that bunch of charlatans,' he had answered testily. 'You'll spend one year painting red teapots and two more learning how to forget what you see in front of your nose. You can't teach painting, any more than you can teach writing or musical composition. Either you've got it or you haven't. No, no, go somewhere you'll meet a few people with brains, like yourself. God knows where you got them from,' he added in an undertone.

It never occurred to me to question this. I had no friends, nothing except books, my parents and him. He was my Abbé Faria, a gigantic signpost pointing the direction where my life was to go. He had gone to Magdalen, and it was to his college that I had applied to read history of art.

I wasn't sure, in my heart of hearts, if I really wanted Oxford, that was the problem. I had seen pictures of the city and, though not up to Italian standards, it looked as agreeable as an English city could get. On the other hand, I had no great hopes that my peers there would be any better than at school: people of my own age having so far proved uniformly smug and dull. Nor was I sure I wanted to go on jumping through institutional hoops for three more years. I wanted life, I told myself. I wanted freedom.

I wanted knowledge of a kind not to be found in books.

Yet the satisfaction of putting everyone else's noses massively out of joint was too great to resist.

'Failure will be good for you, Emma,' said my headmistress just before I sat the entrance papers. 'You need to learn humility.'

'What, from you?' I enquired nastily.

She looked at me with a curious expression. 'I'm afraid you have a hard time ahead of you, my dear. It will be interesting to see what you make of it.'

What she meant, the old bitch, was that she had tried to

scupper my chances, though I hadn't discovered that yet. She could have saved herself the effort, though. Unlike most people, I quite enjoy exams. They suit my nature, sometimes more than painting, which is effortful in its need for stillness and contemplation. I like the feeling of going into a room with nothing but a pencil and my brains, and doing a high-wire act between say, Camus, *Don Giovanni* and 'The Charge of the Light Brigade'. Actually, I enjoyed it so much I began to think I might like it at Oxford, if only intellectually.

I was duly called for an interview, and that was where it all began.

In order to get to Oxford, I had to come down from the northeast to St Pancras and find Paddington station. All would have been well, had I had enough money on me; as it was, I discovered that I had miscalculated the cost of two train fares when withdrawing cash from the housemistress. (We were not, of course, allowed chequebooks.) My interview was not until the following day, but I knew candidates were expected to turn up for dinner that evening. I would have to walk.

As usual, I was petrified. I knew nothing of Marylebone or Bayswater, except their names. I saw nothing odd about this, though it was often embarrassing. Tourists visiting for five days probably gained a better idea of the city than I did in five years.

With a hazy idea that Paddington was off to the southwest, I walked for about an hour without any idea where I was going.

It was very tiring. I felt nauseous with anxiety and the foul smells from fast-food shops, uneasily aware that everything I wore looked schoolgirlish and wrong. Gangs of greasy louts eyed me up, snickering. Black clouds bulged in the sky, as heavy as the bags of rubbish slumped on every street corner. I was too nervous to ask the way, and too poor to buy an *A to Z*, shrinking against the walls to such an extent that I grazed my elbows on two occasions. Whenever people envy the young, they forget that embarrassment is as crippling as arthritis.

I came at last to Hyde Park, and the edge of my known universe. Children played in heaps of dead leaves, joggers pounded past, wheezing slightly in the autumnal air. Every now and again, a mass of small birds rose, shrieking, and practised formation flying for their approaching migration. I realized I had come too far south but kept on walking anyway. I was horribly depressed.

Suddenly there was a great crack of thunder, and the rain began sheeting down. A semi-stuccoed building, the Serpentine Gallery, wavered ahead. I ran for it. Halfway up the steps, I cannoned into something soft.

There was a hiss of indrawn breath, followed by a thud, and a dizzying, exotic scent. I wiped the water from my eyes and looked up.

A woman was kneeling on the floor, her dark-red hair almost brushing it as she collected scattered papers. All around her, a dress of some heavy green material billowed out in stiff, glittering undulations. The top was plain and close-fitting, but its skirt was thickly embroidered with threads of every colour, depicting pairs of animals gambolling in a meadow. Each eye and flower was made of tiny mirrors, or sequins, which cast specks of prismatic light on to the walls and ceiling. It was utterly unlike any garment I had ever seen, and so was its wearer.

'I'm awfully sorry,' I gasped.

'Don't worry,' said the woman, smiling. 'It's only possessions.'

She was very white, almost luminous in the lurid light of the storm, but with the pallor of health, not illness. Her eyes were enormous, the colour of tarnished silver, and rimmed by a thick black line that flicked up at the edges and made them seem incised. She had high cheekbones, a long, straight nose and a mouth like a peony bud.

'Have we met before?'

'No – no,' I stammered, 'but you seem awfully familiar, somehow.'

As soon as I had said it, I knew why. She looked exactly like one of Beardsley's illustrations of Salome.

I said, without realizing I was speaking aloud, 'Perhaps every beauty lives in the imagination first.'

'Why, thank you,' said the woman. 'That's the nicest thing anyone's said to me in this city. Why don't you come and have some coffee when we've collected this up? This rain isn't going to stop for a long time, I guess.'

I nodded and began to help her collect what had fallen out of her folder. There was a postcard, addressed in sprawling black ink to Sylvia from someone called Dave. It had what seemed to be a piece of verse scrawled across it:

> When my love swears that she is made of truth,
> I do believe her, though I know she lies,
> That she might think me some untutored youth,
> Unlearnèd in the world's false subtleties.
> Thus vainly thinking that she thinks me young,
> Although she knows my days are past the best,
> Simply I credit her false-speaking tongue:
> On both sides thus is simple truth suppressed.

A drop of rain fell from my forehead and the ink ran, making a crescent of seven blots in the middle of this. The woman didn't even notice me reading it. I turned the card over and saw a reproduction of Bronzino's 'Truth Revealed By Time', Venus and Cupid, frigidly erotic, entwined in each other's arms: of all paintings in the National Gallery the most wonderful and the most disturbing. It seemed right that this strange woman should have had it chosen for her.

I glanced at what else she had been collecting. In one hand she held an *A to Z*, and in the other a sheaf of paintings. I knew at once they were her own. They were watercolours and they were, unmistakably, of Italy.

'This used to be the old stables,' Sylvia said, flipping two slices of bread over on a toasting fork. 'That's why the fireplace doesn't draw so well down here. Can you imagine, a family of six *contadini* used to live upstairs, with all their pigs and oxen and things down here?'

'The stench must have been appalling.'

'Well, pretty unhygienic by American standards, that's for sure. But I guess it kept them warm in weather like this.'

'Does anyone still live like that?'

'Oh yeah, you bet.' She laughed, a soft, sleepy sound like a pigeon cooing. 'There's a family just above here, the Guardis, who are, like, Neanderthals.' She grimaced.

'I think I met one of them last night. They have a dog on a chain.'

'Yeah. It's never let off, except when Guardi hunts. They're just ignorant peasants, the last left on this hillside. One day they'll be gone, too. You can't make a living up here, it's all stone, and nobody can drive a tractor along half the terraces. Everyone else is a foreigner. Italy is wasted on the Italians, you know, like youth on the young.'

'How sad.'

'It was worse when I came here, years ago. There used to be whole villages, empty and crumbling. So tell me, what took you so long to come out here?'

'I had to finish school.'

'But you got into Oxford, right?'

'Yes. Not to the college I wanted to go, but to an all-women's one.' I didn't add that the don who had turned me down for

Magdalen would still be teaching me, it was a prospect too nasty to contemplate yet again.

'Hey, that's great! But I thought you wanted to be a painter?'

'Yes, I do. But I want to find out if I've got any real talent first; more than just competence, you know. And even if I have, I'm not sure it wouldn't be better for me to be made to look at lots of other people's paintings, instead of doing red teapots and things. But I don't know what I should really be doing, Sylvia. I've run away from home. I hope you don't mind,' I added in afterthought. 'I'm over the age of consent and all that.'

I said the last to make it clear she was not to regard herself as being *in loco parentis*.

'Wow! You said your parents were pretty heavy. So you couldn't hack them any more?'

'No,' I said, guessing what she meant by 'hack' after a brief vision of myself harnessed to a cart and being lashed by my mother and father.

'Most people can't.'

'Really? I thought it was just me.'

'Oh no,' said Sylvia, gurgling with laughter. 'Honest? Did I ever tell you about Dave and his mom? She was a bitch on wheels, believe you me, always on at him. I guess that's why his relationships with women never work out. Anyway, he was driving her one day in England, and they came to the bottom of a steep hill. She was shouting at him and nagging him, and there at the top he suddenly saw this truck coming down, swerving all over the place, out of control. So he slams the brake on and says, "Look, Mom, I've always hated you, and now you can go to hell." Then he opens the door and jumps out. By this time she can see the truck, too, but she's too old to move.'

'How awful,' I said, appalled.

'No,' said Sylvia, 'the really awful thing is that, at the last

28

minute, the truck driver managed to avoid her, and he had to get back into that car and go on driving.'

We both burst out laughing, almost choking on the toast.

'You'll meet him this evening, at the farewell party,' she said in a more sober tone.

'Do you mind a lot?'

'No, not any more. It's a relief, I guess. A relationship between two people is like a living thing; when it goes wrong, you can feel it dying like it's a dead baby or something. It can poison your system. I'll be better when he leaves, that's all.'

'That sounds as if you feel something.'

Sylvia glanced at me. 'The only thing I really mind is what's going to happen about the house.'

'I think I should pay you rent,' I said, in the slight pause that followed. 'If you want me to stay.'

She jumped up, smiling. 'Of course I do. That's real nice of you to offer; I was afraid I was going to have to ask. But listen, don't give me money. If you just buy food for the house, that will be fine. I don't want to feel like some kind of landlady.'

'I know, artists aren't meant to think about money.'

'Who told you that?' she asked, grinning. 'On the contrary, artists talk about money all the time, because they don't have any. It's only rich businessmen who can talk about art.'

I smiled back at her. 'They don't, I can tell you as one who knows.'

She was so easy to talk to, I thought, as we prised the Cinquecento out of the mud and persuaded it to whinge up the hill towards Santorno. When we met, it had been like finding someone I had always known. I remembered having thought at one point, as we sat in the café and worked out my route to Paddington and then discovered we both wanted to become painters, that it was a miracle to find someone so like myself. Or rather, so like the person I wanted to become – so warm, confident, intelligent; so womanly. She had come to painting late in life, she told me; she had just been to see some American charity in London and got a grant to do a course as a mature student at Perugia. I liked the idea of her being officially mature.

'I suppose I'm going to be an immature student, then,' I remarked.

'I don't feel grown up at all, you know,' Sylvia said, and she was the first adult I had ever heard admit it.

Let her go on liking me, I prayed silently, as the car bounced along the rutted road. Let me stay.

'Oh, hell,' said Sylvia. 'A tractor. Great, now the road will be even worse.'

'What's going on?'

'Olive-picking,' said Sylvia, hooting her horn impatiently. 'It's late this year; it's usually over by January.'

A group of people were standing on ladders, picking the brownish berries and putting them into little wicker baskets strapped round their waists; when full, these were tipped into a large sack on the back of the tractor. As they worked, they sang, and the sound echoed up and down the hill between gusts of wind.

'Have you ever seen how they make olive oil?'

I shook my head.

'I'll take you on the way home. I need to buy some more, anyway. Oh, look out, here's the Guardis.'

As we approached the farmyard through which I had walked the night before, the yellow mongrel bounded up, snarling. To my surprise, Sylvia wound down the window, stuck out her arm and made a V sign, hooting her horn. The dog nearly strangled itself in frustration, and someone flung open a window on the upper storey.

'*Rompicoglioni!*'

'*Vafanculo!*' Sylvia shrieked back.

The Cinquecento accelerated, shooting through the yard so fast that a couple of chickens left their tail feathers on the bonnet.

'What did you say?' I asked.

'I told her to go bugger her own asshole.'

'Oh.' I swallowed, weakly.

'That's Maria Guardi, the fucking witch. She's always spying on me, and saying I'm a whore because I don't wear a brassiere.'

Involuntarily I glanced down and saw Sylvia's rather large breasts bouncing up and down.

'Isn't it uncomfortable?'

'All political positions are uncomfortable when they challenge the accepted rules,' said Sylvia fiercely. 'I do not shave my legs, wear a wedding ring or ask men to carry heavy objects for me.'

I looked at the heavy eye make-up round her eyes and said nothing, but resolved to do away with my own undergarments in future.

3

According to a small, blurrily printed pamphlet, featuring an aerial cover photograph of what resembles a pile of vomit on a billiard table, Santorno is thought to have Etruscan foundations.

'Certainly,' the anonymous author wrote,

excavations undertaken in recent years by the archaeology departments of many distinguished universities indicate that there was a city on these bosky hills centuries before Santorno (population 3,999) grew up to become the famous centre of historic interest we know today. Many pottery shards and some coins, all bearing the head of a horned man, have been found, and may be seen in the Museo Felice (closed Mondays).

The origin of the city's name is the subject of much contention. Some, such as Professor Fabrizio Bocca, are of the opinion that it takes its name from the beatific Anthony of Padua, patron saint of Santorno. In 1360 AD, during the course of his wanderings throughout Tuscany, Sant' Antonio founded a monastery which became a well-known hospice for pilgrims travelling to Rome from the Adriatic, and which is now the hospital found in Via del Ospedale.

Others, notably Professor Tiresio Po, are equally convinced that the city was built on a shrine to the god Saturn.

Legend has it that when the besieged Etruscans were defending this city against the Romans, a woman of that race was persuaded to reveal a secret entrance through the walls to her Roman lover. At the last moment, however, she repented and prayed to the god, who sent up a jet of boiling spring water which scalded both penitent and invaders to death. However, this miracle, if such it was, only delayed the inevitable—

'Oh, God, I thought I'd thrown the last of those away,' said Sylvia. 'It's a load of crap for the tourists.'

'Interesting, though.'

Sylvia snorted. 'Have you come to the part about Santorno being the birthplace of Giulio Folconi, Renaissance sculptor, painter, poet, engineer, architect, scientist, philosopher, musician and God knows what else? No? If you look ahead, you can see a marble statue at the end of the parterre they put up to him – a guy like a sumo wrestler sitting on a tortoise.'

I peered ahead. 'Folconi? I've never heard of him.'

Sylvia snorted again. 'Nor has anyone else, and you know why? Because he never existed! At some point the town council decided that it looked pretty bad that Santorno was the only town in Tuscany not to produce a single famous figure during the Renaissance, when every other town did, so they invented him.'

'No!'

'Yeah. Most people prefer their artists dead; Santorno goes one better.'

'Why has nobody exposed it as a fraud?' .

'It's too profitable. Think of all the souvenirs you can sell if you're the birthplace of a genius – even a fake one. How many tourists do you think have actually read Vasari? They even tried to pretend the Palazzo Felice had been designed by him, but the Contessa wasn't having any of it.'

The parterre, where we parked, was broad and flat, but it concealed the entrance to Santorno until the last minute, for the hills in that region are like a row of knuckles on a many-fingered fist. Everything built on them is forced to buckle and twist in accordance with the stone beneath. Buildings that seem poor and narrow open unexpectedly into broad courtyards, whereas long, imposing facades can be suddenly revealed as no more substantial than an opera set. It is a place that defies the rules of perspective, muddles the stranger and enervates the native.

Sylvia and I entered through the main gate, a massive affair of wood and iron, studded with nails the size of hammers. Here, the main street in the town began without preamble: butcher, baker, greengrocer, chemist, florist, stationer. Sylvia strode along confidently, and I kept pace by her side. People stared. Our clothes marked us out as different, I supposed, for in contrast to our long, artistic garb, the Santornese were all attired in the height of fashion. Even in Kensington, I had never seen such bourgeois elegance.

'Are lots of people here very well off?' I asked Sylvia.

'Oh no,' she replied. 'They just live at home until they marry, sometimes even after, so there's more money for making a show. You know, *bella figura?*. This place is dominated by it. They never spend it on art or houses. It's all cars and designer clothes.'

Notwithstanding this, her progress up the Via Garibaldi was a triumphal one. It amazed me how many people she knew, the volley of kisses exchanged on each cheek.

'This is Emma Kenward, an artist from England,' she would

say, over and over. Although confused and a little alarmed at this unmerited advertisement, I began to enjoy myself. Why not? She could have told them I was an international brain surgeon or an acrobat, and none of them would know any better. Truth is not relative but relatives; without a family I was free to reinvent myself any way I pleased.

We bought bread and meat from the shops, but everything else from the market. People spilled down along the Via del Ospedale from the smaller Piazza Felice above to Piazza Venti Settembre below, like blood moving through the valves of a heart. The market was, indeed, vital to the old town, if less necessary to the new. Sylvia told me that *contadini* came from miles around to sell their produce, as Santorno was the only large town between San Sepolchro and Urbino. There were pots spattered with a strange, metallic glaze, giant hams, barrel-sized Parmesan cheeses, baby clothes, crocheted tablecloths, hideous nylon-furred toys, shoes and leather jackets manufactured in the new town, jumpers knitted up in the mountains by shepherds' wives, racks of sunglasses and china figurines, as well as vegetables and fish from the Adriatic. People bought, haggled and sold with frenzied enthusiasm, all dressed up in their best clothes to do it.

'*La dolce far soldi*,' I observed.

'They're Tuscans, what do you expect?'

Both squares were so crammed with stalls that the only building I could make out was the Municipality, a fine stone edifice reached by a flight of steps and topped by a tall, blue and gold clock. Above in the bell tower was a piece of clockwork greatly admired by Santornese and tourists alike, consisting of a devil and an angel who would chase each other round and round, brandishing pitchfork and sword respectively with a jerky motion every fifteen minutes. It had been commissioned, it was said, by a mayor with a turbulent married life, and there

35

was something of Punch and Judy about the two figures even from a distance.

As lunchtime approached, more and more people thronged the street, making their way to and from the market. The cobbles echoed and re-echoed with the shuffle of passing feet; high above, where sun touched the upper windows, bursts of canary song cascaded down into the icy gorge where we stood. Tiny alleyways with extraordinary names – Passage of the Seven Stars, Passage of the Wolf's Mouth, Passage of the White Windows – sprang up and plunged down off Via Garibaldi, allowing glimpses of old women swathed in black waddling home with their shopping.

'Here's Slim's shop,' said Sylvia, stopping just before the main piazza. 'I thought we'd ask him along for a coffee. Slim?'

I remembered that this was the man with whom Sylvia's husband was supposed to be staying, and stared at the contents on display in his shop with some apprehension. They resembled a sort of misshapen cake, as they were all a glutinously bright brown, but the smell of leather proved them to be shoes – quite the ugliest, clumpiest shoes I had ever seen, with gigantic thick stitches done in what looked like mountaineering rope.

'Slim!' Sylvia called archly. 'I'm about to rob your store!'

A man with a ginger moustache and bristling crew cut put his head round the door at the back.

'Ciao, baby. Be with you in a sec.'

He disappeared again. There was a clanking rumble, as if a giant in armour had fallen downstairs.

'Oh, shit, this fuckin', medieval plumbing!' he howled. 'Shit, shit, shit! God how I hate this fuckin' country – no post, no decent telly, nothing but nasty mucky milk to put in my fuckin' tea. Oh, shit!'

Sylvia burst into giggles. 'Poor guy. He used to be an art

director at this advertising agency before he and Izzy decided to quit the rat race and make shoes, but he can't hack not being in London. Hi there, how's everything?'

'Fuckin' awful as usual. Izzy's allowance arrived six weeks late, thanks to the Christmas post. Why the old shithead won't make a standing order to her is beyond me.'

'Probably gives him the feeling of keeping you in suspense.'

'And an excuse to lecture me about not supporting his darling daughter. Christ! Who wants to be married to a millionaire's only child? Who's this, then?'

Sylvia introduced me.

'Halloah,' he said in what, presumably, was supposed to be a parody of my voice. 'Kenward, eh? Any relation to Charles? I once worked on his account, nearly gave me piles, I can tell you.'

Coldly, I informed him I had recently run away from home.

Instead of being impressed, he guffawed. 'Run away? How old are you?'

'Eighteen.'

'Then you're only doing what everyone else does, sooner or later – usually sooner,' he said. 'You're just a late developer, girlie, like all your generation. Christ, it's going to be boring! Everything's going to be handed you on a plate, like it was your parents.'

I thought of retorting that he didn't seem to have done too badly if he'd married a millionaire's daughter, but stopped myself in time.

'Oh, cool it,' said Sylvia, affectionately. 'Come and have a coffee. You're obviously having a bad day.'

'Too right. Izzy's tonto about Dave leaving without making his plans clear.'

Sylvia sighed. 'It was a mistake, his moving in, I guess. Tough on you.'

'Me? Nah. I can take it.'

'Tough on Dave, then.'

'Him? Don't you believe it! The smallest unit of time ought to be redefined as the period in which your sodding husband feels remorse for anything he's done. Look at him, pissing off and saying he'll be back when he feels like it! No, the one you ought to feel sorry for is yourself. I'm OK, any divorce and I'll hit the three lemons in alimony, but what about you? What the hell are you going to do if he wants to marry her?'

I looked from one to the other, bewildered by this conversation.

'I mean, where will you live? Will he just make you homeless, or what?'

The vitality seemed to drain from Sylvia. 'I don't know. But I'll think of something.'

'We'd both better think of something, and fast. Christ, why did you ever marry the bastard?'

'Dave? I guess I must have been in love.'

It was at this point that I decided to add Sylvia's husband to the list, currently headed by my future tutor at Oxford, of people to bite if I ever got rabies.

The Bar Popolare was, despite its name, very nearly empty. Sylvia told me it was regarded by the Santornese as exclusive to foreigners. The air was heavy with coffee and sugar, and beneath the stainless-steel counter, tiny cakes and pastries adorned with crystallized fruit were displayed in cases, like jewels. At the back, mirrored shelves reflected liqueur bottles of every shape, size and colour, so twisted, puffed up or flattened down that I immediately itched to paint them.

'*Buona sera, signori,*' the man behind the counter said in a hoarse, lugubrious voice.

'You know what I love about this country?' said Slim. 'They're all such fuckin' pessimists. The minute it's past noon, they think it's evening. Ciao, Tony. This is Emma, a friend of Sylvia's.'

Solemnly, Tony shook my hand.

He was a most peculiar creature. Everything about him suggested he had been assembled out of lumps of uncooked dough. His head was a bald, floury mound with five curranty depressions for the eyes, nose and mouth; his torso, encased in a bottle-green waistcoat, was like that of a gingerbread man. I wondered whether he would rise like a cake in summer to twice his size.

'And how is the weather in England?' he enquired.

'Rainy,' I answered.

'Ah.' He gave a dim, doughy smile of satisfaction. 'What a terrible country it must be.'

We went to the back of the bar, away from the noise of the market, where an arched window looked out over a jumble of rooftops. A man was sitting before it, long legs bent almost double under the tiny table. English, I guessed, judging by the shabbiness of his cord trousers and tweed jacket. As I passed, he half raised his head. We looked straight at each other. I flushed bright scarlet, and nearly dropped my cappuccino.

It was my *bête noire*, the man who had rejected me from Magdalen, Dr Evenlode.

'I hope Slim didn't get to you,' Sylvia said, after he had driven off in a white jeep to have lunch. 'I noticed you got quiet all of a sudden back there. He likes winding people up, but he's basically a nice guy, believe me.'

'I'm sure.' I didn't want to think about Sylvia's friends just at present, but she took my agreement as sarcasm.

'No, really. Maybe I should have explained, we're kind of in the same boat.'

'I gathered he doesn't like Dave much, either.'

'Yeah, well, that isn't surprising.'

Sylvia kicked a split orange down the cobbled street. All around us, shopkeepers were hauling down thunderous rolls of green shutter over their front windows as the town clock boomed one. Families hurried home, laden with shopping; even in winter, I could hear one or two English voices carrying down Via Garibaldi, a tweedy, white-haired woman calling, 'Oh come on, Donald, that pansy bore is coming to lunch and we haven't a drop of *vino* or *aqua min!*'

We had walked to the western edge of the town. Far below, on the next hill, was a walled cemetery, and after that, mountains. It was a wild place, with only three farmhouses visible from above, and a flock of white doves endlessly wheeling in the thermal currents rising from the shadowy valley.

'Here's the mill. We'll have to carry the oil ourselves, they don't let cars come through on market day.'

A steady rumble came from the building as we approached it. Dark mulch was being ejected in spurts and belches from a long tube. Men were unloading sacks of olives from a tractor on to a rattling, wooden conveyor belt leading up to an open window on the first storey and the sharp air was rendered almost too pungent to breathe by the contents.

Up the exterior flight of stairs, everything was slick with oil. Sylvia started haggling with a man at the counter for a good price. I wandered over to the window and watched a wizened old man there pick each sack up in his corded arms and weigh it in a huge pair of brass scales. As soon as he had done so, the sack would be emptied into a wooden crate marked with chalk, and stacked against the wall. Here the rumble was loudest, and the tops of several ladders poked up over a twenty-foot drop to the room below. I looked over the edge.

It was like the engine room of a ship. Men were working frantically, stripped to the waist and covered in sweat. At one end of the room, I could see a cascade of water and olives pouring into steel vats, to be instantly whirled into a tarry paste by the granite millwheels turning round and round. A minute later, the men would spring forward and coat the paste onto a circular rope mat with a hole in the middle, so each one could be stacked on a steel post. Even as I watched, the oil ran out of this contraption. All the men had to do was screw the plate down on top, and out poured a steady green trickle.

'That is extra-virgin oil, signorina,' said the old man, who had sidled up beside me.

'How can it be extra virgin?' I enquired. 'I thought that was a condition which either is or isn't.'

The old man wheezed. 'Olives are luckier than women, signorina. They are allowed second chances. Virgin oil is what we sell to foreigners.'

'But not to me,' said Sylvia, reappearing by my side. 'Emma, do you mind splitting the cost of this? You'll be amazed how much you use, cooking.'

I gave her my last note; I had changed £50 that morning, but it all vanished very fast.

We lugged the jerry can back to the car with the shopping.

'God, what it is to have money!'

'Not very much. When my £3,000 is gone, I won't have a bean.'

'No, I was thinking of Slim and Izzy.'

'He said something about his wife's father . . .'

'Izzy's the daughter of one of the richest men in England, Sir James Zuckerman, the guy who owns Sucro. That's how she met Slim. She got married real young. It was OK in London, but it all started to go wrong for them when they moved here, seven years ago. Now she wants to divorce him and marry Dave.'

I stopped and looked at her. 'Oh,' I said.

'Yeah.' Sylvia regarded me with an air of resignation. 'I thought you'd better know, because things might get heavy at his farewell party tonight. Not that anyone really expects he'll leave for good.'

'And they're all living in the same house?'

'Slim refused to go, and Izzy didn't want to go and stay in a hotel let alone my house. Dave sleeps in the master bedroom with her.'

'Is he in love with her?'

'Some men like doormats, and some men like bathmats.' Sylvia shrugged her shoulders, dismissive. 'I don't think he's ever been in love with anyone except himself. He's the most self-confident man I've ever known. That's what makes him so attractive to someone like Izzy. He's irresistible to any woman, I guess. That sort of guy always is.'

'I don't think men like that are remotely attractive,' I said heatedly. 'All conceit, all superciliousness is revolting, even in the rare instances where it's justified. It's like people who are rude to servants. Even if they're a thousand times richer, grander, better educated, all they do is expose their own insecurity.'

'Oh, but people usually take you at your own valuation, if you project it strongly enough,' Sylvia contradicted. 'It's like actors convincing an audience they're enjoying a steak when all they've got is a piece of brown bread in front of them.'

'Only the unobservant, surely. Only people who want to be taken in.'

'Ah,' said Sylvia, leaning closer, so I smelled the scent of her hair, 'how young you are! Listen, people always want to be taken in. That's why the richest people in the world are the ones who provide illusions – drugs, films – anything that hides us from reality. And the biggest illusion in the world is love, Emma. It's like those strobe lights you get in discos that flick on and off so fast they make it look like impossible things are happening – water running back into the tap, or clumsy dancers being graceful. You know?'

'No,' I answered. 'I know nothing about these things.'

'Well,' said Sylvia, 'I guess you'll have to find out.'

4

Had I not been so alarmed at the sudden reappearance of the detestable Dr Evenlode, so appalled at the thought of Slim knowing my father, or had gained more experience of parties, I might have found more things about the events at the Dunnetts' that evening strange. On the other hand, something else happened which was so momentous that it would have absorbed all my attention anyway.

Both Sylvia and I prepared for the party with more anxiety than enthusiasm; she, I guessed, because it was the first time she had seen her husband since their separation, I because the last event of this kind had been in my childhood. (I did not count my parents' friends excruciatingly dull At-Homes, nor the stun-gun-style teen discos that had occasionally come my way.) She changed her clothes half a dozen times, eventually calling me in for advice. I did not feel qualified to give it. The mound heaped over the tarnished rails of her brass bedstead amazed me by its quality and quantity; she had started collecting antique clothes long before it became fashionable, and even had a Fortuny, rescued from a dustbin in Venice. Sylvia was the sort of person who only had to open an oyster to find a pearl, I thought.

Her room was all silks, velvet, candles and incense. One wall was covered with postcards of paintings from great galleries all over the world, some battered and franked, some pristine and new. The Bronzino that had fallen out of Sylvia's folder at our first meeting was among them. I could see at once that this was the room of someone who was different from other people, more cultured, more intense.

Clothes were crammed into a gigantic wardrobe, faced with two mirrors whose bevelled edges flashed rainbows.

More clothes jostled along a pole which ran the length of the eaves opposite her window, or lay in attitudes of abandonment on an ottoman. The marble top of a chest of drawers was piled with boxes, small and large, all painted or inlaid with mother-of-pearl.

'They're mostly from India. That's where I met Dave, ten years ago. What a long time ago it seems! We'd both just lost our parents, except that mine were poor Polacks and his father was this Surrey accountant, with a house in expensive grotsville. He bought me these boxes. I keep jewellery and stuff in them,' she said, as I admired them.

'They're marvellous.'

'Aren't they? The craftsmen are incredible. Look, this one has a secret compartment. Wouldn't you have just loved it when you were a kid?'

She pressed the base of the largest, and it slid open. Inside was a small bundle of dollars, her passport, a packet of Durex and a marble-sized ball, wrapped in foil.

'Dope,' she said, smiling her leonine Beardsleyesque smile. 'Only hash, Emma, don't look so shocked! I keep it there in case the police come round unexpectedly though it's legal to have some for personal use. They're far too thick to think of something like this. You know, they say that there's only one test to join the *carabinieri*? They break a floor tile over his head, and if he doesn't pass out, he's in. I really feel like a joint now, but I guess I'll wait until we get to the party.'

'Do you really wear all these?'

'Oh, I'm a terrible hoarder,' she said lightly. 'I never throw away anything that could be useful or worth money. No refugee ever does. When my parents came to America after the war, we lived like snails, travelling round with our things. They kept telling me how lucky I was to be seeing so much of the world, but all I wanted was to settle in one place, you know?'

'Yes.'

'So, here I am, and here I stay. This is my home, right, and I'm not letting him get rid of me. When I think of the guy I'd like to hang him by the balls over a tankful of Amazonian piranhas.'

She began putting on eye shadow the colour of dried blood. I watched in fascination. My mother never bothered with these feminine arcana, and we were not allowed it at school.

'War paint,' she observed dryly, seeing me watch her. 'Want to try some?'

'It never looks right on me.'

'A painter who doesn't know how to use herself as a canvas isn't worthy of the name. Here, keep still.'

She fiddled around with some pencils and a wand of mascara, stroking my lashes. Her fingers made me shiver.

'You should dye your lashes,' Sylvia said. 'I'll do it for you, one day.'

My egg-face was gone. It seemed older, more defined. In fact, almost pretty.

'Sylvia, I think you must be a female Pygmalion,' I remarked, staring.

'Better than a male chauvinist one, any day. Besides, men don't transform women, they only cut them down. It's women who change women, and themselves, Emma. Anyone can change themselves if they want to.'

Could they? I wondered. Sylvia was so confident, so American in her energy. She was more beautiful than any painting of hers I had seen so far, not only physically, but in the understanding of those little ornaments, those grace-notes, as Balzac called them, which make all the difference between an attractive woman and one that is simply mesmerizing. Just now, for instance, she tied a black velvet ribbon round her throat, and suddenly the whiteness of her skin sprang out, astonishing. She stared at her reflection without embarrassment, as well she might.

'Have you ever looked at your asshole in the mirror?'

'No.'

'It's great for the morale.'

'I'll try it.'

'Come on, we're late,' she said.

The drive was all downhill.

'Thank God we don't have to go through the Guardis' farm-yard on a night like this,' Sylvia said. 'Hardly anyone uses this road, but it goes all the way down to the village in the valley. Slim and Izzy are on the hillside opposite. If you look, you can probably see their lights.' She paused, peering through the spattered window. 'When Izzy and Dave started going together, she used to hang a sheet out of her bedroom window as soon as Slim had left for the shop.'

'I'm surprised she didn't paint a red stain on it,' I remarked.

The Dunnetts' house had been a wedding present from her parents, Sylvia told me; it had a swimming pool ('the only reason why they're so popular') and a pair of peacocks called Victoria and Albert who drove neighbours to distraction with their unearthly cries and periodic peregrinations. I didn't know what to expect. My parents are rich, yes, but nothing on the scale of Sucro tycoonery; their money is company money, trust

47

funds not Lear jets and megabucks. I could see little beyond the olives and stone walls lining the lane, but the wooden gate and long, gravelled drive at the end of a bumpy ascent seemed unpretentious enough.

'That was the only thing they put in for security. Izzy's dad's so frightened of kidnappers, he wanted to buy them a villa with, like, cameras and high walls all over the place, but she wasn't having any of it,' Sylvia told me. 'She said it would draw attention to them, which I guess is right.'

To my surprise, the Casa Pavone was merely a farmhouse, not unlike the Guardis' in that it was long and L-shaped, with an outside stair. The stables beneath had been converted into living rooms with french windows. Light from them slicked the wet terrace in buttery slabs.

The roar of sound that came out as we opened the door diminished slightly, though the music was too loud to make much difference. There were only about ten people in the room, some talking, some dancing. I looked hastily around to see whether Evenlode was there, and immediately felt better when I saw he was not. Slim had shown no sign of recognition when we had passed him in the bar, but I didn't dare ask whether anyone else knew him. The chances were, I thought, he was just passing through before the start of the new bout of inflicting misery on his pupils.

'Come in, you're the last to arrive,' said a small, slight woman.

She had frizzy brown hair, large, exophthalmic brown eyes and a receding chin, which gave her the look of a disgruntled domestic rodent. I was astonished when Sylvia introduced her as Izzy. Nobody could possibly prefer this gerbil to my friend, no matter how much money she had.

She was speaking in a curiously flat, nasal voice. I wondered if she was tone-deaf, it was such an unmusical sound. ('Only socially,' Sylvia said afterwards).

'Of course, Dave's whole thing of going away isn't more than a holiday, really. This is just an excuse for a party. We've all been under intense pressure here, as I'm sure you can imagine.'

Both Sylvia and I stared at her, I incredulous, Sylvia inscrutable.

'I can imagine any number of things,' she said.

'I'm sure Daddy's lawyers will be contacting you soon about the divorce.'

'They can try.'

Izzy sighed. 'I do hope you aren't going to be difficult about all this, Sylvia. You can't be possessive about people, and we have to go on living together.'

'Oh, there's Lucio,' said Sylvia. 'I want to speak to him.' She detached herself and sailed over to a young Italian man.

Izzy and I watched her kiss him on both cheeks. 'Americans!' Izzy said, trying, I suppose, to enlist some sort of patriotic solidarity from me. 'That accent, how did he stand it?'

'I love it,' I told her.

'It makes me think of powdered glass in treacle.'

I said nothing. Izzy bit her nails, or what was left of them. Neurosis had left her with no more than tiny scraps embedded in puffy flesh.

'How well do you know each other?' she asked.

'Quite well in one sense, not very in another.'

'Be careful, then. There's less to her than meets the eye.'

'How fortunate,' I said, 'that nobody could say the same of you.'

She was stupid enough to take it as a compliment. 'No, they can't, can they? Of course, that's the great advantage of being luckier than most people.'

Whenever rich people talk about luck, they never mean it. They say it as a propitiatory superstition, like touching wood, but they don't think of it as such. They think they deserve it.

Izzy's house did indeed ooze wealth, though the taste, I guessed, was probably Slim's. Casa Pavone was like the inside of a box of liquorice allsorts. There were angular, outsize chairs upholstered in screaming pink and turquoise, and a strange asymmetrical black sideboard decorated with wavy bits of metal. The sofas were all modern – soft black leather that I knew would engulf sitters in a squidgy embrace and take mean little nips of hair from the legs as you shifted about. Springy silver lamps were poised over them like man-sized question marks, waiting to pounce. Their lights glared down on sitters in inquisition: How much are you worth? Whom do you know? Who do you think you are?

The grace of the old building subdued the worst of it. I persuaded myself that I liked it because it belonged, at least in part, to those friends of Sylvia's who were, she promised, part of the great freemasonry of artists, but my eye cannot be switched off. It was a horrible room.

The other guests did not seem at all nonplussed. They lounged around in clothes ranging from the smart to the shabby, with their feet up on the sofas, spilling red wine on the Persian carpets and dancing about to the music in the next room. Several small sculptures (each carefully positioned beneath its own spotlight) had been used as ashtrays. Izzy did not care, it was obvious, though some of them were good.

I touched a marble baby's head, its features barely delineated. 'Epstein?'

'Slim likes that sort of crap. Have you met him?'

'Yes, earlier today.'

'He's in the kitchen, making hash pizza. It's about all that will make this bloody party tolerable, I think.'

She yawned, rudely, in my face. I looked around for Sylvia in desperation. She had her back to me, and was talking to someone through the archway into the next room. Beyond, I could see Slim in a marble abattoir of a kitchen, slicing tomatoes. No help there.

Someone else saw me, however.

'Well, who's this you've been hiding?'

'A friend of Sylvia's, though she tells me she doesn't know her very well. I'm sorry, I've forgotten your name.'

I had not thought what he would be like to cause Sylvia so much upset, but then, it was logical. Didn't people always choose partners with the same level of physical beauty as themselves? Unless, I thought, one of them was very rich.

Like a gigantic noise, Sylvia's husband blotted out everyone else in the room. I did not find him attractive myself; he was too old, on the other side of the gulf of experience I had not begun to traverse, but I could feel it, all the same. He seemed to concentrate on you and you alone, but in such a way that you knew in the back of your mind he was only granting you an audience for as long as you eluded him; then he'd move on. Dangerous, dangerous man. He asked me questions about myself, and I was quite unable to stop blushing and blurting out all my hopes for the next nine months.

'So, here you are, with Baedeker stars in your eyes. You're really going to Oxford?'

'If I decide to take my place.'

'Oh, you should, you know,' said Izzy with animation, as if she couldn't wait to get rid of me then and there.

'It's a beautiful city.'

'Did you go there?'

'No. I should have done, but I wanted to act.'

'Dave was in *Upstairs, Downstairs*,' Izzy informed me proudly. I tried to look impressed.

He shrugged, and turned up the charm a bit more. 'After about ten years, I decided that what I really wanted to do was write.'

'Dave's quite brilliant, but he can't make the contacts, living out here. But we're going to change all that, aren't we, darling?'

Izzy put her hand on his arm. It was not only a possessive gesture, for she swayed slightly as she stood. Love had rendered her as unbalanced as an infection of the inner ear. I almost felt sorry for her, especially when he brushed it off, irritably.

'Emma hasn't even got a glass of wine,' he said.

'Oh! Sorry.' She became all gerbil. 'Red or white? I'll get you one at once.'

Izzy left, almost running. Dave grinned at me, and I smiled back, warily.

He said, 'Too many people are polite to her just because of her money.'

'Whereas you're rude to her because of it.' I had no idea how to talk to men, but I felt confrontation was the best policy.

'It has a novelty value for her. If old Slim had realized that, he wouldn't be getting the boot. In more ways than one. She met him when she was a spoilt little graphics student from St Martin's and he was the cool art director who had coke delivered by messenger bike. Then, when she found out she wasn't good enough to make the grade in advertising, she decided craft was the thing, and that she was bored with London. So they came out here full time. Slim hates it, but he's gone all soft and middle class. Wants to settle down and have a fambly,' he said, in a perfect, sneering imitation of Slim's voice. 'End of marriage.'

'Are you telling me this as an excuse?'

He put his head back and laughed. 'Why should I have to justify my actions to you? Or anyone?'

I couldn't think of an answer. He grew suddenly and visibly bored. I was ashamed; my first real conversation with a man, which I had thought was going so well, had been a failure.

'Come and meet everyone else at my farewell party.'

I followed him.

The stereo boomed. One or two of the guests started to sing along with Joni Mitchell. I could not see Sylvia anywhere.

'Are you really going to leave for good?'

He shrugged.

'Where will you go?'

'Germany or Greece. I haven't decided. Want to come?' The blue of his eyes was like a kingfisher diving.

'Send me a postcard,' I said.

'I never remember to post them.'

'How long will you be gone for?'

I had my own reasons for asking this; what if he decided he had made a mistake, and wanted to move back in with Sylvia? What if the divorce went through, and the house was sold over her head, as she feared?

'It could be a month, it could be a year, it could be for ever,' Dave said airily. 'I don't want to make any decisions right now. It depends how much boredom I can stand. Don't you sometimes think almost anything, even killing yourself, would be better than everything coming round year after year, and nothing changing except that each year you're a bit closer to falling apart? No? No, of course you wouldn't, you're too young still. I think boredom is the eighth deadly sin.'

'Ah, but can you name them all?' A stocky little man in a blue smock spoke with a slight French accent.

'I'm sure Emma can, she's going to Oxford.'

'Well?' he demanded.

'Lust, sloth, envy,' I began. 'Gluttony, avarice.'

I looked round the circle of unfamiliar faces, with the uneasy feeling of performing a parlour trick.

'Good show,' said an Englishwoman with a stringy ponytail and gummy teeth. 'That's five. I bet you can't remember them all, Louis.'

'I always forget gluttony.'

'Pride. Oh, dear, the last one escapes me.'

'Anger,' said Louis. 'Tell me, are you an angry young woman?'

'Sometimes,' I admitted.

He turned to the rest. 'You know, it is a curious fact that people always forget the sin which they most partake of.'

'Though nobody, but nobody, ever forgets lust,' drawled another woman.

'Who could ever forget it with you around, Mimi darling,' said Dave. 'Even the grapes in your fingers look as if they've been pumped with silicone.'

'It's probably that radiation or something they put on South African fruit,' she answered, inspecting them with a toss of her head. She made great play with her hair, flicking it about as though troubled by an invisible horsefly.

She was blonde, like me, but had, unforgivably, the texture and colour I always hoped for when trying a new shampoo.

I thought she might be South African herself, for she spoke in the curious bliplike accent colonials always have, as if broadcasting their voices over an ancient wireless, but I realized after a bit she was Australian. Her ears and fingers were barnacled with gold jewellery. I wondered what she was doing in Tuscany; Via Condotti looked more her style.

'Here's your wine,' said Izzy, reappearing. 'Have some pizza, guys. Dave, I want a word with you.'

'In a moment,' he said. 'Darling.'

She looked furious.

'You behave like a married couple already,' said Louis. 'Excellent.'

Archly, an Englishwoman remarked, 'No wonder you've never had much time for your book, Dave. You should be like Louis and live like a hermit, dedicated to Art.'

Everyone looked at her in embarrassment.

'Personally, Caroline, I think all writing has become a branch of gynaecology, which any man is wise to avoid,' said Louis. 'What happens to men who write? Either they are homosexuals, or they go mad, like Tolstoy.'

'What about that man staying with the Contessa?' Caroline asked. 'The Oxford fellow.' I felt myself tense. 'Isn't he supposed to be a writer?'

'I don't know,' said Louis, shrugging.

'Is she really mad, the Contessa? My pupils tell me all sorts of strange stories about her and her husband,' Mimi remarked, her face suddenly sharp. 'They say she wouldn't let the Count be buried in the cemetery. You know her, don't you, Louis? Is she a complete kook?'

'How can I tell? Perhaps you think me a crazy man, too, because I prefer animals to people,' he answered irritably. 'I think she's just a little eccentric.'

'That's what you call mad people when they're rich.'

'Mimi's only interested in rich people, aren't you, Mimi?' Dave said. I couldn't tell whether he meant it as a joke.

'Well, I'm not the only one.'

'Dave, you must come now,' said Izzy, who had been listening without interest. 'I'll see you upstairs, OK?'

'OK.'

She left, and he rolled his eyes briefly at me. 'Better have one for the road.'

'When are you leaving?' I asked, trying not to guess what he meant.

'Tonight. There's a mate of Lucio's in Florence driving long-distance lorries this week. I'm hitching a lift with him as far as he's going, then on.'

'Then where?'

'I don't know. Afghanistan maybe. You know the trouble with living like we all do? We're getting stuck in a rut. We should be like little Emma. All you need to walk out is your passport.' He patted a back pocket where his own stuck out.

'And money,' said Mimi, sweetly. 'You won't have forgotten that.'

Dave winked at her. 'You should know, I never look a gift whore in the mouth,' he said.

He went upstairs. Minutes later, a small shower of plaster began to cascade regularly from the ceiling. Someone – Slim, I think – went and turned the music up louder, and we all pretended to ignore it when Izzy's voice rose and fell in a frightful, yodelling ecstasy.

After midnight, the party became a blur. Some people went off into a small, dark room to smoke dope and watch a video about motorcycle gangs in post-holocaust Australia. I rejoined Sylvia. She seemed nervous and withdrawn, but unwilling to leave though I was dropping with tiredness and longing to go home. Caroline's brother Tim (whose face, like a subordinate clause, was bracketed by a pair of long whiskers) had his arm round Sylvia's shoulders and kept trying to kiss her. Everyone was passing round joints made by the Italian, Lucio, who walked in at some point. I tried one and coughed a lot, not being a smoker. They seemed to do nothing to me, though everyone else became either silly or stupefied, giggling at the china ducks flying up one wall. People came and went. I half-dozed on a floor cushion. The room became sweaty with all the bodies in it. A man sat down beside me, and I roused myself.

'This film,' Lucio asked in Italian. 'You understand it?'

'No.' I hardly dared look at him; very beautiful young men seemed to my English eyes a sport of nature.

'Good.'

He was silent for a while.

'I feel hot.'

Automatically I put my hand out to his forehead. He took it in his own fingers instead.

'What a cold little hand.'

Che gelida manina. I thought it must be fate.

'Are you a musician?'

'Yes.'

'I thought so.'

'Are you an artist?'

'Yes.'

'You have a painter's hands.'

I was thankful for the darkness.

There was a pause, in which several motorcycles were blown up.

'I need to go outside, I'm going to be sick,' he said quietly to me.

'I'll help you.'

He put his arm round me, and the shock of it set up a tremor that would not be stilled. I became very brisk and nurselike, once we were out. The living room seemed deserted; I could not see Sylvia anywhere, and for some reason I was glad. I supported Lucio on one shoulder, and opened the french windows with my free arm, helping him out into the icy air. He was not sick, but he fell down in a sort of faint. I put his head between his knees; it was the sort of thing St Crumpet's was quite good at teaching you, because people were always passing out during morning prayers.

'Thank you,' he said after a pause. 'You are very kind.'

'Do you feel better now?'

'Yes.'

I made to withdraw, but he caught my hand. 'What are you doing here?'

'I'm a friend of Sylvia's. I'm staying here with her while Dave is away.'

'Ah. The little English girl she writes to. I remember. You are not so little.'

'No.'

We looked at each other for what seemed like a long time.

'Do you want to go in now?'

'Not yet. Look how still it is, how clear. There's a light on in the Palazzo Felice on the other hill, can you see? And the train down in the valley? It's like a luminous caterpillar, creeping along.'

'I can hear it, too, now. Or is that something else?'

A faint, musical sound came up the hillside, two notes repeated three times. Lucio tensed. 'I think that's a lorry. Dave must be leaving,' he said.

'Without saying goodbye?'

'Yes. That is how he wanted it.'

There was a sudden commotion from inside, and Izzy rushed out. 'Where is he? Where is he? He promised he wouldn't leave without telling me!'

'He has.'

Sylvia glided out of the shadows. I couldn't tell how long she had been there. We all started, and Lucio dropped my hand.

'You!' said Izzy, angrily. 'What have you been doing? Where's Dave?'

'A long way from here,' Sylvia answered. Her face shone in the moonlight. 'You'll never find him.'

'How dare you!' said Izzy. 'I knew we shouldn't invite you, but he insisted.'

'How dare I?' Sylvia asked dryly. 'He was mine for ten years, before you and your moneybags came along. You don't think he ever wanted you for yourself, do you? Who ever would?'

'He was fed up with you and all your scenes. You drove him away, not me.'

Slim came out of the house. 'So, we're having a barney now, are we? Great. Can I join in?'

58

'That depends whose side you're on,' Sylvia said.

'Me own, of course.'

'Oh, Slim, I'm so unhappy,' said Izzy. 'Be nice to me, just for once.'

'That depends on your dad's lawyers, girlie.'

Lucio was standing very still. 'What are they saying?' he asked in Italian.

'Can't you understand?'

'Only a word here or there.'

'They're talking about the divorce. I don't understand much myself. I'm so cold and tired.'

Sylvia noticed us whispering. 'Come on, Emma, let's go. It's far too late for you to be up.'

'Playing mother now, are we?' asked Izzy, sneering, and Sylvia flinched.

Had I not loved her so much, I wouldn't have seen it, but everything about Sylvia concerned me. I turned on our hostess and said, contemptuously, 'Sylvia does not need to play at anything. She and I are friends. It seems you have none, so I'd hardly expect you to understand. We all heard you with him tonight. I think you're the most ghastly woman I've ever met.'

After that, we went.

5

After the party, Sylvia and I saw almost nobody for three weeks. I did not regret my outburst, and neither did she.

'You were great,' she told me. Nevertheless, we did not feel sociable for quite a while.

Every morning, I would get up and make coffee, thick and black, into which we would pour lavish amounts of the thin, bluish milk we bought once a week. If the rain stopped, we would sit outside, looking at the view until the damp rose up our long skirts to knee level. We kept each other company, drawing each other, brushing each other's hair, talking about every subject – except Sylvia's future when Dave came back. That was taboo.

It was a sleepy, private time. With February, rain set in, grey torsions swirling up and down the valley below like gigantic, half-glimpsed deities. The mountains and the plain were cocooned in cloud. Our gravelled road quickly disintegrated to a chalky, bubbling stream. Sounds became muffled and echoing. Even the peacocks on the hill opposite fell silent, and the cock in the Guardis' farmyard was damped down to a single aubade; its increasing hoarseness made us both laugh to hear it, though the dog continued to bark and howl at the moon when the fit took it.

We avoided the *contadini* wherever possible. Sylvia told me, in an unguarded moment, that the Guardis hated Dave in particular because they thought he had cheated them out of the house which a relative had sold, at his persuasion, to the Dunnetts.

'The greed of peasants when they think there is some money to be made or some land to be bought is really amazing,' she said. 'They won't spend any money on what isn't their own. They live for free in one of the Contessa's farmhouses, which could be easily big enough for the whole family if they converted the ground floor, but no way, Jose. They prefer to squeeze six of them into two bedrooms. It isn't even as though they don't have the money – Maria and her husband and parents all work. Just incredible.'

When we ran out of food, we would walk up a narrow path that began outside the old front door on the landing, wriggled up the side of the house through a small wood, and emerged just below the parterre. In this way, a walker could bypass the Guardis and their yellow hound. It was a slippery route, bleached and pleached with dead grass, and seemed almost to have a will of its own if one wasn't concentrating. Even Sylvia could be misled on occasion. One fork brought us out several times beneath the high, spiked walls of the Palazzo Felice. They looked as though they were built by giants, being constructed with boulders or hacked out of the rock itself. According to Sylvia, they were of great antiquity.

'There's a garden inside which hardly anyone has ever seen, full of trees clipped into weird shapes. Dave told me. He bought the house from her, and acted as a kind of agent selling off her estate,' she said. 'The Contessa is some kind of nut, though.'

'What's wrong with her?' I was eager to hear the faults of Dr Evenlode's hostess.

'She had her husband and son buried there, and refuses

to let anyone in from the town, because of what happened during the war. They were in the Italian Resistance, and got caught and executed. Apparently, when the Contessa came back from America, she had them dug up out of the Santorno cemetery and buried in the castle grounds with this huge garden planted round them. It caused a scandal, as you can imagine, especially as she stood in the piazza and cursed their betrayer.'

'Like Verdi,' I said, impressed. 'Who was it?'

'I don't know. Nobody will say. It's one of those dark, provincial secrets,' Sylvia said, arpeggios of laughter trembling in her voice, 'like whether the padre, Don Giovanni, really has a mistress in San Sepolchro, and who embezzled the local Communist Party Funds. Every small town lives off legends like these, for old women to tell when they get together and chew the fat.'

'Do they take it seriously?'

'You know how superstitious Catholics are; you should have seen my parents! The Santornese practically cross themselves when they go past the palazzo gates. The Contessa has never been into the town since. She hates them and hardly sees anyone local, apart from her lawyer and Maria Guardi's family, who look after the house and lands. Even Dave only saw her once. Louis sees her occasionally, but he never gossips. She has visitors now and then, but they're mostly from abroad; she's half English, you see. But this Oxford guy is the first one I've seen under forty.'

It did indeed have a forlorn and somewhat sinister air, I thought, peering in through the wrought-iron gates. The arch in the wall was guarded by a pair of sneering caryatids, each wreathed in garlands of fruit and flowers. Beyond, a mossy avenue of cypress trees sloped up the hill. Nothing seemed able to pierce its gloom, though many streams emerged from secret crevices in the walls, fanged with green, slow-dripping icicles. It amused me to imagine Evenlode and the Contessa living there like the Draculas, emerging only at nightfall, but I was never really easy until we came to the parterre.

Most of the time, we stayed indoors.

We were both very drained: I by the past and my escape from home; Sylvia, I presumed, by worry about the future. I had nightmares about my parents, dreadful rituals of accusation and condemnation in which I was paralysed, unable to defend myself, tears of anguish and frustration pouring down my face. When I woke to see the black beams over my head and knew I was free, it was with an ache that was almost like pain.

Whether Sylvia had nightmares, I have no idea.

It remained painfully cold, too cold to stay outside and almost too cold to stay inside. On bad days, there was the unenviable choice of either choking with smoke from the fire or having to risk hypothermia. Our lives revolved around keeping warm and cooking, an art I had despised at school, but now discovered to be surprisingly satisfying.

Sylvia was shocked at my ignorance of household matters; she even had to show me how to hold a broom when sweeping.

'Didn't your mother teach you?'

'We've always had housekeepers.'

'Does she work?'

'Mummy? No. She did a stint as a secretary, that's how she met Daddy. I suppose she's quite social. She likes organizing and that sort of thing, because she's very bossy.'

'She must be very bored, then.'

'Bored?' This was a new idea. 'I don't know. I've never heard her say so, and she isn't someone who keeps her opinions to herself. I just don't think she likes me, or maybe it's women generally. She's rather beautiful, I suppose, in a terrifying Valkyrish sort of way. Justin and I were always convinced she must have proposed to Daddy, and not the other way about. I'm sure she could have taught me to cook if she wanted to, but she has no interest.'

'She sounds a bitch on wheels. No, chop firmly. Be decisive. You've got to show the fucking onions who's boss, then they don't make you cry. It's like everything else in life. You hesitate and lose confidence for a single second, and the bastards will spring on you.'

'Really?'

'Honest.'

I thrilled when Sylvia spoke to me like this. I amused her with my naivety, I knew, but I felt she was giving me the concentrated essence of all her exotic experience. I had had a vague idea that Americans were brash and stupid, always asking questions in squeaky Bugs Bunny voices and doing idiotic things like taking photographs of Nelson's Column through each other's legs, but Sylvia was the most sophisticated person I had ever met. She told me that she had spent a year on the road in America, picking men up in bars and dumping them. She had been in a commune in Germany and an ashram in India; she had been the mistress of an American history professor in Brighton, cooked for a film star, sung in a jazz band in Greenwich Village and travelled round Europe with an experimental dance company, before deciding to study art at Perugia and become a painter. She had lived as nobody else I knew lived; apart, perhaps, from Pompa, and he had never talked much about his travels.

'I'm old enough to be your mother,' she said once.

'Only a very young one. Would you like to have a baby?'

'I can't,' she said, shortly. Then, after a pause, 'Dave and I tried, when things were OK between us, though he was never very keen on babies. He said that in England, on TV, every time he was in a series with a really slummy setting, like a council block, they always made the sound of a baby crying in the background. So it was never any good. It's probably just as well. I'd only have given it complexes.'

I did not know whether she saw me as an adopted daughter, a friend, a pupil or a paying guest. It didn't matter. I loved her.

We cooked. The blue lotus of the gas rings swayed beneath pots of bubbling meals, vivid with spices and colours. Sylvia believed that food should look as well as taste extraordinary; she had an insatiable appetite for violent contrasts of the sweet and the sharp. She liked mustard on cheese, pepper on strawberry jam and peanut butter on sausages. Some tastes were more predictable. She lamented the lack of jelly in Santorno's supermarket, of giant packets of popcorn, of canned beer, and would gorge herself on pots of a revolting chocolate spread at breakfast, though she never put on weight.

I delighted in these small weaknesses; they made her beauty vital, like the spots on a lily. I tried to imitate everything she did, from the way she dressed to her voice, which was more like singing than speaking, and achieved a transatlantic drawl.

'You sound like someone trying to open a tin can with a silver spoon,' she told me, when she realized this. 'Be yourself, not me.'

Her eccentricities were unique, though. She would howl and moan when the weather forecast on the radio said that another depression was approaching, and encourage the fire to burn by directing blasts from her hairdryer at it. In the morning, she religiously threw balls of hair from her brush out of the window for birds to find and make nests, regardless of the season. She talked to her plants, and firmly believed they understood every word she uttered; once she tried to explain to me how they were in contact with aliens from outer space, but I think we were both a bit high that time.

65

She had the American belief that if you wanted something badly enough, no power on earth could stop you.

'Look at the number of people who've killed Presidents,' she said, 'in spite of all those bodyguards and all that technology. Look at all the great artists who've been born handicapped. You know—' She gave me one of her electric, silvery stares. 'I've sometimes wondered whether I wouldn't be a better painter if I cut off one of my ears, or something.'

'Sylvia!'

'No, suffering enhances. I guess it's the only thing I'm a snob about, the degree to which people have suffered. But maybe being a woman is handicap enough.'

Her literary tastes were no less odd. I had read practically nothing written this century; she had read nothing outside it. I had brought a couple of paperbacks with me, as well as Gombrich, and lent them to her. She was bored by *Great Expectations* ('the guy's a nerd'), and threw *Lost Illusions* down after the first ten pages. For my part, I could not begin to understand the books in her house. They all appeared to be about people who either wandered round the American country drugged to the eyeballs, or who wandered round American cities drugged to the eyeballs, or lived in Hollywood and didn't care whether they were drugged or not as long as they were making millions.

'Well, Dave thought they were really great,' she said, shrugging.

Rain came in through the roof and the chimney. I would listen to the quick plink! plink! as drops fell into buckets all over the house. A velvety fungus crept up the bathroom walls, spattering it with delicate patterns.

'Hey, it's natural flocked wallpaper,' Sylvia said. 'We could make a fortune selling it in spray cans!'

In the living room, half the wall consisted of the naked rock, grey and topaz, the bones of the hillside, and here the rain seeped in like an indoor waterfall, to be carried away by a little stream chiselled in the floor.

'You really don't care?' Sylvia asked, her white skin tinged with blue as she huddled up under a goat-hair rug, while I tried, for the tenth time, to light the fire.

'I think it's enchanting.'

Washing froze on the line and Sylvia's contact lenses in their case. The business of doing sheets by hand in the bath was the most unpleasant chore of the week. Sylvia was terrified of the water heater, which worked off what the Italians gloomily called a bomb of gas, because she was always convinced it would set the house on fire. My fear was less rational: to me, it looked like a witch with a peaked hat and a flame in her navel. I wanted to paint it, of course, with Sylvia in the bath.

But painting was not going well. I tried sketching, the first week, to get used to the change in light, but drawing always makes me impatient. Either you put as much effort into the drawing as into a painting, so you're denying yourself all the sensuous pleasure of colour, or else it's a botch. So I cut some of my precious canvas, made a frame for it, and spent hours shivering in my bedroom trying to paint the view I had first seen from the window. It was scarcely original as a subject. What reduced me to tears of frustration was that I couldn't do it. I would stare and stare, until my hands and feet became chilblained and my eyes would ache in their sockets, but I couldn't see it properly.

Fools and philistines think that you're a painter if you can make your hand follow what your eye sees, because most people don't have that sort of co-ordination. It's a gift, like perfect pitch, but it doesn't make you into a real painter any more than perfect pitch makes you a singer or a true musician. The real thing isn't just reproducing, it's seeing. I had to understand not just the shape, colour, volume, detail, light, but what it was, how it could make a picture, where the beauty was. That was the trouble. There was too much of it, all around; and the beauty I struggled with was not that of nature, but of man.

Lucio had come round five times, despite the bad weather. I did not dare think why; ostensibly it was to sell Sylvia the little balls of Moroccan cannabis which she, and occasionally I, smoked, and which I found myself paying for.

'He's seen a gap in the market, now Dave has gone,' she observed dryly. 'Dave used to go to Florence for everyone and rake in the cash. Trust a Tuscan.'

But there was something else in the air, I could tell. We never touched, or referred to his bout of faintness at the party; he seemed on the contrary to be crackling with energy.

I had to gulp his image down, greedily, in flashes, but it burned on my retina as though it had been seared. He was a creature of light; the locks on his head, the down on his arms were shafted with gold. His irises were yellow, radiant. He was my Apollo, it hurt me to look at him. I tried telling myself it was an accident of flesh and bone, that a millimetre here or there was all that divided him from the rest of humanity, but it was no good. There was still that millimetre.

How could such a person not be extraordinary? He had such panache, from the black star in his earlobe to the Levis tucked into the embroidered cowboy boots on his feet.

Yet he appeared not to care about material possessions. He did not care if his boots became muddy or his clothes soaked. He would turn up with a huge white candle he had taken from the church in Santorno, or a single red rose for us, and, always, his guitar.

Sylvia and I would sit listening, rapt. He would play classical pieces, Villa Lobos, mostly, and songs that belonged to another era. I knew only Bros and Eurythmics – stylish and empty – and the passion with which he sang surprised me, especially as he could not speak a word of English.

He and Sylvia talked politics a lot. This was something I knew nothing about; I had always thought it was a hobby that had been invented by clever people to mop up bores and busybodies. Sylvia supported the Green Party; Lucio was an anarchist. I did not know what I was.

Once, when we had all been arguing about chaos and the need for order, we were standing shivering on the doorstep as he was about to leave. Sylvia went back in to go to the loo, and we were left alone for a couple of minutes.

He pointed up at the night sky. 'What do you see?' he asked me.

'Stars,' I said, and it was true. 'Constellations. My grandfather taught them to me. The Plough, Orion's belt, Pegasus, Sirius.'

'You make pictures even in the empty air,' he answered. 'You think that if you can join the dots out there, you will find shapes and reasons. There is nothing. Just blackness, and balls of flaming gases.'

'I know,' I said, 'but I can't believe it. Besides, there is order even in the natural world, as one of your countrymen discovered. The ways leaves grow on trees, the proportions of your body, the spirals of nebulae, are all reducible to mathematical series. I can't believe in chaos, knowing that.'

'Listen Emma.' He looked into my eyes. 'I'm not talking about science or any of that rubbish you may have learned in your little English school. I'm talking about people. In life, things happen, they happen to people and there is no reason for it, just as there is no blame. There are no pictures and there is no order. You understand?'

I felt sick and breathless, so I nodded; and he smiled at me just as Sylvia came out.

Nothing mattered to him except music, though he hated the Italian operas I so loved.

'It's all bourgeois art, written for a tiny minority. Jazz, folk, rock – these are the rhythms of the people, because they came out of the people,' he told me. I accepted it, as I accepted all he told me, and stopped trying to tune the radio to the Vatican station to hear classical music.

He was full of energy. I loved it when he would become angry about something we were all discussing, for then he would spring up and prowl about, full of tension and grace. All he said and thought was underlined by movement; watching him, I understood something that had puzzled me about the Italian language – why there is one word, say, for a hop, a skip and a jump. An Italian will show the difference with his hands or his body, not just with words, like an Englishman.

He would talk and play for an hour, two hours, then leave. The house was desolate when he had gone; it took days for the mood of peaceful femininity to seep back.

Once, Tim Danby called round, though when he had arrived in the pouring rain, he didn't know what to do, stupid man. I wondered whether he was half-witted. He sat there for an hour, all boots and beard, and a sweater that looked (and smelled) as though it had been knitted out of the hairs of old-age pensioners, talking about the weather and ogling Sylvia. We were not very polite to him. Eventually, he stomped off back to his mouldering farm in the mountains, muttering, 'If there's ever, er, ever any need – call. Please.'

'Do you think, was he dropped on his head as a kid?' asked Sylvia, after he left.

'He got the looks, Caroline got the brains,' I said. 'Or is it the other way about?'

'I wonder what they're doing here, really. I mean, they're not creative people at all.'

Sylvia seemed more irritated than pleased even by Lucio's

visits. I came in, once, and they looked as if they had been quarrelling.

'He's always spying on me,' she complained in explanation afterwards.

'What, for Dave?' Sylvia had told me he had been her husband's greatest friend and admirer.

She smiled faintly at my question. 'Who knows. Maybe.'

She asked me what I thought of Lucio and I was in a panic in case she had guessed. Women only ask that question when they're in love, or think you are. I wondered if he had said anything.

'Don't you think he's a little weird? I mean, he's closer to you in age than me.'

'How old is he?'

'Twenty-three, I guess. He had to do military service for a year when he finished at Florence University.'

'Oh no,' I said. 'I don't think he's strange. He's different.'

'How so?'

'Well,' I said, blushing, 'he doesn't make his eyes go all yuk like most of them. You know.'

Sylvia burst out laughing. *Occhi d'amore*. Yeah, I know. He doesn't.'

'I think someone has hurt him in the past.'

I was probing, of course, in the most obvious way. Surely he could not be celibate? Sometimes I had caught him looking at me, then looking away again quickly. It always surprised me how calm I remained at such moments; it was only afterwards that I started shaking.

Sylvia sighed. 'He had a twin sister, Gabriella. She died while he was away. He's still totally freaked out by it.'

I stared at her. 'A twin?'

She nodded.

'How terrible for him, I mean, I'm not very fond of Justin, but a twin is different. It must be like losing half of yourself.'

71

'Yeah. The parents are shattered. There were only the two of them. Though of course, in an Italian family, the son is the important one. Actually, she was a bit of a pain in the ass, to tell the truth. Always hanging round Lucio, like a ball and chain. A born loser.'

'But he isn't, is he?'

Sylvia's full mouth stretched into a slow smile as she looked at me.

'I guess not, honey. I guess not.'

It became worse. It didn't have anything to do with the heart, as everyone said; nor was it remotely enjoyable. I felt as though my skin was going to burst. At night I would turn and burn until my sheets were wrapped between my legs like a corkscrew. It drove daggers of wind into my intestines, gave me diarrhoea and nausea, twitched and itched until I thought I would go mad. Many of Sylvia's books extolled female masturbation, suggesting a grisly array of implements from cucumbers to vibrators. I knew it would be no good, even if I could bear to try them. Besides, I wanted sin, not synecdoche.

Sometimes I woke up and thought I heard his voice, but it was only Sylvia, murmuring in her sleep. I wondered if it was worse doing without sex when you knew what it was like.

I lived in a suspended frenzy of anticipation. It was impossible to paint other things, for I spent all my energies painting myself. The prospect of his coming made me wash my hair almost daily, despite the cold water, soaking it in camomile to make it fairer. I learned how to dye my lashes and put Sylvia's kohl in them, became thinner and, to my surprise, not unlike a smaller version of my mother. None of it did any good.

Sylvia was away once a fortnight, attending her course in Perugia; she did not invite me to accompany her, and I preferred to stay in the house, hoping for another unexpected visit.

When she was there, I went for long walks. I was afraid that if I stayed, I would blurt it all out, and she would laugh at me, for she was always going on about the cruelty and treachery of love, and what fools it made of women. Besides, there was always the possibility of bumping into Lucio on the way down to see us. She did not seem to mind being left alone, though she warned me to look out for snakes.

'They're not too dangerous now, but look where you tread. Someone dies from snakebite every year, round here. Make sure you carry a stick.'

I did not like the sound of this, but I had to get out of the house, and I never saw any, except once, and that was much later.

It was becoming milder. Waking, the earth puckered and boiled. Flat green iris leaves speared out of arthritic roots. Silent, slow-motion cannon-puffs of blossom went off all over the valley. Almond trees released the sickly scent of cyanide. The tarred road in the valley was littered with the corpses of toads, squashed flat in mid-copulation beneath the wheels of passing cars.

Eventually, the rain ceased. Lazy black bullets of African bees would drone past. Birds whistled and fought musical duels.

'People think they sing for joy,' Lucio had told me. 'But they are like all artists. They sing to warn each other off their territories.'

The patchy grass coagulated, then ran with violets.

Sod it, I thought crossly, decapitating nettles with my stick. Why does everything in the world have someone except me?

I was nervous of going into Santorno alone; my terror of shopkeepers and strangers had not gone, though it was diminished by frequent contact in Sylvia's company. Ordering a cappuccino in the Bar Popolare, however, was not beyond me. I decided to go into town.

I began walking along the path that led to the parterre, but somehow I became lost in the little wood that it wound through, and emerged too far to the right.

It was in this way that I again met the person I most wanted to avoid.

6

I had begun to hope that Evenlode had left. He was never in the Bar Popolare; nobody seemed to know him. With any luck, I thought, he had gone back to his bastion of chauvinism and would leave me in peace. I no longer felt so uneasy round the walls of the Felice estate; indeed, I almost had a sense of triumph, as though I personally had got rid of him.

I was not, however, pleased to find myself on one of the paths that led to the palazzo walls. It was muddy, and overgrown, with brambles sneakily placed at eye-level so that I had to duck and weave to make any progress at all. I became lost and cross, retracing my steps. Finally, the path petered out unexpectedly into a clearing.

I had emerged into a narrow cleft between two hills, invisible unless you happened to walk right into it. Too narrow for tractors, its terraces had fallen into disrepair. Cherry, bay and old man's beard grew in between the olives and tangled vines, with dishevelled dryad elegance. It was warmer than elsewhere. The soil, where it was exposed, was rich and red, and wild flowers came out all the way along a stream in profusion: primroses, periwinkles, violets, bugloss, bergenia, pulmonaria.

The stream rushed out from a semicircular stone pool set in a raised patch of green. It was fed by a stone head set in sheer rock that eventually became the palazzo walls. The only sound was of water falling on water. As I drew nearer, the marble face proved to be that of a man; the water came out of his open mouth.

It was no ordinary garden ornament, that was plain. He was carved with delicacy and precision, each lock of hair and curl of horn etched out to match the beauty of his features. I wondered who had put it there; whether it was a whim of the Contessa's or one of her husband's ancestors. It looked old and must surely be valuable. What really shocked me, though, was his expression. There was a wildness, an air of not being confined by normal human considerations. The ooze of some passing snail had left a glistening track of moisture across the eyeballs; I could almost believe the sculpture would blink, for he gave the illusion that good paintings have, of following an onlooker around.

It made me acutely uneasy and at the same time excited. I began to notice things in the way I normally do only when concentrating hard on a painting. The damp lichen on the trees flashed and glowed like jewelled lace. The grass crackled with insects. In one tree, I could see the Dunnetts' peacocks roosting, Albert's tail hanging down in galaxies of iridescence. Things shimmered at the corners of my vision as if a migraine was coming on. I put my hand out to wash my face.

Immediately, something that was all teeth and claws leapt up on my shoulder, pushing me over. As I fell, banging my kneecap against the side of the pool, my hand entered it. I had a surprise so intense that the pain shooting through my leg almost left me. The water was red, and as warm as blood.

The next moments were fairly confused. I ended up sitting on some very muddy grass, with the Guardis' yellow dog all mixed up in my cloak.

'Down, Tonto, down!' said a woman's voice in Italian.

'As far as I'm concerned, he should be put down.'

'The signorina is hurt.'

'Is she? He's a bit overenthusiastic at being let off the leash. Down, boy!'

The peacocks let out a shrill, chilling shriek and took off down the valley, making everyone jump.

Dr Evenlode struggled with the dog.

'It would be you,' I said, trying to stand up. My knee hurt. 'I was beginning to hope you had left.'

'Why? Have we met before?'

Even though he might one day be in a position of authority over me, I was in no mood to be trifled with.

'You know perfectly well we have. You interviewed me a year ago for a place at Magdalen.'

'Did I? I thought you seemed dimly familiar.' He lay stress, I thought, on the word 'dimly'. 'Did you get in?'

'Yes,' I said, through gritted teeth.

'Oh, well, that's all right, then.'

It was not all right, but I was not going to start haranguing him from my position at his feet.

Maria Guardi came and knelt beside me to examine my knee. 'Does it hurt very much?'

'Yes.'

'Do you think it's broken?'

'How should I know?' I asked irritably. Then, after a pause, while her fingers probed it through my worn woollen tights, 'I think it's only bruised. But I can't walk. Will you tell your dog to go away?'

The dog, Tonto, was poking its head in everywhere, sniffing with great interest. Evenlode whistled, and it trotted off to stand by his side. He slipped the chain back on.

'I've forgotten your name. Ermintrude or something, isn't it?'

'Emma.'

'Can you really not walk?'

'What do you think? You think I'm hanging around here because I like your company?'

'Do you think I'm staying because I like yours?'

This was so rude I would have hit him if I could. 'So you do remember me!'

'Why should I bother to lie to you? I can't remember all the hundreds of adolescent girls I see, coming up for interviews every year. As far as I can tell, there's only one difference between you: either you're reconstructed round your eyelashes like the Bionic Woman, in which case you've gone to a comprehensive, or else you're looking like terrified hares, in which case you've gone to a boarding school. Either way, practically none of you has any real interest in or knowledge of the cinquecento, which is all I care about. Personally, I'd get rid of the lot of you and make the college single-sex again. The boys are duller, to begin with, but they tend not to think scholarship is a prop for their wretched little egos.'

'So you admit you discriminate against women.'

'Not at all. My job as an examiner is to find whether you are going to amuse me for an hour once a week for the next three years, or whether, beneath that air of superficial maturity, you're going to go off and do tedious things like discover sex or commit suicide.'

'Suicide must be a great problem among your pupils,' I said, with irony.

'Oh, it is,' he agreed, apparently without it. 'Every morning when I wake up and realize I don't have to deal with the miasma of undergraduate solipsism for a whole year, it puts me in a perfectly wonderful mood.'

He bared his teeth at me in what he no doubt thought was a smile. I scowled back.

'The palazzo is too far,' said Maria Guardi. 'We had better go to my house. You ugly rascal!' I had a vain flicker of hope she might be addressing Evenlode. 'Here, *professore*, I will take the dog, you help the signorina.'

'All right. You go on ahead.' He spoke some more, in a curious Italian, which I could barely understand, though Maria seemed to catch on well enough. Then he turned to me. 'Want a piggyback?'

'I'll hop,' I answered coldly. 'I wouldn't want to burden you with the miasma of my solipsism. Just give me your arm.'

It was a long and awkward business getting back on the road that led to Maria's house. I was determined to suffer in silence. He was too tall to be much support without practically lifting me off my feet. I was sure I could hear his teeth grinding with impatience; it was my only consolation.

He had the sort of face that is made to express irritation and hauteur. It would have looked well in an eighteenth-century steel engraving, being all forehead and cheekbones and chin, with a long beaky nose and heavy, ironic eyelids. His hair needed cutting, but it did not soften the impression of will and wilfulness. I could not imagine him ever having been a child.

'Nearly there, thank God,' he said.

'I know, you've simply loathed every moment.'

'You don't expect I'd enjoy it, do you?'

'Oh no,' I said sarcastically. 'Not when you could be back at the palazzo, hobnobbing with the Contessa. Snobbery takes up such a lot of time.'

A flicker of amusement crossed his face. 'Actually, I've always thought snobbery a rather harmless pursuit, like stamp-collecting,' he said.

I could not think of any reply cutting enough and fast enough. 'Why do you speak such funny Italian?'

'It isn't Italian, it's Latin, mostly. There was a time when every educated person in Europe could converse in it; far better than that rubbishy Esperanto. I suppose nobody your generation learns it any longer.'

'Not at my school. And anyway, you can't be very much more than ten years older than I am, even if you do dress like an old man.'

'I merely wear the traditional clothes of an English gentleman, which is what I feel comfortable in.'

'Exactly. You have the soul of an old man.'

'Whereas you wear what looks immensely decorative and Pre-Raphaelite, but dreadfully cumbersome from the way you keep tripping. What does that say about you?'

'That I'm a martyr to aesthetics. Everyone should be.'

'You must meet my godmother. She thinks the same way.'

'Who's she?'

'The Contessa.'

'Oh.'

We hobbled up the steps into the Guardis' kitchen on the first floor. It was a most peculiar place. There was a gigantic fireplace, much like the one on the landing in Sylvia's house, where an ancient couple, like animated bags of rags, sat on either side, warming themselves. In the middle was a table, covered with a red and white checked plastic cloth. A worn wooden dresser stood at one end, next to a window overlooking the yard where pigs and geese wandered in the mud. At the other a huge television set, watched by two fascinated teenaged boys, swam with pictures of Fred Astaire and Ginger Rogers tap dancing across Hollywood's notion of a Venetian bridge. A kind of Aga bubbled with soup or stew by the door; sniffing it, Tonto whined and salivated, and got automatically kicked in the ribs.

Maria had made some camomile tea, and had got out a wooden box of bandages. I wriggled out of my ruined tights, avidly watched by the Guardi grandparents, and exposed the knee to her, feeling silly. She knelt down to examine it. Evenlode sipped his tea looking bored.

'*Si*, it is very badly bruised,' she said. 'Not broken, thanks be, but it must hurt. I am so sorry, signorina.'

'*Mea culpa*,' said Evenlode, surprisingly.

Maria sighed and smiled, exposing a row of gleaming false teeth. 'Yes, very naughty. You English, you think animals have souls, like us! The Contessa is just the same, always nagging me to let Tonto off the chain. Look what happens when I do! He runs away! Stupid beast! Drink, drink. The tea will make you calm. Have some cake, signorina. I make it myself.'

There were strands of white in the shining dark bun piled on her crown, and a reek of sweat surrounded her like musk. Her old print dress was worn and bunched, but there was a glow about her like that of a healthy animal.

She disinfected the cuts, then rubbed some ointment into the knee and bandaged it tightly.

'The pain lessens? It is made with water from the spring where we found you.'

'That marble head. What is it?'

'Who knows? Old things,' she answered shortly.

'I think—' Evenlode began, then stopped. 'What were you doing there, anyway? It's private property.'

'So am I. It didn't stop Maria's blasted dog from attacking me.'

'Didn't you see the sign?'

'No.'

'The hunters must have shot it off again. Do you know, in Italy you're trespassing unless you have a gun. Extraordinary, isn't it?'

I ignored him.

'You live with the American, don't you?' Maria said, not so much a question as a statement.

Warily, remembering the mutual ill will, I nodded.

'Is it true her husband has left her?' This came from the grandmother, in dialect so thick and sibilant I could hardly understand her.

'Yes.' It must, after all, be common knowledge, but the smile on my face dried like egg white.

The old man said something incomprehensible in even thicker dialect, accompanied by an explicit gesture and a deep, coarse laugh. I felt annoyed and rose to go.

'Quiet, *nonno*,' Maria said. 'Signorina, I am sorry about your knee. If you leave your tights with me. I will mend them.'

I thanked her.

'Where were you going?' Evenlode asked suddenly. 'Was it just a walk, or were you going into the town?'

'Town. I got lost.'

'I'll give you a lift, then. I was coming down to collect a Cinquecento. Maria's lending me a spare so I can phut-phut around the countryside. I may as well try it out now.' I thought of telling him he could phut-phut off, but he was too waspish for me to be certain of victory. Besides, I was aching to have even a glimpse of Lucio, whom I had not seen for a week.

Midafternoon, midweek, the parterre was deserted. Chestnut trees all along it unfolded tiny viridian parasols. The wind sliced past Evenlode's head, which had to stick out through the sunroof in order to accommodate him. I looked at his arms and thought how much I disliked herringbone tweed, how utterly smug and hateful he was, and how I'd really rather not go to Oxford than have to amuse him with my thoughts on history of art for an hour a week for three years.

'How's the knee?' he shouted, as we passed the squat statue of Santorno's fictional genius.

'Throbbing.' Actually, it wasn't too bad, now.

'Sorry about the dog. I can't stand seeing it chained up like that all day.'

Normally I would have approved wholeheartedly of this sentiment. 'You know the saying, in Italy they're cruel to animals and kind to children, in England it's the other way about. I prefer the Italians.'

'Oh, animals expect less.'

'And vegetables require light and water. Why not give up on the animate altogether, and concentrate on minerals?'

'There are parts of art history which are just that,' he said cheerfully. 'My favourites. This where you wanted?'

He stopped in the piazza.

'Yes. Please don't wait, I'm sure someone else will give me a lift back.'

My eyes were looking up and down Via Garibaldi in search of Lucio; I had already spotted someone I thought might be him, going into the Bar Popolare, and was desperate to get away.

'Fine.' He paused. 'If you're not doing anything next Monday night, why don't you come up to my godmother's for dinner? Maria is rather a good cook. You can collect your lingerie' (he pronounced it 'Lynn Jerry', with affected Englishness) 'at the same time.'

I was so surprised, I looked at him directly, and caught a glimpse of humour in the ascetic disagreeable face. It was on the tip of my tongue to refuse; why should I bother? But curiosity about the Contessa and her mysterious garden won over antipathy.

'All right.'

'Good. See you at eight, then. Goes like a little bomb, doesn't it?' He turned the Cinquecento round, and took off.

'Well!' I said aloud, not knowing whether to be more gobstruck at his invitation or my acceptance of it. What on earth had possessed me to even think of going to the don's donjon? I must be mad.

I hobbled over to the Bar Popolare.

Lucio wasn't there. I wondered why it was that when in love with a particular person, I was always mistaking complete strangers with only a passing resemblance to him. Vaguely I recognized this man as Max Vincioni, a depressed, spindly character with huge moustaches who owned Santorno's only hotel and restaurant, and who was, according to gossip, a self-made millionaire. Sitting at another table was Louis. I ordered a cappuccino from Tony, and went over to join him.

'Italian men,' he sighed, jerking his head in Max's direction. 'They go out of their mother's house, into their wife's. Then they spend the rest of their lives trying to get away from both.'

'Why do you live here and not in France?'

'Ah, that is a long story. I was born in Canada, you see. All my life, I dreamt of going to France, where my grand-parents came from. I was so proud of being French, I refused to speak English. I despised the colonialism, the bourgeois provincialism of Toronto. Then, one day, I finally had enough money to go. I went to Paris, the city I had dreamt of for twenty years, and what did I find? No artistic life in the Latin Quarter, nothing of originality or intellect; all that was over before I was born. Nothing but filth and Algerians. So I came here. And you?'

'Oh, I'm not sure. I'll stay until my money runs out or Sylvia gets sick of me. Then I have to choose between the university of Oxford and the university of life,' I said, lightly. Louis's cynicism was temporarily infectious.

'At your age, that means you want to find out about love.'

He looked at me, his dark little eyes twinkling like industrial diamonds. 'Or perhaps you think you are in love already? Tell me, do you have pains here, in the heart?' Louis thumped the left side of his barrel-like torso dramatically. 'You are breathless? You feel sick? You cannot paint?' I nodded.

'Then, my dear girl, you have not love, but indigestion.' He roared with laughter. I wrinkled my nose crossly. 'Do you think I can't see you're like a ripe peach, ready to be plucked? Ten years ago, I'd have tried it myself. Ah, you lucky, lucky girl. All those hormones going round and round, like the *pallotti* in a pinball machine. Where will they land? Whom will they shoot down?'

'Oh, Louis, for God's sake!'

I was really irritated now, and embarrassed.

'What is it that gets into northern women as soon as they come to the Mediterranean?' he mused. 'All of you, without exception, throw your knickers in the air and cry "Yes!" after years of saying "No". Is it something to do with the temperature? Yes, I wonder if at heart women are not reptiles, needing to be warmed by the sun before they are fully alive?'

'You must be thinking of the sort that like swallowing frogs,' I said, but Louis only grinned.

'Have you heard about Izzy?' he asked.

'No. What?'

'I thought everybody would know by now. She's pregnant.'

'By who?'

He shrugged. 'The betting is, it's Dave's.'

'Oh no! That's torn it!'

Tony, who had turned his head at the mention of Dave's name, now creaked slowly over to our table, holding something in his doughy fingers.

'I forgot,' he wheezed. 'This came for Sylvia. It's a postcard from England, no?'

'Is it from Dave?' Louis enquired. 'How amusing! Izzy will be absolutely furious if she knows. She hasn't heard a word from him.'

85

I took it. It was indeed a postcard, with an English stamp franked the week before. But, when I read the inscription, I saw a familiar seven starred ink-blot blurring his verse about love and, when I turned it over, I saw the Bronzino reproduction that had fallen out of Sylvia's folder over a year ago, and which had until recently been Blu-Tacked on the wall of her bedroom.

Why should Sylvia pretend her husband was writing to her? I puzzled over this as I walked back with the postcard in my bag. The only reason I could think of was that she did it as a cruel practical joke, knowing that her husband never sent letters and Izzy would be in a ferment waiting. We had seen her in the street once or twice, and she and Sylvia had kissed each other like boxers shaking hands. Slim always looked horribly embarrassed.

In a way, I felt sorriest for him. He was awful; needlessly offensive, and with that terrible pseudo-Cockney whine which I suspected had taken years of practice to perfect. Yet he did at least try with his hopeless shoes. Whenever I went into town, there he would be in his little shop on the piazza, fiddling about with sickly-smelling pieces of unnaturally natural leather. Occasionally, when a party of youngish German tourists descended on the town, he would even make a sale.

'He only sticks it to get away from Izzy and her flaky nut cutlets,' Sylvia said sourly. 'Imagine staying a vegetarian in Italy! Like wearing earplugs at Woodstock. You know, whenever I look at most Britishers and see how ugly they are, I think it must be because of the food they eat.'

'The worst of it's American,' I pointed out.

'Oh, come on! Did we invent Spam? Or kippers? Or, my God, faggots? Look at Mimi, both her parents are British, and she turns out looking like a Barbie doll with a breast reduction. If that isn't the Australian diet, I don't know what else it can be.'

I did not argue; the formative properties of food was one of Sylvia's hobby-horses. She put far more energy into domesticity than she ever put into her watercolours.

She was stirring a pot of something in the stove when I got back, the blue steam rising up to her intent face.

'You know, two hundred years ago, a woman who looked like you and lived alone would have been burnt at the stake. I'm not surprised Maria Guardi thinks you're a witch,' I said.

'Me? Ha! That would be the pot calling the kettle black, as Dave would say. If I were, I'd put a hex on that darned dog of hers.'

'Why? Did it attack you, too?'

I told her about my encounter that afternoon beneath the palazzo walls, though not about the pool and the marble head, which I wanted to keep to myself for some reason.

'You mean, you know this Oxford guy? And he's asked you to the Contessa's? Oh, wow! He must fancy you.' She looked very happy at the thought. I was touched by her concern.

'Like a hole in the head. He'll probably grill me slowly over a bonfire of examination papers.'

'I hope you didn't tell Maria anything about me.'

'Only confirmed what she already knew, about Dave leaving.'

'Great. Now we'll have every man in Santorno coming round to peer through our windows.'

'Only Lucio.'

'Why do you think he always comes by the path, not the road?'

'I'm sorry.'

'What you have to realize, Emma, is that this place is full of people with nothing meaningful to do in their own lives, so they make up stories about their neighbours. Communities, they drive you crazy. They spend the whole time spying on each other. You know what you should do if your car ever breaks down in the middle of the empty countryside? Take your clothes off. I can guarantee that in half an hour, the road will be crawling.'

'I don't think I'd have the same effect as you.'

'Don't you believe it. You've come on a lot since you arrived. Don't think people haven't noticed.' I wondered whether she meant Lucio. 'Have your heard about Mimi?'

'No.'

'Someone in Santorno has denounced her to the police.'

'What happens? Will they get out the tumbrels?'

'No, she just has to leave Italy for a month, drive to France or Germany. She hasn't got a proper *permesso di soggiorno*, see, and she's working here. They make difficulties for you if you're not from an EEC country. That's why I had to enrol as a student at Perugia. Anyway, I thought I'd go with her, hitch a ride for a week. I haven't been out of this shit heap for months.'

'By the way,' I said, taking the postcard out of my bag. 'This arrived for you.'

I watched her as she took it and pretended to read what she must know already, wondering whether she would share the joke.

'Oh. Well, shows he's still alive.'

'It will make Izzy awfully cross. Have you heard, she's pregnant?'

7

Sylvia's rage when I told her about the pregnancy astonished me. I had known she felt ill will towards Izzy, even if she said that her marriage was over and that she cared little for her feckless husband. This, however, was something new. I had been used all my life to being the most volatile personality around, but Sylvia cast my own puny tantrums into the shade completely.

I began to wonder whether the artistic temperament was not a little overrated. The tears, the smashing of crockery, the long periods of gloom were things quite outside my experience. It was with difficulty one night that I persuaded her that going round to the Dunnetts' with a Sabatier knife was not the best course of action.

She wept in my arms.

'It's all her fault, everything's her fault, she's destroyed our lives. How can we ever go on? I think I'll kill myself. What shall I do?'

'I thought you didn't love him any more.'

'I don't, I don't'. She raised a face streaked with kohl. 'It's the baby. It's so unfair. Why should I be punished, while she's rewarded? She started the whole thing. I'll never be able to have one, and she's having his.'

'You don't know it's Dave's. It might be her husband's.'

'Slim? No. That – that – titless bitch was completely crazy about Dave. No way could it not be his.'

I tried to be sympathetic, but I couldn't cope with this sort of thing; besides, I had my own misery. It was hard to concentrate on someone else's problems when the urge to confide my hopeless passion rose up so strongly that I had, literally, to bite my tongue. Often I would sit there, nodding and looking sympathetic, but not hearing a word. Sylvia was no longer the lodestar of my internal life, as she had been for over a year. I think she sensed this somehow; at any rate, although I listened to her invective for hour after hour, we were never as comfortable or as trusting towards each other again.

One other unfortunate effect of Sylvia's grief was that she lost something of her quality of remoteness, so essential to beauty. The volume of anger swelled her until she seemed to become larger. Small blemishes in her skin became noticeable; I saw for the first time that there were grey roots to her hennaed hair. When I had first met her, I felt as if I had been drunk; now I was hung over. I realized, guiltily, that I couldn't wait for her to leave.

She went two days later, driving off in Mimi's car at the crack of dawn. Mimi seemed a bit down, too, though she still managed to look impossibly glamorous in a leather flying jacket and diamond earrings.

'Ciao. Take care,' Sylvia said, raising swollen eyes to mine. 'I'm sure you won't have any visitors, but make sure you lock up at night.'

'Yes Mummy.'

'Byee!' Mimi called. 'Don't do anything I wouldn't do!'

I thought, waving goodbye, that this probably didn't leave much. What on earth was she playing at, burying herself as an English-language teacher in Santorno? No wonder wives and girlfriends became jealous and suspicious. I felt quite jealous myself that she was able to offer Sylvia something I could not. Still, it was good to have the house to myself. I did a fatal thing, which was to take possession by spring-cleaning. There was some excuse: everything smelled of kippers, thanks to the smoking fire, and there was a coating of dust as thick as fur in some places. Scrubbing, I worked myself up into a sanctimonious lather about Sylvia's sloven-liness; she was always nagging me about washing up and not throwing tissue paper down the lavatory, but the place really was a disgrace.

All day, I banged and thumped and swept and washed, until clouds of dust motes hung in the air like sequins. It was a glorious day, the first of April, and wild daffodils were putting out snaky buds from their transparent hoods up and down the terraces. I found a scorpion like a miniature black lobster in one corner; when I swatted it, it split in half like a burnt match, which cheered me up still further. I was becoming better at co-ordinating my movements when sweeping, though I wondered how on earth all the women who were nothing but housewives managed not to go mad.

By the afternoon, every floor and window was spotless.

I had checked on the wall of postcards in Sylvia's room; the Bronzino was back there, looking innocent. The table held a jug full of cherry blossom and flowering rosemary, which I thought I might paint if the blossoms held. I was struggling to light the fire when Maria Guardi tapped on the open door, and called:

'Poss' entrare?'

She came in, very hesitantly, with my tights in her hand.

'How pretty.'

'Have you never seen inside?'

Maria shook her head. 'Not since it was bought. It was once

my great-aunt's. All the houses in this valley had my family in them. My grandmother told me that, fifty years ago, there were wolves in the mountains, and when the winter was long and hard, they would come down and prey on the farms. Then all the men of my family would get together and hunt until they killed the wolf and roasted it, delicious to eat. There were nearly fifty of us then.'

'What happened?'

'Some moved away to the cities, some died, some were killed in the war. And now our enemies, the Germans, are buying our land everywhere, putting in swimming pools so that our own wells dry up.'

'I'm sorry.' What else could I say?

Maria shrugged. 'Everything changes, for a little while. We wait, and one day the invaders are gone. Many, many battles have been fought here: Hannibal, Napoleon, Garibaldi.'

I wondered how she knew so much history; whether she had learned it at school, or whether stories had been passed down through the generations. She was not short and squat, like some of the peasant women I had seen in Santorno, but fine-boned, with eyes like dates.

'You are trying to light a fire? No, no! You will never catch a husband like that, signorina!' She laughed at me slyly as I blushed. *'Posso?* Look, the wood has to go like this, up the chimney, with air beneath. There, now it can breathe, though it is not happy here. This is a new chimney, yes? It catches the north wind.'

New or not, the fire was drawing better than it ever had done before. I thanked her for her help and for the tights, which had been exquisitely darned, and she prepared to leave.

'You are coming to the palazzo next week? Good. The *professore* is a young man, he should not spend all his time alone with his books.'

I couldn't care less what he did, and thought of telling her so, but restrained myself.

'Is the Contessa very formal?'

'Yes, but wear your green dress, the one with little flowers.'

I wondered how she knew about it; she really must be a witch. Then I reflected that she must have been spying on us, as Sylvia claimed, and said goodbye.

It was very still. Outside, the clear, cold air had faded to a pale jade, with a single star low on the horizon. I could hear the sound of a waterfall, perhaps one fed by the hot spring, and an occasional ruffle of silver leaves in the groves all around, like birds settling down for the night. A moth rapped against a pane of the french windows overlooking the valley. Maria's fire continued to draw, murmuring to itself and sending little sparks dancing up the black chimney. Half-asleep in front of it, I dried my hair. It still resembled carded wool, long enough to sit on; not quite Rapunzel length, but thick enough to make a good strong rope. I wondered who would climb up it and if there were something seriously wrong with me, to have reached eighteen and not have been disembarrassed of my tedious innocence.

The moth rapped again, harder. I looked round. It was Lucio.

'Posso?' he said, as Maria had.

I opened the door for him.

'Were you going to bed?'

I was in my nightdress; long, white cotton, not transparent but still not the thing for receiving guests. I took an old blue blanket from the back of the sofa and wrapped it round me.

'Sylvia is away,' I said awkwardly. 'I've been cleaning the house all day, as a surprise for when she gets back. Then I found I was covered in dust ...'

'I like it,' he said. 'It is very delicate, like the Madonna in old paintings. I think you would look very beautiful pregnant.'

A wave of heat coursed through me; not just embarrassment or lust. For the first time, I realized I was capable of bearing children, and the strength of the desire to do so utterly appalled me.

He did not apologize, as an Englishman would have done, though he flushed slightly, too, the old gold of his skin deepening as he stared at me.

'You want a baby, don't you? All women do.'

'I am not any woman,' I said, mechanically. 'Any woman can have babies. Few can paint pictures. That is what I am here to do.' As I said it, I knew I was lying; had I not been mooning about, thinking of him instead of getting on with work?

'I did not come here to be—' he made a wiggling motion with his hand – 'viscido.'

'Slimy?' I said, in English.

'Slim-ey?' We both laughed.

'You've heard about Izzy?'

'Yes.'

'Sylvia is very upset.'

'Yes. She would be.'

I could not stop looking into his eyes, huge and yellow-rayed, like an owl's, paralysing me. They came closer and closer, and the bang of blood in my ears was almost deafening.

The fire cracked, twice, and we both jerked backwards.

'I thought somebody was here.'

'Would you like some wine? Some food? I was about to make supper.'

'I will help you.'

It was just like any of the evenings he came round when the three of us were there; yet unlike. We were both smiling too much, drinking too much wine. Everything had become distorted. I had bought a chicken breast and thigh for my supper. They seemed obscene in their fleshy nakedness; I would have cooked anything else, but eggs, the only alternative, seemed worse after his remark about babies. I began to stew them, chopping onion, staring at the concentric white rings, tinged with violet, as they fell into the sizzling oil.

'Onions are like people, they have no centre.'

I contradicted him, not to be contentious, but because I knew conversation is the best chastity belt.

'So Ibsen thought, too. You are both wrong. At the centre of every onion is just a smaller onion, the original one from which all the layers grew. Not a vacuum.'

'And at the centre of men?'

'A child. So a psychiatrist would say. A priest would say a soul, and a psychologist a snake.'

'What?'

'I read somewhere, we have three layers of brain, each one a stage in evolution. The first and smallest, the one our deepest feelings come from, is a reptile's. Perhaps that's why dinosaurs died out; they didn't die of cold, but of passion,' I added, as the thought struck me.

'This I do not like. I hate snakes.'

'Me too. An absolute phobia. Is it true they're all over the countryside?'

He nodded. 'In summer, you see them shoot across the roads, like black lightning, in the mountains. You have to be very careful, too, when you stop your car. They like the heat in the engine, they wind themselves round it, and then, when you open the bonnet, psht! They bite. They will even come into houses.'

'Really?'

I shivered, and drew closer. We both became very still. All of a sudden I felt a sharp pain in my upper leg and nearly jumped out of my skin.

'Oh, God, I've just been bitten! Quick, quick, where is it?'

Lucio burst out laughing. 'It was only me, Emma. I was teasing.'

I glanced angrily at him, saw his expression and began to laugh, too.

'Listen, if a snake did get into this house, I'd be far more dangerous than it, believe me.'

'You could never kill it fast enough. You said yourself, they move like lightning.'

'Oh, but I would. I would make up my mind that it was either the snake or me. You can do anything, once you've made up your mind.'

The chicken was done; we carried it to the living room and sat in front of the fire. It had burnt low and gave the only light in the room apart from a pair of candles. Neither of us could eat a mouthful. I had a bread roll, and kept tearing it into smaller and smaller bits.

'You sound like Sylvia when you talk like that.'

'Don't let's talk about Sylvia. What is it, are you in love with her?' His voice took on a cruel, bullying tone.

'No,' I said quietly, my eyes on my plate. I did not dare look at him.

'Good. I hate lesbians. I hate them even more than I hate snakes.'

I did not like the way this conversation was going, did not know what to do or say. After a moment, he apologized.

'You are different from other foreign girls. You don't seem to behave like them, so people think you must be ...'

'Why can't they mind their own business? I left school a few months ago, if you must know; a kind of convent, though not religious. I've hardly ever met any men of my own age. Why should I be any different from an Italian girl, just because I'm foreign?'

'You are right,' he said, after a pause. 'They are little people,

96

with little minds. They judge people by their appearances. If you dress differently, or have different-coloured skin, they think you are their enemy.'

'Is that why you once said you wished you were black?'

'You understand me, then? You do? I knew you would. We are the same.'

There were only crumbs left on my plate now.

'Look at me, Emma.'

I looked, and was lost.

He was so beautiful, so beautiful, but it was not only a beauty that struck the eye. His skin smelled of new-mown grass. I shook with great, shuddering, convulsive tremors, before and after he kissed me. They wouldn't stop, they were like hiccups.

'That's good,' he said, softly. 'Feel them, they're like an orgasm.'

'Yes, yes.'

I did not know what I was doing. I only felt safe when we were kissing, tongues darting and whirling. Things became vast, without sense or proportion. I could feel the cavernous ridges along the top of his mouth, the suck and flow of saliva. His hands pushed and kneaded me into a different shape, a woman's shape that ached and burned, slime and fire. All the hardness went out of my body and into his, the bones knitting into that strange new limb at his groin, soft and raw as it grew.

'You like it?'

'It is, after all, the basis for a great deal of architecture.'

'Oh, you are beautiful,' he said; and for that I would have given him anything. 'Shall we stay here or go upstairs?'

'Upstairs. Someone might come.'

'I saw you through the window.'

'I know.'

'I have been dying for you, I was afraid to touch you.'

'And I you.'

My virginity was very nearly ended on the narrow stair. I couldn't walk, my legs were locked around his hips. He carried me into Sylvia's room, and we fell on her bed.

'The pill, you take the pill?' he said suddenly, urgently.

'No.'

'What day of the month are you?'

'What?'

'When did you last? You know, the blood.'

I was bewildered. 'I don't know, a week.'

'Oh, God.'

'Wait, wait.' I scrabbled about in Sylvia's boxes, found the one with the hidden drawer, and jerked the whole thing out. 'Here.'

He took a long time, and it was painful. They never tell you this, how much it hurts and goes on hurting for days; a dull, deep pain, like menstruation but worse. The joints at the top of my legs ached, and my jaws, and my lips, which were bitten by his teeth and mine until the skin cracked. There was a great deal of blood, sweat, and a white sticky stuff like cuckoo-spit.

It was not gentle, not tender, not, in a curious way, erotic at all. It was violent, a struggle to postpone pleasure, which became pleasure itself. Yet when pleasure arrived, it was the annihilation of sensation, like death.

When it was done, and he was asleep, I lay for hour after hour, thinking, staring at the unfamiliar beams of Sylvia's ceiling. The night paled, and birds began to squeak and flutter; or perhaps it was rats. Our breaths curdled, so that I had to breathe out at the same time as he did, as if on an artificial respirator. He was heavy, soft and damp, now, his penis curled into a snaily lump. The creature that had snarled and grimaced above me, terrible as lightning, was gone. I felt a love for him that was different, maternal, as though the strength he had

98

drawn out of me to begin with had been returned, made mine for the first time.

I wondered, half-dozing, about a great many things; his life, my life, whether my parents had ever known anything like this, how he would be when he woke up.

But also, I wondered why it was that in the drawer of Sylvia's box, beside the packet of condoms, I had seen a roll of money and her husband's passport, when he was meant to be abroad.

8

Lucio and I stayed in bed for three days, getting out only to wash and drink water.

I said, 'I thought it would make me feel older, but I feel like a child again.'

'I can't believe you've never done it before. Why not?'

'I didn't like anyone. I didn't like myself. Nobody wanted me to.'

'They must be blind, Englishmen.'

'Not blind, exactly. They mostly start off on boys, I think. What was it like for you, the first time?'

'Terrible.' He laughed and stretched and light slid along his skin in bursts. 'I was like a stick of wood, I was so nervous.'

'Who was she?' I asked. 'Someone in Santorno?'

'No. From San Gimignano. It lasted a year, and then she wanted to be *fidanzato*, get married, though we were only sixteen.'

'Do people really marry that young, here?'

'Only *contadini*.'

'And how many others have there been?'

'You have breasts like vanilla ice cream, with a strawberry on top, which I must eat.'

'How many others?'

Lucio raised his head and gave me a level, yellow stare. 'You don't need to know. They were not virgins, like you.'

'But now I'm not either.'

'You will always be different. I think, in some way, you will always be a virgin; not in your body, but in your head, where it matters most.'

'Why?'

'Because all that happens here—' he began to stroke me with his hand – 'is nothing to what happens in your head.

It is a thing of the mind far more than the body. It makes you dream, like a drug. Haven't you found that yet?'

'Yes,'I said. 'Yes.'

The sheets became grey and filthy, despite our frequent baths. We bathed a great deal, not only because it helped me recover but because Lucio was scrupulously fastidious. He would even go out of the room to blow his nose.

'I was always told by my parents that Italians were dirty.'

'Dirty! Why do you think every Italian bathroom has a bidet?'

'Sex.'

'No. Well, that too. But it is to use after the toilet. We don't just use paper, we wash. We think you English are filthy because you don't.'

'Don't include me with them. I've never felt English.'

'What do you feel?'

'Italian. I don't know. Different.'

'As I feel different from Italians. Yet you seem so English to me; you are so romantic, you have so many ideals. An Italian woman would be thinking by now how to get a ring on her finger, or how to make me jealous.'

I blushed faintly, for I had been thinking of one of these, in a soppy, sentimental way I despised myself for. I had not told him I loved him yet. It would make me too vulnerable, when I was so much at his mercy anyway.

'Do you like the English?'

'I like them when they don't come here to live. The ones who come here to live are the worst in the world.'

'Not the tourists?'

I had seen them starting to arrive by the busload, as Easter came; desiccated spinsters in flannel skirts and brogues, clutching their copies of guidebooks and exclaiming at the picturesque piazzas; balding, tweedy fathers trailing whiny brats and domineering, razor-voiced wives. They always made me wince with shame at their arrogance, their ignorance, their pretensions to culture. How I agreed with E. M. Forster that nobody should be allowed to cross the Channel without taking an examination in art history! One of the things that really made me laugh was seeing a whole party of them pretending to have heard of Giulio Folconi.

Whoever invented him in Santorno had obviously had a better sense of humour than I initially suspected.

'They bring money, and leave. You are mostly poor, and stay.'

'Is that all that matters to you, money?' I was distressed; this was something new.

'To me personally, no. I would like to have a house like this, in the country, to get away from my parents. Foreigners have made that impossible.'

'It's the same in England. It's just people with money, buying more than they need.'

'But wouldn't you, if you had the money?'

'No. I don't want to become like my parents.'

'Are they rich, then, your people?'

'So-so. Not like Izzy's.' I didn't want to think about my parents, though the bitterness of my mother's parting words, about taking it as a welcome sign of normality if I had a lover, still set my teeth on edge. Well, I had one now. I wondered whether she had ever been kissed from the top of her head to the smallest toes on her feet, by my father or anyone else. It was quite unthinkable.

Sometimes we would get out of bed and watch ourselves making love in the mirrors of Sylvia's wardrobe. I was more embarrassed doing this than anything else, but he said I had to see my own beauty as he saw it. Mostly I watched him, but when I had the courage to look at myself, I was astonished by how much I had changed.

'There used to be terrible red marks, all over. Have you made them go?'

'These?' Lucio ran a finger along a faint, silvery line scrolling across a hip. 'That is time, not me. They are the scars of growth. You should be proud of them.'

'You are so golden, and I am so white,' I said. 'Don't you think whiteness is ugly?'

'It would not be good if we were both the same. You're almost as tall as I am, that is the only thing wrong with you.'

'Are Italian women better?'

'Italian women have wonderful bodies and faces like rats. American women have beautiful faces, and bottoms like elephants. You are all perfect.'

I knew it wasn't true; but he had what he claimed for me, perfection.

What drove us out in the end was hunger, that and the recollection that it was Monday, and time for Sylvia to return. We had eaten the chicken, all the eggs, and even spaghetti with nothing but onion and tomato as sauce.

Lucio had to go anyway, to rehearse with his band for a gig later that week. It was called Stella Nera and there were only four of them, with a few hangers-on. I didn't like the sound of this.

'I'll bring some food back this evening,' he promised.

'I'd better change the sheets on Sylvia's bed,' I said reluctantly. 'Lucio, what are we going to tell her?'

An expression of extreme disquiet clouded his face. 'Say nothing until I have spoken to her first. There are some things I should explain, but not until I've talked to her.'

'What things?'

'Don't worry, they don't concern you.'

The prospect of Sylvia's return filled me with apprehension. How would she react to Lucio staying the night? Could we go on sleeping in her room, or would we have to cram into my narrow single bed? Would she have calmed down as a result of her week abroad?

I worried, too, about Dave's passport and the bundle of money which had not been there before. After Lucio left, I looked at them again. How could someone go through customs without a passport? Was it different because of the EEC? I thought not; perhaps his friend the lorry driver had smuggled him out. But why leave it behind if he had one? I had a feeling that something was wrong, but I didn't know what. The money was mostly Italian, and there was nearly £2,000. Where had it come from? I knew it had not been there before, any more than the passport; I remembered the night of the party distinctly, at least the early stages of it.

Lastly, there was the dinner with Evenlode, which I realized with irritation was this evening. It was far too late to cancel, though for two pins I'd have done so. How could I endure an hour, two hours of that pretentious, affected, condescending piffle, when I could be with Lucio?

Not knowing what else to do, I began to strip the sheets from Sylvia's bed to soak in the bath. Glumly I poured half a box of detergent on to them and began to tramp. The lukewarm water went brown, then grey, but the stains wouldn't budge. I tramped for an hour, until my feet were red and itchy from detergent, then gave up and poured bleach over the lot. Even after another hour, there was still a faint mark when I hung them up to dry.

The house was a mess again. We had not bothered to wash up; I couldn't bear it now. Lucio had been gone for five hours, and I was starving.

I got dressed. It was strange to be wearing clothes again. The first couple of nights I would wake up suddenly and think, heavens, I'm naked with a naked man, my heart pounding with fright, but I had got so used to it that it seemed strange not to be so any longer. I was missing Lucio terribly already. I took up my sketchbook and drew him from memory – a thing I had never been able to do before – rampant on Sylvia's bed. Then, when he still did not reappear, I went into Santorno. It was after the siesta, and the main street was crowded.

I thought people looked at me strangely as I passed, but I told myself this was just because I must radiate happiness.

I went in and out of a dozen shops, buying food and looking for him. He had not, I suddenly realized, told me where he lived in the town. I went into the Bar Popolare. Tony was there, polishing his stainless-steel counter to the rumble of the TV set, and Slim.

'Ah, there you are,' he said. 'Sylvia's been looking for you. She's in a right fandango.'

'She's back? I didn't know. Is she still upset?'

'Still? She's heard about you and Lucio.'

'What?' The unease that had been hanging over me all day deepened. 'How could she? We've only just—'

'Do you think people round here are blind or somefink? He's done you like a kipper. Everyone knows it. Even if they hadn't guessed where lucky Lucio's been these nights, he's gone round telling all his mates.'

My heart blanched, like meat dropped in scalding water.

I tried to tell myself that it didn't matter, that I was proud they knew, but I felt sick all the same. No wonder people had looked at me so oddly. All my fears about being in a public place returned, redoubled. In the mirror behind Tony's rows of coloured liqueurs, I could see my face had become chalk white.

'There, don't take on so,' said Slim, more kindly. 'Have a cognac. It was bound to happen, sooner or later. Anyone could have told her, you being so young and all.'

I couldn't bear to listen to any more, I picked up my shopping and ran out. I managed to keep running until I reached the parterre, then I burst into tears.

The gravelled road and my humiliation seemed to go on for ever, but eventually both came to an end. The sun was setting; the houses and cars in the plain below were clear and tiny, a child's world. Rows of black cypress bent in the wind, like falling skittles; then righted themselves again.

I felt older, calmer. What did it matter if Lucio had told one or two friends? We were in love with each other, it was only natural. The first thing I had wanted to do was tell Sylvia I was in love, even before Lucio and I had slept together – so why should I be so upset? Probably, what had happened was that he had told his best friend, as I would tell Sylvia, and then the best friend had told someone else, and so on. Slim was an envious, frustrated, nasty old man who wanted to cause trouble for other people because his own wife had gone off him, that was all.

I walked back down the little path in the twilight. It was full of noises, unlike the still, crystalline evening when Lucio had come to me; the Guardis' dog yapping, the cock crowing, the Dunnetts' peacocks screeching, the leaves hissing, the waterfall bellowing. There was a scent of aniseed from the tall, feathery fennel that grew everywhere between the olives. My feet dragged. I did not want to see Sylvia. Why should she be angry about Lucio and me?

I found out.

*

'I come home, after a long and difficult journey, and what do I find? Every plate in the house is filthy. Every pan is covered in crap. There is no food, not a scrap. The john is blocked with paper. My bed is stripped and stained, and the sheets are still wet on the line. And then I find this.'

Sylvia held out my sketchpad with the drawing of Lucio. 'This piece – this obscene piece of *shit*. People told me in town he'd been screwing you while I was away, but I thought, I thought, it's just their evil minds, Emma is my friend, she wouldn't do that to me.'

'I bought some food,' I said stupidly. 'I cleaned everything else. I'm sorry about the dishes.'

'You're sorry about the *dishes*!' Sylvia's voice rose to a shriek, like a kettle coming to the boil. She began to laugh hysterically. 'I don't give a fuck about the *dishes*. What about Lucio? What have you been doing with him?'

I smiled. I couldn't help it. I smiled like the cat that has got at the cream, and Sylvia seized my shoulders in a maniac grip. I stopped smiling.

'Sylvia,' I said, seriously. 'You mustn't mind. It isn't that you aren't important to me any longer, but Lucio and I are in love. I've been in love with him for weeks and weeks, ever since I first saw him at the party.'

'The party,' she repeated.

'Yes. I thought you knew. I thought you guessed.'

'No, I never did. Stupid of me.'

'Anyway, I never thought he was interested. Well, I did, I saw him looking at me sometimes, but nothing happened. Then, when you went away, he came round. And I found out – oh, Sylvia, you mustn't be unhappy, but it's so wonderful. I never thought it would be like that. Why aren't people doing it all the time?'

'I can't believe this,' she said. 'I really cannot believe this. You mean you don't know? You haven't guessed?'

'Know? Know what?' I began to feel panicky. Her grip on my shoulders lessened, and I seized her as hard. 'Tell me,' I said, starting to pant. 'What is it? Why are you being so strange?'

Sylvia looked at me with a terrible, cruel smile, but behind it was a kind of sadness.

'Lucio is my lover,' she said. 'He's been fucking us both.'

I remember standing there, counting the panes in the window quite mechanically: one, two, three, four, five, six: over and over, making noughts and crosses with my mind.

Sylvia had left me and was sobbing on the sofa, deep, racking sobs, like those I had wept on the parterre. I felt quite calm, in a dead sort of way, but listening to her, I felt pity, and with it the return of love. I went in.

'Can't we talk about it?' I asked, hesitantly. 'Can't we be friends? I'm sure there's been some terrible misunderstanding.'

Sylvia gulped and said in a hard, muffled voice, 'There's been no misunderstanding, honey. None at all. You saw him, and you finally got hot pants, so you took him.'

'Sylvia, it wasn't like that, it really wasn't. I didn't know.'

'You're lying. I don't believe you!'

'It's true.'

'Liar!'

'How was I to know? You never said anything!'

'I thought you'd heard us in bed together.'

'No. Why didn't you *tell* me?'

'Because I'd have lost the house of course. Dave's so mean, he would have kicked me out if he'd known. Why do you think Lucio was always coming round?'

I looked at her, her face puffy and swollen, and said quietly, 'I thought – I hoped – he was coming to see me. I really ... ' My voice started to creak, and I stuck my chin out. 'I really didn't know. You must believe me.'

'I wish I could, but I can't.' Sylvia stared at me, her face suddenly vulnerable. 'You have to see, I can't. Otherwise I have to blame him.'

'Yes,' I said, dully. 'I see.'

'You can't stay here any more.'

'No, I'll start packing.'

I went upstairs, into my room with its narrow white bed, its black beams and red floor. I had loved it so much, three months ago, and now I saw its bareness as a symbol of my barren virginity, my primness. I began to pack. It didn't take long.

When I got to my green dress, sprigged with the little white flowers, I paused. I was still hungry; the storms of the past two hours had not altered that, and I had nowhere else to go. The idea of booking a room at Max's hotel filled me with fear and horror, and I couldn't stand the idea of a night on my own. I stripped, shivering, and crept into the green dress.

Then I went downstairs.

'I'm going now.'

'I didn't mean you have to leave like tonight. Where will you go?'

'Don't worry. I'll find somewhere.'

I didn't want to remind her about my invitation to the palazzo, in case she told Lucio. But why should she? I reflected. She had every reason in the world not to; to let him think I had simply disappeared, like Dave.

I pushed the thought away. I couldn't cope with much more.

'There's food in the bags. I'm sorry about everything. Goodbye.'

She did not bother to answer. I began lugging my suitcase up the hill and into the night.

9

The gates to the palazzo were open. I passed between the sneering, garlanded caryatids, and nearly jumped out of my skin when the gates closed silently behind me.

Even without the weight of misery and my suitcase, the walk up the drive would have been a dismal one. The cypress trees were very black in the twilight, seeming to bulk the air. They grew so thickly, from the base up, that they formed an impenetrable hedge, some fifty feet high, through which I could see nothing. A narrow, susurrant stream ran on either side in a white marble channel, periodically interrupted by classical statues which had a ghostly look in the gloom.

I began to remember my fantasies about Evenlode and his godmother; they no longer seemed quite so funny. Even if they would take me in for the night, I thought, I would probably be found stark, staring mad in the morning. The idea held some appeal in my present state of mind.

Why had Lucio not told me? I could understand, with an effort, why Sylvia had not; perhaps she assumed a greater degree of perspicacity than I in my ignorance and inexperience possessed. But Lucio knew I didn't know about the affair. Perhaps he had enjoyed deceiving us both. Perhaps – this was a really dreadful thought – he had simply used me as a stopgap while she was away, had never meant a single word of all those things he had told me.

I was so wrapped up in wretchedness that when the avenue came to an end and I was suddenly in front of the palazzo, it took me by surprise.

It was a square, graceful building of dove-coloured stone, not immense, but built round an inner courtyard where, through an archway, I could see orange trees and a fountain. Apart from where I was standing, it was surrounded by gardens which fell away in terraces. I could not see much, but the air of the place was so completely different from that of the avenue that I actually wondered whether I had come to the right house. It was full of the scent and shimmer of blossom; up here, the night was gentle, unoppressive, and broken by a large, bright lamp.

'Come in, signorina, come in,' said Maria.

'Hallo there.'

Evenlode appeared behind her, his head grazing the lintel, and took my suitcase. The blood rushed back into my cold hands, painfully. 'This must weigh a ton; no wonder you've taken such a time coming up the drive. Have you brought us a present, or are you coming to stay?'

'Dr Evenlode,' I said, my voice creaking. 'I'm awfully sorry, but—'

'Maria, could you tell the Contessa that we'll be a few minutes? Now, then. Don't tell me you've run away *again*?'

I gave a watery smile. 'How did you know about the other one?'

'Oh, the grapevine. You know.'

I did indeed. I gulped and stuck my chin out.

'I didn't run away this time, not exactly. I got chucked out, more or less, by the woman I was living with.'

'Don't tell me you're yet another silly girl to fall for the dubious charms of the dreadful Dave.'

'No, he's away, and it's Sylvia's boyfriend, Lucio. You see, I didn't know they were having an affair, and he – well, he came round the other night, and he – we . . .'

'Oh, spare me the blow-by-blow details. I can quite imagine what you got up to. Or maybe,' he added more kindly, as I went bright red, 'I can't. There must be some compensations for age. You have got yourself in a pickle, haven't you? Go off and do whatever it is you need to do to make yourself look less doleful, and then come on into the drawing room. Don't be so wet, girl.'

I had no option but to go into the bathroom he showed me to, though when I had locked the door, I was so angry I made faces at it for a minute before starting to wash my red eyes. I looked appalling, the ghost of the self who had preened at her reflection only hours before. What a pushover Lucio must have found me, I thought bitterly.

The floors under my feet were of black and white marble; I had the sensation of being a pawn as I followed Maria into the Contessa's drawing room.

I had expected drapes, dust and heavy furniture, but here, too, I was pleasantly surprised. It was no bigger than my parents'; the walls were painted a light, sunny yellow, so that even with the last sliver of light fading out of sight beyond the huge, arched french windows at the far end there was no sensation of darkness. The furniture was old – mostly eighteenth-century, judging by its grace – upholstered in opalescent silks. The ceiling was powder blue and gilded—

'Oh, how lovely!'

'When I was a child, I was always afraid of the dark,' said the woman on the deep, damasked sofa. 'So when I came here, I had stars painted on the ceiling of every room that wasn't frescoed. I'm glad you like them.'

She was tall, slender and slightly stooping, walking without

112

the aid of a stick. Eighty? Sixty? Her thick hair was white, and her strong long hands meandered with blue veins, but she was elegant beyond the dreams of fashion. It wasn't just the heavy gold bracelet weighting down one arm, or the flowing simplicity of her black velvet dress; it was something in her.

I had thought Sylvia my ideal of womanhood; beside the Contessa she seemed as garish as a fairground figure. I was glad Maria had warned me to be formal. She was a terrifying old thing; not in the way I had imagined, all Miss Havisham and vampire teeth, but much worse in that I instantly wanted her approval, and was afraid I was unlikely ever to merit it.

'So, you must be Godfrey Kenward's granddaughter, yes?' Her English was quite perfect, it was only the last word that gave her away; and even that, I thought, might be deliberate. She was not one to show any mark of weakness without calculation.

'Did you know him?'

'Many of the most lovely lilies in my garden came from him. You have something of the same eyes as he had. Are you a painter, too?'

'Trying to be.'

'Andrew tells me you are to be one of his art-history pupils later on.'

'That's a long way off,' I said, casting an apprehensive glance at Evenlode, who, having stood up, was now toasting his feet before a fire of pine cones. A large, dark painting on the chimneypiece behind him made his beaky features stand out even more sharply.

'Don't prod Emma too much, Claudia; she's just fallen out with the American doxy.'

'Mrs or should I say Miss Lurie? How very interesting.' The Contessa's eyes and cheeks brightened at the prospect of gossip. I did not like Andrew Evenlode calling Sylvia a doxy, but I was grateful for anything that made the old woman more human.

'Why do you call her miss?'

'Because,' said the Contessa, with the relish of one imparting a really juicy bit of gossip, 'she and that English confidence trickster she calls her husband aren't married, and never have been.'

When I finally got to bed that night, I fell instantly and dreamlessly asleep. The dinner had worn me out, on top of everything else.

It wasn't that they were unpleasant or unkind; far from it. Even the demon don had been unexpectedly tactful. I had thought he would be foul, snide and gloating, but he could not, within the parameters of his acerbic nature, have been more courteous. The Contessa had seemed to tolerate me, too; at any rate, she had made no demur over my staying the night, or even several nights in the palazzo.

'You will be the youngest person in here since my son,' was all she had said.

No, what had terrified me was the conversation at table. I had never been in the company of people so articulate and erudite, witty and serious, who could disagree on a thousand matters of opinion without losing their temper or their affection for each other. It was like watching a dance, perhaps the kind that had evolved out of armed combat but which was now performed for pleasure. They were not even showing off to each other, or to me.

'Is that what high table is like?' I dared to ask, after.

'No,' Evenlode told me. 'I'm not flattered you should think so, either. It's a remarkable thing in universities, the way they can bring together some of the finest minds in, say, physics, philosophy and classics, and not only will they not discuss their own subjects but the only topic on which they will venture an opinion is the local nursery school.'

'Oh.'

114

'But I'm sure you will find other students to discuss the meaning of life, there.'

'You may laugh at me for having ideals, but it's worse to be without them,' I said.

'I don't laugh at you any more than you deserve, and certainly not for that.'

'Why do you always seem to be laughing at me, then?'

'Do I? Perhaps you remind me of myself at your age. Good night.'

'Good night. And thank you.'

'For what? Just don't sob too loudly into your pillow. This is not the place for disappointed calf love.'

Curiously, I found it was not. I knew rather than felt I was unhappy the whole time I spent at the Palazzo Felice. Its lightness, its brightness, the very air seemed conducive to a peculiar tranquillity. According to the Contessa, it had been built by one of the Count's ancestors who had served with Federico de Montefeltro, and was modelled in a smaller scale on the ducal palace at Urbino.

'Have you never seen it? Andrew must take you. It gives the lie to all those who claim that great architecture is a matter of passing fashion, not a question of discovering divine proportion. This, though, was built on the foundation of an ancient town, the Etruscan Santorno, I believe, and has something of an older feel.'

'What about the old town below?'

The Contessa waved a disdainful hand, protected by a suede gardening glove.

'That – that is a piece of Roman trash, overlaid with medieval religiosity. My husband's ancestors built the parterre to keep us separate, not that any of them dare to come near here.'

'How old is the garden?'

'Old. At least, the bones of it, the terraces and the topiary are. The rest I planned myself as a memorial to my husband and my son.' The Contessa's voice was deep and sweet, like a cello, but the diamond drops in her ears quivered slightly.

'It's exquisite. I hadn't realized gardening could be an art.'

'It is the greatest of arts, because it takes shape over time. Music takes an hour, books a day, but gardens – with gardens you have to see for twenty, a hundred years, and your materials are living things, vulnerable to sudden frosts and baking summers, to slugs and snails and insects and, most of all to man. Go and explore, my dear,' she finished, dismissing me.

The Contessa's garden was indeed an extraordinary place. My grandfather had never bothered much with his, being away so often, and my mother's idea was to pave everything and have a few pots of hydrangeas; but had I been born in Sissinghurst this would still have been remarkable.

It was built on three levels, like a wedding cake: the smallest and highest being where the palazzo stood, the largest and lowest at the base. It was completely walled in. The true extent of its size was impossible to ascertain, for it consisted of so many mazes that you could wander for hours without being certain of where you were going. Each square, rectangle or hexagon of clipped box was like a room – some tiny, filled only with grass, some as big as a football pitch and dazzling with spring flowers.

One garden consisted of spirals, obelisks and orbs clipped out of bay; another was a herbarium, laid out in the shape of interlocking pentangles. One was an orchard, buzzing with blossom-intoxicated bees, another a shadowy avenue of topiary giants: men, women, children, animals. Nothing could be anticipated, yet every garden within the garden seemed like a logical sequence or balance to what had preceded it. Each changed, like shot silk, according to the direction in which you looked at it. From one end, an enclosure could seem as innocent and romantic as an English herbaceous border; at the other, you suddenly saw a pattern so dominant that it could only have been Italian.

Yet it was not only a garden of plants, but of water. I searched for the hot spring, without success. There was a circular pool surrounded by narcissi, a series of fountains arching into a marble stream, a grotto encrusted with shells and tiny, trembling ferns, its windows made of transparent malachite, but nothing with the water like blood.

I stopped wondering, after a while, how the Contessa could possibly maintain all this with only the Guardis to help her. It had an enchanted air, like something out of time.

Though much of the wall was pierced with windows, allowing views of the hills east and west, only one faced south and on to Santorno. I looked down on the rooftops, the colour of red mullet, jumbled on top of each other. Somewhere down there was Lucio; unless, that is, he was with Sylvia. I hoped she was lying, as she had about being married to Dave (why? I couldn't begin to think) but I had no real illusion that she had spoken other than the truth. The thought of her and Lucio in bed together, doing the things we had done, made me feel quite ill; but then, so must Sylvia be when she thought of me and him, I told myself, trying to be reasonable. From her point of view, I was the wicked intruder, the guest who had betrayed her trust. No amount of protestation on my part would persuade her of my innocence, that was clear.

So, what was I to do? Should I go back to England and spend six months eating humble pie to my parents? The idea was unendurable. Should I spend yet more of my legacy, now whittled down to less than £2,000, going somewhere else, another country perhaps? My courage failed me as I thought of going through all the business of trains, planes and taxis again. And why should I? I had a right to be in Santorno just as much as Sylvia did. I loved it with a passion. It had deepened and overlaid the landscape of my childhood, and it was now inextricably bound up with my love for Lucio. Whether I could stand all those nudging, smirking shopkeepers was another matter, but I had to learn how to cope, somehow.

Also, I still craved Lucio. The knowledge that he was unattainable because he belonged to someone else made it worse. I hated hating Sylvia. When I thought of her letters to me, so different, so vivacious (so illiterate, too, another part of me admitted), of her kindness, of the way she had been my first and only friend, of the way she herself had changed me from a plain little English girl to someone capable of attracting her own lover, I was tormented by guilt. Yet there was no contest. Sylvia hated me, and I had to hate her back.

Dr Evenlode and the Contessa were nowhere in evidence for most of the day. He spent his time typing, presumably working on his book, while the Contessa was no doubt attending to her vegetable loves.

The evidence of so much industry prodded me into getting out my easel and starting to paint again. I had expected it would be impossible now, but for some reason it was easier than it had ever been. My room was north-facing, towards the highest peaks that formed the chain known as the Mountains of the Moon. Their remoteness, the steadiness of the light and the comfortable silence of the castle helped me to concentrate.

I did a self-portrait. I wanted to purge myself of the narcissism I had enjoyed with Lucio, to see myself as truthfully as possible. People think that the camera never lies, but it is paintings that do not – even if what emerges is not immediately recognizable, as a photograph is.

Andrew Evenlode's description of public-school girls as looking like frightened hares had annoyed me, but it was no longer applicable. If not precisely haggard, my face was becoming sharper, less innocent, more watchful. The eyebrows helped; the extent to which eyebrows denote the key to character was something I had only recently noticed, following my own acquisition of some. The Contessa's were fastidious arches, my mother's a thin, irritable wisp, my father's and grandfather's thick bristling clumps, Lucio's . . . Lucio's were perfect.

I worked without stopping until the light went, not even bothering to let layers of paint dry. It took three days. My hosts did not enquire how long I intended to stay. I told them I was painting.

'Is this the Before or the After?' Evenlode enquired in his usual mocking manner when I showed it to him.

'Guess.'

'Well, on the one hand, you've given yourself a soppy look, so it might be the Before, but on the other there is a certain air of the tragedy queen, so my guess is, it's the After.'

'Dr Evenlode, I think you're the most hateful man I've ever met.'

'Miss Kenward, you may well be right, but you must learn not to take yourself so terribly seriously.'

'But if I don't,' I said, beginning to lose my temper, 'who will? Not you, that's for sure!'

'I take people on my own estimation, not theirs.'

'What's so wonderful, so infallible about your estimation?'

'It is based on dispassionate observation.'

'Nobody can be that dispassionate, it's against human nature.'

'Ah, we're on to that, are we? And what do you make of human nature? Do you think it's something that can be systematically analysed, categorized and co-ordinated? Or do you think it's something wholly spontaneous and unpredictable in every circumstance? The latter, I suspect, like all romantics.'

'I think you can tell a great deal about people from their faces.'

'Now that really is a foolish error, and such a common one. You disappoint me; I had thought better of you than that.'

'If you have any sisters, I hope they boxed your ears regularly and with vigour,' I said.

'I do, and they didn't.'

'Why not?'

Evenlode looked haughtily down at me, and replied, 'Because I'm stronger, and bigger.'

I could not repress a smile. 'So you learned to be a bully in the nursery.'

'Am I? I thought I believed in benevolent despotism.'

I could never be entirely sure when he was serious. That was his chief weapon, as well as his wits, which I knew were too quick for me. Now and again I was surprised at my own temerity in talking to him as I did, considering his age and my position there, but fear always makes me refractory. I was frightened of him, though I didn't want to admit it, more than of my mother or headmistress or even Pompa.

We only really met in the evening, for dinner. Maria was an excellent cook, as he had promised, though she was scarcely unobtrusive as a servant. She seemed to understand much of what we said, though she couldn't speak English, and was not one to keep her opinions to herself if it was a subject on which she felt strongly.

In the middle of serving up some mouthwatering concoction of fresh pasta, shaped into butterflies or twisted into shells, she would stop and deliver fierce little monologues on the corruption of the Catholic Church, the necessity of fidelity in marriage or on the inferiority of everything emanating from the modern Santorno. The more heated she became, the more she would slip into the sibilant sing-song of Tuscan dialect, her date-shaped eyes glistening as she swayed from side to side, staring into the pot from which she was serving like a haruspex.

'That supermarket, trying to cheat honest people with all its machinery from the day it was built, the owner had nothing, he borrowed it all from his cousin, the wife of Max Vincioni, *la cattiva*! She was deceiving him for years, and now he's made a sack of money, *managg' alia miseria*! Excuse me, Contessa, but he has, and he's making the town into a brothel down there!'

The Contessa would wait, smiling faintly, for the diatribe to finish; at which point Maria would simmer down and start serving again. I could not quite understand their relationship. They seemed to hold each other not just in mutual respect but in a kind of alliance against the world. Maria could have cheated her employer all over the place and demanded vast wages, knowing her detestation of the townspeople, but she was rigidly, transparently honest.

'I've tried many times to give them their farmhouse, but they won't take it as a gift,' the Contessa told me. 'They're too proud. The place they wanted was where the English couple, the Dunnetts, live. It was to come to them by inheritance, but Mr Lurie cheated them out of it.'

'How? Sylvia mentioned something of the kind.'

'Maria's great-uncle married again, to a woman not of these parts. She was greedy; Mr Lurie knew the Dunnetts were looking for a farmhouse to buy, and persuaded Maria's relatives to sell up and move out so he could take a commission. They moved to a flat down below, and died there.'

'I see. But surely that sort of thing must happen quite a lot?'

'Not round here. Most of the land is mine, up in the hills. As I have no children and my husband's estate is not entailed, I have been selling off abandoned houses to one or two people who take my fancy; Louis Marchand, whom I think you know, and a couple of middle-aged people who work in Rome and only come at weekends. But I do not wish for another Chiantishire. The tourism in summer is quite bad enough. One day, too, the farmers will come back. The wines will improve; already people realize more and more how good and healthful olive oil is. This is a working place. I intend to see it remains so.'

She spoke with great charm, but also great authority. I would not have dared contradict her in anything. The force of her personality had nothing to do with her class, for she would have been just as impressive in Maria's position. Indeed, I thought I could glimpse a kind of similarity between them, now and again; not physical, but as though they were both driven by the same thing. Maria's husband, Guido, was a quiet, gentle man who worked all day in the garden, weeding and trimming the topiary. I wondered how he stood it, being the buffer between two such terrible women.

It was he who came to me on the fourth day of my stay and told me that there was someone at the gates who wanted to see me.

10

'Emma, forgive me.'

I gripped the bars of the gate. He looked drawn and exhausted, reeking of cigarettes.

'I should have told you before. I meant to, in the evening. I didn't want to think about her while we were together. I didn't want to think about anyone except you.'

'You only thought about yourself, not me.'

'No! No, I promise to you, I swear it, on my mother. You must believe me, I am telling the truth.'

'Sylvia thinks I let you do it deliberately, to spite her. How could you, Lucio?'

He seized my hands and stared at me with his yellow-rayed eyes. The touch and smell of him made me remember too much.

'How could you?' I repeated.

'Ah, don't look at me like that!' he pleaded. 'What have they done to you in this terrible place, those two witches? Come away from here, come away with me, my angel, outside where they can't watch and hear, and I'll explain everything.'

Well, of course, it sounded better in Italian.

'I don't know how to open the gates.'

'There's a little gap at the bottom, where it's wider. My

mother told me, she used to come in as a child. Look, here. If your ears get through, the rest will follow.'

I felt idiotic, coming out like this, but it seemed logical at the time. That's the trouble with sex: once you've accepted the ridiculousness of it, you're on to a law of diminishing returns. Lucio scorned caution and inhibition, in any case. I never thought of asking someone to open the gates.

As soon as I was through, Lucio seized me and pushed me roughly round the corner, out of sight, and down into an olive grove beneath. Then he slammed my back against the terrace wall before I could begin to protest.

I went limp and stupid, like a fish hit over the head. He didn't even take off his clothes, or mine, driving into me with such force that, afterwards, my buttocks were indented with the sharp projections of stone. I could hear lizards rustling about, swisser-swasser, like miniature dragons in crevices of the wall. Over his shoulder, the yellow fields of some crop became incandescent.

'That's better,' he said, breathing hard.

'Oh, bloody hell, what I have done?' I muttered, coming to. I couldn't believe what had just happened, and in broad daylight. I thought of what Louis had said about Englishwomen behaving like tarts in Italy, and wished for a bottomless pit.

'Now,' said Lucio, 'listen to me. I am going to tell you everything.' He was shining again, a second sun in his hair.

I looked at the long, springing muscle in his thighs, like the bow of a violin, and stopped berating myself. 'Sylvia and I started going together after Dave went off with Izzy. We were both very upset.'

'I can understand about her, but why you?'

'Because he was my friend for years, just like you and Sylvia,' Lucio said. 'All that time I was a teenager in Santorno. I thought they were both wonderful.'

'She's wonderful. He's a creep.'

'You never saw them together, Emma, when it was good between them, but they were special. They never seemed to quarrel or talk about boring things like money, they were always having parties and making music.

'The first real music I ever heard was with them, you understand? I can't tell you what it did to me. None of the big bands come to Italy any more, because of all the kidnapping and corruption, they haven't for years, and the radios and discotheques play shit, Iglesias and Gianni Morandi, *che schifo*. When I heard Dave's music, I felt as if it was made for me. It became mixed up with how I saw him.'

'Yes,' I said. 'I see.' I had the same thing about Sylvia and painting; to a degree.

'I didn't really notice Sylvia at first, except as part of Dave. Oh, he went off and fucked other women, American tourists especially; he was the sort that only had to see a hole in the wall and up he'd go, but it didn't seem to matter to him or to Sylvia. He would sit there, typing his book sometimes, and she would cook for him, or draw, and they both seemed like the perfect couple, the new way people were supposed to be, not like my parents or my friends' parents.

'Then, something happened. I was away a lot, doing military service in Calabria. I came back, and there was this situation with Izzy' (he pronounced it 'easy') 'and there was Sylvia. She had always been a little distant to me, mysterious, but now she wanted to be consoled. So,' Lucio said, smiling a little and shrugging, 'I consoled her. We kept it secret because she hoped Izzy would give her money to buy the house from Dave if she seemed the abandoned woman.'

'I don't know why you're telling me all this,' I said, riven with curiosity and jealousy. 'Why didn't you just tell me about her? If you want this to go on, why didn't you finish with her first?'

125

'Because, firstly, she became obsessed by me. Yes, really obsessed, it disgusted me, but it was like a fantasy, too, it excited me. She won't – wouldn't let me go. And I thought for a while, well, why not? She's older than me. It was a conquest. You have to understand, for a man, the attraction of novelty. Even an ugly woman can fill you with desire for a time, and Sylvia is not ugly.'

'No,' I agreed, 'she is not.'

'But she is old, and dark, and neurotic. She is not natural, like you.'

'No,' I said, trying not to think of my eyelashes. 'She isn't.'

'I was getting bored, anyway, even before the party. Then you came, and I found I was visiting to see you, not her. You are so different, so intelligent, so romantic. A virgin. Every Italian man dreams of a virgin, and in this I am like them. Emma, I love you.'

His eyes swam with tears. It was impossible not to be affected. In opera, women were always forgiving their errant lovers, so how could I not do the same?

'Have you ended with her, then?'

I could hardly speak; I knew I shouldn't give in, but he had been so honest. An Englishman would never have been so honest. He had always been beautiful, but now it was as if a mask had been removed, and I was looking through the palimpsest of his features to the truth.

'Yes. She told me where to find you.'

'Oh, Lucio, then I love you, also.'

'Come away with me now, if you mean it,' he said.

I returned to the Palazzo, sliding through the gap in the gate, and went to collect my things as quietly as possible. Luckily, neither the Contessa nor Evenlode was about; if the latter had cross-questioned me, I don't think I'd have had the nerve.

The ever-vigilant Maria was not so easy to evade, however.

'So, you're off, then? With that traitor?'

'Maria, he's explained everything, and it's all right again. I love him,' I said. 'You can't stop me. Tell the Contessa thank you, thank you for everything, but I must go.'

'And the *professore*? What about him?' She folded her arms, glaring at me.

'Oh, he'll be glad to see my back. He thinks I'm a nuisance, he hates me. He's got his book, and the Contessa's got her garden, and I've got Lucio, so everyone's happy.'

'Signorina Emma, you are making a mistake,' said Maria, but she let me pass. Her voice floated down the avenue as I hurried past the ghostly statues. 'Come back . . . '

'Evil old witch,' said Lucio as the gates swung open, then closed. 'She's always hated me and my family.'

'Why?'

'Oh, she hates everyone, except the Contessa,' he said, between kisses. 'Perhaps her husband had his balls shot off.'

A week ago, such crudeness would have shocked me; now I laughed. 'I don't think so, she has two sons.'

'Well, something else, then. Who cares?'

'Where are we going?'

'To Mimi's flat in Santorno, Max Vincioni is waiting with the keys.'

'Won't she mind?'

'She won't be back for at least three weeks; after France, she decided to go back to Australia. Oh, and if you want it, you can have her teaching job while she's away.'

'Lucio, that's wonderful!'

'Am I clever?'

'Yes, you are, and I love you.'

I couldn't stop saying it, now it was out. It was such a relief. He carried my suitcase down Via Garibaldi. We had our arms round each other; my hand was in his pocket. It was the siesta time, almost nobody was around, which was just as well.

Max was waiting. His long moustaches shook with sentiment.

'A young couple, how beautiful,' he said. 'Take them, take them. Be happy in this miserable town!'

We couldn't wait for him to leave, and after shaking our hands solemnly, he clanked off like a jaundiced skeleton, leaving us in fits of nervous laughter.

'Poor man, is he very unhappy? With the Michelin star and all the money from his hotel?'

'He has a terrible wife,' said Lucio, locking the door behind us.

Living in Santorno was very different from Sylvia's, or the Palazzo.

To start with, there was the noise. I had got used to living in the countryside, which, though it has its own rumours of things stirring about, eating and being eaten, is not intrusive as a city is. The first night in Mimi's flat I couldn't sleep, not only because of Lucio, but because of all the racket inside and outside.

The flat was on the ground floor, overlooking one of the streets that sloped down from Piazza Vend Settembre to Santorno's south and lowest gate. The lower you went geographically in the town, the lower you sank socially; Mimi's place, though only just below the piazza, caught the full blast of vomiting drunks, quarrelling couples, whining scooters, and TV sets loudly tuned to pornographic satellite shows. The ludicrous passion and heavy breathing of the last was at first an entertaining counterpoint to our own activities, but as it went on, hour after hour, it became tedious, and then infuriating.

Water swished and trickled through pipes in the building. Steps shuffled across the reconstituted marble-chip tiles outside, and at three o'clock a pack of small, yapping dogs appeared to go suddenly mad.

We dozed and slept; dozed and woke. It was nearly midday. 'I must go.'

'You're always leaving me.' It was with difficulty that I prevented myself from clinging to him, so I made it into a joke.

'No,' he said. 'One day it will be you who leaves me. You will go off and marry a lawyer, or a banker. I know it.'

'Never, Lucio, I promise!' I exclaimed, horrified.

He gave me a long look, then lowered his lashes. 'If you ever try it, I'll kill you,' he said, smiling. I laughed, and after a moment, he laughed too.

'When will you be back?'

'Later. This evening. And you, you have to see Mimi's pupils, don't you?'

'Where do I go?'

'Ask Nastri, the chemist. He organizes all that.'

The flat echoed with emptiness after he left. I was nervous about going out, but I knew I had to. I got dressed, put on my pearl necklace to try to make myself look respectable, and emerged into the hall. Another door opened and a woman peered out, staring. When I tried smiling at her, she hissed, 'Putana!', then whisked back inside like a lizard.

Nastri, the chemist, all too obviously shared her opinion, though his reaction was a different one. A plump, middle-aged man whose grey hair was combed into tinny corrugations, he held my hand too long in pinguid fingers, and made hateful Italian cow's eyes at me.

'You understand, what will be expected of you is the same as for the Signorina Mimi?'

I sighed. I could guess only too well what Mimi had got up to with a dozen lecherous burghers of this kind. No wonder she always looked so well turned out.

'I am perfectly capable of teaching children English,' I said. 'I am shortly to be a student at Oxford.'

This visibly impressed him, for he dropped my hand. 'I can see you are a serious person. But,' he said, ogling again, 'let us hope not too serious!'

'Why not ask the Contessa,' I went on, despising myself for sinking into snobbery, but what could I do? I needed the money, and I was determined not to take any nonsense from him. 'She is a friend of my family's.'

'We are honoured, then,' Nastri said, practically grovelling by now.

After that, it was all plain sailing. He told me the children were still on holiday, after Easter, but that the lessons could begin the next week, and that I would be paid 5,000 lire a child on the day.

'They are all children of good family,' he said, anxiously. 'They wish to learn English so that they can get good jobs, later, perhaps in a bank or in the Hotel Max. It is important, you understand?'

'Yes,' I said. 'I understand, and I'm so glad you do too.' Signor Nastri gave a sheepish little smile and a shrug, as if to say, who could blame him for trying it on?

'The other English lady, Signorina Danby, she teaches the older ones. She recommended you.'

I could not hide my surprise. 'That was kind of her.'

'She's in the Bar Popolare now, I think. Good afternoon.'

Tony had put out some tables in the piazza, now it was warmer, and Caroline was sitting at one of them. She waggled her fingers coyly as I approached.

'Ciao. Come and join me. Isn't it lovely, feeling warm again? I think I'm getting a tan already. You'll soon have to be careful, with that Carrara marble skin of yours. I'm always seeing English girls getting frazzled because they think it's like sunbathing in Green Park. D'you know what Tony calls you round here? *Nuvola bionda*, blond cloud. Isn't that sweet? But you mustn't float about too much, you know.'

I hate it when women tell me I float about; the St Crumpet's headmistress said the same thing. It always means they hate me and wish I were a plodder like them.

Caroline continued, blithely. 'You know the marvellous thing about Italian weather is that even when it rains, it never does so for more than a couple of days in a row, so unlike England and those awful grey skies. When I came out here on holiday, I vowed I'd never go back there, and I haven't.'

'Thanks for the job.'

'Oh, well, it was more than I thought I could cope with, the children and the teenagers, on top of the farm, and I thought the children would like you.'

'Possibly.'

I was by no means certain I would like them. I had not been lying when I told my parents I loathed children; partly because all the girls at St Crumpet's were so soppy about them, but also because I can never see why people make such a fuss over what are really dwarfish, calculating and grotesquely ill-behaved adults.

'How's the farm?'

Caroline made a face. 'Well, its okey-dokey now, with the spring rains, but it gets really frightful up there in the summer.'

'Where are you?'

'Way, way up in the mountains, the cemetery side of Santorno, past the rubbish dump. Have you never been there? It's an extraordinary place, the dump, I mean, a whole hillside covered in stuff. It never stops burning day or night; Timmy calls it Mordor. Anyway, if you go on a couple of kilometres, you get to the farm. You really should visit, I know Timmy would like to see you, and it's a lovely little valley.'

'What's wrong with it, then? Snakes?'

'Oh, there are oodles of those. No, it's the water. The well dries up completely in summer, which is a nightmare for the crops. You see—' Caroline brought her horsy face closer to mine, and spoke through teeth that were even more tightly clenched than usual – 'when we bought it, we were complete innocents. I mean, Timmy had always wanted to farm, but in England, even in Wales, it's so expensive. So we came here, and Dave showed us the farm, and he never told us that the reason why it had been abandoned for thirty years was because it's dry as a bone for four months in the year!'

'Oh no!'

'Oh yes. It took all our money, too. That's why I have to teach English, you see, to keep us afloat. We've tried letting out rooms to tourists in the summer, but they're mostly Americans, and you know what Americans are like about showers. And, of course, nobody else will buy it, because we couldn't possibly not tell them about the water. I mean, could we?'

She looked wistful for a moment, like a horse considering a Polo mint just out of reach.

'Couldn't you drill another well? A deeper one? There seem to be springs all over the place in the palazzo.'

'Ah, the palazzo. No, that's an exception. Besides, there are all sorts of regulations about drilling these days, because the water table keeps dropping. The Dunnetts had to pay out the most massive bribes to get their swimming pool accepted by the commune, and even so, it's officially listed as a farm reservoir. No, it's all hopeless. I just have to keep on soldiering on.'

'Poor you.'

I felt some sympathy for Caroline now. She was very plain, with those awful teeth and the ratchety voice, but not a nasty person, really; the sort of woman doomed to spinsterdom, I thought.

'No, what I'm really worried about is poor Timmy.'

I wondered how her brother liked being called by this baby-ish name; it struck me, suddenly, apropos Justin, that it couldn't be all that easy being a younger brother.

'I do so wish he'd settle down. It would take a huge burden off me if he found someone, then I could come and move into town.'

'I'm afraid I'm otherwise engaged,' I said, in alarm. Caroline smiled gummily. 'Oh no, dear, I didn't mean you, you're far too young for him, and besides, you'll be going to university later on this year, won't you? No, I was thinking of Sylvia.'

'Sylvia!'

It was all I could do not to laugh. Sylvia and Tim, what an unlikely combination!

'Yes, you see, he's always, well, fancied her rather, and I thought that now her marriage is over, well, it might be the solution to all our problems.'

'I don't think it would work.'

'Oh, but are you sure? I don't know her very well; I've always been closest to Mimi, and Sylvia is rather distant in a way.'

'I've never found her so.'

'No, well, that's why I thought I'd, so to speak, sound you out.'

'Why don't you ask her yourself? Or better still, why doesn't Tim?' I could just imagine the reception he'd get, too. Stifling a fit of giggles, I continued, 'I'm afraid I'm the wrong person now, anyway. Sylvia and I have, well, we've fallen out.'

'Yes, I'd heard. It must have been rather difficult for her having a pair of lovers under her roof when she's still so upset over Dave,' said Caroline censoriously.

So that's how she's explained it, I thought; well, I wouldn't complicate matters by telling the truth.

'But I'm sure things will be cleared up. She's very fond of you, anyone can see that.'

'She threw me out of her house, she's totally out of control,' I said, wearily.

Caroline looked at me and said, 'You think so? Well, people are always hardest when they see their own faults in others. Remember that.'

After Caroline had left (without, I noticed, paying the bill for her cappuccino, but I could be said to owe her that), I sat at the café table and watched the pigeons wheeling like confetti round the blue-and-gold-faced clock in the Municipality tower. It was a handsome building like many in the town. The Contessa had dismissed Santorno as medieval trash, but it had its share of romance and the Renaissance. I could imagine Mercutio dying on the Municipality steps, or Figaro bounding around one of the little alleys with perfect ease. Instead, I saw Lucio.

'How was Nastri?'

'Slimy. But don't worry, I took care of him. Lucio, there's a woman who lives opposite Mimi's flat, who called me a whore this morning.'

He looked black. 'I know the one. She saw me when I came out this morning. We'll go and see her.'

'Oh no, don't let's make a fuss. She's probably mad anyway.'

'You English! You complain, then you don't do anything about it,' he said affectionately. 'But that one I can stop.'

We walked back to the gloomy apartment in Via delle Finestre, past the withered pots of clivias and a cheeping, lard-coloured canary, and he knocked on the door opposite Mimi's.

A pair of black eyes bored out at us from behind a chain set in the mahogany veneer.

'Good evening, signora. I wish to present you my *fidanzata*, Signorina Kenward from England. She will be staying here a few weeks, while the Australian teacher is away,' said Lucio politely. 'She thought she heard you say something to her this morning, signora, but not speaking Italian as well as you or I, she couldn't quite understand it. What was it you said, signora?'

The black eyes blinked and made to withdraw. Lucio put his embroidered boot in the door.

'You can't remember, signora? That's good. Because, you understand, if she hears it again, then so will I, and if I hear it, then the story of what you and your uncle do together might be told to a few people. Good evening.'

'Lucio!' I said, when we were back in the flat. 'How did you dare?'

'Oh, my mother told me her uncle's been screwing her for years,' he said carelessly. 'She knows everyone's secrets, my mother.'

'I didn't mean that, I meant telling her we were engaged.'

'Well, it will stop their tongues from spitting poison at you.'

I wanted to ask if he meant it, but I didn't get the chance. Someone rapped sharply on the door. I opened it and saw Tony from the bar, puffing and wheezing on the doorstep like a collapsing meringue.

'Signorina, this has just come for you. It's a telegram, from England. The postman didn't know where you were. I hope it's not bad news?'

He watched avidly as I opened it.

'Yes,' I said, 'it is.'

FATHER ARRIVING LUNCH MAY TWO STOP, it said. It was unsigned, but I had no doubt that it was from my mother.

11

Mimi's flat drove me to distraction in a matter of days. Worse than the noise was the furniture: the porridgy bed with its mahogany-veneered headboard, the feeble, unstable lamps with their tasselled fringes, the Formica kitchen, the bathroom with its *Psycho-style* starfish-spattered shower curtain, the stainless-steel cutlery, the matted cream flokati rugs that looked like cats' sickballs.

The first week, I moved all the furniture except the bed into the sitting room, and locked the door on it. The bed I covered with my cloak, the table from the kitchen with a white sheet. I filled jugs and jam jars with wild flowers culled on walks beneath the city walls. Even then, I felt miserable.

Lucio thought I was mad.

'What's wrong with it all?' he kept saying. 'It's furniture, isn't it? You're only going to be here for a couple of weeks; why does it matter so much to you?'

I tried to explain to him that ugliness is like a physical pain to me, that I cover up pictures in hotel bedrooms with hand-towels, that even the knowledge that such furniture existed in the next room was like a sore tooth. He couldn't understand. He was, I supposed, protected by the glamour of his own beauty; the things that appalled me could no more touch him than darkness could afflict light.

It was the lack of light in my new home that was worst of all. When Lucio was there, it didn't matter, for the perpetual gloom at the bottom of the street then became a thing of intimacy, secrecy, candles. But as soon as he left, I plunged into despair.

I couldn't paint. It wasn't like being at Sylvia's, where, despite my obsession with Lucio, I had still managed to keep my fingers supple, do something every day, and, no matter how indifferent the results, this had been a source of self-respect. To become a painter, you need great physical strength in your arms and shoulders to enable you to stand there, hour after hour, in the waking dream; but the mental discipline required is even greater. The most effortful thing you do every day is to win the battle over inertia: to pick up a brush and start painting is like moving a mountain. It never seems to get any easier. Either a painting is going badly, and every brush stroke is agony, or else it's going well, and any brush stroke could ruin the whole thing, irrevocably. But this was far worse. I could not paint.

I have heard of English people who suffer acute depression in winter because of the paucity of light, but mine is not just a question of happiness or sadness. Light is all in all to me.

Mimi's flat suffocated me, paralysed my will, yet I was frightened of going outside. It was not only the irritation of having passers-by rudely stop and peer at my progress, or interrupt a train of thought with their idiotic questions, it was the constant pestering to which any woman, remaining stationary in a public place, is subjected. I could see now why Sylvia had pretended all these years to be married, for the status of a young and single woman, known to be sexually active, is not an enviable one in Italy. Though Lucio had declared me to be his *fidanzata* to the hag across the corridor, I still knew that she and others spat venom when they saw me.

Crossing the piazza to teach my pupils became an ordeal worse than any in Kensington. I began to wonder what it was I had been so frightened of in London shops, where rude assistants at least minded their own business and didn't start tittering as soon as my back was turned. The mothers of the children I taught would not meet my eye; the fathers stared too long. Often, there would be telephone calls to the flat when I was alone. They went like this:

'*Buon giorno*, signorina, I understand you teach English.'

'Yes, I do. Do your children need lessons?'

'Can you teach me privately?'

'Yes, though it's more expensive.'

'Can I ask, could these lessons be *incontri d'amore*?' Encounters of love. It made me laugh, afterwards, the extreme propriety of such improper suggestions, but every time I went cold with shock, slamming the telephone down wordlessly. I wondered if English lessons had the same connotations as French lessons did in England, or whether I was being watched all the time. It was possible to see straight into the bedroom by standing on the Municipality steps, I discovered. This made me even more tense about going out, though freedom and the countryside were only down the road, beneath the city walls.

To my surprise, the Santornese never went for walks, confining themselves to promenades along the parterre before and after the siesta. They regarded the peasantry with absolute contempt, and the olive groves all around as fraught with peril, to be ventured into only armed, and in the pursuit of *la caccia*. The more I came to understand the profound revulsion the townspeople had for the countryside, the more Lucio's determination to visit Sylvia and myself on foot flattered me. I wondered whether she had appreciated it, and thought, with some satisfaction, she had probably not.

I longed to lie with him in the fields of wild barley, of a green so tender it made the heart ache. The terraces rose and tightened, swirl on swirl, like the fingerprints of a giant. The groves echoed with the sound of cuckoos, blackbirds, even nightingales, though it was a miracle any survived the hunting season. It was too rich, too abundant to absorb and control on canvas, but irresistible to attempt.

The people were different there, too. In country lanes, the men played a version of bowls, winding a leather strap round a piece of wood in the shape of a *pecorino* cheese, and hurling it as far as it would go. When I stopped to watch and sketch, their wives would ask me in, plying me with glasses of sweet, brown *vin santo* and thick feathery slices of Easter cake. It was a different world, the one poised between the old Santorno and the new; eventually, everyone had no doubt, the two would fuse together, but for the time being it held tranquillity. Yet I was desperate for a studio, along with a nicer place to live. I could endure Mimi's flat only by forcing myself to go out of it most of the day, and this restlessness made concentration impossible.

'Why don't you come with me?' I would ask, but Lucio always found an excuse.

'Out there is Africa,' he would say. 'I want to see animals and green things either in cages or on my plate.' It was the only subject on which we seriously disagreed.

I did not go near the palazzo or the parterre, in case I bumped into Sylvia. Lucio had warned me to stay away from and not speak to her, and, recollecting her violent inclinations towards Izzy, I felt this was probably wise.

Once, when I was walking back along the road to the old city in the evening, my hands full of white and blue iris, I was followed by a car with two young men in it. They leered and jeered, trying to persuade me to get in with them. I was terrified that at any moment I would be dragged off and raped. Only a narrow lane, arrowing down between vineyards from the old town to the new, spared me further persecution: a car could not squeeze through it, and they were too lazy to run.

I arrived at the flat on the verge of tears. Lucio was furious when I told him.

'Who were they? Why didn't you take their licence number?' he demanded. 'They must be enemies of mine, from Santorno *inferiore*.' (This was what the inhabitants of the upper, *superiore* town called the industrial zone down below, with a curl of the lip.)

'I don't think so, Lucio,' I ventured. 'I think they just thought I was fair game. You've said so yourself, they think foreign girls are all tarts.'

'It was aimed at me, I tell you,' he said angrily. 'You understand nothing about this town, nothing. We will find out who they were, and burst their testicles, the band and I.'

The band I had met only briefly, though he promised to take me on a gig. There were three of them, besides Lucio: a huge, oxlike drummer, Sandro; a small, hairy saxophonist, Marcello; and Chiodino, the manic-depressive bass guitarist, perpetually coming down from one drug or climbing up on another. It was in Chiodino's cellar that the Stella Nera would practise. I had yet to hear their music, though I had no doubt it would be good. Lucio spoke of his compositions with such confidence and self-assurance that he could only be gifted beyond measure.

'How they will fawn and cringe, all the people in Santorno who have not believed in me,' he exclaimed in a passion on one occasion. 'The children in the streets, who think I must be crazy because I don't cut my hair short, will be proud they come from Santorno, one day, because it is my birthplace. Success is the best revenge, Emma, don't you think?'

This had certainly been my creed at school; yet increasingly I was less certain, both of its efficacy and of its merit as a motivating force. Recently, the idea that an activity like painting might be an end in itself had begun to creep into my thoughts.

'If you do something for another purpose, like making love

just to have children, isn't that a corruption of the act?' I asked him. 'Isn't it a good thing, to love and be loved?'

'You are talking about what exists between people. Making love and making music or a painting are quite different things.'

'Yes, but . . . When I look at an object to paint it, I have to learn to see it with love. You have taught me that, in a way. Ideas of revenge have nothing to do with it. I have to see what is special about a particular object, or combination of colours and shapes, just as I see what is special about you.'

'But when you've done it, and it's good, don't you think, Ha! this will show them! After?'

'No, because I'm never pleased with what I've done. But even if I were, that wouldn't be the point.'

Lucio laughed, in a good mood again, and began to undress me.

'So, my serious one, you paint without any idea that you might one day be a Michelangelo? Without ambition, without the craving for glory? I don't believe you! You live for praise and admiration, the laurels, you've told me so yourself. All those ugly virgins in your little English school by the sea, you wanted to show them, didn't you? Why do you suddenly disagree with me when I want the same thing for myself in Santorno?'

'Because . . . oh, Lucio, listen, stop tickling! It should be more than that.'

'Should be! We're talking about what is, not what should be. You said once that at the heart of every human being is a child. I'm telling you, what exists in us is the same as what lives in the centre of the earth, a boiling fire of hope and fear, ambition and vengefulness. It is these things that give life, and life in art.'

'Perhaps that's why I can't paint, I'm too happy with you, it makes me forgive everyone.'

'But your parents, you haven't forgiven them, have you?'

'No.'

141

The mischief faded out of his face. 'Emma, you should.'

'Why should I, when they're so hateful to me?' I cried. 'They're supposed to be the grown-ups, not me. Why can't they accept me for what I am, or want to be?'

'You should love your family, Emma,' Lucio said earnestly. 'I know they love you. Your mother and father love you more than anyone will ever love you, even me.'

'Now you're being very Italian,' I said, sulking. I did not like to think of anyone loving me more than he did. 'You think it's enough for them to love me, you don't know what kind of love it is, how hard and selfish. They don't love me for myself, as you do; when they're proud of me, it's only because I reflect well on them, because they can boast about how many Alphas I have to other parents.'

'Emma, you are wrong,' he said.

I was looking forward to my father's visit with dread. Of the two of them, he was by far the easiest to deal with, being inclined to sentiment rather than censoriousness. On the other hand he was, unlike my mother, less in control of his emotions, and liable to explode into violent, hectoring rages. Restaurant meals were a perennial ordeal; I had known him on one occasion to suggest to a waiter who brought warm white wine that he stuff the bottle up his bum. He had the businessman's complete lack of sensitivity towards what he called the service industries and, I felt, an equal disregard for the sensibilities of his children when contradicted on any matter.

'You think you know it all, because of the education I paid for. Well, you don't,' was his favourite refrain.

I had hoped, in a way, that this trip had been made especially to see me. It would have argued some genuine concern, if only for his investment, had he come out off his own bat. Walking up the hill from Piazza Felice to the Hotel Max, I kept trying to keep calm, telling myself what Lucio had said, that he really loved me, despite his truculence, despite his domineering manners. Lucio sent me off reeking of semen, with a love bite on my neck, and promised to wait for me in the piazza in the afternoon.

As soon as I walked into the hotel courtyard, however, I knew it was going to be a disaster. There, occupying at least three parking spaces, was a giant, shiny, black Mercedes, complete with chauffeur. This could only mean one thing. My father was on a business trip; he had dropped by only because it happened to be convenient. For two pins I would have gone straight back to the flat, but I was determined not to be cowed.

The dining room was dancing to the musical chink of china and money: acres of marble and white linen everywhere, and a coach party of superannuated Miami bimbettes swapping notes, and probably husbands, along one wall. They stared at me in my long skirts and straggly hair, and the waiters looked ready to double up as bouncers. I rolled my eyes and stuck my chin out.

My father had his chin stuck out, too; I could tell because there were only two instead of the usual three. I sat down at his table, overlooking the plains, and we glared at each other with deep suspicion.

'How are you?'

'Fine. And you?'

'Fine.'

'That's good. And Mummy? Don't tell me, she's fine.'

'She's been made a magistrate.'

'Oh, she really must be fine, then. What is she sentencing, a diet of bread and water for anyone who appears without a tie?'

'I doubt it,' said my father, 'She sits with two others on the bench.'

'I'm sure she'll bulldoze them into doing whatever she wants, too.'

My father sighed, and rubbed his oyster eyes. He looked so tired that, for a moment, I had a pang of pity for him. He saw it, and was on to the moral high ground in a flash.

'There's no point in having this meeting if you're going to take such an aggressive stance. Can't we try to act like civilized adults?'

'As long as you remember I am an adult, not the little girl you so mourn, we'll get along fine,' I said. 'The moment you forget it, I'm off.'

'What do you think makes you an adult, then?'

'Being eighteen, for a start. Having a job. You didn't know I was teaching, did you?'

'No. I hope it gives you an insight into what your own teachers had to put up with.' My father summoned the waiter, and ordered lunch for both of us. I promptly changed every single thing for my own. For once, he didn't rise to the bait, but smiled.

'I remember when you were a little girl and I took you to the Connaught for your birthday. You ordered steak tartare. I kept asking you if you were sure you knew what you were ordering, and you said, impatiently,' (he put on a sickly, lisping voice) '"Yeth, yeth, Daddy, of course I do, everybody knows what steak tartare is." You'd been reading about it in some book, I think.'

'Then, when it arrived, I couldn't eat it,' I finished, irritably. 'Of course I remember. You never let me forget it. Is that what you call being grown up, knowing about steak tartare?'

My father's eyebrows began to resemble a pair of caterpillars advancing on each other, but he kept his voice level.

'No. I think it's when you learn to admit your mistakes, and laugh at yourself.'

'How frightfully profound,' I mocked. 'And you do that all the time, I suppose? You just wake up, look at yourself in the

144

mirror when you're shaving, and burst into raucous peals? Come off it, of course you don't!

'Do you know what I hate, hate, hate about being a teenager? It's that everyone thinks you're so bloody funny all the time. Oh, it's just Adrian Mole, it's just a phase she'll grow out of, it's just that she takes herself too seriously! You're so full of sententious advice, of being wise after the event, of being so frightfully pleased with the way you've turned out. You never dare to look at your own lives and think, Christ, what a failure I am, how gross, how stupid, how asinine. How would you like it if we saw you looking depressed and said, Ho, ho, it's the male menopause, let's all barf! I mean, would you?'

'Tell me something,' he said, his jowls wobbling. (I shall never, never marry a man who will run to fat, I thought.) 'Why do you hate us so much? What have we done to you?'

'What have you done?' I was outraged. 'Oh, absolutely nothing, I suppose. Only messed up my life. Only sent me to a school for snobbish morons. Only spoilt Justin rotten and been a Scrooge to me. Only kicked me in the teeth the moment I showed any sign of self-confidence – cheek or conceit, in your book. Only made it patently obvious that you valued me less because I'm a girl.'

'Good God, you really believe all that?'

'Can you deny it?'

'What do you think it's like, being a parent? Do you think it's so easy? Just you wait, my girl, until you have some of your own, then we'll see!'

'Not bloody likely,' I interjected.

'If you think I'm such a terrible father, you should have seen mine.'

'Pompa! Pompa was a saint compared with you. He understood everything,' I said, fiercely.

'A saint! Ha! My father was the most domineering old coot

that ever walked the earth! Do you know what he used to do, on the rare occasions when he was at home? He used to put his shoes outside the door every evening for me to polish. Imagine, as if I were his fag! He would demand that I iron his newspaper every morning. He would go over every word in my school report and cane me if I fell below an Alpha. He was an utter bastard.'

'I don't believe it.'

'Oh, by the time you got to know him, he'd mellowed. Also, you were always a chip off the old block. He never forgave me for not going to university. How do you think your mother and I felt, watching him push you through the same hoops he tried to push me?'

'He didn't. How could he? He was hardly ever there, and when I saw him all we talked about was painting,' I protested.

'Pompa was a tyrant, a very charming, brilliant tyrant, but still a despot. I don't think you fully realise how much influence over you he really had. I used to hear you parroting the same things he would lecture me about, in my own home! It was like a nightmare. As soon as I thought I was free of him, along you came, as his catspaw. He despised me for making money, you know, when he threw away all his inheritance, and mine, on expeditions. Mama and I were so poor in that freezing Shropshire house, we spent the whole time in the kitchen. She was an asthmatic. He killed her with his obsession.'

My father's oyster eyes brimmed with sudden tears. I was shocked and embarrassed; he had never told me any of this. I didn't believe a word of what he had said, but I felt sorrier for him than I had ever done before. Tentatively, I reached out, but at that moment the waiter swooped down with the second course.

'There's a woman here who knew him, I think quite well. She has lilies Pompa gave her, in the most beautiful garden.'

146

'Oh? Who's that?' My father took out a handkerchief and blew his nose – *poot!* – to the horror of several waiters in the restaurant. Relaxing slightly, I tried not to laugh. 'The Contessa Felice. She lives above Santorno.'

My father put down his knife and fork. 'Not Claudia Felice?'

'Yes. And Daddy—' I fiddled with a toothpick, drawing on the tablecloth – 'that man, the Oxford don who was so foul, is here, too. He's her godson.'

'Claudia Felice, good God, I haven't seen her since I was a young man. She came to our wedding, gave us that foul Ayrton you so admire. I always meant to look her up when we were living in Rome,' he murmured; then, with a sudden snap of his businessman's mind, like a turtle spotting a fly, added, 'So you've seen something of your future tutor, eh?'

'I don't think he will be.'

'Oh, come on now. You're having your little show of independence, but once your nine months are up, you'll come back and go to university, my girl.'

'Will I?' I asked, sweetly. 'I really haven't made my mind up yet, Daddy, but I think it's highly unlikely. I haven't just been painting and teaching English, you know. I've got a boyfriend.'

My father stuck his chin out so far that he was down to one of them. 'Oh? Who? Who?'

'You can meet him, if you like.' Nervously, I began to make a little house out of the toothpicks.

'What is he, one of these damned waiters?'

He glared round the room with such ferocity that they all sprang to attention, and the head waiter came over. 'Everything to your satisfaction, signore?'

'No, Daddy, he isn't,' I said, alarmed. 'He's a musician.'

'The bill, please,' my father bellowed, sending the man scurrying. 'Is this why you ran away from home, then? To get off with some twangling jack?'

'No, Daddy. I went to stay with a woman friend, the one you didn't believe existed, and this just happened. Anyway,' I added, pouring salt all over the toothpick house, and remembering what Slim had said, 'I didn't really run away from home. I just did what most people do, sooner or later, and left. I want to see if I'm any good as a painter.'

'Waste of time. If you want to do that, why didn't you apply to art school?'

'Because I don't think it can be taught,' I said, patiently. 'Also, I'm not interested in Modernism, Post-Modernism, and all that hackneyed rubbish about Hockney and photography being art. I'm just interested in becoming a good, figurative painter, which still seems to me to be the most difficult thing of all to do well.'

My father looked blank: it was plain he didn't know what I was on about.

'You know, the sort that ordinary people can look at and say, I don't know much about art, but I know what I like, and this is it?' I quelled an internal wince.

'You mean,' he said dryly, 'you want to appeal to philistines, is that it?'

'Yes, if you like.' (I always forgot he had brains, too, of a sort.) 'They have eyes, too, they just don't know how to use them.'

'Oh, God, spare me the moralizing of the young!'

'Spare me the blindness of the old! If you really cared a jot about me, you'd help me find somewhere to live where I can paint,' I said. 'I had to move out of Sylvia's, and I'm going potty in this beastly little dark flat I've borrowed for a month.'

'Oh, you want a love nest, now, do you?'

'You always did have such a tabloid mind.'

'At least it pays the bills,' he said, letting fall a plastic cascade of credit cards. I looked at them, and him, with loathing.

'I didn't ask to come to lunch here. You've just guzzled a

whole month's rent, as far as I'm concerned. I'd far rather have just been given the money. But no, you thought you'd drop by, on one of your company freebies, for a quick sneering session, didn't you?'

He ignored me. 'Come on, I'll drop you off.'

'I'd rather walk. It's better for the figure.'

'I want to see what this young man of yours looks like.' The waiters heaved audible sighs of relief as we left, and the chauffeur jumped out, trying to pretend he hadn't been smoking. My father snarled at him, and I wished to sink into the ground. The doors of the Mercedes clicked like the lid of a jewel box.

'Where to?'

'He's just in the piazza. We could easily have walked.'

'I'm going straight on to Milan. I hired a car especially because the Rome-Urbino railway is so bad.'

I said nothing; I was in a panic at the idea of my father meeting Lucio like this. The latter had wanted to present himself, as he put it, to my family. I had tried to put him off, until he asked whether I was ashamed of him. Then I had no option.

It was as bad as I had feared; worse.

'He didn't even get out of the car,' Lucio said.

'It isn't his, it's hired.'

'Porca Madonna. I've never seen such a car!'

'Absolutely hideous. He was just showing off, as usual.'

'The father of Izzy has such a car.'

'Lucio, will you please stop going on about my father's car? I'm very sorry he was so rude to you.'

Lucio shrugged. 'What can you expect?' he asked disdainfully. 'He's English, and he's rich. One day, you will be the same.'

'No, I won't. Not ever.'

'Then, my angel, I know you better than you know yourself.'

12

My father's visit rapidly faded from memory, but it had two consequences. One was that I became determined to do my best as an English teacher for the duration of Mimi's absence.

Twice a week, I would trudge up the Vicolo del Ospedale to a room in the Municipality and give English lessons to the infant progeny of Santorno's bourgeoisie. The room itself was charming, frescoed with the seduction of Europa and the rape of Leda, but neon-lit and stuffy. The children would read aloud in droning, sing-song voices, each dressed in a little white smock with a navy bow which I remembered from my own schooldays in Rome. They were only moderately cute, and I spent the whole time watching the clock. By the end of every lesson, in which we ground through chapters of a staggeringly dull book about the domestic chores of Jane and Henry, sibling morons in a fictional English village, I was ready to scream. It became obvious to me that most people are paid, not to work, but to endure boredom.

The money was useful, though. I bought myself a couple of new things in the market and replaced a tube of rose madder. The expense of painting equipment in Italy horrified me; I was running out of canvas, and my palette became increasingly muddy with browns and umbers, because these were the cheapest. It was good discipline, but depressing to have to be so careful and monochrome, when the struggle to keep going in Mimi's oubliette was already so exhausting.

It was not just the lack of light, it was the difficulty of developing my own style. Everyone, even a beginner drawing matchstick men, has a different style, which changes, backtracks, goes down false alleys and dead ends before – if one persists – permitting sudden, dazzling glimpses of possibility. Dazzling, that is, only to the painter, for as soon as you step back, you see the ineptitude. Despite Giotto, despite Giorgione, a painter does not usually begin to find the lode of individual style in adolescence: to arrive at that point, it is all work, work, work and hope. My style would take years to develop, I knew that already. It was fluid, precocious, ambitious (but what is the point of being modest as a learner? At least badness on a grand scale teaches you something), inclined to self-indulgence and lack of structure. I knew these were feminine faults, for women are generally best at colour and detail, and bad at form.

Oddly enough, the children helped. Tiring of textbooks, I drew rapid cartoons for my pupils, making them identify people and animals in English. Eventually, this became a game we would all play; to my surprise they actually learned a bit of English as a result. I was amused at the primitive awe children have for anyone who can represent an object: it was magic to them, and practice for me, encouraging purity of line and a speedy grasp of essential lineaments.

'I hear the children like you, Signorina Kenward,' said Nastri one evening, bowing and washing his hands in invisible soap.

'Oh, really?'

'Yes. My daughter says you are better than the Australian *dottoressa,* even if you never give them sweets.'

'Yes, well,' I said, ungraciously. 'There's no need to treat them like half-wits.'

Nastri beamed; where his own children were concerned, he was obviously the optimist who saw a glass as being half-full, not half-empty.

'Have you heard when Signorina Mimi is returning?'

'No. But soon, I think.'

My imminent homelessness was a cause for intermittent despair. As summer and the tourist season approached, the rents for even the tiniest rooms soared beyond my reach, to 100,000 or 200,000 lira a month.

'What shall I do? Where shall I go?' I moaned to Lucio.

'Don't worry, we'll find somewhere. I'll ask my mother.'

To me, the solution was for him to move out of his parents' and live with me, combining resources, but the one time I suggested it he looked at me in horror.

'I can't possibly do that, Emma. They need me, they're still in mourning for my sister. It would break my mother's heart. Already, she is angry that I have not presented you to her. She has heard from the old witch at Mimi's, you are my *fidanzata*. She wants to meet you.'

'Oh, God, no!'

'Don't worry. You are so full of anxiety and indecision, Emma. When you learn to trust yourself, then you will be a woman.'

'Like your mother?'

'My mother is a wonderful woman, I tell you. She had me and Gabriella when she was nearly forty, after twenty years of marriage, but you'd never believe it. You should see her when she comes out of the hairdresser's every week. She is the most elegant woman in Santorno.'

'Oh, bloody hell,' I muttered, remembering what Louis had said about Italian men and their mothers. 'All right.'

I hadn't seen much of the expatriate community since my move, though I had bumped into the Dunnetts a couple of times. Bumped was the word where Izzy was concerned, for at five months she had begun to swell unmistakably. It didn't help being so short, of course, but she took care to wear expensive jersey wrappings which emphasized her stomach. I found it quite obscene, though Lucio, like all Italian men, was charmed by the mystery of procreation.

'Perhaps one day we'll have a little *bambino biondo*, like you,' he would say, sentimentally.

'I'm more interested in not having babies than in having them, right now,' I reminded him.

The fact that Izzy was happy being pregnant, nobody could mistake. A blaze surrounded her, like flaming brandy round a Christmas pudding. She had completely forgotten my rudeness on the night of the party, and positively beamed at me when we passed in the streets on market day. What was even more astonishing was that it appeared she was forgetting Dave.

'Women,' mused Slim in a philosophical moment at the Bar Popolare. 'I'll never understand 'em.'

'Women are like life, unpredictable,' Max told him. He was looking frightfully depressed, as usual.

'Yeah,' Slim concluded. 'Life: it's a cunt.'

I had hoped Max wouldn't understand slang, but it was all too clear that he did, for he went puce, bowed slightly, and walked out.

'For God's sake. Slim,' I hissed.

He looked at me with a foxy grin. 'Thou shalt not take the name of the Lord in vain,' he intoned. 'How's life with the Italian stallion?'

'Brill. Have you seen Sylvia? How is she?'

I felt unhappy, asking. Sylvia hardly ever crossed my mind these days, but when she did it was like a shadow.

'Not so good. She came into the shop earlier this week. Looks terrible. I wonder what'll happen when Dave gets back? D'you think they'll patch things up?'

'I don't know. I shouldn't think so. Gosh, what a mess everything is.'

'Not from my end, girlie. Izzy's mum and dad are so thrilled about the baby, they've actually put her allowance up, on condition she comes back to England to give birth.'

'Do they think it's yours?'

'I don't think they care, much, it's still their grandchild. And you know? Neither do I. It could be either of ours.'

'Could it?' I strongly suspected Izzy had spun him a yarn on that one, but he nodded.

'Yeah. We worked out, it happened the night of the party.'

'But I thought—'

He shrugged, and went slightly pink. 'She was so upset, afterwards, see … It seemed quite natural.'

We caught each other's eye, and burst out laughing.

It was hard to avoid such a fate myself. Contraception is impossible for unmarried women to obtain in Italy, at least it was round Santorno, where even married ones had a hard time getting the pill prescribed. Lucio rapidly gave up, telling me that sex with Durex was like eating chocolate with the wrapper on, and that I must count the days after menstruation, like an Italian woman.

'It's the second week that's dangerous,' he said, knowledgeably. I ticked it off on Mimi's glossy two year calendar, noting, with some amusement, that she had done the same herself the year before; but often, when the second week occurred, I wouldn't tell him.

The strangeness of sex was beginning to wear off, but not its delirium. I was like a fish that had swallowed a hook; as long as I followed where he led, I didn't feel it, but as soon as I resisted it tugged at my guts.

There were refinements and debts to pleasure. He would sit

154

naked on a chair, neither of us allowed to touch except where my tongue glided up and down his body, up and down, until the pain of desire became too great, and I would be seized and impaled in a single convulsive twist. Sometimes, he would make me lie spread-eagled across Mimi's bed, while he drew an X over and over on my skin, from my breasts to my thighs with a feather dipped in oil; or lift me up by the knees so that I walked with my hands on the floor. He taught me gutter slang (which to me were just sounds) to say to him, he made me call lovemaking fucking (*scopare*), he allowed no modesty of thought or action.

'I am your lover, there's no need to pretend you don't go to the toilet,' he said. 'Nothing I do before you or you before me is shocking. Modesty is a bourgeois concept.'

He said that he only had to think of my virginity to become excited. When I laughed, he became furious.

'I told you, you would always remain a virgin in your head,' he said.

He believed that pain was only an extension of pleasure, or its spice; he would bite and nip, forcing his fingers under my arms, along my buttocks, between my legs, tickling, plucking, probing, pinching.

'Abandon yourself, give yourself to me,' he would say in his hoarse, singing voice. 'Sex is like dancing, if you don't feel it down to the last finger, you become clumsy and foolish. You must feel me everywhere, like music.'

He would never spend more than three nights in the week with me, for propriety's sake, he said. I could not sleep with him, and I could not sleep without.

'Where do you go all the time?' I complained. 'You can't always be practising or with your parents.'

'I need to be alone some of the time, like you. Listen, don't behave like a wife, OK?'

I subsided. He was practising hard for the *sagra*, the feast of St Anthony, Santorno's patron saint, on 13 June, and the time we spent together was too precious to waste quarrelling, even when it led, like everything else, to making love.

We would rock back and forwards, like the valves of a shell, hour after hour, slippery with saliva and sweat and the fishy slime of sex, while the bed became littered and rumpled as a beach when the tide is out, and our own cries were as strange and distant as those of seagulls. His body was to me a thing of infinite variety and wonder. I knew each archipelago of moles, the tectonic plates of muscle, the ranges of bone, the jungles of hair. I could have drawn him with my eyes shut, though when I tried with them open, it never worked.

'You did better in the beginning, with the one that Sylvia unfortunately saw.'

'That was before I knew you. The more you know a person, the less definable they become.'

'And then, in the end, you see only faults.'

'Is that what you see in me now?' I asked, alarmed.

'To me, you are even more beautiful than in the beginning,' he said. 'But less strong. When I first met you, I thought you were so confident, leaving your parents, so sure about what you believed. Now I see you are vulnerable and full of doubts.'

'Do you dislike it?'

'No, it makes you softer, more feminine. It makes me want to protect you, as well as fuck you,' he said.

I was touched, but also disturbed. It was true, I was losing my wilfulness, and it made it harder for me to paint. I don't think you can paint as a woman (what's wrong with flowery Blackadder and slushy Kauffmann) or as a man (what's wrong with randy old Renoir and that tub of blubber, Rubens), only as a painter.

Increasingly, everything revolved around that, the difficulty of painting. I would spend hours rereading Gombrich and looking at the reproductions in *The Story of Art,* trying to catch the rhythm, the balance, the detail, the vitality of the Renaissance. I began to understand the arrangement of symbol and rebus, that other language to which the modern observer is deaf and blind, but which still contains significance, like a riddle to which you can only guess the answer. It was no good going out into the groves and doing endless landscapes, or attempting portraits of Lucio in the gloom and grunge of Mimi's. I needed a studio.

At the end of May, when my anxiety about where I was going to live reached a peak, Lucio told me it was time I met his mother. I was invited for lunch, he said, and I should wear my pearl necklace.

Accordingly, I went.

The Ferrantis lived in the Vicolo delle Sette Stelle, above Via Garibaldi, that all-important dividing line between the upper town and the lower. I walked up Via del Ospedale through the Piazza Venti Settembre, dazzling in the sun, as the clockwork angel and devil chased each other round in the belfry, and the blue and gold clock boomed twelve. All the plates in nearby kitchens began to chink and clink. The scents and smells of Santorno came in overlapping waves: fierce bleach, frying steaks, rank cats' urine, peppery geranium leaves, washing soda from the lines hung up to dry across the street on pulleys, crushed garlic, fresh plaster, old paint, liquorice and menthol from the tobacconist, varnish and glue from the carpenter's, coffee and sugar from the bars, paradise from the amethyst clusters of wistaria up one side of a building, sewage from the gutters underneath.

I dawdled, nervous of my reception. The Ferrantis' apartment block was old, one of four facing a small courtyard set back from the cobbled street. Lucio, equally nervous, opened the door to their first-floor flat and, after introducing me to his mother, disappeared.

Signora Ferranti and I locked grins, like a pair of duellists. She was a small, solid woman, dressed in a beige silk dress printed with little red compass points, flesh-coloured tights in beige court shoes and a choker of (patently false) pearls. Her hair was jet black and lacquered into a bouffant helmet; her nails were so long and red that, when she moved her hands, they left the illusion that she had drawn blood from the air. Her skin was coarse and heavy, her teeth short and square. All this I noted with a mixture of interest and satisfaction, yet she had one weapon before which I was rendered powerless: she looked like Lucio.

I recognized every shadow of expression that flitted across her face, his musician's hands, his brow, his yellow-rayed eyes. It was infinitely disconcerting, as though he had dressed up as a woman, then stood in front of a fairground mirror. All families of friends, enemies, acquaintances are distortions of the familiar; I had seen this already on school parents' days. Some random act of genetic jumbling goes on, and presto! the beauty becomes the beast, the beast the beauty. So it was with Lucio and his mother. This female dwarf, this embossed carbuncle, had produced my shining lover, who hid in his bedroom, playing his guitar, while the two women in his life confronted each other.

'I am pleased to meet you,' said Signora Ferranti. 'Lucio – and a number of others – have told me a great deal about you.'

'Thank you,' I said, knowing perfectly well that she meant the hag next to Mimi's, and all the other old crones of the town. 'I'm afraid Lucio has not told me a great deal about you.' I smiled, sweetly. 'So we will have to get to know each other better, alone.'

'I hear that you and my son have got to know each other very well – alone,' she replied, with equal sweetness; then, with a sudden disconcerting swoop into crudeness, 'He calls you his *fidanzata-*, tell me, are you . . . ?' She made an arching gesture, indicating pregnancy.

I raised my eyebrows, like my mother, disdainfully. 'No.'

'Of course, you foreigners are so much more, how shall I put it, knowledgeable about these things,' she murmured.

'Really? Have you known many?' I asked, innocently.

I had meant to imply that she was a woman from a provincial backwater, but for some reason this shot seemed to go deeper than I intended, for she flushed a deep, unbecoming purple.

'I – used to know a few, yes. When I was a girl. But perhaps the Contessa has told you of that?'

She watched me, running her pale tongue over her lips, Lucio's lips.

'The Contessa?' I repeated, puzzled. 'Do you know her? She never mentioned you.'

'Ah.' Signora Ferranti let out a sigh, shook herself, and fixed her smile back on. It seemed more friendly this time. 'I misunderstood you, my dear. So – Lucio tells me you are looking for somewhere to live?'

'Yes.'

'Well, it so happens that a friend of mine might be able to help you.'

'Really?'

'She has two rooms at the top of her house, across the courtyard, with a small balcony, which she would let to you for 50,000 lire a month. There is no toilet, but it has a sink. It was a playroom for her children when they were small, but now it is used only to store things. It would take a little time to make ready for you, about a week, but you can have it if you like.'

I couldn't believe my ears. 'That sounds perfect, signora.'

Too perfect, I thought; why has she suddenly decided to be nice to me?

'Lucio has told me how important it is for you, as a painter, to have light,' she explained, with a charming smile.

I had mistaken her nature, I thought, ashamed.

'Thank you so much. When can I see it?'

'After lunch.'

It was a tense affair, that lunch. There was the best china, the paper doilies, the crispest linen arrayed. Signor Ferranti, a quiet, sallow man, arrived promptly at one. He wore a dark three-piece suit on which a black arm-band barely showed up, and seemed sunk in indifference or apathy throughout. I tried to ask him about his life as a tax inspector, not that I had the faintest idea what that entailed, but all he did was roll his eyes and say. *'E tutt' un casino.'* (It's all a brothel.) Then he carried on noisily sucking up his minestrone.

Nobody spoke after the food arrived; in Italy, plates are not heated, and everyone races to finish what they have before it can get cold. Signor Ferranti needed the large napkin tied round his neck; after he had polished up every scrap, he sighed, and began to read his newspaper at the table.

Lucio's mother, on the other hand, could not have been livelier, at least between courses. She prattled, she sparkled, she tossed her head and gnashed her teeth in a display of amity more unnerving than her earlier manifestations of ill will. She drank quite a lot of red wine, too, which stained her teeth and eventually encouraged her to drop the gentility of her manner.

'Lucio tells me you've been having problems with telephone calls and *ragazzi*,' she said. 'Let me tell you what to do. You go like this—' she put her left hand over her right forearm and brought her right fist up sharply – 'and you say *"Vafanculo, figlio di putana, o ti rompo gli scatole!"'*

'*Bravo, Mamina!*' Lucio applauded.

'Repeat it, now!'

'Go do it in your bottom, son of a whore, or I'll break your boxes,' I repeated, mystified.

Mother and son rocked with laughter.

'*Cafè?*' demanded Lucio's father, emerging suddenly from behind his newspaper.

'Yes, my angel,' cooed Signora Ferranti, regaining her sobriety in a flash. 'At once.'

'Isn't she wonderful? Didn't I tell you?' Lucio demanded, as he walked me back to Mimi's flat.

'She's very lively. It's immensely kind of her to find me somewhere to live next month,' I said, diplomatically.

'She is all woman, my mother,' he said proudly. 'She even finds you a flat. Tell me, will it be all right for you, now?'

'It's lovely,' I said, hesitantly, for it was: two huge rooms at the top of the block owned by Signora Ferranti's friend and neighbour, overlooking the rest of the town and the plains below. I had recognized my future landlord, however, with a sinking heart, as the awful taxi driver who had first driven me to Sylvia's. Luckily, he appeared to have no memory of me.

My other worry I told Lucio.

'It has plenty of light, but it's south-facing.'

'So? What does it matter? It's still light, isn't it?'

'Yes, but north is steadier, better. South means it changes all the time as the sun moves. I can't use a south-facing room.'

Lucio threw up his hands with one of those electric gestures of anger I found so delectable.

'Madonna, will nothing satisfy you? Do you think none of the artists of the *Rinascimento* had to endure poverty or discomfort? No? Well, then, be happy with what you have been given!'

'I'm sorry, Lucio, you're quite right,' I said, humbly.

But, as it happened, I need not have worried. When I got

back to the flat – that hateful flat, which thankfully I would see no more of in a week – I found a square white envelope of thick, ribbed paper addressed to me in exquisite copperplate. The Contessa had written, offering me the use of a folly in her garden, as, she said, my father had informed her I needed somewhere to paint.

13

In early summer, the palazzo gardens were full of roses. It was a shock, seeing them at the end of the cypress avenue, like going into a dark church and coming upon stained glass. I had not noticed them previously, but now they billowed everywhere. These were no garish modern floribundas, either, but old gallicas, damasks and centifolias, opening petal over petal, quartered and crumpled with velvet abundance.

The main rose garden was just below the drawing-room terrace, down a curving flight of stone steps. Looking from above, I could see that it had been laid out to a design I recognized: Michelangelo's pavement for the Capitoline Hill in Rome, a still centre radiating a twelve-pointed figure of interlocking curves, enclosed within a circle. In the middle, however, where the Capitol has a statue, the garden had a spiralling fountain, which sent down a continuous corkscrew of water.

The Contessa was wandering around with a basket and a pair of secateurs, under a battered straw hat wreathed with yet more roses and a veil.

'Good morning, my dear, and welcome. Isn't this scent heavenly?'

'I thought heaven was all lilies,' I said, daring to tease.

'I have those also, but they come later. Come, tell me how

you are. Your father came to see me, after all these years, and told me you were desperate for somewhere to work. If only I'd known!'

'You are too kind. I'm sorry I left so suddenly, last time. I always meant to write and say thank you,' I stammered.

'It is nothing,' the Contessa answered. 'You have other concerns, I know.'

She looked at me kindly, and with such compassion that I said, 'It's very ... It's so confusing, being in love and all that. I suppose, after a bit, you get used to it?'

The Contessa's diamond ear-drops trembled. 'Ah, my dear, some spend their lives surrounded by love, like a child floating in the womb. First, there is the love your parents give you; then the love of a friend; then that of a lover; then that you receive from your children. In the end, it all drains away, and there is only the love of the earth. Then, it is to earth that we return.'

I did not understand much of this.

'Is that why you like gardening so?'

Her tiny arched nose and bright eyes made her look like a miniature bird of prey: a merlin, perhaps.

'It grows on you,' she said, smiling at her own joke. 'In the beginning, I merely had the topiary and yew walks pruned back into shape. This, however, was my first garden, which I made after the war. My husband and son are buried here.'

I stared at her.

'You mean, right here? Where we are?'

'Yes, what was left of them. I did not see why they should fertilize the graveyard in Santorno. Bonemeal is exceptionally good for roses,' she added calmly. 'Apart, that is, from the hot spring that rises here.'

'The hot spring? The one that comes out of the head at the bottom of your walls?'

The Contessa nodded. 'It is very good for growing things; it has a lot of iron in it, which is why it leaves red traces.'

I laughed. 'You know, the first time I saw it, I thought it was blood. It gave me a tremendous shock.'

'Did you?' She bent her head, so that her hat obscured her expression. 'How very interesting. It stains the marble of the old fountain quite badly, I'm afraid.'

'Where does it go to, in the valley?'

'Nobody knows. Probably into the Santorno water reservoir in the plains, like most of the streams, to get pumped up to the town again.'

'Did you put the fountain here, too?'

'No. That has always been here, and the head in the wall, and the pattern to which the roses are planted. It's shown even on the first plans for the palazzo. My husband used to call it the whirligig of time.'

'It's very lovely.'

We stood, sniffing the roses, then I added, 'May I see the folly?'

'Come,' she said. 'I will show you, and you can tell me if you would like to use it for a studio.'

It was perfect, of course: out of sight of the palazzo, and with two fifteen-foot arched windows facing north, to the mountains. I sighed. Lucio had made such a fuss about my going, I had half hoped I would be able to turn it down.

'You make me feel very spoilt, Contessa.'

'It is my pleasure, to watch the young of others. Andrew is always telling me off for fussing over him. I nag him to eat more, you know. Writing seems to make men thin and women fat: the opposite effect to alcoholism, yes?'

'Does it?' I answered vaguely. I had thought little of Evenlode; his importance in my life receded, the more certain I became that I would never return to England, and Oxford.

I longed to begin work. Lucio was practising all day for the *sagra*, at which his band would play their first official event in the town. If it went well, he said, Max Vincioni might offer them a contract to play at L'Incantevole, the nightclub he owned down below.

'He's being very friendly; I think he likes you,' I had observed.

'Perhaps he likes you, instead. He's always had a taste for blondes.'

'I shouldn't think so, after the way my father behaved in his restaurant.'

'So? Your father shouts at a few waiters, but he still pays the bill. That is what counts.'

The Contessa watched me as I prowled around, inspecting the stone basin tucked away in one corner, and the scarred wooden table on which I could put my things.

'You like it?'

'Oh, yes, yes. Thank you; it couldn't be better.'

'There's just one condition attached.'

She paused, and I thought, she's going to ask me to pay her rent, and I can't afford it.

'This is for you, and you alone, you understand? You are welcome, any time; but the palazzo is a private place.'

'Yes, of course,' I said, blushing scarlet. What did she think I would do, bring Lucio's rock band?

'Nobody else from the town must come. You must excuse my rudeness; there is no love lost between us, and never has been.'

'I understand.'

I went in, at her invitation, for a drink. The chequered marble floors were already a relief against the heat of the day.

At the sound of our voices, Evenlode put his head round a door, which I assumed led to the library.

'You again?'

'Hallo.'

I avoided his eye. I had forgotten how tall he was, and how intimidating. Maria appeared, and the Contessa ordered us long glasses of lemonade. I sipped mine, and looked about the now familiar drawing room.

Even in summer, it smelled faintly of woodsmoke and linseed oil, but more of the wide cloisonne bowl of potpourri. This was placed in the middle of the great white marble chimneypiece, carved with dancing putti. Above it hung a large, dark painting in an elaborate gold frame. When I had been there last, in the shadowy spring evenings, it had always been too dim to examine, but now, with the summer sun pouring in through the windows, I could see it more clearly.

It was executed in a rich, dramatic style, flickering with light and shade. A woman, standing, was holding up a candle to examine her lover, just waking up from sleep on a damasked crimson bed. They were both very young, and exquisitely beautiful, but on her face was an expression of astonishment, and on his one of sadness or anger. The radiance of the candle lit little beyond their two faces, making it seem as if they floated in the surrounding blackness; but it was just possible to discern that between the shoulders of the young man were folded a pair of wings.

'Caravaggio?'

'No,' Evenlode said. 'Good guess, though. It's by someone who learned quite a bit from him. Artemisia Gentilleschi.'

'I've heard of the surname, but I thought it was Orazio.'

'Her father. She was lucky, you see; she learned in his studio.'

I looked at it again.

'It's beautiful, quite wonderful. Goodness! Why have I never heard of her?'

'Because she's a woman?' Evenlode suggested, surprisingly.

'Very few of her paintings survive,' said the Contessa. 'There's one in London, in the Wallace Collection, of Judith holding the head of Holofernes. She painted two or three; you might say she was obsessed by the subject of vengeful women. She had an unhappy life, poor thing. She brought a case against one of her father's pupils, who she said had raped her. When she lost, she began painting the Judiths.

I think this is from another period.'

'You recognize the subject, of course?' Evenlode's voice took on a didactic tone.

'I may not speak Latin, but I can still read mythology in translation. It's Cupid and Psyche, isn't it?'

'Yes.'

'It's strange how in every culture, even as far as Norway, that story is repeated,' remarked the Contessa. 'The bear, the snake, the frog prince . . . So many women's experience of men is the complete opposite. They kiss the prince, and he turns into the frog, yes?'

'Alas, Claudia, and I was hoping to prove the opposite.'

'Are the Judiths as good?' I asked.

'One is, in Naples. But anger is not good for artistic expression.'

'Isn't it? I thought art was all about self-expression.'

'You think *what?*' Evenlode jumped up, suddenly furious. 'Good heavens, here I am thinking you've got at least some brains, and you trot out a half-baked notion like that!'

'Andrew, Andrew, calm down,' said the Contessa, laughing. 'You mustn't be a bully.'

'Don't worry, I'm quite used to it,' I told her. I looked mulishly at Evenlode, sticking my chin out. 'So, if you don't think it's about self-expression, who d'you think paints a picture or writes a book? A robot?'

'Of course I don't, you ninny; it's created by an individual with particular memories, feelings, ideas, misconceptions, quiddities and kinks, just like you and I, perhaps even more so.'

'So?'

'And, of course, all those will be a part of what goes into the act of making.'

'So? You haven't disagreed with me yet.'

'Yes, I do, quite violently, in fact.' He put up a hand and brushed away the hair that had flopped down onto his forehead in his excitement. 'That is simply some of what goes into a work of art; the ingredients, if you like. But it has no more to do with what it's about than if I were to look at you and say, aha, Emma Kenward is an organism consisting of 98 per cent water and a few chemicals. It's the combination, the ordering, of those elements, impregnated by the energy of inspiration, that counts. *That* has nothing to do with the self; indeed, it's an escape from it. Picasso said that art is a lie that makes us realize the truth, and he was right: the truth not about the particular creator, but about something fundamental to everyone's life.'

'I don't see how that could possibly be so,' I said. 'To start with, people are so different, and truth so various, you can't possibly hope to find a single denominator. Besides, an artistic temperament is so different from that 'of an ordinary person, I fail to see how they can have anything in common.'

'The artistic temperament! The artistic temperament is the luxury of the amateur,' Evenlode retorted.

'Oh, really? What about Michelangelo, then or Van Gogh? Or even Caravaggio?'

'I'm not saying artists behave like members of the Women's Institute,' he snapped. 'What I am saying is, the better their art, the more invisible the artist's personality. The dyer's hand, in short. That's what undid Gentilleschi, and Picasso himself. You can *contain* an idea or an emotion, but it's the beginning of the end if you try to express it. Artists aren't meant to have intelligence; it's a positive handicap to them. Nor are they meant to have large personalities and exotic wardrobes. Why

169

do you think that, in an era surrounded by scribblers and snappers-up of unconsidered trifles, we know practically nothing about Shakespeare? Or that the Renaissance artist we know most about is that mediocre braggart, Cellini? Self-expression indeed! What do you think the self is, anyway, some sort of pimple to be squeezed?'

Privately I had to admit that this was all too close to my idea of my personality, but resolved to deny this.

'I would choose a less ejaculatory metaphor,' I said in my nastiest manner.

'Then you must choose a more penetrating argument.'

From then on, whenever Evenlode and I met, our conversations became something between a tutorial and a battle. He could be as rude as I was, but with the added ingredient of wit, which I, in my passion, always lacked. I would think of us as being like two boxers, slugging it out, but suddenly he would run rings round me, turn cartwheels and jump glissades before returning for the knock-out. Doggedly, I went on defending my patch, until it seemed as if we had not only agreed to disagree, but were disagreeing in order to agree.

'What do you know about it, anyway?' I complained once. 'You're not a painter; I am.'

He quoted Dr Johnson, a favourite of his. 'You may scold a carpenter who has made you a bad table, though you cannot make one.'

'That still doesn't mean to say you know exactly why a good table is good, though,' I retorted. 'It's not enough merely to attack the bad.'

'Then be good, sweet maid, and let who will be clever.'

'Ha! I'd far rather be clever than good, at least in the sense you mean.'

'And what sense is that?'

'Why, nonsense, Dr Evenlode, of course.'

I fell into the habit of accepting lunch from the Contessa; she said it amused her to listen to the two of us, though when things became too heated, she would slide in with some remark which took the wind out of both of us.

'Children, children,' she would say, reprovingly, her earrings trembling with suppressed laughter.

Despite this bludgeoning, which often gave me headaches and invariably left me cross, I enjoyed coming to the palazzo more than I would have thought possible.

The walk, morning and evening, along the parterre was delicious. As it became hotter, the cicadas started up; the sound they made was like listening to a bicycle endlessly freewheeling into summer. The chestnut trees on either side produced a mass of creamy flowers before shirring them with green foliage.

All along, the outer walls of the palazzo were twined with morning glories, deep violet on the walk out, limp mauve on the way back. I did not mind my evening classes nearly so much, now they took place in daylight.

Preparations for the *sagra* of Sant' Antonio proceeded apace. At the end of the parterre, by the statue of Giulio Folconi, was a small civic garden, consisting of neat, heart-shaped municipal flowerbeds, edged with box and filled in with frightful, glaring marigolds and red salvia, so that they resembled jam tarts. Beyond this, before the twist that revealed the town, was a small, semicircular amphitheatre built into the hillside.

As the 13th of June approached, I would pass a group of a dozen brawny, good-natured, groaning young men every evening, bending their knees and shuffling their feet minutely forward beneath the weight of a wooden table to which a chair was lashed. Seated in the chair and bellowing at them with an expression of ineffable complacency was Santorno's obese

171

priest, Don Giovanni. The resemblance to Santorno's fictional genius was so striking, I wondered whether he was a descendant of the original model.

Once, when I was a little later than usual, I saw them just as he was being lifted down from his lofty perch. He bowled over to greet me, holding out his ringed finger for me to kiss with such assurance I found myself making a sketchy sort of bow.

'You have seen us practising to carry the holy relic, yes? It is all a great secret.'

'Don't people see it every year, though?' I enquired.

'They forget,' he said, happily.

Lucio, when I told him of this, snorted.

'What he means is, everyone gets too drunk. I only hope they won't be too crazy to appreciate good music.'

'What will you play?'

'Oh, something for everyone. Old tunes, pop, rock music, some of my own. Everyone will be dancing, you'll see.'

'I won't be able to dance with you, though, if you're playing, will I?'

'No, though I might permit you to dance with one or two others.'

'What is this, permitting me? I don't need your permission to do anything, now, do I?'

'Don't you?' he asked, in a bullying tone.

He caught my arm and jerked it up and back, playfully, until I said yes. I was surprised at the violence of the gesture.

'I can feel the shock, inside you,' he explained.

We would lie across two mattresses on the floor, kept together by a double sheet tucked in round the side. It gave a gymnastic dimension to sex, though I still insisted on keeping it quiet because of the Pistoias downstairs. The mattresses were old and dusty, inclined to slide apart under exertion, but made tolerable by the fact that they were in my new home. There were a rickety old cupboard and a cane chair, to fill the emp-tiness; next door, across a small landing, I had a stove, fridge, table and two more chairs – all bought, out of my diminishing funds, the day after my precipitous move there.

Mimi had returned, suddenly and without warning. I had heard of it in a slightly surreal way.

Living alone in her flat, I had taken to listening to a small transistor radio which Lucio lent me for company. Mostly I kept it tuned to the local radio station, run by (who else?) one of Max's employees at L'Incantevole. This churned out an uninterrupted diet of pop, with special soppy stuff for the siesta. Lucio told me that all over Italy, radio stations play special music for the siesta, to assist copulation. I didn't know whether to believe this, but it was true in Santorno, where Julio Iglesias reigned supreme from one until four o'clock every afternoon. In between songs were advertisements, and the mindless patter of Max's disc jockey, occasionally assisted by Max himself. ('Anything to get away from his wife,' Santornese would agree.)

I had been listening to some execrable new record by Paul McCartney, hoping that Lucio would turn up, when suddenly the music was drowned by a shriek:

'Mimi! *Sei tornata!*'

Then there was a crash, and yowling silence as the station went off the airwaves.

I realized at once what it meant, of course. Mimi had returned from Australia and gone straight to the hotel to collect her keys. Despite my being there with Vincioni's per-mission, I doubted whether she would be pleased to find me in her home.

Frantically, I began to pack; then realized that all her fur-niture was still crammed into the locked *salotto*. I went to the door to drag it out, and horrors! there was no key.

173

I lost my head. The prospect of encountering Mimi in such circumstances was too much. I piled all my belongings into my suitcase and dashed out, leaving the key in the front door.

('Strange,' Mimi said afterwards. 'I think I had burglars while I was in Sydney, but all they did was move the furniture around.')

I had gone at once to the Vicolo delle Sette Stelle, to see if Signora Ferranti's friend's flat was ready for me. For about ten minutes, I banged and rang the bell, without success.

In the somnolence of the afternoon, nobody had answered, though I suspected I caught a glimpse of Signora Ferranti's glittering eye observing me through one of the net curtains of the first storey. Windows which in the morning had carpets hanging out of them, like tongues, were shuttered fast against the heat. In desperation, envisaging a night on the streets, I had retraced my steps to the Bar Popolare. Tony's green shutter was only two thirds down, and his door was open.

'Tony?'

'Shh! Only Louis and I are here, playing cards. What's the problem? Has England been swept away by floods yet?'

He wheezed with laughter, lifting the shutter up enough for me to enter.

'Tony, Mimi is back, and I can't find Lucio anywhere.' Tony and Louis exchanged glances. 'His mother has found me a sort of flat,' I explained. 'But nobody's in, and I don't know whether it's ready yet. What shall I do?'

I didn't want to cast myself even more on the Contessa's (and Evenlode's) charity; it already stuck in my throat too much at times. If I had been thinking clearly, I would have seen that the sensible thing would have been to leave Lucio a note and sit quietly in the bar, waiting for him. But my head ached, and I was rank with the perspiration of panic.

I began to cry; I couldn't think why, when everything was going so well.

Tony creaked forward in concern, proffering a handful of paper napkins from the stainless-steel holder on his counter.

'There, there, *nuvola bionda*, save your tears for when it gets really hot, eh?'

'It's being too much in the town,' Louis said abruptly. 'Come, my friend, we can finish our game another time. I'm taking the *Inglesina* for a drive back home with me. You can tell Ferranti that, if he comes looking for her.'

He was as good as his word, for a few minutes later I sat, sniffing, in Louis's navy Citroen as it shot out of Santorno's north gate and up the mountain.

'This is a nice car,' I said, after a bit. 'It's new, isn't it? Are you successful as a sculptor?'

'In terms of money, yes. It's an expensive business, carving in marble. You don't keep doing it if you can't make it pay.'

'Do you enjoy it, though?'

'When it's going badly, no. Then, the noise, the danger – you can cut your hands open any time – the dust! Pah! You make one mistake, and the whole block is ruined. But when it goes well, I cut through the stone like butter and don't even notice the rest.'

I looked at his stubby hands on the steering wheel. The nails were cracked and filthy, and two of the fingers had bandages on them.

'Now, then, why did you dissolve into tears, eh? Tell Papa. What is worrying you so much on such a beautiful day?'

I looked out of the window. We had climbed above the Palazzo Felice, even, though it was hidden by a fold in the hill. The rubbish dump went past, reeking with foul smoke and the detritus of consumerism.

'Oh, I don't know. I'm worried about the future, I suppose. That, and running out of money. Having Mimi's job for a month was a godsend. I've spent nearly three quarters of my legacy, you see, and it wasn't very much to start with.'

'So, you need another job, if you are to stay. What can you do besides paint? Can you type? Can you drive a car?'

'No,' I confessed. 'My parents wanted me to learn ... but I turned it down.'

'That was foolish of you. So, your one skill is that you speak a foreign language?'

'Three but only Italian well.'

Louis shook his grey head. 'Not good enough. Caroline does any translation work round here. Ah, she's a good woman, that; her brother doesn't deserve her! She keeps the whole place going.'

I was not interested in Caroline.

'But Louis, can't I make a living, well, selling my paintings?'

'Selling them?' He put back his head and roared with laughter, narrowly missing a truck. 'No offence, my dear, but where do you think you are? The Florence of the Medicis? The kind of picture people buy here is mass produced, from furniture stores. You must have seen the kind of thing: an old man with a pipe, or a busty gypsy in a red dress?'

I knew what he meant only too well: they had both been on the walls of the Ferranti *salotto*.

'So, how do you make such a good living, then?'

'You don't think I sell my work here, do you? What an idea! No, my work goes to New York, or Germany, sometimes even Canada – my countrymen are so patriotic, they even forgive renegades. But that takes years and years, to build a reputation, an oeuvre. And that is impossible to do in anything but a capital city. Even if it is only Toronto.'

I could see his point. It was what was being gradually borne in on me, and which I persistently tried to ignore. There was no future for me in Santorno as an artist. Either I had to support myself as an English teacher, or I had to leave.

14

It was evening by the time Lucio found where I was, and he was furious. He burst in on us as Louis was showing me round his studio. Neither of us had noticed the sound of his car. I was too absorbed in examining Louis's work.

I knew little about modern sculpture and still less about abstract art beyond the fact that I detested anyone after Cezanne who attempted it in painting. I liked Louis's, though. He was doing a series of fine, semitransparent slices of marble, carved to suggest clouds, brains and the bodies of women all at once. They were beguiling not only to look at but to feel, and he did not dress them up by long explanations of his own genius. Earlier, he had taught me how to make proper omelettes, which we ate under a fig tree hung with stone wind chimes, overlooking the hills below. I was happy again. Simply to see that it was possible to achieve the life I desired through working as an artist was inspiration.

Lucio's arrival interrupted this tranquil exchange. I felt the familiar nausea of desire when I saw him, forgetting everything. He was incandescent with rage, bundling me and my suitcase into the car before I had time to thank Louis for his kindness. Louis had shrugged his stocky shoulders, and waved.

'What do you want to do, kill me?' Lucio shouted, as soon

as we rejoined the mountain road. 'That old toad, he's like all Frenchmen, he talks as if he's vomiting and he was only waiting to get you into bed!'

'He was only being kind,' I protested. 'Mimi's back. I had nowhere to go.'

'Kind! *Porca Madonna*, how can you be so stupid! He wants to fuck you, that's all.'

I was silent. Louis's remark about how he would have tried to pounce, had he been younger, came back to me, casting a less agreeable light over our afternoon together.

'I promise, he didn't do anything.'

'That isn't the point. Can't you understand, you're a woman, and you're in Italy? Any woman who spends more than fifteen minutes alone with a man in this country is assumed to have been had by him! Half Santorno knows I've been looking for you. You've damaged my honour.'

'Oh, don't be so silly!' I gasped. My stomach felt as if it was performing somersaults. He was driving at breakneck speed now, shooting round the hairpin bends. 'Slow down, Lucio, you'll crash!'

He seized my head by the hair and dragged it down. 'If you love me, show me.'

'Lucio, no!'

'Show me, or I'll kill us both.'

'No, Lucio, I can't, not while you're driving.'

'Do it.'

I was gagging before he pulled over to a lay-by overlooking the rubbish dump, and stopped. The taste of his semen was like thick tears. I was humiliated, but also flattered; I took it to be a sign of passion that he was so violent. There was another car in the lay-by, which I recognized as Max Vincioni's. I hoped he had not seen through the windows of Lucio's car.

'You shouldn't be so afraid of what people think,' he said when I pointed.

I was silent, looking at the hillside of burning tyres, plastic bags, rusted-out cars, paper, all flickering with blue flames that walked up and down the slope like wraiths.

He suddenly became gentle.

'Emma, my angel, when I can't have you, it hurts me so much I can't walk,' he said, sliding his hand in, rolling my nipples as deftly as he rolled cigarettes. 'I want you, all the time, it's like a sickness, a fever in my veins. It makes me do crazy things. Don't you feel it, too? Look how much you want it, now.'

'Yes,' I said, and it was true, for I let him do it to me right there, though the seats were squeaky and plastic, and the shame afterwards was as great as any pleasure. 'Please, please, don't drive so fast. It's very frightening.'

He took my face in both hands and kissed me. 'You are right. We all drive too fast. My sister died like that.'

'Did she?'

'Yes, on the road to Santorno *inferiore*.' He was silent a moment; Gabriella was a subject we did not discuss. 'Just before Christmas. Her car went round the bend and off the road.'

'Were you very much alike?'

'People said so, though she was blonde, like you. You have something of her quality, at times. She was very beautiful, but too thin, always too thin, like a boy.'

'Did you see her before it happened?'

He shook his head.

'No. After I came out, I needed some time alone. It's diabolical, military service. Everybody tries to get out of it, but unless you can go abroad, or plead Article 79, saying you're insane or a drug addict, in which case nobody will ever employ you, you have to do it. They won't give you a passport before, and if you ever come back to Italy without doing it, they arrest you. They get you by the balls and they twist them until they drop off. It's a nightmare. The first day, they line you up and strip you, and the army doctor walks up and down with a big needle and a bucket, giving injections. The pain is so bad, most people faint.'

I was shocked, and said so.

'Yes. And then they put you in with all sorts of low types, criminals and homosexuals, and send you all over Italy. It's so stupid, they teach you nothing, you do nothing, it's just a way of keeping unemployment down.

'So, when I came out, I felt I couldn't face my family for a few weeks. I stayed with a friend, a cousin of Chiodino's in Florence.'

'The one who gave Dave a lift?'

'What?' He seemed startled. 'Yes. Yes, of course. Then I heard.'

'How terrible for you.'

'Terrible for all my family. Worse for them, because soon after, I started with Sylvia.'

'So you needed consoling, too. Poor you. Poor Sylvia. Do you ever see her?'

Lucio started the car and began driving again. I was glad to leave, and hoped the windows had been too steamed up for passers-by to see in.

'Now and again. I can't walk right past her, can I?'

'Is she very unhappy?'

He shrugged. 'She is the type that is always unhappy, don't you know that? She always wants something just out of reach, like so many Americans.'

'How I wish it hadn't all been so nasty! Lucio, what am I to do about moving into your mother's friend's flat? I haven't got any furniture or anything, and, now Mimi's back, hardly any money.'

'Don't worry,' he said. 'Marga Pistoia has cleared it all out,

180

and, look, I've got some money you can have. Sandro paid me back what I lent him to buy his drums.'

He handed me 50,000 lire.

'I can't, Lucio.'

'Why not?'

'My mother told me I must never accept anything from a man but flowers, restaurant meals and theatre tickets,' I said seriously.

Lucio put back his head and laughed. 'Listen, you're my *fidanzata*, aren't you? Take it, take it. In two days, the band and I will be paid a sack of money for the *sagra*.'

'Well . . . all right, then. But only as a loan.' Another thought struck me. 'Lucio, will Sylvia be there?'

'I expect so,' he said.

The feast day of Sant' Antonio was a much bigger affair than I had supposed. It was an excuse for a holiday – there are more holidays than working days in Italy, some say – but it was also a way of welcoming the summer. People looked forward to it for weeks.

As soon as the sun was up, all the bells in Santorno started ringing. My new bedroom being right above the municipal belfry, I caught the full blast. I tried burying my head in a pillow, but it was useless. Eventually I got up.

It was going to be a blazing day. Stripes of heat were already penetrating the shutters; when I opened them, the plains below shimmered in a blue haze. In between the clamouring boom of the big bells and the cries of the swallows, I could hear cicadas tuning up like an orchestra.

I made some coffee, dressed, and wandered out.

All the shops and bars in Piazza Venti Settembre and Piazza Felice were closed, but the two squares simmered with people. Children rushed around, wild with excitement, playing tag, while their parents and grandparents, dressed in their best clothes, gossiped and fanned each other. The closer to Piazza Felice, the more crowded it became. I looked everywhere for Lucio, but only caught his mother's eye in the crowd as she was chatting to the Pistoias.

She smiled and jabbed a scarlet-taloned hand back in the direction of the parterre. By this time, however, it was too crowded to retrace my steps. The piazza was jammed; I had a family of *contadini* on one side and a couple of English tourists on the other.

'Oh, darling,' the wife shrieked above the jangle of the bells. 'Don't you wish we could live here all the time?'

'Absolutely,' he bellowed back.

At eleven o'clock the bells stopped, and the church doors were thrown open with a thunderous bang. Out came four vergers in white surplices, waving incense, and Don Giovanni, resplendent in gold embroidery, holding a gold and silver staff in his hand. Behind him, dressed in their best suits, shuffled the twelve men I had seen practising for the occasion. Scarlet with effort and shyness, they bore aloft a remarkable concoction of precious metals topped by a crystal orb and a gold cross. The crowd cheered, and Don Giovanni, like a giant bullfrog, raised his voice above the bewildered shrieking of swallows and babies to chant blessings on the town's founding saint.

'I suppose that's the holy relic,' the English husband bellowed. 'What is it?'

His wife screeched with laughter. 'It says in the tourist brochure, Saint Anthony's foreskin!'

'No!'

'Yes!'

'Catholics!'

'I suppose it's got Mass appeal!'

Everyone began to move, swept along by the crowd. After

182

Don Giovanni had blessed the crowd, the choir behind him burst into hymns, barely audible over the renewed clangour of the bells.

Slowly and with immense dignity, the little priest and his retinue circled the town, then began to descend to the south gate.

'Where are we going?' I asked the baker's wife beside me.

'Eh, *figliola*, we're going down to Santorno *inferiore*, now!' she shouted back. 'Along the pilgrims' way, then we return to the Ospedale, and then the mayor makes his speech.'

My heart sank. It was becoming hotter and hotter as the sun blazed high in the heavens.

The pilgrims' way turned out to be the narrow lane I had used on the evening of my harassment by the two louts. We were jam-packed into it, jostling and treading on each other's toes. Sunk between groves, it was at most a metre wide, but shaded by walls and overhanging vines, which occasionally caught at the priest's staff and even the relic itself.

'*Sanctus! Sanctus!*' he bellowed.

'Cri-cri! Cri-cri!' sang the cicadas.

'*Sanctus! Sanctus!*'

'Si-si! Si-si!' shrieked the swallows, wheeling and diving.

'Can't understand a word of it, can you?' said the English couple to each other.

Halfway down, the lane crossed the main road, winding down to the station. Fearful of being run over by honking cars, the crowd fragmented, and I was able to escape. A slow tour round Santorno's industrial zone was not my idea of a nice time. Parched with thirst, I plodded back up the hill by the tarmacked road.

The crops between the olive trees were slowly ripening. In winter, the trees had seemed to chequer the hills with white; now they were squares of darkness against their bleached surrounds. There were vegetable patches and some kind of pea, and barley the colour of steel.

I walked and rested, panting. The road wound around so much, it seemed to take three times as long to return to the town, for, by the time I got back, so had the priest. His turn was over, now: it was time for the mayor's speech.

Much to my surprise, the mayor of Santorno turned out to be Nastri the chemist.

I had no wish to hear him speak, though it was hard not to, as he was blasting his address down a megaphone. I had a boiled egg for lunch, tried to catch up on lost sleep, then made my way out to the parterre to find Lucio. The mayor was still going strong. I caught fragments of it:

'*Dunque* . . . brothers and sisters, we must all join together to . . . socialist vision of Italy . . . Renaissance . . . Garibaldi . . . *Dunque* . . . this historic city . . . mysteries and secrets . . . so many respected and respectable citizens . . . a richer and more prosperous place!' (Enthusiastic cheering.)

The amphitheatre was busy with electricians stringing up coloured lights. Members of the Stella Nera were trying out their microphones, which howled and shrieked agonizingly. Sandro's and Marcello's girlfriends, Nina and Tina, watched the proceedings with dull interest, chewing gum and giggling. Lucio wasn't there.

'Have you seen him at all today?'

'Oh yes, he was around earlier.'

'He went off some time ago.'

'Where?'

'Don't know, really.'

'Off there, I think.'

Tina raised an arm clanking with brass bracelets, and pointed further down the parterre.

'Thanks.'

They looked at each other, smirking. I knew they didn't like me, and I disliked them also. Though barely sixteen, they were physically far more mature than I, and of a type. Nina was the daughter of a fat, dyed blonde who ran the pizzeria down in the lower town; Tina a waitress at L'Incantevole. I found them coarse and silly. When I had first been introduced to them, Tina had asked. 'Is your hair really blonde, or is it dyed?'

Then, when I told them, Nina asked, 'And between your legs, is that blonde, too?'

I could hear their shrieks of laughter as I walked away; it reminded me of what I had heard at school as soon as my back was turned.

Lucio was nowhere to be found. I thought he might have gone to the gates of the palazzo, looking for me, but there was nobody.

I didn't feel much like going in; I had just finished a still life of old, black Penguin paperbacks with classical paintings on their covers, which I was quite pleased with for half a day before seeing that, as usual, it wasn't good enough. Instead, I wandered down the familiar dirt track below. I didn't want to take the path to Sylvia's, so I found myself in the Guardis' farmyard. The yellow dog was dozing in the sun; for once, he did no more than yawn amicably and rib the dust with his tail.

'Enter, enter,' Maria greeted me. 'The *professore* is here.'

'Hallo,' said Andrew Evenlode. 'Are you escaping the noise as well?'

'I can't bear all this bourgeois self-congratulation,' I said.

'Bourgeois in the Marxist or Flaubertian sense?'

'I don't know. What's the difference?'

'Marxist describes an economic class, Flaubertian a spiritual one.'

'Both, then. They're equally hateful and ghastly. All those smug, stupid faces.'

'So tell me, who do you think is going to buy your paintings one day? People like Claudia are rare birds, you know.'

'I know.' I didn't want to start one of our perennial arguments, so I asked Maria what she was doing.

'Making tagliatelle. Have you never seen it?'

'I've only bought them in packets.'

'Watch, then.'

She kneaded a lump of dough from a peak of white semolina flour, into which an egg and two drops of oil and two of water were poured. Her strong fingers pushed and pulled, until she was left with a yellow, fine-grained ball.

Next, she whipped out a huge rolling-pin, and began flattening the dough into a perfectly round circle.

'That's what she hits Guido with if he disobeys her!' quipped the grandmother, much to the amusement of the grandfather, who nearly choked on his cigarette. He was smoking it the wrong way round, with the lighted end in his mouth; when I asked why, he said it stopped the wind that came down the chimney from blowing it out.

By now, the dough had been rolled out into a circle two feet wide and the thickness of parchment.

'Look,' said Maria, holding it up so the late afternoon light came through it. 'When it looks like the full moon, then you can cut it.'

'Can you cook it right away, after?'

'No, it has to dry for a couple of hours.'

The two old people cackled. 'She doesn't know anything, this one!'

'She's a foreigner, what do you expect?'

'Foreigners, what do you know about them?' Maria sniffed. 'The furthest you've ever been is when you bicycled to Arezzo for your honeymoon.'

'We should have stayed there, too!'

186

'Go, then, the bicycles are still here!'

Evenlode let out a crack of laughter.

'Your Italian must be improving,' I observed.

'Difficult not to, with Maria around. So tell me, are you going to the *sagra* this evening?'

'Of course. Lucio will be playing. All the Ferrantis will be there.'

At the mention of the name, the squabbling Guardis fell silent.

'He's got bad blood, that one,' croaked the grandmother.

'They're all traitors, my daughter,' the grandfather added.

'*Nonna, nonno,* be quiet!' said Maria. 'I forbid you to say any more. I'm sorry, signorina. Memories go back a long time here.'

I shrugged and supposed it was some old family feud; Lucio had mentioned something of the kind. After a moment the unpleasantness passed and we stayed there, chatting of this and that. Maria taught Andrew and me how to make tagliatelle ourselves; we were both covered with flour by the time we finished. He laughed when he saw me.

'It's all right for you, you always dress like a tramp anyway, but I've got to go before Lucio's mother's beady eye,' I said, trying to beat flour out of the Liberty skirt I had donned for the occasion.

'And who do you think will be looking at you? as my nanny used to say. Come on, we'd better go. Apparently, the tables get crammed.'

They were, but by coming from the opposite direction to the rest of the town, we managed to squeeze in before too long. Andrew paid. I put up a show of protestation, but my funds were so low I was losing my pride in such matters.

Row after row of pigeon and rabbit were sizzling over a vast, red-hot brazier, sending off mouthwatering smells, and pretty girls rushed around, serving. Evenlode and I found a place on a long trestle table. It was impossible to talk. The town brass band, beaming and melting in scarlet and gold, was playing oompah-oompah with tremendous brio. The trombonist kept playing half a beat behind the rest; every time we heard it, we grinned at each other.

'Snouts in troughs!' he shouted at me. I nodded. On either side of us, along the long trestle tables, the Santornese were eating their subsidized supper with infectious, lip-smacking enjoyment. Lucio, when I had told him of Louis's omelette, had turned his nose up and remarked, quite accurately, 'The French, what do they know about cooking? It's all sauces and butter with them. You could be eating an old boot and never know it. Tuscan food is the best in the world.'

It may have been hunger, for I could not afford to eat much these days, but that meal did indeed seem the most delicious I had ever tasted.

'Gosh, I feel a pig myself, now,' I said, after bolting it down.

'Well, you don't look it.'

'Oh, listen, the band has begun playing, the real one! Lucio must be here.'

I glanced around. The sun had set, blazing, and the crowd was illuminated now by the strings of coloured lights hanging between the chestnut trees. I could see Louis and the Dunnetts on one table talking to Tony and his wife. Izzy, to my surprise, was eating meat, and looked as though she was enjoying it. (Slim said, later, that she had felt irresistible cravings during pregnancy, and had been persuaded that nut cutlets alone were not good for the growing foetus: a triumph of diplomacy which did much for their malnourished married life.) Elsewhere, I caught sight of the Danbys. They were talking to Sylvia in the queue; my heart sank as Caroline immediately dragged the others over.

'Hallo, Sylvia,' I said, in as friendly a voice as I knew how.

'Hi.'

Slim had been right; she looked awful. Normally so slim, she must have put on at least a stone, her features sinking into a Mongolian flatness. Uncorseted as always, her breasts sagged. Grey roots showed in her hair, now unmistakably hennaed.

'How are you?'

'OK.'

Caroline was gushing, through maniacally clenched teeth, at Evenlode.

'Of course, it's the simple life here that is so marvellous, don't you find? Timmy and I feel we're getting back to our roots, living from the earth, like St Francis.'

I listened with half an ear for Evenlode's response, fully expecting him to wither her with some shaft of sarcasm, but he was perfectly polite. Tim barely paid him any attention; he was ogling Sylvia like a goat, and as usual smelled like one, too.

'Sylvia, I'm sorry.'

'You'll be sorrier.'

'Is that a threat?'

'It's a fact.'

The ground between us shifted. Wearily, I began buckling on the mental armour of bitchery I had worn for so many years at school. I didn't want to fight a battle that had, as far as I was concerned, already been won.

Evenlode looked at me suddenly, breaking off his chat with Caroline.

'I think it's time for us to give up our seats,' he said. 'There are still people queuing to eat, like your friends here. Come on.'

He took my arm and almost dragged me from my seat.

'Let go of me at once, please.'

'With pleasure, as soon as you're far enough away. I thought you two were going to fly at each other like fighting cocks.'

'I'm perfectly able to look after myself, thanks. In any case, you misunderstand the nature of feminine antagonism. One never comes to physical blows with another woman.'

'No, I know. That's why men are nicer than women, in the long run. We bop each other on the snoot and shake hands afterwards, whereas you lot do it all with words and have it festering for a lifetime.'

Evenlode's retreat had brought me to the edge of the amphitheatre, where the Stella Nera were playing polkas over the heads of whirling Santornese and *contadini*. Mimi was there, in a kind of cotton brassiere and white trousers, surrounded by eager young men, and flirting tenderly with half a dozen at once. The Ferrantis swept past (the sight of Signora Ferranti tangoing was indeed a sight to behold) and the Pistoias, and dozens of other people I vaguely recognized from either shops or English lessons. Even Slim and Izzy managed a sedate jig, though Slim said loudly that she looked more like a limbo dancer, she was bent back so much under the bulge. Sylvia allowed herself to be manhandled by Tim, and Caroline tittered and quivered in the soapy grasp of Nastri, who used her to try and edge closer to Mimi. I saw Lucio at last and tried to catch his eye, but he was rapt in the dream that playing music always cast him into.

'Come, now,' Evenlode said, 'Why don't you work off your temper by dancing instead? A much more civilized solution.'

'I don't know how, to this sort of music,' I said, sulkily. 'Or any, come to that.'

'You must have gone to dances.'

'Yes, but I always frightened off prospective partners as soon as I started talking.'

'You may indeed be an ogress and the descendant of ogresses, but you certainly won't intimidate me. Besides, you don't have to worry much. I lead, you follow.'

'Oh, bloody hell, all right.'

I consented chiefly because I thought it would serve Lucio

190

right, but once we began dancing, it was different. Against my will I sank into a kind of dream while he held me, not even conscious of moving to the same rhythm until I thought about it, and stumbled.

'You know, the secret is to look your partner in the eye.'

'Is it? I suppose,' I said, unthinkingly, 'that must be the chief difference between dancing and sex, then.'

As soon as I realized what I had said, I went scarlet. Evenlode let out a snort of laughter and stopped dead on the edge of the dusty ground, so that other couples nearly banged into us.

'Now you have succeeded in terrifying even me. Go on, I'll release you.'

I suddenly became very angry.

'Why?' I asked, glaring at him. 'Wouldn't you like to?'

He stared at me; then a curious look came down on his features.

'Don't make a fool of yourself, Emma.'

I lost my temper.

'Go away,' I hissed. 'You've ruined my life, and then you come out here and ruin it all over again.'

'Is there a problem?'

Lucio had stopped playing and came over, while the rest of the band carried on. He put a hand on my shoulder and drew me to him, looking up at Evenlode with cold eyes. Until that moment, I hadn't realized how small Lucio was, by English standards; it really was quite brave of him.

'No, no, it's nothing,' I said, hastily. If there was a fight, I had an uncomfortable suspicion Goliath would win. 'Just an argument about something.'

'Whoever argues with you, argues with me,' said Lucio, in a loud voice. Several heads turned. He was still bristling and eyeing Evenlode up. The latter continued to look down on him, as though inspecting a rather uninteresting insect.

'It was nothing. Leave it, it doesn't matter,' I pleaded. 'Does it, Andrew?'

He gave a shrug and his sneering smile.

'Sorry,' he said, in English. 'A slight misunderstanding.'

Lucio nodded his head, dismissing him, then took me by the upper arm and frogmarched me up to the raised platform where the band was playing. I was getting tired of being manhandled in this way, but as soon as I tried to resist, he tightened his grasp until it hurt.

'You shouldn't be dancing with other men,' he said. 'Where were you this afternoon?'

'Practising.'

'I don't believe it. Nina and Tina said you'd gone off—' a sudden thought struck me like ice – 'in the direction of Sylvia's house.'

'They were lying,' he said. 'You will hear what I was practising, now.'

The band had finished with the country dances that had kept everyone whirling. It had gone well; there was applause at the end of every number. Couples looked flushed and happy, even the young girls who, out of propriety or want of partners, had danced together. Lucio took the microphone.

'Signore, signori, the time has come for you to make requests,' he announced. Several hands and voices were immediately raised, which he grinned at. 'We're hot this evening, yes?'

'Yes!' some of the couples shouted back.

'But first,' he said loudly, 'I have a song for someone else, for my *fidanzata* over here.'

Lucio waved a hand in my direction, and whistles broke out. I scowled. No doubt he meant it as a compliment, but I hated it, the corniness, the showing off, the publicness. My skin went goosepimply with embarrassment. I hoped he wasn't going to sing something he had composed himself. That would,

192

I thought, be worse than having someone read their poetry to you. But Lucio took no notice of my frantic grimaces, which made the Santornese guffaw. He began to play.

'O vien' alla finestra, o mio tesoro,
O, vieni a consolar il pianto mio:
Se neghi a me di dar qualche ristoro,
Davanti agli occhi tuoi morir vogl'io . . . '

I had almost forgotten the enchantment of his voice, which I had not heard since living at Sylvia's. It made me think of the days when I had loved him so painfully and innocently, and without hope. He sang without effort or affectation, as though light was streaming from his throat.

Everyone listened. It was an astonishing thing. In a country where opera is as popular as football, nobody could remain indifferent. I was not the only one who had tears in my eyes. Sylvia was openly weeping, and Signora Ferranti, and even the brazen Mimi.

All the long midsummer day had been gathering up into this. It radiated out over his audience in glittering swathes, layer upon layer of sound, waxing in power and beauty. One by one, people fell silent, stilling their chatter and the cries of infants: listening, until the only other sound was that of the fire that leapt and hissed to itself in the gathering dark.

15

After Lucio had so publicly called me his *fidanzata*, the attitude of those in Santorno altered noticeably.

To call someone your *fidanzata*, or *fidanzato*, in Italian is not the same thing as in French or English. It means you're serious about someone, it gives you a semi-official licence to have sex, but it doesn't mean to say that you are definitely engaged, only that you might become so.

The shopkeepers knew this, of course, and with varying degrees of kindness, cupidity or malice would ask me when Lucio and I were actually going to get married.

'I don't know,' I would say. 'He hasn't asked me yet.'

They all thought this very funny, though it was perfectly true.

My putative engagement was useful, though, when it came to furnishing the new flat. I had to buy everything for it: crockery, cutlery, cooking things, dustpans, detergent. Now that I was no longer an interloper, a foreigner, the shopkeepers gave me discounts, especially when I was accompanied by Signora Ferranti.

Evenlode had called me the descendant of ogresses, but nobody in my family would ever have behaved as she did. She was the terror of butchers and greengrocers, inspecting every sliver of meat and piece of fruit before it was wrapped.

'What's that hole there?' she would demand, jabbing a long red talon at a peach with a slight dent in it, making the hole bigger. 'Don't you try fobbing this innocent young woman off with some of your fruit from the bottom of the box, now! Shame on you! If you want to sell damaged goods, go to the street market!'

Through her good offices, though not quite as she intended, I acquired a set of Santorno plates and mugs, decorated with a strange, glittering glaze that was the secret of a single family of potters, the Lottos. Their last surviving member was a small, gentle young man with a harelip. It made him hard to understand, and dreadfully shy; Signora Ferranti bullied him mercilessly.

'We want this, but at a lower price, you understand? What are you, as stupid as you are ugly?' she kept saying, until the poor potter was shaking and blowing bubbles of spittle through the horrible gash in his face.

'*Thi, thi, prendetelo,*' he said, cringing away.

'What do you mean, take them? You will deliver them, this evening, to the house of Signora Pistoia,' said Lucio's mother, sweeping out of the shop. 'These people, they're all the same, they think they can cheat you right and left! As if I would allow my son to eat off anything but the best! But why you must buy this peasant stuff, when you have the beautiful English Wedgwood, I don't know. I'm sure your parents have that, don't they?'

'Yes,' I admitted, reluctantly.

'And the Irish crystal, like diamonds, the one that the President Reagan has?'

I hate cut glass above all things, my parents' possession of it was a source of deep shame, but I nodded.

'Ah,' Signora Ferranti exclaimed in satisfaction, nodding her coiffed head. 'I knew you came of good family!'

I was trying to like her, as she was me, but remarks like these made my task almost impossible. As soon as she left me, I turned round and hurried back to the potter.

Fie was sitting, throwing a jug on a wheel which he pumped with his foot; when he saw me, his hands faltered and his face fell.

I said, 'I don't think you stupid at all, and your plates are lovely. Signora Ferranti means well, but all the time, she's thinking of her son ... '

'I understand,' he said, smiling suddenly. The harelip gaped, but it was such a sweet smile it didn't matter. I looked at him properly, then, for the first time.

He was saying something about Lucio's mother, which I couldn't quite understand, though I nodded, and smiled back.

'Don't worry about delivering it,' I said, when he had finished. 'I can carry the box myself.' I thought of Sylvia saying that she never let men carry heavy objects for her.

His face fell again. 'For you, willingly,' he said. 'I will give you extra plates and bowls, gratis.'

'No, wait.' I was looking at his face, which was pure and regular above the cleft palate, with innocent blue eyes. Earlier in the week, I had been studying one of Velásquez's dwarfs in Gombrich. 'Have you ever had your portrait painted?'

He blushed and shook his head, his hand straying up to cover his upper lip.

'No, don't,' I said. 'One day, you will go to the hospital and have it stitched up so it disappears – you know they can do that, don't you?' To my astonishment, he shook his head. Italian medicine, I thought, in disgust. 'Well, they can, it's very easy, a cousin of mine had it done. But before, I would like to paint you.'

I hadn't wanted to go back to the palazzo after the incident with Evenlode; it would be too embarrassing. Now, however, I

196

had a subject which was different from those I had previously attempted. I thought of Velásquez again, and wondered whether I had not been pursuing the right thing in the wrong places.

Sometimes, after months of struggling on a plateau, one makes a sudden leap of understanding why things have been going wrong. So much of painting is the elimination of faults, rather than the acquisition of new ideas; when enlightenment comes along it's like being drunk. It makes up for all the other times, this feeling: nothing else gives such satisfaction.

Painting Lotto was like this. I loved him, his ugliness, his poor, naked lip, the sweetness which became increasingly apparent to me. I was in love with Velásquez, whose greatness of spirit and technique seemed to me to surpass even my Italian masters. I was in love with the paint on my plate, with the words on their tubes: burnt siena, crimson lake, viridian. I began to experiment with the surface of the paint, scumbling the background and applying various thicknesses of colour, sometimes scraping them off to the canvas itself. When it was done, it was little more than a homage to Velásquez, but it was mine, too.

At any rate, it made the young potter very happy, and even Lucio could not be jealous of such an ugly man.

Lucio was becoming increasingly moody and violent, especially when we made love. I could not understand what was going on in his mind. He would be cold and unresponsive to my caresses, then, when I was cold towards him in turn, he would jerk my skirts up and fuck me suddenly and in uncomfortable positions: on the kitchen table, against the cooker with a pot of boiling water close enough to scald, or, when the Pistoias were close by, down the stairs. I did not enjoy such ungentle embraces, nor the expression of snarling ferocity that crossed his face at the end.

As soon as he had finished, he seemed to forget all about

it. Bruised and trembling, I had to make an effort to pretend I had, too.

I wondered whether it was caused by the heat, which made everyone tired and irritable. The cicadas started to grate on the ears like sandpaper; it was stiflingly hot in my attic rooms. Sometimes I would lie in bed until noon, watching a gecko advancing, millimetre by millimetre, on a large black fly which hovered just out of reach.

I tried, unsuccessfully, to tame the gecko with little pieces of meat. When Lucio was away, I felt bored and lonely. It became more and more of an effort to go out, not to be dependent on him for all my pleasure and entertainment. After the potter's portrait, I felt drained and irritable. I tried to repeat the pleasure I had felt, and it wouldn't come. There were excuses: my canvas had run out, it was too much work scraping unsuccessful ones off; most of my paints and brushes were at the palazzo, where I didn't want to return. The high point in my day was always the evening, when Lucio might or might not turn up for supper. I always had to cook two meals, which meant not having lunch myself, to save money. Sometimes he would turn up, ravenous; at other times he would complain he was already full.

'Mamma makes me eat her suppers, too,' he would tell me.

'Then say you're coming here.'

'I can't, it would upset her. Besides,' he said, grinning, 'she's a better cook than you are.'

I was childishly wounded by this.

'She has more money to spend on food than I do. Lucio, I don't know what to do. I've only got £200 in traveller's cheques left, that's barely enough to pay the rent for the next quarter.'

'So? You can teach English, can't you? Or else make the potter pay for his portrait.'

'I can't do that,' I said, shocked. 'I asked him to sit for me, not the other way about. It's a present, in return for his crockery.'

'So? Make him pay for it. He's in love with you, anyway. No woman has ever paid him so much attention before. It makes me a laughing stock, I tell you. Make him pay.'

'No.'

Lucio shrugged. 'Then advertise yourself as an English teacher. Perhaps some of Mimi's pupils will leave her and come to you.'

This, in the end, was what I did. I drew up a series of placards, advertising my services, with Signora Pistoia's telephone number, had them franked by a smirking Nastri ('You should have come to me for help,' he said, but I could guess what that would entail) and fixed them up all round the upper and lower town.

They brought the usual telephone calls. Marga, my landlady, was more shocked than I was. 'It's all these American students, Signorina Hemma, they think you must be like them.'

It was true, the sexual temperature of the town had gone up, as well as the physical one.

An annual art class for Virginia debutantes, or their equivalents, had descended upon Santorno. I could hear their voices drawling to each other in the streets. Every young man for miles around followed them about, making bedroom eyes. I was quite outclassed by these Amazonian goddesses, who cast even Mimi into the shade with their long, brown legs and dazzling white teeth. The women of Santorno watched their men with vigilance, and became even friendlier towards me.

'It isn't just our sons, it's our husbands, too,' Marga confessed, one evening. 'These girls, who knows whether they have AIDS? We are all in danger.'

She was a worn, washed-out woman, her children all grown up and married, very much in the shadow of Signora Ferranti and her own husband. The latter I avoided whenever I could; luckily, he spent most of the time glued to the television, especially when there was a Disney wildlife film on.

'*Dio*, look at that great brute of a tiger!' he would shout, over the commentary. 'If only I had it in front of my gun!'

'Yes, dear,' his wife would reply.

'Look at him, the great brute, waiting to spring. *Pan! Pan!* Ah, if I could only go to Africa!'

Signor Pistoia was a fanatical hunter; not even his mortal fear of snakes would prevent him from going out with his gun from the first day of the hunting season to the last, and the ban on shooting from February to October chafed him unbearably.

He kept a blackbird in a tiny cage on the balcony of their kitchen. I had discovered this only by chance, after enjoying its liquid song for several weeks while sunbathing on my own balcony above.

It was a wretched, bedraggled bird. I assumed at first he must be keeping it because it had injured itself; when I asked how it was doing, he stared at me, then bellowed with surprise.

'This here, he's a hunting bird,' he explained. 'I keep him with a cover on, and when I take the cover off in winter he thinks it's spring, so he sings, and brings the others to him. Then I shoot them.'

I was appalled, and said so.

'You eat meat, don't you? What's the difference? In any case, he will soon be dead. They usually don't last more than a year.'

I did not argue, as his tenant, but from then on, the sound of the poor creature was a torment to me as we sat in the sun; it on one balcony, I on the other.

Eventually, I acquired two pupils in Santorno *inferiore*. They were both young men, and it was obvious their only reason for having private tuition was that they thought it would give them the edge over their rivals for the American girls at L'Incantevole.

Usually, I walked down the pilgrims' lane, wilting in the heat, but occasionally Lucio would give me a lift. Since his success at the *sagra*, the band were playing all over the plains, as far as San Sepolchro. There was even talk of their making a record.

I would accompany them, quite often, in the black van which carried the seven of us, plus instruments, to the nightclubs. Lucio would drive at his usual breakneck speed, his arm round me when he wasn't passing a joint. Once we were stopped by a policeman, and were in a panic he would notice the smell. However, when the man sniffed the air, Lucio asked him, with imperturbable cheek, whether he liked Nina's mother's new pizzas.

'Smells good,' said the policeman, waving us on.

As soon as he disappeared, we all collapsed.

'They're so stupid, you could get away with murder and they'd never notice,' Chiodino said.

I was both happy and unhappy in the band. They had accepted me as one of them since I painted their name and a shooting star on the van; but I still loathed Tina and Nina.

I missed feminine companionship. After five years of having it forced upon me, this came as a surprise; but when Mimi walked into my attic one morning, I was more pleased than I would have thought.

'Neat,' she said, wandering around.

I reddened. 'Mimi, about your furniture. I've been meaning to apologize.'

She laughed when I explained, and said she had thought it must be Max's wife, snooping around.

'She's a kook about foreign women,' she said. 'It's strange to be back in all that. I'd forgotten how alive Sydney is.'

'Didn't you miss Tuscany?'

'Well, yes and no. The guys there, they're still from the boondocks. One of them took me to dinner and ordered sherry the whole way through, instead of the usual Fosters, because he thought it showed sophistication.'

Mimi and I laughed, companionably. I made her coffee, and we bemoaned the chores of English teaching.

'Oh, by the way,' she said, as she got up to leave. 'You can have this. I brought back one of the outback, to remind me of home, and I reckon you seemed to need it.'

It was the calendar, the one from the kitchen by which I had worked out my safe periods.

'Thanks. It's kind of you to let me have it.'

'Gabriella left it, when she came to live with me.'

'Lucio's sister? I didn't know about that.'

'No, well, it's not the kind of thing they'd tell you. She was one of my English pupils, and came round to me in tears, a month before the crash, asking if I could help her.'

'So she ran away from home, too? Yes, having met her mother, I can see why.'

'No,' Mimi said. 'It wasn't that. At least, not only that. She thought I would know where she could get an abortion.'

It became hotter. Even with the shutters closed tight all day, my attic was stifling. I had the illusion that I was not walking, but wading through the thick air. Lifting so much as a finger made me break out into perspiration.

Outside it was worse. The glare hit you between the eyes like a hammer. Santorno baked and stank. People scurried from one patch of shadow to the next, or flopped from bar to bar, fortifying themselves for the next ten metres with long, cold glasses of sugared lemon juice. Beyond the city walls, the earth cracked and curled back parched lips. Even the fields of sunflowers in the plains became too dazed to wheel their heads round, hanging black and heavy on their stalks. Grass and barley alike became thin and white, though poppies flourished like specks of blood.

There were stories of dogs going suddenly mad and expiring

with the froth of rabies, and of husbands, happily married for years, who became so irritated by trivial household affairs that they knifed their wives. The newspapers reported cholera in Naples, an invasion of giant algae along the Adriatic, UFOs in the mountains, earthquakes near Calabria. It was too hot even to pursue the traditional siesta pastimes of watching football on television; the bars tried putting their sets in the coolest part, at the back, but nobody came to watch.

I was in despair about the Pistoias' blackbird, which in its tiny cage was wholly without protection for the hottest part of the day. On my dusty journeys down to my two pupils, I would pick vine leaves to drop on top of the cage to shade it. They always shrivelled up within a day, but I knew that if I were to drop a cloth, it would mean I could not pour down additional water, for it was often left untended by its captors. Every time I did this, the poor bird would go into a panic of fluttering and cheeping, breaking a few more feathers.

I was not sure whether I was not prolonging its misery. What did it have to live for, after all? What was the point of seeing the miracle of the Tuscan spring, if it was behind bars, luring its own kind to death? Better for it to die, I thought. I would console myself imagining Pistoia and his fellow huntsmen all shooting each other by mistake, up there in the mountains. He couldn't wait to go hunting again, but the laws governing the rule of trespass out of season were so strict as to deter even him.

'Before the war, Letizia Ferranti's father went hunting in the grounds of the Count, one day before the season began, and one of the *contadini* cut his hand off with a scythe,' he told me. 'He nearly bled to death, but the *contadino* got away with it, because of the law and the Count's protection. The next day, the lads all went round and slaughtered every bird in the man's farm, but it didn't bring the hand back, did it?

'Ah, this accursed law! Game needs a couple of months

to breed, to be sure, but we can always import more where it comes from. They say there are more snakes in the hills, now the hawks are gone, but only last year, the Comune released a batch of German boar, and they'll do the trick. They trample them with their feet, you see, and they have skins like a tank. Have you ever tasted wild boar, Signorina Hemma? It's delicious, the best meat in the world. Wait until the *vendemmia*; then, hunting season or not, you'll taste some.'

I couldn't be bothered to think about food, which was just as well, as, despite my two pupils, I had barely enough money for one meal a day. Where did it all go? I couldn't think. I no longer bought myself oil paints or clothes, only the bare necessities of life, yet still it seemed to drain away like sand in an hourglass.

To have to choose between half a loaf of bread and three eggs is an ill fate. I had to make these choices now, every day. Meat I stopped eating soon after the *sagra*, and cheese also. I replaced the mocha coffee with chicory, stopped taking milk, and used the cheapest soap instead of my favourite Roger & Gallet.

What was really hard was limiting the amount of fruit and vegetables I bought. The markets and greengrocers were overflowing with produce: vast, ribbed tomatoes, striated fennel bulbs, six different kinds of lettuce varying from a kind of green barbed wire to white and purple radicchio. Oh, and the peaches, peaches the size of two tennis balls, their pinks and reds and yellows melting into each other beneath the silver fuzz; and the watermelons, with their striped skins pierced to show a grinning row of black pips embedded in pink flesh; and the misted grapes from Sicily like living jewels dangling from their stems . . . Everywhere I looked there was food, from the silvery slither of wet fish netted in the Adriatic and lake Trasimeno, to the steaks that sizzled in the Pistoias' kitchen below me.

Lucio occasionally treated me to a pizza at Nina's mother's pizzeria down in the new town. The band were playing at

L'Incantevole every week now, and I would often walk down to hear them; as much because I was a little worried about what the sight of all the dazzling American girls would do to Lucio as anything.

He admitted to having slept with a few, in previous years, which did little for my peace of mind, though he insisted it meant nothing to him.

'Foreign girls, Italian men, it's so banal,' he said, shrugging. 'You both see something else to what is really there: they want romance, we want sex. I suppose we both get what we want, and we are both disappointed.'

This comment struck coldness into me, for how different was it from what I wanted from him, and he from me? I had told myself in the beginning I wanted sin, but now I understood that what addicted me to him even more than his beauty were the caresses that healed the self-loathing left by my parents and my school. Yet often, in his arms, I was more lonely than I had ever felt then.

We did not talk so much. That period of mutual discovery had come to a stop, because he had not read the books I had, and I did not really find rock music enjoyable, though his was good of its kind. I supposed that initial intoxication had to end, just as it had started to peter out with Sylvia; perhaps it was true that at the centre of people there was nothing, a vacuum.

We would quarrel, now, in order to make it up in bed. That obsession, the fascination with each other's bodies, had not gone; it grew and strengthened, even as it coarsened, like the stem of a plant.

'Nothing two people do together in private can be wrong,' he told me; but I wondered, and resisted. This modesty, or inhibition as he called it, alternately inflamed and quenched his desire.

'You're like all northerners, the ice has entered your heart,' he shouted at me once. 'An Italian woman would do as I ask, and enjoy it!'

When I laughed at him, he became angry and violent; when I burst into tears, he was contrite. Gradually I found myself crying more and laughing less. It was a way of manipulating him, but, at the same time, I became weaker and less confident.

I wondered, once or twice, whether his strange behaviour towards me was due to another woman; but, after inspecting every student with an eye sharpened by jealousy, I could see nobody he paid particular attention to.

They were very friendly, those beautiful Americans; that was half of what kept getting them into trouble with the men of Santorno. Friendship between members of the opposite sex is unheard of in provincial Italy, where any woman who hitches a lift is assumed to be asking for something more. Some undoubtedly came out for a holiday romance, but others were there simply to enjoy the life and have a good time, even if none of them, as far as I could see, were remotely serious about painting.

They were the life and soul of the discotheques, that was for sure, lending the glamour of their country to the tacky dives of the plains. Every discotheque was the same: a darkened concrete building with a whirling mirrored ball in the ceiling and tracks of coloured lights. Sometimes they had semitumescent red plush seats for clients to sit on. At others, there were just plastic stacking chairs. The band would always have a raised stage, and a separate entrance at the back where they would all retire to smoke marijuana or, in the case of Chiodino, heroin.

'You didn't realize, he's an addict?' Lucio had asked, amazed, after I had found the other guitarist being sick during an interval. 'That's why he's so thin and crazy, and not interested in women. But a good musician, as long as he's kept supplied. The rest of us – well, we stick to hash, instead. I'm going to Florence soon, to pick up some more dope for the band. With all the money we're making, we can buy the best, now.'

Every Friday and Saturday, the Stella Nera would play to a packed house. Lucio was jubilant.

'You've brought me luck, *Inglesina*,' he would say after a good gig.

The teenaged sons and daughters of local farmers, *contadini*, shopkeepers and professionals would come in their best clothes and mingle with these bejeaned maenads. The country girls were so fresh and charming in their neatly ironed skirts and little flat pumps – not altogether different from the denizens of Kensington, I thought at times – but they didn't stand a chance next to the Americans.

They reminded me of Sylvia, a little, with their conventional unconventionality. I yearned to see her and indulge in those endless lessons about life which she had given me. I thought that, if I told her about Lucio's behaviour, she might be able to tell me what I was doing wrong. But, in the circumstances, she was the last person to ask. So I watched, and longed to talk to them, but pretended to be Italian when they approached me. I could not afford any more complications.

16

The band's trip to Florence to buy drugs had to be postponed until mid-August. They were not addicts (though Chiodino often took off alone) and there were so many engagements to be had during the long summer break.

I did no work myself, apart from the dreary English-tuition classes. It was too hot, and the light that came through the windows made everything syrupy. Most of my paints were still at the Palazzo Felice, and I had no energy to fetch them. It was too stifling to sleep until midnight, when the mosquitoes were out in force, and then I would wake when it was nearly noon, and baking again.

I would sit and stare for hours at the jumbled, lichen-splashed rooftops and the plain below, not thinking very much, though my brain felt as if it were boiling. The gecko became tamer with the stillness, but I had lost interest in it, though I still tried to save the sinking blackbird, which now sang only at dawn. My pastime was watching the express trains as they glided along the plain from Urbino to Florence and on to Milan, Paris, Vienna: places that now seemed unimaginably distant.

I could understand now why people in Santorno talked of someone like Lucio's father, a Cortonese, or even someone from the next hamlet as being a foreigner, 'a foreign body' as they put it, as if we were a disease. From Lucio to Signor Pistoia, they all drove with tremendous speed and panache, but they would never leave their own area of a few square miles: beyond the city boundaries was another country. Garibaldi might never have existed, for it was not just north against south or province against province, but city against city, village against village, zone against zone, fragmenting into smaller and smaller units of social, geographical and political animosity. The Santornese being less wise than the Sienese, these differ-ences were never formalized, but remained and rankled down the centuries.

I was becoming like them. I shopped where the Ferrantis shopped, smiled on their allies (other local dignitaries) and ignored their enemies from the north and east of the town. Signora Ferranti did not hesitate to give me helpful hints on how to dress; I resisted, having no money for hairdressers and the like, but took to wearing my grandmother's pearl necklace at all times. The idea of walking in the countryside had now taken on a tinge of ludicrous eccentricity. I confined my strolls to the evening promenade along the parterre.

These were not so much walks as a daily fashion parade, as far as most of the Santornese were concerned. The stars of the occasion were an aged pair of identical twin sisters, still handsome but unmarried, who would never appear in the same outfit twice, and who would walk along, talking exclusively to each other with tremendous animation. What they had to say that was of such interest, after all these years, was a subject for continual speculation on my part and that of most Santornese Lucio confined himself to the remark that, in his experience, twins did not need to speak, but knew what was passing in each other's minds.

Next came a gaggle of matriarchs, farded and bedizened up

to the roots of their immaculate hair, practically kebabing their small, hairy dogs with every stiletto-heeled step. Then pairs of girls and boys, eyeing each other up across the gravel. Then the young couples, wheeling squeaky, chrome-plated perambulators in which reclined the latest household god, lovingly cocooned in crochet blankets and scarlet in the face, bellowing for a time when he would grow up and fulfil his parents' dreams – if he did not expire from the heat first. Sometimes, these miniature thrones would be wheeled by the mothers alone. Every year, Lucio told me, there would be at least one virgin birth to a young woman who swore that no man had touched her, yet swelled up and was delivered for all to behold. The shame of this, for the families, was terrible: every effort had to be made to discover the culprit and make the girl confess, so that she could be decently married.

I wondered who it had been in Gabriella's case, and whether Lucio knew about her pregnancy. Mimi had been unable to tell me whether she had obtained an abortion or not; the girl had moved back in with her parents after a week, and a fortnight later she was dead. Whether it had been accident or suicide, Mimi couldn't tell. I was convulsed with anxiety myself, every month, if I was only a day late.

'What shall I do if it doesn't come?' I wept, on one occasion when my cycle was a week late. Lucio shrugged, and said that in that case he would marry me.

'I'm sure your parents would make some provision for us, like Izzy's.'

Izzy's parents were increasingly desperate to get her to have the baby in London, but she had refused obstinately, saying that she wanted to have it in Santorno, despite the hospital's lack of modern birthing facilities. Baffled and wounded, the parents rang both Slim and their daughter daily now, warning them of the terrible things they had heard about Italian medicine, and wanting to send out the Queen's gynaecologist to attend her, all of which had vastly impressed Pia, the Dunnetts' gossipy maid, and thence everyone else.

I tried to explain that my parents weren't like hers, but he couldn't understand this.

'They're your parents, aren't they? Whatever you think, they must love you better than anyone else in the world,' he insisted.

'Then heaven help me if nobody else's love will ever measure up to theirs,' I answered bitterly. 'How can you say they love me, when I haven't received a single letter from them in all the time I've been away?'

'Your father visited you here.'

'Only because it was convenient.'

The prospect of my going to university in the autumn was even more remote than the knowledge that I had once lived in a world elsewhere, in London with its double-decker buses, and the Hard Rock Café of which Lucio dreamt.

'You could go back, and I could follow,' he said once; but I knew it would be no good. For me, he was Italy, he was Tuscany. Even his increasing cruelty seemed natural to me, like the blows of the sun, the burning light which turned my skin almost as golden as his own, if I could endure its sting.

'We go to Florence tonight, before everything closes for Ferragosto,' he told me one day. 'You can come, if you want, and stay with Chiodino's cousin.'

'Oh,' I said, sitting up, 'will there be time to visit the Uffizi? I haven't seen it since I was a child.'

'You saw the Florence of tourists and children,' Lucio said. 'Come with me, and I will show you the real city, just as I have shown you the real Santorno.'

We drove off, the three of us, when the night was thick with stars. Fireflies hovered above the ditches pulsing with cold heat. Chiodino kept shivering; he had lost even more weight than I had, and was desperate for a fix.

'Faster, faster,' he kept saying to Lucio.

'I can't go any faster, this is my father's car and the brakes need replacing,' Lucio responded, though he put his foot down on the accelerator so the dial touched the limit.

I was terrified, but excited. Santorno fell far behind. I realized that it was the first time in eight months I had been more than a mile beyond it; its invisible tentacles in the mind seemed to stretch thinner and thinner, like a piece of elastic. The wind whipped the hair around our heads into long banners. This was what it was to be young, after all; this must be what people missed when they grew old and cold, and settled in their ways. No wonder Dave had wanted to break free and travel once more, before it all caught up with him.

It was strange when I saw Florence again, so familiar and unfamiliar from expeditions with my parents and grandfather. The great, rose-red dome of the Duomo, belling out from its humbug-striped base, the Arno glimmering with lights. The most perfect of cities, I had always thought. It was, if anything, even hotter here, and packed with tourists in the centre. I looked at them and felt smug, for I was no longer one of their number.

We stopped at Vivoli's for an ice cream. It was packed with elegant, rather affected Florentines, whose clear Italian made me realize how much dialect I had acquired from the Santornese. Impatient, Chiodino split off to find the dealers on the Ponte Vecchio, agreeing to meet us later at his cousin's.

'I'll come back with all the dope I can find,' he promised, teeth chattering, but we knew he would spend everything on heroin.

'He can't control it any longer,' Lucio said sadly. 'A year ago, it was just an experiment, after he came out of the army, but now it's eating the flesh from his bones. I'll buy hash for the rest of us later. If only Tim had done as Dave suggested, and grown marijuana up in those mountains of his, what a lot of trouble it would have spared us all!'

'Tim Danby? Wouldn't someone have found out?'

'Up there in the mountains? You've got to be joking! It's the perfect climate, much better than for tobacco, which the government subsidizes, and nobody ever goes up there to snoop about. He's a fool, that man.'

It was indeed a different Florence that I saw with Lucio that night. Away from the Piazza della Signoria, down dark alleys, there were beggars, pimps, prostitutes and what I took at first to be exquisite young women, who Lucio told me were transvestites.

'I tried picking one up once, when I was a student, and he had me fooled, *porca Madonna*, right until the last moment, I tell you! There are clubs all along here, especially on the other side of the Arno.'

Once, we crossed Via Tornabuoni, its illuminated caverns glinting with famous names for window-shoppers to gaze at. Passing Gucci, I saw, to my horror, a giggly, buck-toothed redhead I had been at St Crumpet's with. Of course, I thought, this would be her natural stamping-ground. She saw me, and I could not avoid exchanging greetings.

'Are you doing the course at the British Institute, too? I haven't seen you yet, but people do gang up so fast, don't they? Gosh, you have lost tons of weight, how do you manage, with all the vino and pasta? This is Nico, my boyfriend, by the way. He's a prince, has this really fab villa in Fiesole.'

A fair, languid young man in a yellow cashmere jumper kissed over my hand.

'Delighted,' he said, while Lucio watched, bristling. 'Who's your friend? Doesn't he understand English? Gosh, he is dreamy, isn't he? Just your luck.'

Both Lucio and Prince Nico, who understood English quite well enough, thankfully intervened at this point by dragging us away.

'Ciao-ciao! Come and see me soo-oon,' called the girl whose name I could not remember, though I knew we had disliked each other at school.

'You were right, the English who come to Italy are the worst,' I said.

The business of buying drugs from the dealers on the Ponte Vecchio was conducted with astonishing openness by souvenir-sellers, who kept pairs of brass scales on display at all times. Tourists thought the men were itinerant jewellers, an illusion which the pedlars did nothing to dispel, for they all displayed velvet-lined cases of oriental silverware as a cover. They had the faces of rats. I could hardly bear to look at them.

There was not much to be had. The tourist season had cleaned them out, and the customs officials were becoming more vigilant. Eventually, Lucio boasted that he had the entire supply of Florence's hash stashed away in his cowboy boots, and it seemed a fair guess he was right. I was too nervous to watch, convinced we would be arrested at any moment. Waiting, I wandered up and down looking at the gold jewellery in the shop windows, pretending to be just another tourist, though I felt cut off from them by a wall of glass. Dark water flowed under the bridge, reflecting the wavering ochre buildings all along the banks. I felt tired and was longing to lie down and sleep, but it was nearly midnight before his commissions were completed.

'Do you still buy for Sylvia?' I asked, as we walked to Chiodino's cousin's flat, across the Arno.

'Why, would it bother you if I did?'

'I'd just like to know.'

'Yes, then.'

'I wish you wouldn't.'

'It has nothing to do with you, or what you want. It's just business, OK?'

Cats, liquid as their shadows, stared out at us with reflective eyes from the rank alleys. There were burst bags of cold spaghetti, used condoms, empty syringes, rotting fruit. Someone had vomited on a street corner, and the smell mingled nauseatingly with that of the sluggish city sewers.

'*Oh, che bell' far l'amor con un' bionda come quella!*' sang out one young man, walking past with a group of his friends.

'*Soltanto co' l'uccelino su'l' cazzo tuo!*' Lucio answered, quick as a flash.

Hardly pausing, they both turned, crouched, and raised their fists at each other before walking on.

Yes, a different city from the one I had seen before.

Chiodino's cousin, or rather his girlfriend, Laura, lived in a modern flat near the hospital. She was a nurse there and, according to Lucio, supplemented her income by filching drugs from the stores. Though I had come to think of what the band took as relatively harmless, I was horrified at this.

'But that means she's a thief.'

'So? Everyone does it, in Italy. I bet you they do it in England, too. Everyone steals from their employer. It's part of your salary. You're so naive, Emma.'

'I know,' I said. 'Forgive me.'

Chiodino was happy again, his eyes sparkling, if pinned. His cousin, Gianni, and Laura, had both been reading *Lord of the Rings* in Italian, and were full of praise for it.

'It's a great romance, an exceptional romance,' said Laura excitedly. She was crop-haired, with white teeth that gleamed against an olive skin, and as modern as Gianni looked dated. 'Have you read it?'

When I told her I had, at Sylvia's house, she became even more enthusiastic. 'If only I could read it in English! Tell me, Lucio, have you been learning English from your girlfriend?'

Lucio, who was rolling a joint, smiled and shook his head.

'I've tried to teach him, but he won't learn,' I said, yawning. 'Sylvia says Italian men never learn unless they're forced.'

'Are you trying to say I'm stupid?' he asked, scowling.

I looked at him in surprise. 'No.'

'Good. It's foreigners who are stupid, not Tuscans.'

'Hey, man,' said Chiodino's cousin, 'talking of foreigners, what happened to that one you wanted me to give a lift to a few months ago? I waited and waited for him, but he never turned up.'

Lucio put the joint between his hands, lit it, and inhaled deeply.

'Didn't he? I walked with him down to the crossroads, and then I heard you sounding the horn.' The smoke made his voice squeaky.

'Yes, I did it to remind him he was supposed to meet me. But he never turned up.'

Lucio took another inhalation and started to cough before passing the joint to Chiodino's cousin.

'He must have got a lift with someone else, then.'

'I suppose so. It was stupid, though. I went all the way to Munich that night. I could have taken him a long distance.'

'He was crazy, that one.'

I looked from Lucio to Chiodino. Things stirred in my memory, despite tiredness: the postcard, the passport, the roll of foreign money.

'But Lucio,' I began, 'this could be serious, if he never turned up. Perhaps you don't know – when I was at Sylvia's—'

'Sylvia, Sylvia, what is it with you this evening?' he suddenly exploded. 'What are you, obsessed?'

216

'No,' I said, half laughing. 'But listen—'

'Listen to what? More of your jealousy? More of your garbage about her?'

I began to feel the blood drain from my face at the hatred in his. 'Lucio, you know I never – you know I never discuss – Lucio, this isn't fair . . . '

Chiodino, Gianni and Laura were watching us in varying degrees of stupefaction, drug-induced or otherwise. I was more embarrassed than alarmed, then became frightened.

'Do you know what I think?' Lucio shouted. 'I think it's her you wanted to fuck all along, not me! You're obsessed with that woman, you're a lesbian and you don't know it.' I stared at him.

'Is that really what you think?' I asked, unable to believe my ears.

'Hey, man, cool it,' said Chiodino's cousin. 'This isn't the time or the place . . . '

'Are you really a lesbian?' asked Laura, with sudden, predatory interest.

'Oh yes,' he said. 'You are, aren't you? That's why you'd never had a man before me, isn't it?'

'Lucio, you know that's a lie,' I said, quite calmly, though I felt I was dying of misery. 'Tell them it's a lie. Although,' I couldn't help adding, 'I can't honestly see what's so terrible about women loving each other in that way, if they happen not to like men. But I'm not one of them.'

He stared at me with red eyes, glowering. There was silence in the room; it stretched on and on. I felt that the three of them had ganged up against me, a foreigner. I raised my chin.

'Well, if you won't admit it, then I'll leave, and make my own way back,' I said.

'Go, then.'

'Lucio, you can't turn her out in the street, not at this hour,' Laura protested. Chiodino just giggled.

'This is all crazy,' Gianni said. 'Thinking too much makes you old.'

'I'm going.'

I picked up my bag, walked out and down the steps. When I got to the street, I waited for him to call me back, but the only sound was that of the door slamming. It echoed and re-echoed up and down the stairwell of the apartment block, and in my memory.

I began to walk in the direction of the railway station. It was only when I had crossed the Arno that I remembered I had no cash in my purse and no traveller's cheques left.

It was a time of nightmare, those hours I spent walking round Florence. The streets were deserted, apart from roving louts, who thought I was a prostitute and followed me for block after block, while I tried not to lose my nerve and run.

I became hopelessly lost, though I hardly cared, such was the misery I felt. It burned in me like a red-hot coal, keeping me warm and careless. For the next hour, I was full of fury towards Lucio, so much so that I muttered aloud as I walked, which at least kept my persecutors away.

Then I began to think, perhaps that's what he really believes, that I was in love with Sylvia; he asked me that right at the very beginning, perhaps that's why he's been so strange all along. Then I began to pity him, and myself, and sank down.

I was in the Piazza della Signoria by now. It was floodlit but utterly deserted, the bars closed and shuttered, their tables stored away inside. The sky looked the colour of blood. Half the square was dug up because archaeologists had found some old remains and were determined to leave them exposed. Rack and ruin everywhere.

If he loves me, I thought, he will come looking for me here; he must know I have no money and that I can't catch a

218

train at this hour. I waited and waited, and the blue and gold-starred clock on the Signoria struck three, then four, but he did not come.

I could see the floodlit statues of the Renaissance in the loggias all around me: Cellini's Perseus, holding up his head of the Medusa, Michelangelo's giant, noble David with his head so like Lucio's, Giambologna's Rape of the Sabines, the metamorphosis of Daphne in Apollo's arms, the fountain of Neptune. I had dreamt of them all at boarding school; and now they were only decoration, offering no consolation.

Sitting on the stone steps to the Uffizi, I thought I would freeze to death in my thin cotton dress, the green-and-white-sprigged one Maria Guardi had admired, which I had altered by cutting the sleeves off and shortening. That seemed such a long time ago, that evening at the palazzo. I was always getting kicked out, I thought, smiling a little; for the absurdity of it was beginning to strike me.

Did everyone go through this at eighteen? Oh, God, I hoped so, or things were worse than I suspected. I would be nineteen soon, and then twenty; and then ninety, like the Contessa.

How Andrew Evenlode would laugh if he saw me now! My own worst enemy. He saw right through me, as my father had said, even in half an hour at that dreadful, dreadful interview at Magdalen, and I had hated him for it. Don't make more of a fool of yourself, he had said.

The Dunnetts' peacock opened his beak and screeched with laughter, before flying off.

The water from the fountain trickled on beneath its spotlights, then exploded.

Bang!

I could see Evenlode's face bending over me, and he didn't look at all amused.

'Emma, are you all right?'

219

I rubbed my eyes and blinked.

It was morning. I had slept through the dawn on the steps of the Uffizi. The depression of months hit me with the heat and light of the day. It was now ten o'clock, and Evenlode was crouched down in front of me. I put my hands out to him.

17

How Evenlode got me out of Florence, I can't remember. I was so stiff and exhausted I could hardly move, and shrank under the stares of passers-by. He wanted to pour coffee down me and take me back to Harold Acton's villa, where he had been staying, but I burst into tears and said I only wanted to leave.

He made no objection, though later I discovered he had set aside the day for looking round churches and museums for his book. He asked only one question.

'Emma, are you on drugs?'

I shook my head. He sighed, and took my arm.

Maria's Cinquecento was parked near the Pitti Palace. I was in a daze, my hair matted and tangled, my eyes still itchy with tiredness. As soon as he had folded himself into the car and started the engine, I fell asleep again.

When I woke up, Florence had disappeared and we were up in the hills. It was cooler but still glaringly bright. I looked at the cypress trees rising and falling on the horizon, black against the enamelled sky, heard the cicadas singing in the silver groves, and felt peaceful.

'If you're awake now, I wouldn't mind the use of my right arm back.'

'Oh, sorry.'

Evenlode looked at me and smiled. I smiled back, though my face felt stiff.

He was a ridiculous sight. I had forgotten that he was so tall he had to fold back the Cinquecento's sun roof to fit his head in, and to shade himself from the sun he now wore an ancient Panama hat jammed down on a roll of handkerchief.

'You should try kirby grips,' I commented, yawning. 'What happens if it blows off?'

'Then I drive even more slowly, because I won't be able to see the road so well.'

'I like this speed. You notice more.'

'Mmm. Like being on trains instead of planes, or bicycles instead of cars.'

'Lots of bicycles in Oxford,' I remarked, cautiously. 'Yes. I sometimes think it's the exercise that keeps students mentally active, not the teaching.'

'If every one of your pupils is as demanding as I am, I'm not surprised you needed a break.'

It was the closest I could come to an apology.

'Well, no, you are a particular case.'

We smiled at each other again. Really, I thought, he looked quite different when he did so.

'Have you missed Oxford?'

'Yes and no. The palazzo reminds me a little of a college, the way it's built round a courtyard, and the countryside is so wonderful, both in itself and because it's stuffed with some of the paintings that are my life's obsession ... But it's a distracting place to try and work in. One keeps wanting to look out of the window at the view, and once you do that, you've had it. I don't know what it's like to paint in, but for writing, it's a disaster. You know, I'm sure the reason England and Russia and northern France produce the best literature is because of the diabolical weather ... '

'What about Germany?'

'Ah, yes. Germany. I've just been reading Goethe's Italian journal, and he says that if the Apennines were smoothed out, the weather would be sublime and the region comparable to Bohemia.'

'Silly ass.'

'Yes, but then, it must have been hard work, being a German poet. Claudia tells me he was a brilliant botanist; but, as I've said before, intelligence is almost as fatal as ideas in such matters.'

The mention of hilliness was bringing on a bout of carsickness. It was now stiflingly hot, the tar melting and making slushing sounds as we drove over it. Pools of heat shimmered in the road ahead, mirages of cool water that moved for ever out of reach.

'I'm aching for a wash. I must smell horrible.'

'Why do you think I've got my head sticking out of the sun roof? Don't worry.'

There was a pause. Well, here goes, I thought: nag, nag, nag.

'Aren't you going to ask what happened?' I asked, wearily.

Evenlode glanced down. 'You'll tell me, if you want to. Otherwise, it's your own business. You're a grown-up now.'

Surprised, I squinted at the road ahead.

'Am I? Yes, I suppose I am. Legally, that is. But I can't get used to the idea.'

'It does take some getting used to,' he agreed, but without the usual barb to his voice.

'I used to think it would be so wonderful. Nobody telling you what to do any more, absolute freedom ... But we aren't really free, are we? I can't bear the way everyone in England is so connected.'

'It's less of a burden, in the end, than complete freedom, you know,' he said quietly. 'You don't realize yet how lucky you are – oh, I don't mean materially, though you are that too. I mean, in having this great network of family, and friends of family. It's what people try to create all over the world, and you've been born into it. It's the closest thing most people come to the love of God, you know, all that judgement and approval, or disapproval.'

'But it's so stifling, so stupid! How can they judge, when most of them are too thick even to run a business? The arrogance of it!'

'I think you'll find many of them are less stupid than you suppose, though their individual intelligence may be different from yours. Think of it as being like trying to write a sonnet. You have a rigid form, but perfect freedom to do what you want within that. Or like painting, since you are a representational painter.'

'If I were to go back,' I said.

'Yes?'

'Andrew, what if someone, say, someone like me, had got mixed up in something really awful?'

'How awful is that?'

'As awful as can be. Say ... terrorism, or child pornography or something. I mean, he or she couldn't go back, could they? In theory, I mean.'

'It depends how much the person was involved, I should think,' he said, keeping his eyes on the road.

'Well, not at all. Not directly, that is. But if you've found something out that feels wrong ... When I'm painting, you know, I sometimes try to cheat. I think how convenient it would be if that little bit there was dark, instead of light, or something; but when I do it, I see at once that it's all wrong. Everything depends on everything else; once one thing is a cheat, it puts all the rest out. Oh, I'm not explaining things properly. It makes me miserable, anyway.'

Evenlode glanced down, and smiled at me again. 'Does it? Good.'

'So what do you think I should do?'

'I can't help you decide on such a small amount of information, and certainly not before lunch. You interposed yourself between me and my breakfast at Doney's this morning, and I'm ravenous.'

'I've suddenly realized I am too.'

'Good. Let's buy a picnic before the shops close.'

'Are we driving straight back?'

'More or less. We stop off at Monterchi. I haven't been there since I was a student, and I want to see the Madonna del Parto.'

'You're very young to be able to take a sabbatical, aren't you?'

'Only somewhat. Every five years, if it's unpaid, otherwise every seven,' he said. 'I have a bit of my own money, which helps. To be honest, I wanted to get away for a bit. I was having a rather dour affair which ended quite suddenly when she decided to marry someone else.'

'Bad luck.'

'No, it was a relief on all sides. Things sometimes just run their course. Also, Claudia won't last much longer, and I wanted to see her and the gardens.'

'What will happen when she dies? She said it isn't entailed.'

'Oh, I expect she'll leave it to some relative; or else to the Royal Botanical Society. Or even to the Comune of Santorno, if they can bury the hatchet, now that they're Communist.'

The road wound down, down, down through wooded mountains to a valley were poplar trees swayed and sparkled in the sun. We stopped in a small, dusty hamlet called the Palazzo di Pero, an exotic name for a modest place. Under the interested gaze of villagers, drinking beer beneath plane trees on the dusty verge, we bought wine, transparent pink slices of prosciutto and *coppa*, two mozzarellas floating in square plastic sacs, more cheese, fresh bread, and a bagful of tomatoes and peaches and grapes. We loaded these into the car and went back up the mountain until we found a dirt track that led off it to a small green meadow with a stream and a series of pebbly pools at the bottom. Here we unpacked and put the wine in to cool. Longing for a swim, I washed my arms and face and tried to untangle the worst of my knots before we began eating.

We ate and ate. Ants crawled up his blue-striped shirt. The cicadas, which had quietened down momentarily at our approach, resumed their cheepings. I began to feel more cheerful.

'It's like Porphyro's feast,' I said.

'Those damned Romantics,' Evenlode answered irritably. 'I wish to God they'd take them off the syllabus, the trouble they cause! I'm always trying to get my students to plan essays, but no, they've all read Wordsworth at sixteen, and they think it would be so much more interesting to find out what they think as they go along, like blithering idiots, so what comes out is a mess.'

'I don't.'

'No, I remember.'

'Do you? Perhaps you remember why you turned me down for your college, then.'

I hadn't been meaning to raise the issue, especially not now, when he had been so nice to me, but once it was out, I was glad.

Evenlode lolled back on one arm, chewing a stalk of grass, his face remote.

'Perhaps I was just in a bad mood that day. It's so easy, at the end, just to dismiss people. You get so bored and tired. Besides, it wasn't my decision alone. I was only a junior fellow, then.'

'It was you who said I was my own worst enemy.'

226

'So that got back to you, did it? That's the trouble with what we were talking about earlier, there aren't any secrets.'

'If you knew what a misery that remark made my life, for months and months, at home!'

'Did it?'

'Yes, it did. It was one of the reasons I ran away from home, in fact.'

'I'm sorry, then. It was never meant to reach your ears. I thought your mother's relation would have been more discreet.'

'Well, he, or his wife, wasn't. You know how malicious they all are, the Ansteys. And now I'm condemned to go to another St Crumpet's, full of lino and girls in winceyette making Ovaltine at bedtime. Well, I'd sooner not go, thanks.'

'Really?'

'Yes, really.'

'That would be a pity. At most, you'd only have to put up with that for a year, before you moved out into town. Besides, you misunderstand the college system. It isn't like being at school, you know; everyone moves around. It's a positive advantage not to like your particular college, sometimes, because it gets you out and about. Magdalen can be awfully insular.'

'I don't care!' I said, my voice shaking. 'I won't put up with ugliness any more, or the company of women, I've had them stuffed down my throat until I feel – I felt – like a Strasbourg goose! Why did you do it? You know perfectly well I wrote good papers!'

Evenlode put his head back and laughed, properly for once.

'Do you know, your mixture of supreme confidence about academic matters and extraordinary timidity about everything else is one of the things I most remember about your interview? Though it's by no means so uncommon. How you have blossomed since then ...'

'Don't try and oil round me,' I said angrily. 'Of course I've changed, what do you expect in nearly two years? Bloody hell!'

'Yes, your papers were good, at least the art-history ones were. Excellent, in fact.'

'Ha! So why the hell didn't you take me? Sex discrimination again, I bet!'

'No, not exactly. Languages you were clearly bored by, that didn't go down well with Piston. Though possibly we took too much notice of what your teachers said, especially the head-mistress, from what I recall. Emma, it was all a long time ago. Can't you accept it?'

'So that was it, the old cow! She always hated me. Yes, I remember her saying something about how failure would do me good.'

'I'm sure she would not have allowed her judgement of you to be clouded by personal feeling.'

Lord, he could be an old stick!

'Oh, just as yours is always based on dispassionate observation, I suppose?'

He laughed, in the peculiar way that he had, through his nose.

'That was a bit pompous, I admit, though I do try. Look, to be accepted by one Oxford college instead of another doesn't constitute failure. It doesn't even constitute failure if you don't get into any. I live by academia, it's my world, I'd fight against its erosion to the last drop, but I don't make the mistake of thinking it's the be-all and end-all of life. Try not to care so much.'

'How can I not care?'

'Well, try to put it in perspective, then.'

'Perspective? You forget, I'm a painter. I know the artifices that employs. Besides, in order to create such an illusion, you need a vanishing point. How can I hope to find such a thing, when everything in my life is so close up? I know so much, but

228

I have no experience, no time, no distance to put between me and what I see.'

'Don't you? But you have enough to recognize that is the problem. Why else did you leave home and come out here?'

I fell silent, pondering.

All around us, the heat simmered and crackled.

'Heavens, it's hot,' Evenlode said, yawning. 'They say storms are coming, but I can't see any sign of them.'

'I think I'll die if I don't have a swim,' I said, presently. 'I still feel filthy from my night on the streets.'

'Go ahead. I might join you.'

'Well ... I haven't got anything except knickers, actually.'

'So?' he said, lazily. 'I'm not bothered. I should think boxer shorts are pretty transparent, too. Go without. I won't look.'

'Promise?'

'I thought you despised conventions.'

'Oh, bloody hell, all right.'

He tipped the Panama over his eyes and I stripped off, hurried and self-conscious. Hard, round pebbles underfoot. The relief of entering cold water. I gasped a little, then began to splash. It wasn't deep, a yard or so, but fast-flowing from some mountain spring.

'Good, isn't it?'

He was brown, though not as brown as Lucio, I thought; broader and hairier, too ... I hadn't expected hair. It ran from his chest down to the groin, a narrow Y of darkness. I knew I shouldn't look at him, but it was only the second one I'd ever seen in real life, and I was curious. Evenlode raised his eyebrows and, to my surprise, went rather red.

'You look better without your clothes on,' I said, almost accusingly.

'So I've been told,' he answered, with mock complacency. 'That's why I conceal my charms behind the old man's wardrobe you so deplore. If the truth were known, I'd never be able to go out again without a hundred harpies panting to rip them off . . . '

We both burst out laughing. He swam away, adding, 'You too, as a matter of fact. So English. All that shapeless cotton.'

'My mother said it made me look like a bog quivering with pretty flowers.'

'Did she?'

'Yes, she did.'

He floated downstream, to my side. It was an odd feeling, neither likable nor dislikable. I noticed his eyes were greenish, not brown as I would have expected.

'Then she must be as terrifying as Claudia says.'

'Does the Contessa know her as well as Daddy?' I asked, surprised.

'She came to their wedding.'

'Oh, yes, he said so. They look so odd in the photograph you know, in those funny clothes with big collars, and kipper ties. I can't believe they were ever my age. It seems so peculiar.'

'We'll seem just as peculiar to our children. What a pity parents can't pass on what they learn. Everyone keeps on having to start all over again, making the same mistakes, over and over.'

'The trouble with my family is, we all behave like most people do only on Christmas Day.'

'Rude, you mean?'

'Fearfully.'

'Whereas mine are all so desperately polite, we hardly know one another. I have to make a tremendous effort to break away.'

'Your rudeness appears to be quite spontaneous to me,' I said dryly.

'Thanks, that's a compliment, though I know you didn't mean it to be. You think I'm beyond redemption, don't you?'

I swam upstream to a clump of willows.

'Well ... Actually, I think you're quite nice. At least, you have been, recently.'

'Emma, what are you going to do when September comes? It's your decision, but you can't really just chuck it in because you don't like the college that took you on.'

'It isn't just that.' The light dazzled me, a galaxy of pinpoints, coalescing. 'It's painting.'

'You can still do that.'

'And, well, Lucio.'

'The Demon Lover. I see.'

We were both silent for a bit. The river rattled on, clearing a pebble from its throat now and then.

'Does he have anything to do with the moral dilemma you mentioned earlier on?' Evenlode asked, presently.

'I don't know. I don't think so. It's just – well, if you must know, it's Sylvia's husband.'

I told him about the postcard, the passport and Dave's disappearance, feeling more and more silly. By the time I finished, I felt sure he thought I was telling it to make myself seem more interesting.

'It's not very much, is it? I'm probably just doing what Sylvia says people in Santorno do all the time, out of boredom and ignorance, making up a story. But why should she lie? Why does everyone hate him?'

'He seems to have had a genius for making enemies. Even Louis.'

'Really?'

'Yes. Maria told me. Louis adores the Guardis' dog. He found it running wild and starving in the mountains, and nursed it back to health. They looked all over the place for it – they're quite valuable, hunting dogs, you know – and Lurie told them where it was. There was no end of a scene, apparently.'

'That's another thing. Why did she tell everyone they were

231

married? I thought it might just be to stop unwelcome attention, but she isn't that sort of a person. She's so proud of being unconventional, it doesn't fit. Oh, Andrew, if you could have seen her, when she found out about Izzy's baby! It was like living with a lunatic. I was really frightened she was going to go round with that knife. I'm so afraid she's done something awful.'

'The passport bit does look bad, I agree. Though he could have just left it and not bothered to come back. There's a rational explanation for it all.'

'Why would Sylvia have it, and not Izzy?'

'He could have dropped it in Santorno.'

'No, he had it at the party. I saw it in his back pocket.'

'Sylvia could have stolen it, to make life awkward for him at the border.'

'I suppose so,' I said, reluctantly.

'It takes a lot for someone actually to commit murder. I know everyone sees it so much in films, the horror of the idea is less than it was to an age that lived with real violence. But it is still an almost incredible step to take. People don't usually scream and shout and kill each other, you know.'

Oh, don't they? I thought, wondering if he ever opened a newspaper, or had known a family other than his own.

'Nothing has turned up, has it? I mean, just supposing Sylvia had bumped him off for some reason, I'd have thought it would be almost impossible to conceal a body for so long.'

'Would it?'

'Heavens, yes. Look around you. You don't think you can dig a hole in this lot, do you? They say you take out more stone than earth, in Tuscany.'

'But what about all those abandoned houses and things?'

'They may be abandoned, but they're pretty well known,' he said. 'Shepherds and people camp in them, lovers . . . '

The word hung in the air between us. I had to sort

something out with Lucio, I thought. Things couldn't go on as they were. He was destroying my will, eating away at it as heroin consumed Chiodino.

'I'm getting crinkly fingers.'

The Madonna del Parto was a tiny chapel on a cypress-lined hillock outside Monterchi. Fields of maize surrounded it as though it was any old building, a farm shed, perhaps. A grumpy, halitosic man demanded an entrance fee. I had none.

'How did you plan to get back to Santorno?'

'I thought of selling my grandmother's pearl necklace. I wear it all the time, these days.'

'I noticed. Even in the river.'

'Did I? Damn. I expect the string will rot, then.'

We looked up. There she was, revealed by two angels, each the exact reverse of the other and holding up the crimson corners of her quilted pavilion. She seemed to float above the ground, at once solid and weightless. The halo above her head looked flat as a loaf of bread. Her face was broad, beautiful only in its serenity, the curve of downcast eyes. A young peasant face. That bent arm, was it out of pride, or pain? The white, vulva-shaped split in her blue robe.

I did not relish the prospect of pregnancy myself, despite that dazzling moment with Lucio. As far as I was concerned, fertility was an enemy, particularly for women artists: Sylvia and I had agreed on this point at our first meeting. It was obvious, that one sort of productivity cancelled out the other in all aspects of art. Yet now, looking at this faded fresco, I could understand Sylvia's grief at being sterile, and Izzy's pride.

We left, eventually, without saying a word.

The drive back was long and winding; I had cause several times to think more kindly of Goethe and his wish to flatten the Apennines. The little car became hot and uncomfortable.

Andrew and I made desultory conversation. It was a relief to have told someone else of my worries about Dave; but even if they were groundless, I still had a great deal else to think about.

We came down through the pass that led past Louis's house and the rubbish dump. I thought at first it had become unusually active, for as we rounded the corner, a great pall of smoke hung over the valley.

'Oh, God,' said Andrew suddenly.

It was not the dump that was sending up the smoke. Beneath the Palazzo Felice, the whole hillside was on fire.

18

Nobody ever found out how it started. A piece of broken glass, a carelessly thrown cigarette, spontaneous combustion, even arson, were all suggested. It began during the siesta, while everyone slept, just below the Dunnetts' house.

Later, I learned Izzy had been the first to hear it. It was the maid's day off, and the Dunnetts were alone in the house. She had been lying, swollen and restless, while Slim slept beside her, grateful for the slight breeze coming in through the window. She was eight months gone; her parents still rang her every day to beg her to fly to England on a specially chartered flight (no normal airline would now take the responsibility of carrying her), but she remained steadfast in her resolution to have the baby in Santorno. She had become placid and vast, inured even to the savage kicks of the child inside her, which fascinated Slim in the way they made her belly quiver.

'It'll be a right Kenny Dalgleish,' he would say, delightedly.

Everything had changed in their marriage, she told me (for Izzy was not one to keep any feelings to herself; she believed everyone must be fascinated by her simply because she was rich, and perhaps she was right). She, who had been petulant and domineering, was now utterly dependent on her husband, and in a curious way at peace with herself because of it. He, in turn, had become noticeably more protective, the foxiness of his expression softened into something approaching sentiment. They both lived for the child, endlessly discussing its future.

Izzy had lost sight of her feet weeks ago below the swollen bulge of her belly, but when she heard a sharp crack, she had thought someone might be knocking on the door, and, rather than wake Slim, had shuffled down to see who it might be.

When she saw the line of tall flames advancing up the hillside, she let out a great shriek. Slim, jerked out of sleep, immediately scrambled up, dazed and panicky. He could hear her shouting below, so he ran barefoot down the stairs. Halfway down he tripped and fell. Izzy found him at the bottom of the stairs, white as marble.

She squatted down to see if he was still alive, and then a gush of water wet her legs and feet; pain went through her, sharp as knives, and she thought she would faint. Gasping and sweating, she dragged herself, on her hands and knees, to the nearest telephone. But the line was dead. The flames had long since consumed the wooden pole that held the cables running down from Santorno. Two hundred metres away, they danced like a thousand yellow devils, advancing in the breeze.

Izzy, perhaps for the first time in her life, thought hard and fast. She was not stupid, only spoilt, and she had inherited her father's determination to survive at all costs. Her first thought, she told me, was to get out, and save herself and the baby. She realized that if she and Slim stayed in the house, all three of them would probably die. Even if stone did not burn, it would heat up like an oven and roast them. It had happened to an abandoned house in the mountains near the Danbys' a couple of years ago; she had seen the charred ruin.

The pangs of her labour were coming faster now. Every time it happened, her body took over. There was no control; all the stuff about counting was nonsense. The baby was going to

236

come out, whatever she wanted, even if it killed her. She could keep crawling between contractions, but it was important to do what she had to do at once, before they got worse.

Somehow, she managed to roll Slim onto a rug, a kelim that had been a wedding present. Then she gripped its fringe and began to drag it, very slowly, to the swimming pool.

Lotto, the young potter, had been the next to see the fire, I think. He had just delivered some garden urns in his van to the Palazzo Felice, for he was one of the few townspeople the Contessa admitted through the gates. He had unloaded them while she went off to rest, and neither of them had noticed the smoke ascending the sky, or the smell of burning, which a breeze blew away from the palazzo hill and hid from the town on the other side.

Seeing the Contessa and her garden always made him happy. He was ardently romantic, but nobody knew this. Most women assumed, like signora Ferranti, that he must be stupid because his cleft palate made him inarticulate and agonizingly shy; his parents, who had tried to protect him from the taunts of other children, had assumed the same, despite his gift for the craft.

'It's lucky his hands are the Lotto hands,' he told me his father had said to his mother. 'Even if he's an idiot, they will earn his bread.'

He was in a dream, driving out of the gates and down the slope to the parterre. When he saw the shimmer over the valley below, he thought it must be that of the sun's heat, but then his mind took in the smoke and the bright, jagged line of flame.

Lotto acted at once. The Contessa was safe, for the wind was blowing away from her house, but he could see the doll-like figures of the Dunnetts in their slab of turquoise swimming pool, the one that had caused so much envy in the town and made people mutter ominously about how the foreigners were causing the water table to drop. He put his foot down on the accelerator and shot off along the parterre to the town, hooting his horn.

By the time he had got to the main gate, he was in such a lather of excitement, I doubt whether anyone would have understood him. Unfortunately, the first person he encountered was Signora Ferranti, fresh from the hairdresser and off on a post-siesta stroll.

'Ffff-o!' Lotto shrieked, jumping out of his van and seizing her in a maniac's grip.

Signora Ferranti let out a screech.

'Rape! Rape!' she cried. 'Let me go! *Vafanculo, figlio di putana, o ti rompo gli scatoli!*'

Shopkeepers, just opening up, poked their heads out all along the Via Garibaldi.

'No, fff-o!' said Lotto desperately, clinging to her as she hit him repeatedly with her stiletto-heeled shoe. Eventually, as people crowded round, he caught sight of Nastri, the chemist. Lotto made a dive for him instead, and the crowd, muttering, took a pace back.

'Ffff-o!' he said, pleading, his harelip frothing and gaping.

The mayor, believing he was confronting a madman, swelled and put his fingertips together, fixing the little potter with a commanding eye.

'*Dunque* . . .' he said.

Maria Guardi came down from the palazzo shortly after Lotto, wheeling her little scooter. Unlike the potter, she was fully alert: her nostrils had already caught a faint scent of burning, but she thought it might be the rabbit she was roasting in the oven at home. Guido's great-grandmother was getting sleepy with age, and couldn't be relied on to keep an eye on such matters. The boys, who slept in their grandparents' bedroom on foldaway mattresses, complained that both of them snored at night, *nonna* worse than *nonno*, but what were they to do? The only other room, besides the kitchen and the two bedrooms, was the *salotto* in between, and this, however rarely used, Maria would defend to the death as a sacred mark of respectability.

If only, she said after, that *maledetto* Lurie had not persuaded her uncle to sell his house to the millionaire's daughter! The only member of her family who had saved up enough after the war to buy his own land and home, and childless. She and Guido had looked on it as her dowry, and then her uncle had to marry a greedy foreigner from Grisi, five miles away, and the next thing, it was gone.

Maria cast a resentful glance at her uncle's former home, and saw the fire. Unlike Lotto, she immediately thought of going back into the palazzo, which had a telephone.

Lifting her voice in a piercing yell, she called for her husband, who came running to the gate with a pair of shears in his hand. She told him what to do, and he scurried back up the avenue.

As he did so, Maria noted with alarm that the wind was veering round in the opposite direction, bringing the smell of burning clearly to her, driving the flames away from the Dunnetts' and back up her own hillside. She kicked her scooter and raced down the dirt track to the farm. The boys were working as waiters at Max's, but Guido's grandparents were in there. She had to start trying to beat out the fire before the *pompieri* arrived; they were only a voluntary force, heaven knows how long they would take to assemble with the siesta only just ending.

'*Nonna*, take the scooter and drive into town,' she said. 'Tell them there's a fire, in case the Contessa hasn't got through. *Nonno*, we must run and tell the American. Get blankets, anything.'

The old man and his granddaughter raced down the hill, while the old woman wobbled into town, screeching. When she was almost at the main gate, she collided with Signor Pistoia in his taxi. He was bringing Izzy's parents from the railway station.

'Get out of my way, you mad old bat!' he yelled at Guido's grandmother, sprawled on the cobbles.

When they recognized each other, they were even angrier, for they were ancient enemies.

'You should have been dead years ago, you old witch!' Pistoia yelled. 'Stay in my path one more moment, and I'll make sure you are!'

Guido's grandmother forgot everything in the fury of her indignity.

'Bad blood, bad blood, I curse you!' she said, pointing at him with a trembling finger, while he made the sign to ward off the evil eye.

'Excitable lot, these Italians,' Izzy's father observed to Izzy's mother, who sighed. He had seen the screaming knot of people further down Via Garibaldi, struggling to hold Lotto the potter down, and was highly amused.

It was at this point that Andrew and I appeared.

We were luckier than the rest, descending into Santorno by the north gate. The road down to the Piazza Felice went past Max's hotel, and we saw him in the street.

'Max!' I shouted, standing up inside the sun roof. 'Call the *pompieri!* The valley below the palazzo is on fire.'

Max disappeared back into the hotel in a flash, and not only called the fire brigade, already responding to the Contessa's call, but rounded up all his staff, though we didn't see them until much later.

The Cinquecento raced on, bumping over the cobbles of the two piazzas and down the Via Garibaldi. Here we had to halt, for the crowds surrounding Nastri, Lotto and Signora Ferranti were all enjoying the fight hugely, and wouldn't budge. Signora

Ferranti, quite beside herself, was hitting indiscriminately with her shoe, convinced they all wanted to abduct her, and Tony had now waded in to try to calm everyone down.

I yelled at them, but by now my voice was hoarse with tension, so Andrew stopped the engine and stood up. The whole car nearly overbalanced, and the movement was so sudden that everyone fell silent.

'There's a fire in the valley, and it's coming very fast towards the town,' he said.

'*Si, si, fff-o!*' the battered Lotto agreed, pointing at the sky, where billows of smoke were now ascending.

Instant commotion. The crowd dispersed like magic. Creaking and puffing, Tony helped Lotto from the ground. The sight of him reminded me of Slim and Izzy.

'Tony,' I said. 'Do you know the way to the Dunnetts'? Then quickly, quickly, find a car and see if they're all right. There was a fire all around their house when we looked down.'

Lotto made a great effort, and spoke clearly. 'I have a van,' he said. 'Show me.'

The small potter and the fat barman ran to Lotto's Fiat van, reversed it out of the gate (almost crashing into Pistoia and the bewildered Zuckermans) and raced off down the road to the lower town, and thence to the next hill.

'The Contessa,' I said, as Andrew followed, and drove along the parterre, 'will she be safe?'

'Yes,' he said with certainty. 'Nothing can get through those walls, and it's full of water. It's your friend Sylvia I'm more worried about, and the Guardis above her.'

We bumped jarringly down the track, and stopped in the farmyard. It was a cacophony of noise, pigs squealing, oxen lowing, geese yammering, chickens clucking, dog howling. Tonto had smelled the smoke and was maddened with fright, straining against his chain.

'Get out and let him loose,' Andrew said, keeping the engine running. 'If the fire gets this far, he won't have a chance.'

I did as he said, and the dog took off at once. The pigs came out of their sty in a greasy stampede, following, as did a pair of milk-white oxen.

'Get sacks, anything we can beat with. The Guardis must be down there already,' Andrew said.

We stopped off at Sylvia's house, but she was out, for there was no reply. Andrew parked the Cinquecento by the kitchen, afraid that if he brought it too close to the fire it would be dangerous, and we ran down the road to the valley, clutching our sacks. His long legs far outstripped mine, as did the sheer strength of Maria's husband, scurrying down from the palazzo. I was the last to arrive.

I could hear the fire now, and the sound of it struck terror into me. It roared and spat, shooting up flames of twenty feet or more; sucked the air from the lungs and licked the face with its burning breath even at two hundred metres. Nothing could withstand it. Row after row of olive trees went up like hair, the dry, oily wood burning fiercely. The brambles on the neglected land helped to spread the fire, as did the desiccated decades of old man's beard. It jumped up from terrace to terrace, showering sparks.

I didn't want to go on, but I knew I had to, because of the others. Andrew, Maria, Guido and Maria's grandfather were all beating furiously. They had broken open an old well at the bottom of the valley, but weren't drawing water from it.

'Has it dried up?' I yelled at Guido. He shook his head, too exhausted to speak.

We beat and beat. I thought my back and arms would break from the strain. I was dying of thirst, we were all coughing in the smoke, and half blind. Where was everyone else? It would have been useless, except that the fire was all concentrated, by some fluke of the wind or the land, into a gulf some twenty

242

metres broad, though it kept trying to send out sneaky little lines to get past us. I made it my job to stop these; I was more effectual like that.

Then something terrible happened. The Dunnetts' idiotic peacock, Albert, suddenly broke from cover, like a pheasant, with its tail feathers on fire.

With a scream, the poor bird took off, clumsily, into the air. Normally, it couldn't fly more than a hundred yards at a stretch, but pain or terror gave it supernatural strength. Up, up it went, aflame, then fell, like Icarus, just below Sylvia's house.

At first, we didn't realize that the line of defence had been breached. We kept beating, hoping to hold the fire back until the firemen arrived, not noticing that our backs were getting as hot as our scorched fronts. I turned.

'Look,' I croaked, touching Andrew's arm.

He saw, and then we all stopped. Despite the breeze, the fire was now coming down the hill, as well as up. The fire engine was stuck on the narrow road below the Guardis', bell clanking uselessly. We were cut off on an increasingly narrow isthmus between two impenetrable sheets of flame.

We all realized that we had probably had it. Andrew and I just stared. Guido and his grandfather, with grim faces, turned back, and kept on at their hopeless task. I was determined to go on looking until my eyeballs fried. Andrew started to move forward to beat back the new fire.

But Maria did something extraordinary. She walked past him in a dream, until she stood facing the second line of flames, and spread her arms, black against the blinding heat and light. Then she cried, with a great voice that seemed to rise even above the howls of the fire, and echoed and re-echoed all around the curve of the hills, 'O *Padrone, salvateci!*'

She has gone mad, I thought, holding tightly to Andrew's hand. This is the last straw.

For a moment, nothing happened. Then there was a rumble that shook the earth, and a singing roar. Behind the second wall of fire, a pillar of water began to climb, higher and higher, twenty, thirty, forty, a hundred feet into the air, up and up until its crest caught the sun, flashing gold on silver. The wind came and ruffled its surface, turning the column every colour of the rainbow, scattering droplets of water over the fire, which hissed and shrieked, turning this way and that.

Higher and higher the water still climbed, while we gawped, and tears or spray, or both, ran down our faces, cooling the harsh air. Then it fell, with a roll like thunder, rushing down into the valley in torrents, not silver now, but muddy, and sinking fast into the parched earth from where it had sprung.

After that, of course, Maria's reputation as a witch was confirmed. It was a miracle, everyone agreed, even though the astonishing jet that had risen out of the earth at her command turned out to be that of the main water supply to the town, so that everyone watching on the parterre above was cut off for the next three days, and very cross they were, too.

'Even if there was some rational explanation for the presence of water,' old men would say in bars, 'how come it came out like that, just when it was needed?'

Later, it was claimed that the Santorno fire engine, trying to navigate down the narrow country road between the Guardis' and Sylvia's house, had been too heavy for the road, and had ruptured the pipe of the water supply ... but the firemen, who had not exactly covered themselves with glory, were not believed on this point.

Those who did emerge with full credit were Tony and Lotto. Carried away by the idea of a lady in distress, they had heroically driven through a wall of flame and found the Dunnetts in the shallow end of their swimming pool. In fact, they were hardly needed, except to cut the umbilical cord of the Dunnetts' new daughter. Slim had regained consciousness and had held Izzy while she had had her baby in the water – 'the most dramatic Leboyer birth ever,' as she told everyone afterwards. There was a horrid mess of blood and stuff in the pool, which Leboyer had never mentioned, and which the maid complained about, and they both needed a doctor, but the baby was fine, and the birth had hardly been painful at all. Or so Izzy claimed, later. They were both nauseatingly soppy about the whole thing. Lotto and Tony got them into the van and up to the hospital before the ambulance even realized there might be a crisis.

One consequence of their heroism was that Tony was unanimously elected mayor the following year; another was that Izzy's grateful father paid for the potter to have his harelip stitched up in London. The sweetness of his face became plain to see, and he made his fortune when two of his remarkable pots (of which he made a present to the Zuckermans) were spotted by a woman at Clifton Nurseries and became all the rage for fashionable town gardens.

The hills beneath the palazzo, and facing it, were black and charred, but not for long. The water that spread over the devastation encouraged seeds to grow, and within a month the gaunt slopes were green with new grass. Most of the vines had escaped, being above the Dunnetts' house. Even the olive trees would survive, springing again as young trees from their bases as they had done elsewhere in Tuscany after the bitter winter of 1986. They were hundreds of years old, and it would take more than fire or ice to destroy them. The Contessa told me that it may even have done them good by freeing them from the slow, strangling growth of convolvulus and ivy.

The peacock that had caused the conflagration to spread survived, and came somehow to the Contessa, to be nursed and nagged back to a full set of tail feathers by the insufferable peahen, Victoria. But one effect of the fire could not be eradicated: Sylvia's house had been utterly destroyed.

One of the culprits was Andrew's Cinquecento, the tank of which had exploded when the heat was at its worst. It melted the glass so that it ran from the window frames, causing the wooden beams inside to catch fire and collapse, particularly on the side where I had once slept. It was as well that Sylvia had not been there, for, though her bedroom was the least damaged, it had collapsed onto the living room beneath.

Nothing was left, despite the best efforts of Max's staff to stop the encroaching flames of the second fire. It was they who had prevented it from spreading as far as the Guardis' farm; and if Maria's sons acted with greater energy and enthusiasm defending their own home than that lower down, who could blame them?

Sylvia had arrived after it was all over, driven by Lucio. She had pushed her way through the goggling crowd, assembled at the top of the parterre to defend their own properties if need be, and viewed the devastation of her home in bitter silence. Eventually, Tim and Caroline Danby found her and led her away.

The crowd took longer to disperse. They stood around, talking of miracles and witchcraft; the old poison tongues of Santorno had never known a day like it. Nastri, Pistoia and Signora Ferranti, were all loud in condemnation of the whole thing: their dignity had been affronted, they had lost *bella figura* and were frantic to scramble up to their former position as leading members of the professional classes. Nastri even claimed that Maria's invocation had not been to her dark master but to the fire brigade struggling with their equipment halfway down the road. Few took any notice of them, however. Guido's grandmother, hobbling back, was treated with unprecedented courtesy, but she disappeared, with the rest of us and

246

Max's staff, to the palazzo to bathe and have our burns treated by the Contessa herself.

The taciturn Guido, however, went at once to the telephone to call the police. They must come at once, he said. When breaking open the cover of the abandoned well in the valley to try and stop the fire, he had discovered the decomposing body of a man.

19

Coming dose to death is supposed to produce a state of abnormal alertness. It does not. My energy lasted only until we got to the top of the avenue, and then I was like a sleepwalker. Unlike Maria and the men, whose hands and heads had been blistered by falling cinders, I was not in need of anything but rest. The Contessa sent me off to my old room. I was out until nearly midnight with the acrid soot of the fire blackening the sheets of my bed.

It was disconcerting to be back in such luxurious surroundings: everything so crisp and clean and smooth, like living inside an airing cupboard. I despised myself for enjoying it, after my spartan attic rooms. The best thing was having a real bathroom, with a huge porcelain tub, Floris oils and that nirvana of all wallowers, bulgy brass taps to turn on and off with the toes. At the Pistoias', there was only a smelly thunderbox of a lavatory downstairs, haunted by the taxi driver. I had to wash with a sponge in my basin. The artist's garret was also low on creature comforts like towelling dressing gowns and cayenne biscuits, so I made the most of them while they were available before putting my dress back on. It had been laundered while I was asleep.

It was very spoiling, being waited on hand and foot again.

The Contessa and Max's staff had cooked dinner for us all, stripping the hotel canteens and infuriating a group of German tourists beyond endurance. I came in at the tail end of the meal, and had to make do with cold pasta and salad, but it had all the air of a successful impromptu party, with young couples dancing on the terrace to jazz records cranked up on an ancient gramophone. I felt an ache, watching them; most were even younger than I, but engaged ... Lucio kept creeping back into my thoughts. I wondered whether he had even known I had been one of the people trapped by the fire, when he had got back from Florence, whether he had known I had had no money for a train, or felt any guilt about his behaviour towards me.

The Guardis had gone home to sort out the farm and search for their livestock as soon as the sun came up, though the poor old grandfather's hair was half burnt off, and Guido's hands clubbed by bandages. To my disappointment, Andrew was nowhere to be seen. I hoped he wasn't too badly burnt; I had noticed him limping, for he had been wearing espadrilles on his feet.

Max and the Contessa got on like a house on fire, so to speak. She had known his grandparents before the war; but then, she knew everyone's grandparents, including my own. I must ask her about Pompa, I thought.

Once she unbent, the Contessa was open in her enjoyment of the young Santornese, observing that a garden without the young was like a flower without scent. They in turn lost something of their timidity, though none of their awe of the old woman. For generations, she had been a figure for mothers to frighten their children with when they misbehaved. Few had seen, though all had heard of, her sinister garden, nourished by the corpses of the dead and popularly believed to be haunted by the devil. When they discovered the wonders hidden behind

249

the palazzo's high stone walls, they marvelled over them, which pleased her very much.

'I had thought they had no appreciation of such things,' she told Max and me. 'I remember, when I first arrived here as an idealistic young bride from Urbino, I was convinced that the instinct for beauty must be natural to all Italians, whatever their education, and my disillusion was swift.

'"Why else do you build your houses so they blend with the landscape?" I asked Maria's great grandmother, expecting to hear some wise treatise on peasant aesthetics.

'"Contessa, it is cheapest and most practical to use the stone provided by God," she replied.

'"Very well, but your lands. Why make them into hillsides more resembling the hanging gardens of Babylon than farms?"

'"Contessa," she said, patiently, "we build terraces in order that the little soil we find should not be washed away when it rains."

'Finally, I saw her tending a bed of iris.

'"This, at least, must be for beauty, and not practical use!" I exclaimed.

'"Oh no, Contessa," said Maria's great-grandmother dolefully, "these are for funerals."'

We all laughed.

'All the same,' said Max, 'I am sure it is inbred. My parents were *contadini*, as you know, and they would have said that everything they did was practical, too. Yet I remember that even the patterns in which they arranged the scythes on the stable walls were those of symmetry, not use. The times when my father would gaze and gaze at sunsets! He would say it was to see what the weather would be the next day, but it was more than that. A man is only a cloud in trousers, he would say, never put your trust in him . . .'

'I thought it was women who were supposed to be inconstant,' I remarked.

'Ah, no. Women may be unfaithful, but only to protect or revenge themselves,' he answered, with unshakable chivalry.

'Signor Vincioni, where is your Rosinante?' the Contessa asked, her earrings twinkling.

'Alas, Contessa, I have no need of a nag,' he answered.

I recalled the rumours I heard about his wife, and was silent. He was a strange man, Max, an autodidact full of unexpected quirks and overwhelming melancholy. His rise as a hotelier and businessman was the stuff of local legend, as were his wife's flagrant infidelities. It had been virtually an arranged marriage, a means of establishing a toehold in the society of the old town, for she was a second cousin of Signora Ferranti's. None of these respectable bourgeois couples were as stable as they seemed, according to Lucio. A few years ago, there had been a huge scandal about orgies and wife-swapping parties, which Santornese society, some twenty years behind the times, had only recently discovered. You could see it, after a bit; they were all obsessed with sex, one way or another. Max appeared the exception in having put the Machiavellian Tuscan mind towards business, not adultery.

Later, I had been unable to sleep. Whenever I closed my eyes I saw Lucio's, glaring accusingly, the glitter of the river with Andrew black against it, the crack of the fire, the cavernous arcades in Florence, a black and rotting corpse. I tossed and turned, the cold pasta heavy in me, listening to the high-pitched squeaks of bats. A wire grille over my open window kept insects out, but they would have been a lesser torment. I hated sleeping alone. How could I go back to that, if everything was over between Lucio and myself? He was always so pleased when he got an erection, shaking it in my face like a cat bringing home a dead bird to lay at your feet, demanding that I worship its full size and beauty, thinking I was mad for sex because I liked to drift off to sleep holding his penis; but mostly, it was the comfort of holding and being held I valued. I could remember what it was like, that electric charge of eroticism, but it was slipping away. I blamed myself for his violence, which had a current of desperation about it, even though it was the cause of my own increasing detachment, too.

Eventually I got up, wrapped a sheet round me, and wandered downstairs into the garden. It was cooler, but still warm. The night prickled with thousands of stars. Every now and again, a small bright tear would appear in the darkness, only to be instantly mended. I wandered down the first flight of stone steps to the rose garden. A figure was seated by the edge of the corkscrew fountain, dangling legs in the water.

'Can't you sleep either?'

Andrew shook his head.

'Are your burns hurting a lot?'

'Incurable insomnia. I usually come down here, listen to the water. In England I get through a detective story a night.'

'You must read a lot of detective stories.'

'Mmm. Luckily, one forgets the plots after a couple of years, which means you can reread them. This is better.'

'Do you want to be left alone?'

'Not particularly. I am social, but not gregarious. Most people are the other way about. Come and count shooting stars.'

I sat down on the edge of the pool and put my feet into the water, too. It was warm, like the pale marble surround, and faintly fizzy.

'I always thought they were terribly dull, detective stories. I mean, it's always the least likely person, isn't it? The girls used to read Agatha Christie nonstop at school; it was the only thing apart from *Tatler*.'

'Were they really that bad or are you exaggerating?'

'No. Snobbery, sexual frustration and the stench of burning sanitary towels, I swear. The teachers were prone to say things like, "Now gels, always remember you're the cream of British womanhood."'

We were both quiet for a bit, listening to the gurgle of water.

'What's it like for men?' I asked, suddenly.

'What? School? I survived all right because I was good at sport. There were no sanitary towels, but lots of old socks.'

'Frustration. When you stop having sex after having had it.'

'Oh, that. Well . . .'

He was silent for a bit, and I thought he wouldn't answer. When he did, his voice was light, but odd.

'Sometimes I think I'll never feel another twitch of randiness for the rest of my life, and other times all I want to do is fuck my brains out,' he said. 'Lust isn't a constant condition for anyone over sixteen, though it seems worse recently.'

'It's the heat, isn't it?' I said with a rush.

He laughed, not kindly. 'Oh is this why you've come shimmying down in a sheet, then? I thought you might be dressing up as the Count's ghost. Want to try?'

'Don't make more of a fool of yourself,' I quoted, shivering. 'All I did was ask what it was like in the abstract.'

'Women are useless at dealing with abstract concepts,' he said. 'You make a generalization to a woman, and she always thinks you mean it personally.'

I kicked water at him. 'Don't make me barf. That's as stupid as the theory that we can't be astronauts because we can't mentally rotate three-dimensional objects in space. If you've ever seen a man trying to manoeuvre a chair through a doorway, then a woman, you'd know that isn't true.'

'The object I am thinking of manoeuvring isn't a chair,' he said, leaning closer. I could hear a kind of laugh in his voice.

'No, but I dare say you wouldn't hesitate to use it as a footstool. Or even,' I said, nastily, for I was starting to shake, 'a pouffe.'

'Oh, is that what you think?'

'The English vice.'

'A typical Continental fantasy, my dear.' He leant back on one arm. 'For your information, buggery is usually more popular in countries where contraception is difficult and men are fixated on their mothers. Or haven't you found that out yet?'

'Oh, you utter *pig*, you!'

I sprang forward into the pool to box his ears, got caught up in my wet sheet, and slipped, drenching us both in water. Evenlode got up, laughing quietly through his nose, and went back to his room while I was still trying to untangle myself. I glared at his retreating back, and resolved not to speak to him again.

Great as the excitement had been over the fire, the discovery of a corpse in a well was sufficiently bizarre to warrant full coverage by *L'Etruria* and small front-page paragraphs in *La Nazione* and the *Corriere della Sera*, both desperate for items of news during the silly season. For three days Santorno basked in the attention of the press, as everything from the Mafia to the depredations of a serial killer known to have struck repeatedly in Tuscany over the past ten years was suggested to explain the murder.

Suicide, according to the local coroner, could be ruled out at once. The corpse was that of a man in his late thirties or early forties, who had been killed by severe blows to the head and neck. The body was substantially decomposed due to its immersion in semi-stagnant water, but was estimated to have been dead for seven months to a year. He had been dressed in jeans, a woollen shirt and a green, hand-knitted jumper. No dental records could be found to correspond to the man's teeth.

I read these reports in the newspapers scattered around the Bar Popolare, tearing one out. Tony, who normally only bought

Oggi for his clients, had proudly framed every mention of the part he had played in rescuing the English millionaire's daughter from the conflagration, so it was hard to avoid the rest.

Oh, August in Santorno, the enervating heat, the misery and drabness of it all. The leaves of the chestnut trees along the parterre were limp, the little municipal garden parched to a crisp since the water supply had been cut off and drought set in. The roads were so thick with dust that any car travelling across the plains left a blinding white trail, like the exhaust of an aeroplane. The stench from the sewers, the blare of radios, the sullen glare of the sun. The shops closed down for Ferragosto, the streets babbled with tourists, snapping at pots of geraniums with their cameras. On Saturdays the market was blocked by Saabs and Volvos bearing middle-class English families, with their rented villas in Lucca or San Gimignano and their assumption that Italians were simple and warm, that life was kind, that they were welcome for anything but their money. How I despised and envied them!

Yes, August in Santorno, and the long, sweltering walk down to the lower town to teach my stupid English pupils, the flicker of lizards or snakes wriggling up dry-stone walls just out of sight, the crickets jumping around fields like hot grease in a pan, the ripening of black grapes under blue leaves, the acrid scent of figs, sleeplessness, looking for Lucio, longing for rain, looking at couples drifting along the brightly lit streets, the bats twisting and flickering through the air, the moon floating in the sky over the piazza like a slice of lemon in Pepsi Cola; longing for ice-cream, for rain, for Lucio.

I would not knock on his mother's door like a beggar, so I went to the hospital. It was a long, arcaded stone building rising up from the main piazza and decorated with a della Robbia plaque of the Madonna and Child, which was greatly admired by visiting tourists. The monks had long departed, but the nurses all wore high, intricate, starched caps, reminiscent of wimples, and there was great competition among the young women of Santorno to be accepted for training there.

Izzy and the baby remained under observation for a fortnight, mostly at the insistence of Izzy's parents. They had flown out the Queen's gynaecologist after all, to make sure everything was in order (which it was: the great man told them testily to stop upsetting the mother in case her milk dried up), had special meals trolleyed down from Max's, imported dozens of tiny, lace-trimmed baby clothes, and even wanted to pay for the repainting of Izzy's hospital ward when she complained that the pale-green colour made her feel she was living inside a lettuce. Eventually, Slim asked Sir James and Lady Zuckerman to go back to England.

'You know Slim, he doesn't mince words. He told them to fuck off back to Weybridge. They were absolutely livid,' Izzy said, with satisfaction. 'Mum was OK, funnily enough, we're getting along better now, but Dad told Slim he wasn't going to take any lip from a freeloader too idle to earn his own living. Typical. So Slim told him that we're going to sell up here, and go back to England, and start up a business of our own. He's got an idea for a franchise designing children's shoes, which he thinks will work better than us trying to make them ourselves.'

'I could never understand why he chose shoes in the first place. I mean, it's quite different from advertisements, isn't it?'

'Have you ever seen his feet? They're a sight, I can tell you. When he was growing up in the East End one pair of shoes had to last for years, so he had football boots that were always too small for him. The result is, bunions and a foot fetish. Everything goes back to childhood.'

'You're really going to sell up?'

'Yes, next month.'

'It shouldn't be difficult to find a buyer. The town seems

to be full of English and Germans peering at the estate agent's window.'

Izzy shook her head, making her curls bounce, and the small snout snuffling at her breast protested sleepily.

'No, we aren't going to have anything to do with them. We're selling to the Guardis. We never knew about Maria expecting to inherit it, and all that. To tell the truth, it's never really felt like our own home.'

I thought of the terrible liquorice-allsorts furniture. 'Have you ever heard from Dave?'

'Yes,' said Izzy, to my surprise. 'I got a postcard from him, months ago, from France. It was a slight shock, actually. You know, I've almost forgotten about him. I mean, I remember being crazy about him, but it's like another existence. I suppose all I wanted was a baby, really. I knew he was only after me for the money.'

She looked so smug, with her gerbil face and her bulging breasts, I couldn't repress a question.

'What about Sylvia? She's lost everything.'

'Oh, she's a survivor,' Izzy said dismissively. 'That sort of woman always is. They trail disaster in their wake like a comet, but they always do well out of it. She's living with Tim and Caroline, while they check on the insurance. I bet Dave didn't cover it. He was a bastard. I don't think anyone will be sorry if he never comes back.'

The baby began to mewl in the squeaky, fretful voice, spewing up on Izzy's plump shoulder.

'Isn't she gorgeous? Mum says it's very fashionable to have babies now.'

'Mmm,' I said, noncommittally. (An epaulette of sick: what the well-dressed woman is wearing.)

'Slim and I just spend the whole time gazing at her, she's so perfect. Aren't you, Gabriella?'

'Gabriella?'

'Yes. We both decided that's what she was called as soon as she was born. It's such a pretty name, don't you think?'

'Yes,' I said. 'It is.'

It was lonely, back in the attic, with only the gecko and the crackling radio for company. I checked anxiously to see whether the Pistoias' blackbird was still alive, pouring some more water down into its bowl from above, which elicited a feeble cheep. The air was thick and dull, unbearably stuffy. Going to open the shutters of my bedroom window, I saw why.

A storm was coming. I could see it approaching all the way across the plains, black and grey and forked with lightning. It was like living marble, it was like the wrath of God, it was like the end of the world. Field after field was blotted out. The olive trees blanched silver, streaming before the wind, before disappearing into the murk.

On and on it came, shutting out the light. Everything turned sepia brown, like an old photograph. A blast of icy wind came through the window, followed by the stinging slap of rain. A heavy roof tile was picked up and whirled about like a piece of cardboard before shattering. The air became black; I put a light on, but it blew, instantly, with a popping sound. Rubbish swirled up from the street, higher and higher, and a bedraggled swallow dashed itself against the far wall of my bedroom and lay still. The thin whistle of wind made me think how cold it would be here in winter, without a fire.

I felt a touch on my shoulder, and turned. It was Lucio. The storm had covered the sound of his approach. He went down on his knees before I could stop him, and buried his face between my legs. I could feel his tongue, flickering; it seemed like the only warm thing in that room.

There was no need to say anything, and in any case, there

was too much noise. We shed our clothes without stopping, frantic, frantic, in front of the window, the rain ice cold and his penis red hot. I could have sworn it hissed like a poker as it sank in. I locked my legs round his hips, and then he walked to the bed, falling down on the mattresses with a bang that drove all their dust into the air and the breath from my lungs, ramming into me, again and again, faster and faster until he was a blur of motion. Everything was banging and moaning and crashing. I had a confused impression of a ball of blue fire rolling round the room, of someone thumping on the door to the stairs, and of Signora Pistoia's horrified face as she saw us in a flash of lightning, rolling over and over, blind, deaf and dumb in the act of devouring each other, and then the whole house shook as the storm arrived.

20

Andrew Evenlode would have found it hilarious, of course. I could just imagine him, hooting with laughter and saying 'Oh, Heathcliff! Heathcliff!' in acidulous tones, but I didn't care. Passion is elemental; you don't stand there snickering when it lifts you up by the hair. Lucio understood that. Sylvia had told me, long ago, 'You can't combine a sense of the absurd with the suspenders of disbelief: that's why Englishmen are such bad lovers.' I had no experience of anyone but Lucio, but I knew at once she was right. Evenlode would have been a disaster in every way ...

Later in the night, there were explanations.

'It's the heat,' Lucio said, first. 'It drives everyone crazy, it makes me feel as if I'm bursting out of my skin.'

'I know.'

'It concentrates everything, even the poison in snakes. If you get a bite in the lion's month, it's always deadly. I went nearly mad with jealousy of you and Sylvia, you and the Englishman, you and the Contessa. I want to possess you, all, not just your body, and you won't even let me come to London with you.'

'Oh, Lucio, nobody means more to me than you.'

'But why do you need them? Why can't you just stay here to paint? Why do you lock yourself away in that old witch's castle?

Are you so bourgeois? Is it so much to you, that a countess should speak to you?'

'No,' I said, with a touch of impatience. I did not want to explain about my own family. Andrew was wrong: snobbery is not harmless, because it elevates people for no good quality of their own; social nobility no longer has anything to do with nobility of conduct, which is the only thing that counts. I knew peers' daughters with less courage, kindness and dignity than Maria Guardi. 'It's nothing to do with that. I admire, I like her for what she is. She reminds me a little of my grandfather.'

'And the Englishman? You like him?'

'No. Yes. I don't know. He was kind to me after that horrible night in Florence.'

'I didn't know you had no money for the train, my darling. I drove round and round the station; they said the last train had gone. Then I drove back to Santorno to pick you up, and you weren't there. Then I heard you'd come back with the Englishman.'

'He means nothing to me,' I said, violently. 'He's homosexual, I know it.'

'How?'

This was a facer. 'I just know it, the way women do,' I said. 'Lucio, why did you tell that lie about me and Sylvia?'

'Oh, that!'

'Yes, that. It was terrible.'

'Nobody believed it, except Laura, and that was just wishful thinking. You are too beautiful, and a beautiful lesbian is like a beautiful nun, an impossibility. You are like a rose just opening out, made for men to pick. It shows in your skin, your walk, your smile, your eyes ...'

'Oh, don't tickle and say silly things! Why are you so jealous that I care about poor Sylvia, then? She won't even speak to me, you know.'

261

'You should be above such a person. Forget her. She's a fat, American whore, without talent.'

'How can you say that when you loved her once, too? Why are you so contemptuous? She's fat now because she's unhappy, and she's unhappy because she's loved you.'

'It isn't love, it's lust.'

'How do you know what I have for you, or you for me, isn't just lust, too?'

'I don't.'

The bleakness of this response made me withdraw from him again.

'Can't you be certain of anything, Lucio?'

'Only death,' he said.

My dreams were full of death. I would dream I was floating in a quilted red tomb, and a slit of blinding white light would split it open and force me out into agony. There were faces, dimly recognizable, suffering behind sheets of ice, but I could not remember whose they were. I heard footsteps on the stairs, of a man getting closer and closer, and when I saw him he was not human at all, but composed of barley and corn, olives and grapes, roses and thorns. He would reach out to me, beckoning, with a stench of rotting verdigris that haunted me even on waking, mingling with the foul vapours from the Pistoias' lavatory below.

I became afraid to sleep. Lucio took to spending the night more often; now that the Pistoias knew for certain he was fucking me, instead of just suspecting, it was easier. Well, easier in some respects. Signora Pistoia blushed bright scarlet every time she saw me (she had come up to close the windows during the storm, thinking I was out, she explained), and Signor Pistoia developed a disagreeable obsession about sniffing my dirty laundry. ('Mi piace le mutande, he told me, leering, when I caught him at it; Lucio and he then had a most unpleasant quarrel.) But, on the whole, it was a relief, and my semi-engagement protected me from too much scandal.

Lucio bought me food to cook, instead of going home to his mother across the courtyard; he said he had no idea I had been nearly starving myself. We became domestic, calmer, happier.

'You need to paint again,' he said, at the end of August.

I had no canvas, but the carpenter in Via del Ospedale gave me an idea.

'Why not paint on wood?' he said. 'I've got lots of old panels I can't use for anything but firewood. You decorate a cabinet for me, and I'll pay you.'

That was how I found a secondary source of employment in Santorno, congenial if not as well paid as teaching English. It was laborious at first, for any art is nine tenths craft, and craft needs to be flexed and exercised like a muscle, in order not to atrophy. I missed the rhythm that builds up when painting on canvas, the slight bounce of it against the brush, but wood, once prepared with gesso and glue, has its own charms. Its stability made possible all sorts of technical changes and bolder experiments with texture, so that I began to mimic surfaces by means of different thicknesses and brushstrokes. I never went back to canvas, afterwards.

I did a portrait of Tony behind his counter, swelling up inside his green silk waistcoat with his mirrored rows of liqueur bottles in the background and the glass shelves of little cakes in front. It pleased us both enormously: me because I made him look like a particularly large and grotesque bottle, him because he thought it showed him as a hero. He insisted on paying me 100,000 lire, which I was exceedingly grateful for and which increased my self-confidence, though I suspect that Louis put him up to it.

Louis was a happy man. Tonto, the Guardis' dog, had run

to him during the fire, and this time they let him keep it. His adoration for the scrawny yellow hound was as ridiculous as it was touching, but there was no doubt that both of them looked a lot better for it. Louis still wore his cynicism and his filthy blue smocks on all occasions, but he lost something of his rebarbative expression. Tonto was positively sleek with good living. His round, brown eyes rolled in doggy ecstasy, his tongue drooled and his unpleasant habit of dragging his anus along the ground by his two front paws disappeared with a change in diet. Louis refused to eat meat, but the dog's ribs were only just visible. I guessed that a lot of omelette had been going his way.

'I think he was more for protection against poachers than anything,' Louis told me. 'Now that Maria is held in such awe, nobody will dare go near them without permission. I hear she has a steady stream of people visiting her these days for medicines and love potions: Nastri is furious.'

'She doesn't really make love potions, does she?'

Louis chortled. 'If she does, I'm sure Tim Danby will be banging on her door. He's driving Sylvia crazy. She said he even proposed marriage to her.'

'Doesn't he realize that women simply loathe bores with beards?'

'Apparently not.'

'Someone should say something. I mean, in a way, it would be quite a good thing for Sylvia to marry and have security, wouldn't it?'

'Why don't you tell him?'

'Perhaps I will.'

'After all,' Louis said, looking at me, 'it isn't likely Dave will come back, is it?'

I stirred my lemon juice, watching the sugar cloud the base.

'Are you thinking about the man in the well?'

'It must be in all our minds. The postcards prove nothing.'

'Louis, shouldn't we do something about it, then? I mean, it's wrong not to.'

'And cause more trouble for Sylvia? She's the one with the legal duty to report him missing.'

'But Louis, they aren't, weren't, married.'

I told him what the Contessa had told me, and about the passport.

'Are you sure it wasn't Sylvia's, the one that you saw? It seems such a stupid thing for her to keep.'

'Yes, absolutely, it was English, with his name on the top. Sylvia's is American, and in her maiden name, Polanski. I know because she showed me, when she went off to France with Mimi.'

'Whatever you saw,' said Louis, sighing, 'it will all have been destroyed by the fire. My advice is, forget it, unless the police find out.'

'But you can't just do that!'

'Can't you? Who misses Dave, really? Whose life did he make better, rather than worse? Izzy's? Slim's? Yours? He was a bad man, Emma, believe me.'

'How bad does someone have to be in order for his murder to be condoned?'

'He got your friend Chiodino onto heroin, for example.' I was silent.

'How do you know?'

'I know. He bought drugs for everybody stupid enough to take them round here. Even the Santorno police had started to cotton on; it was one of the reasons why Dave wanted to go away for a bit.

'Emma, there is nothing worse or more destructive than someone who has the perceptions of an artist without the talent or, more important, the discipline to realize them. That was what Dave was like. Failed writers are even worse than

265

failed actors, and he was both. He was fascinated by people, he wanted to find out always what made them tick; but he didn't understand that people aren't like clocks. You can't take them apart and put them together again without killing something.'

'He didn't kill Sylvia.'

'Didn't he? How do you know what she was like before? Why do you think she paints so little?'

'Because she doesn't make herself, she's too in thrall to her emotions.'

'No. There is a difference between sowing wild oats and going to seed. He did that to her.'

'Lucio says they were the perfect couple, before the affair with Izzy.'

'Lucio! He's another one.'

'What do you mean?' I demanded, starting to lose my temper. 'Just because Dave told the Guardis where their dog was, of all the silly things, you hate him? Why shouldn't he? Tonto was their dog.'

Louis looked at me, his little eyes hard.

'Anything done in a spirit of malice is unforgivable,' he said. 'Stupidity may be more destructive, but malice – that is blackness, true evil.'

'I don't believe in such absolutes. There is no such thing as black and white, only colour.'

'Yes. But you should know, black absorbs all the colours of the spectrum into itself, and white reflects them. You may think that painting is only a matter of trying to capture what you see, but it is a moral activity, also. You are not only recording truths, you are judging between them. That is one difference between an artist and a machine.'

I had cause to doubt these words when I saw the exhibition the Virginian art class put on in the Santorno Comune.

The Comune was a tall, thin building in Piazza Felice, next to the Teatro della Commedia (now a cinema showing pornographic films). It was plain enough, pierced by a rising series of arched windows, but its main feature was a balcony, tacked on to the front and supported by two marble, muscle-bound giants: the sort who in real life would have had a tough time trying to get a shaving brush near their cheeks because of their bulging biceps. They were the butt of endless practical jokes, these statues. Hardly a week passed without some wit draping them with sausages, sticking cigarettes in their hands or painting their genitals bright red. They had the irresistible comedy of great bad art. Periodically, their removal was mooted by the Comune, especially as they had been erected during the Fascist era. However, they were never got rid of because incoming mayors liked making speeches from the balcony so much.

Inside, it was cool and white, with plenty of spotlights, for an antiques fair was held there in autumn, and sometimes wedding receptions when more than one family wanted Max's. It was the ideal place to have an exhibition, but nothing could improve the standard of what was on display.

There were vast, violent daubs of colour, which might as well have been executed in Virginia, for all that they were given pretentious titles like 'Chiaroscuro 1 and 'Rinascimento'. There were lifeless copies of well-known postcards on display in the tobacconist's, and twee cats sniffing pots of geraniums. Complexions were rendered in seagreen or livid mauve, as if the sitter were the victim of acute nausea (which they probably were after, if not before). There were olive wood sculptures with long, typed explanations in English and Italian expounding on the artist's view of creativity; and collages and embroidered tapestries of the Tuscan landscape which made it appear to be a mass of animated vegetation from another planet.

I was tremendously cheered by the badness of what I saw,

then depressed. They were four or five years older than I was, and the sheer degree of technical incompetence staggered me as much as the lack of aesthetic judgement. Yet the dignitaries of the town and some newspaper critics were all standing round looking grave and approving. Why did nobody else stand in the middle of the room, as Andrew Evenlode was doing, and grin?

'The sculpture makes me wish, as Randall Jarrell once said, that wood had less grain.'

'Thank goodness someone else thinks they stink.'

'There's nothing wrong with this lot that more education and less exercise wouldn't cure. It never seems to strike anyone there that glowing good health and intelligence are strictly incompatible. Look at the Japanese, tiny and dying of cancer, but twice as bright as these Amazonian bird-brains.'

'That could just be genetics.'

'Nonsense. Think of Proust, Schubert, Hawkins, Einstein, Keats. When science abolished syphilis and TB, heaven knows how many poets went down the drain. Ditto with manic depression and dwarfism. By the time we have genetic screening, we won't stand a chance. The Greeks knew what they were about when they made Hephaistos a cripple.'

'So your theory is, we should all strive to be syphilitic, tubercular, manic-depressive homosexual dwarves? What about those born to such affliction, without the talent or willpower to compensate for it?'

'There's a price for everything, unfortunately. Which would you have, a hundred healthy morons with perfect eyesight and no idea how to use it, or a single Degas?'

'Just because they can't paint doesn't mean they might not do something good or useful.'

'Like the girls you were at school with? Be careful, that sounds as though you're mellowing. I prefer you green and sour.'

'Or dry to wet?'

'Do you want an apology?'

'Not if I have to ask for it.'

He looked down at me, beakily. 'What a lot of trouble you're going to cause when you get to Oxford.'

'If I go.'

'If you go. How much longer are you going to dither like this? It isn't fair on others, you know. Think of all the disappointed candidates who'd jump at the chance to take your place. You really are behaving like a spoilt brat.'

'I can't decide, I can't decide,' I said, my voice becoming shrill.

Several Santornese looked round and began to whisper among themselves when they saw us talking. I lowered my voice.

'Don't nag me, Andrew, please. I can't cope with it now.'

'I didn't mean to nag,' he said. 'Actually, I meant to ask if you'd accept a commission. I'd like you to paint a portrait of Claudia for me.'

That was the infuriating thing about Evenlode: whenever I had made my mind up he was an absolute stinker, he'd do something kind. I accepted, of course, and as soon as it became known, my stock went up no end. Louis had been wrong: if I cared to, I could have kept myself afloat painting icky pastels of the wives and daughters of the professional classes until kingdom come, after that. Of course, good portraits don't come for the asking. I preferred to turn down my chance to paint the little Nastris, and continue decorating furniture with cabbage roses for the carpenter.

Signora Ferranti was impressed beyond measure, even before I began work on Evenlode's commission. Nothing would now satisfy her but that I paint her, too.

The trouble was, I longed to paint Lucio's mother, but not in such guise as she would have been pleased with. It was one thing to fool Tony or perceive something different in Lotto, but

269

Signora Ferranti's eye was sufficiently sharpened by maternal jealousy to know a gorgon when she saw one. She would ask me to make her thinner, or younger, or something, and then we would end up having the ding-dong battle that always loomed in the air without breaking whenever we met. She was not, however, to be deflected.

'Mama says, will you come and have dinner with us, just a plate of pasta, *in famiglia*, one night?'

I had to say yes, of course. There was no evasive action, with the Ferrantis living just across the courtyard; she could see exactly who came and went.

The evening was a disaster from beginning to end.

It all started when Signora Ferranti cut her finger making bolognese sauce.

Now, I had gathered, more or less, that Italians think the possession of good health the single most important thing in life. Where English people talk about the weather, Italians will discuss their livers with the liveliest anxiety, going into long monologues about how many eggs a week their doctor permits, and the overriding necessity of eating meat every day. (Lucio used to tell me, most of Italy's foreign debt is to Argentina, to pay for the importation of beefsteak.) Scars in the most intimate places will be publicly revealed by icons of respectability, following convalescence, and the slightest alteration in bowel movement or digestion is discussed before the entire family in gruesome detail.

Nobody is immune from this neurosis, least of all doctors. Caroline had told me that the man in charge of the hospital, Dottor Mantovani, was a quivering wreck of hypochondria.

'You go to see him with backache, and he nods his head and says, "I know, Signorina, I can hardly bend over myself." It's useless trying to complain of fatigue, he'll tell you he can barely stay awake without twenty cups of coffee a day, and as for blood pressure, as soon as he reads your result, his own shoots up far higher than anyone on the verge of a heart attack. I know, he showed me,' Caroline said, through more than usually clenched teeth. She did, indeed, look quite exhausted these days, for between them, Tim and Sylvia were not giving her an easy time.

'I thought that when Izzy came in with her baby, he'd be foxed, but damnit if he didn't go down with phantom puerperal fever on the spot. The nurses spent far more time looking after him than they did Slim or Izzy combined. The one good thing is, he always suffers so much more than you do that you go away feeling much better. Italian medicine is quite, quite extraordinary. Izzy's parents were perfectly right to be so worried about her staying here. She was lucky to get away with it as she did.'

So, when Signora Ferranti cut her finger chopping an onion, I really should have known better than to remark, gaily, 'Never mind, signora, I'm sure a little blood will add flavour to the sauce.'

There was a deathly silence. Signora Ferranti made a frightful grimace at me, and Lucio, who had been discussing the chances of Juventus winning the European cup with his father, jumped up at once and made a great fuss of her.

'Poor Mamma, poor Mamina,' he crooned, running the afflicted finger under a cold tap, while Signor Ferranti cranked off to get the first-aid box. It was only a little cut, but he came back with half a pharmacy of ointments and iodine bottles, all of which were tenderly applied. Last, a gigantic white bandage was wound round and round and tied at the top with an elaborate bow, rendering the whole hand quite useless, though the long, crimson talon of her forefinger still protruded at the end.

I could not help giggling, watching this, for Signora Ferranti's eyes rolled like a duck's in a thunderstorm; I really did think it must be a joke, because it was such a small cut. But, when it was finished, Lucio turned to me with a black look and beckoned me out of the room.

'You have insulted the three most sacred things in an Italian house,' he hissed. 'My mother, my mother's health, and my mother's cooking.'

I began to laugh, then realized he meant it.

'Oh, Lucio, I really am most terribly sorry.'

'You will have to apologize, and finish making the supper yourself, now,' he said, in a tone which brooked no argument.

I did not relish displaying my culinary skills to a woman whose son believed her to be a better cook than me. Lucio poured scorn on his own countrymen, but it was at times like these that I realized how foreign we were to each other. It was like trying to understand the difference between the sexes: I would bowl along, thinking that we were pretty much alike, and then some kink or predilection, in bed or out of it, would reveal that we belonged to utterly alien species. Most of the time, this shock of novelty was exciting or intriguing, but on other occasions, such as now, it was just a bore.

I wondered what it would be like to be Signora Ferranti's daughter-in-law. It was not an agreeable prospect.

She recovered soon enough, once I offered to take over the cooking, though the injury to her finger appeared to have affected her legs as well. From then on, Signora Ferranti sat in a chair like a female general, pointing with that long red talon protruding from its cocoon of bandage to direct me, getting more and more impatient by the minute. Signor Ferranti had gone back to his newspaper, now the drama was over, but popped his head round every three minutes to ask how supper was getting on. He had an ulcer, his wife told me, with an accusing glare, and must on no account miss the prompt arrival of meals.

I had not been so nervous since I left school. My hands shook as I chopped and stirred and peeled and boiled. If I had had any sense, I'd have chopped my finger, too, and taken the wind out of her sails, but I was determined not to be cowed. How I would have loved to have painted her, seated in that high plush chair, her jet-black hair standing out like an enamelled nest of vipers, her square, gold-filled teeth flashing and gnashing in her hard red mouth as she barked out directions in that deep, raucous voice! She was the Medusa of the provinces. No wonder, I thought, Lucio only liked strong women.

'Chop more finely! No, with that knife, not the one you're using. No, with the other knife, are you blind? Keep stirring, I can smell something starting to burn. Are you sure nothing is sticking to the pan? I'm sure I can smell something burning, Hemma. Burnt food gives Signor Ferranti indigestion, it keeps us both awake all night, everyone in this family is a martyr to it. If only I hadn't cut my finger, not that I'm complaining, but the onion juice went into it, I'm sure it's infected, I'll have to see Dottor Mantovani tomorrow, I don't trust that man Nastri any longer after the disgrace when he tried to molest me. I'm sure something is burning. Lucio, *caro*, check to see whether your *fidanzata* is burning your dinner. No, not that pot, this one. *Porca Madonna!* I'm sure Gabriella would have done better than this in an Englishwoman's kitchen!'

It was the first time she had mentioned Lucio's sister to me. A spasm passed down her husband's face and made his Adam's apple quiver as if swallowing a bolus of bile. He was a dry old stick, but now I suddenly saw that his quietness, his faddishness, his insistence on routine were ways of coping with an overwhelming emotion. There was no doubt in my mind that to Signora Ferranti, Lucio was the important one, but her desiccated husband still wore his black armband for the dead Gabriella, though it was, like his grief, almost imperceptible. I wondered how my own father would react if I were to die so. A vision of his oyster eyes brimming with tears at Max's welled up in my memory. It struck me, with the force of revelation, that my father might after all love me, and be as incapable of expressing it as Lucio's father; but I dismissed the idea immediately as sentimental. If either of them loved me, they would have written. There was that ineradicable fact. They would have tried to mend matters between us, not rely on me crawling back to them when poverty demanded it.

Oh, the agonies of that dinner! I can't cook much at the best of times, and when distressed, all dexterity deserts me. Lucio made a joke of it afterwards, saying that I should sell the recipe to the Mafia as an alternative to concrete boots, but it was utter humiliation at the time. He and his father chomped valiantly away at my half-cooked mound of spaghetti in the manner of Laocoon and his sons struggling with the Hydra, but Signora Ferranti pushed her plate away with a bright smile after a single mouthful, and ostentatiously confined herself to a diet of bread and wine until the fruit course.

I was reduced to a glowering silence. There was no doubt about it, her triumph would have been complete – except, of course, that she wanted me to paint her portrait. She only remembered this while I was making coffee.

'Well, now!' she said archly, watching my struggles with the espresso machine. 'What if I give you cooking lessons in return for a portrait, Hemma? You're certainly going to need them if my son isn't going to die of indigestion every evening.'

'Mamma!' said Lucio, but she took no notice.

'I understand now why he has such terrible constipation. I hear him groaning away in the mornings, it's been a real worry to me, I can tell you, but after what I've seen this evening—'

'Mamma!' Lucio implored. 'Please, these are not things which the English think proper to discuss.'

'The English! The English! And what are they, pray? We were discovering America while they were still swinging about in the trees,' said Signora Ferranti with magnificent disdain, twitching her bandaged talon. 'You can't possibly compare them to us! We are civilized; they are barbarians!'

'Mamma, in England everything works,' Lucio said patiently. 'The post gets delivered, they have pop concerts, the trains run on time, the—'

'So they did in the days of Mussolini,' Signora Ferranti interrupted. 'People can say what they like about the Fascists, but they made this country work. I was there, and I know it! Now what do we have? The Red Brigade in the north and the Mafia in the south, and Africa in Rome. To think I should live to see the day when a Hungarian *putana* is elected to the government because she stuffs a python up her arse! It's a casino!'

Lucio rolled his eyes at me. I admired him for putting up with her as he did. I would have been at her throat hours ago, had she been my own mother, but that habit of filial obedience was too strong in him.

Yes, too strong.

'I am an ogress and the descendant of ogresses,' I told myself, but in Signora Ferranti I had met more than my match. My heart misgave me, my confidence vanished, and I sank back into gloom.

21

The skies turned hazy at the start of September. Mornings and evenings, the air was tinted with a luminous, Byzantine gold, making the near seem far and the far near. From my bedroom window, the small hills dotting the plain below became islands again, floating in mist, though the cicadas continued to sing and the sun to glaze the enamelled heavens an even deeper blue. The last sunflowers bloomed, and turned black. Crops of maize were harvested, and the fields ploughed up, mostly by tractors but occasionally, up in the hills, by a pair of milk-white oxen dragging a rigid share. The greengrocers' were full of ripe figs. A red and yellow tinge appeared on the ends of certain vines on the Dunnetts' hillside, like a slow-burning fuse.

In the palazzo gardens, Guido and Maria's grandfather were busy all day with the electric pruners, trimming the yew giants and their children into shape for winter.

'I always feel they should be allowed to grow a winter coat, like animals,' said the Contessa, 'but it would mean too much work in spring. And who knows, besides, how many more springtimes I may see?'

'Don't say that, please.'

'Why not? We are too afraid of death, these days. I look forward to the grave, you know: it seems to me the most comfortable of beds. "Ay, but to die, and go we know not where"; what nonsense! We go into the earth and decay, and a good thing it is, too. What heaven could be better than to be transformed into the lilies of the field? I would far rather nourish a bee than play a harp!'

She nodded her head so vigorously that her earrings flashed, like tears that never fell. What a pity it was that she and Sylvia could not become acquainted, with their common love of nature. Yet the Contessa's was that of an informed and active mind, whereas Sylvia's was passive and contemplative. They would probably only irritate each other, as Andrew and I did.

I sighed, and dabbled my brush around two blobs of colour on my china plate.

'You don't use a palette?' the Contessa asked.

'No. It wastes paint. This way, I can cover it over with cling-film at the end of the day.'

'So necessity is indeed the mother of invention?'

'Well ... mothers are a necessity, but I'm not sure about the reverse. I'm not too good on mothers.'

She smiled briefly, revealing the brown stumps of old ivory. Her hooded lids, veined the colour of autumn crocus, her withered skin and merlin's nose gave me infinite pleasure. I never realized how much greater the ruins of beauty can be than beauty itself, until I began to paint the Contessa. Even if Andrew were not paying me, I would have wished to do it above all else, once begun, for every day that I worked seemed to bring about great leaps of understanding.

I had longed for beauty with all my heart, venerated it, turned it almost into a religion, only to be confounded by it. I had hated and despised most contemporary painters because they had given up this struggle in favour of depicting political opinions or the arcane symbols of their inner worlds – subjects which an artist has no business inflicting on anyone else, any more than a dancer should get up and display her broken toes instead of dancing on them.

I still despised their cult of deliberate ugliness and obfuscation, but now I had come to see that the beauty which hit me between the eyes, like Sylvia's or Lucio's, was not the only kind worth having. There were subtler gradations, the palimpsest of personality, as astounding as any aesthetic arrangement of form or feature once I began looking. My grandfather had told me to look for the darkest dark and the lightest light, but it is not a question of searching for extremes. When I began painting Lotto and Tony, I started to understand the intense satisfaction of plainness: how the bulge of a fat belly could be as mesmerising as the Renaissance ideal, how the little broken veins could be as delightful as smooth and unblemished skin.

The Contessa sat very upright in her dark-blue dress, with the autumnal hills and plains of Tuscany behind. On the inlaid marble table beside her was a basket of eggs, a wine glass half-filled with water, a bottle of red wine with a corkscrew known as a Cristo in the cork, and a Lotto bowl of roses. Andrew had given me no guide to what he wanted, but I knew he would understand such language, the pattern in which the objects were arranged, and this thought gave me a deep satisfaction. He had finished his book, but I hardly saw him at all these days.

'He is delaying his return again, until the last moment,' the Contessa told me. 'He has such love for this part of the world, you know. He insists on travelling back by train, which I tell him will take twice as long, but he has a detestation of aeroplanes. It amuses me, these young men pretending to be old ones, while so many of the old cling to their youth.'

'Tell me about my grandfather, please.'

'What do you wish to know?'

'Everything.'

'I would not tell you everything, my dear, even if I could.'

'Well, then, what you can. How did you meet him?'

'The winter after the war, I returned from America, where my husband had insisted on sending me because of my English mother,' the Contessa began, in her soft cello voice. 'I was convulsed with bitterness. Ah, yes, it was a bad time for everyone in Europe. So much poverty, so much grief, so much guilt. People were stunned, first by victory, then by the understanding of how much evil had been at work. A cruel winter. I had lost everyone, my father, my mother, my husband, my son. What that means, my dear, I pray you will never know ... My marriage had been arranged between our two families, but my husband and I became lovers. I was sixteen at the time of my marriage, and nearly forty when he was murdered. I had no existence, no personality beyond my life with him, or so I thought.

'It is a miracle, to marry for money and find love. Too much; it tempts the gods. I had more than most, yes, twenty years of happiness, and then it was all lost and gone. I thought it would have been better never to have known it, that it is better never to have loved than to love and lose, whatever the poets say.'

I sat up at this. Andrew had refused to tell me, that evening, about what it was like to live without. He had spoken lightly of his past affair, but I wondered now how much it must have affected him, to make him leave England for nine months. No, decidedly, I could not cut myself off from Lucio and return, if that was what it felt like. In my perturbation, I missed what the Contessa was saying.

' ... Italy again, though I longed for it also. I spent some time in Chelsea, with my mother's family. A strange, wild part of London it was then, half bombed, and haunted by the ghost of Augustus John or his many children. The buildings that were left huddled together, street after street of slums. I did not know what I was doing, half the time, but it seemed to me that if I could not kill myself, I must be waiting for some sign ... I fell

279

into the habit of going to the Chelsea Physic Gardens; the high walls reminded me of the palazzo, they made me feel at home, though I had no courage to return to Santorno.

'We met there, your grandfather and I. It was over a clump of hellebore, I remember. I knew nothing of gardens or plants then. I saw this strange, delicate white flower, in the middle of so much winter desolation, and it seemed to me a kind of miracle, the sign I had been waiting for. He told me it was the Christmas rose, which was said to have blossomed the night of Christ's birth, alone of all plants, in His honour . . . He was the most charming young man, with such fierce blue eyes. He was just about to go up to university, like you, my dear. We became friends, and later he came to stay at the palazzo. He was a great storyteller and adventurer; but this you must already know.'

'My father says he was a tyrant.'

'I fear he was not a good husband or father. He did not understand women. That was one of his charms, I may say. There is a fatal belief most women have that they can change men; it is what leads us to love alcoholics or criminals, and it is worse when it has something to do with a man's nature. As a friend, he was ideal, but as a lover he must have been dementing. Yes, I can see that. He was too solitary by nature, too impatient. He had the habit of finishing off other people's sentences. Your father was of a different temperament. He always struck me as longing for the warmth he had lacked in childhood.'

'Why did he marry my mother, then?' I burst out. 'Andrew called her an ogress, and he's right.'

'Who can tell why anyone marries? I do not know either of your parents well. Perhaps she is not as cold as you think. Perhaps she has altered to become so, or hidden her true nature. She has great energies and nowhere to direct them, I suspect. It is a problem for women of the generations before yours, my dear. We were not educated to use our intelligence for anything other than getting a husband and making a home, and people of your parents' kind were, and are, the most conservative. It is not true that to understand all is to forgive all, but if you love them, you will understand more.'

I pondered this. The nature of everyone I loved or knew was an endless puzzle to me. I kept thinking that, if I had enough information about their lives, all would suddenly become clear and sharp. Instead they became magnified into an abstraction, as faces dissolve when seen too close. My family and my fellow pupils had irritated me beyond endurance, lacking the gloze of distance. Yet living with Sylvia, and even with Lucio, I had begun to lose sight of the way they had first seemed to me, and I regretted it. Lucio said that nothing about him should disgust me, or vice versa, but how could it remain so?

'Contessa, is it really possible to continue loving someone despite their faults, no matter how bad they are?'

'Why, yes. It is not only possible, but essential,' she said, sharply. 'When one falls in love, my dear, one does so as the kings and queens of countries used to do. You are shown, not the real person, but an idealized portrait of them, as they, or you, would like them to be. Then, when the reality appears, there is the terrible shock. The hair that was gold is bleached, the spirit that seemed happy is sad, the smile that delighted has teeth like a line of washing on a windy day. For some, the shock is so unacceptable that they spend their lives moving from one person to the next, always looking for the image, not the truth.'

'But there must be people who fall in love, who really are incompatible,' I interrupted. 'People who really do discover they can't live together.'

'Yes. If it is something fundamental in their nature, it cannot work, and it is better it should end. But, more often, lovers part because of a lack of self-knowledge in the first place as to what will really make them happy, and what they themselves have to offer. So much of love is misplaced self-love, my dear, not the acceptance, the delight in a particular otherness. To love another not despite but because of all that is different: that is the real test.'

I thought about this, walking down the gloomy cypress avenue in its eternal twilight of marble statues and whispering streams. Conversations with the Contessa always made my head buzz and ache. I was too frightened of her to adore her, as I had done Sylvia, but I respected her more than anyone since my grandfather.

Sylvia had told me about life, but the Contessa somehow showed it to me, always taking what I knew and changing it, as a prism splits light into the spectrum. Listening to her strange, poetic English, or to Evenlode, I had the sensation of shifting around great half-comprehended thoughts and feelings, an act at once exhausting and exhilarating. Had I loved Sylvia because of myself, or because of what I had seen in her? In a way, I conceded, the former.

I had loved in her what I had wanted myself to become: just as, really, I had hated my parents because they were all I did not want to become. But was Sylvia in herself lovable, or my parents hateful? And, surely, the Contessa's observation did not apply to sexual love, which must, by its very nature, involve this mysterious appreciation of otherness she seemed to find so important?

Without intention, I found myself on the little path that led down from the parterre to Sylvia's house. The wood had escaped the flames, so the shock of what I saw was all the greater on emerging.

It was a desolate sight. The house was black, with charred and tortured stumps of olive trees all around. I could look straight down into it, as if reading an architect's plan. It was a heap of rubble – beams, smashed tiles, scorched stone, nothing but the shell with empty holes for windows. I was astonished at how small it was: just three rooms above and three below.

It was indescribably strange, seeing it like this. I knew that house and its surroundings so well, it was like seeing double, the vision of how it had been rose up so strongly to my inner eye. How happy Sylvia and I had been, those three months, in the wind and cold and rain! Was it because we had both been in love with the same man, or would it have been the same without him? She had said, once, that it was only possible to appreciate a landscape when one was in love, which should have made me realize.

She had seemed so tranquil; surely, if the body were Dave's, and she had put it there, she would not have been so? But then, I had noticed so little, absorbed as I was in thoughts of Lucio, and trying to paint. How bad had her sudden bouts of depression been? I had put habits like howling at weather forecasts down to the artistic temperament, but I could easily have been mistaken. The depths of my naivety humiliated and appalled me, the more I plumbed them. I had thought I knew everything, because I had read such a lot, but really in some ways I was stupider than the girls I had been to school with.

What did I really know of Sylvia, or anyone, come to that? 'A man is a cloud in trousers,' Max's grandfather had said. How could there be any constancy, any consistency? I had quite liked Dave, but both Louis and Izzy, who knew him far better, insisted he was destructive, a bad man, better gone. Yet their own perspectives on him were far from objective. How could Lucio love me, or I Lucio, when neither of us knew what we were, or would become? Although he believed he would never change.

He insisted that character was fixed from the moment of birth, and that nothing short of a knock on the head would

283

alter it. He said I disagreed because I had no interest in children, otherwise I would see how different they were, right from the start, just as he and his sister had been, even though they were two halves of the same being. People changed only in that their personalities became more concentrated with time: reduced, he said, like a pot of sauce on a stove. I thought they altered beyond recognition, as new ingredients were added.

'In seven years, every cell in your body will have changed, so how can you still be the same? How can you judge what is a different being?' I asked.

'You can, and must,' he said. 'Change is an illusion.'

Idly, I began to kick over bits of rubble in the ruins of the living room. No illusion here. It was like sifting through a jig-saw puzzle; I recognized fragments of familiar objects: the head of a small blue vase in the shape of a bear with open jaws, the rim of a jug, a lamp split exactly in half, the charred cover of a paperback now called *Bright Li*. The fire had turned *Success* into *cess*; a blockbuster announced itself as *tiny*, while another warned, *ages*. So much dust and paper. Bits of Sylvia's portfolio, delicate watercolour landscapes I had seen nearly two years ago in the Serpentine and now recognized as this hill or that. Postcards, a carved wooden bow from her wardrobe, wire hangers, glittering fragments of bevelled glass.

Ashes and twisted nails. I kicked some more, and uncovered what I least expected to find undamaged: Sylvia's Indian box.

The clasp had come undone in the fall, and her jewellery was scattered or crushed, but the drawer was still intact, with its secret inside.

After my conversation with Louis, I had begun to doubt what I had seen in Sylvia's room, but there it still was: the bundle of money, thinner now, and the blue and gold English passport with the name, David John Lurie, inscribed in the barbarous hand of some Foreign Office clerk in Rome. It had seven years left to run, gave his height as five foot eleven and his eyes as blue. I remembered those eyes, their intensity, the way they had focused on me as though I were the only person in the room. Nobody had looked at me like that, not even Lucio . . . certainly not the elusive Andrew Evenlode.

Someone else was coming down the path, a man, to judge by the noise. I didn't know what to do, so I put the passport into my bag, leaving the money, and shut the drawer again.

'Found anything?'

It was Tim Danby, all whiskers and sandals, clambering down the steps.

'Not much,' I lied. 'A jewellery box of Sylvia's. Here, give it to her. Nothing of mine. I left a painting or two behind.'

'Bad luck.'

He thumped down, grinning and sweating. Poor Tim, I reflected; he had the sort of open, unimaginative masculinity that was so outdated as to be utterly repulsive to any woman with a shred of imagination. You could see he was bewildered by his lack of success. He wasn't that bad-looking, he was nice enough, decent enough, but not enough. His eyes had that puzzled, oxlike look at the back of them. You see men like Tim everywhere in England: good blokes drinking their blokish pints in pubs: men who approach women like a mechanic trying to fix a bicycle with a pair of tweezers, then wonder why they never get anywhere.

'How's Sylvia?'

His face lit up, though he frowned at the same time.

'Well, she's not very good. Cries a lot. I've been trying to get her to contact Dave through the embassies, to find out whether the house was insured, but she won't hear of it. Too proud, you see.'

'Yes, I know. I wish I could do something.' If she knew that

Dave was dead, I thought, the last thing she would want was to draw attention to the fact through official channels.

Tim sat down on what remained of the steps. 'I didn't realize they weren't even married.'

'Didn't you?'

'No. She always gave the impression that they were. He never told Izzy, neither.'

'I wonder why.'

'I suppose he thought that that way he might, um, screw more money out of her,' Tim said, with surprising shrewdness. 'Though I doubt whether Sylvia would have seen any of it. Christ, that man is a bastard. You know, every time I hear of another disaster, an earthquake here or a train crash there, I hope he's in it. It seems so unfair that innocent people should be killed when there's someone like him walking the planet.'

This was the longest speech I had ever heard him make, and I looked at him with sudden interest. What if –? How long had he been in love with Sylvia? I thought. Before the party, that was certain; I had seen the way he had behaved towards her that evening. Hopeful, faithful, dogged, men like him never stood a chance and they were probably the ones most deserving of love all along.

'He cheated you with the farm, didn't he?'

'Yup. Trusted him. My own stupid fault. I should have checked.'

'Had you farmed before?'

'Our parents did. Rhodesia. They left for England in the seventies, when we were teenagers. Caro and I couldn't stand the weather. But it's a hard life in the mountains. I'd do something else now, if I knew what.'

'Why don't you take over Slim's shop?'

'And do what?' he asked, drawing lines in the dust with his sandal.

'Not make shoes. Do something, provide something everyone wants.' I thought of the last morning I had spent in Sylvia's house. 'A launderette, for instance. I'm not the only person who has to wash sheets and clothes by hand in Santorno. Those Americans were always complaining about it. Hardly anyone has a washing machine in the lower town. I'm sure Sylvia would help.'

'She doesn't like staying with us,' he confided, awkwardly. 'I hoped, if she came to live ... I can see her looking at things, criticizing.'

Now for it, I thought. 'Well, she is a very fastidious person, Tim.'

'She didn't keep her own house very tidy, though, did she?'

'No, but she's extremely sensitive to, well, smells.' Oh, sod it, I thought, why not tell him the lot? 'She likes people to be clean, and wear clean clothes, and, well, shave.'

'What's wrong with a bit of pong?' he asked, sulkily. 'It's natural. Besides, I hate shaving. It makes my face itch.'

'Well, you'll have to decide which you like most, beard or Sylvia,' I said in a brisk, encouraging voice. It was, after all, one thing for me to perceive beauty in a Lotto, and quite another for someone like Sylvia to perceive lovability in a Tim.

'D'you think that's really all it is?' Tim asked, looking like a goat spotting a rosebush.

No, of course it isn't, you silly twit, I thought; you know nothing about art, or making love, or anything but your boring farm. Oh, why isn't conversation taught in schools, instead of all those useless lessons on periodic tables and capital cities? Why don't you go off and read something other than *The Hitchhiker's Guide to the Galaxy*, learn to play the guitar, get rid of your blackheads, realize that your unvarnished self simply will not do? Why don't you fill her bathtub with flowers or take her to a hotel in Venice? Why are Englishmen so hopelessly bone-headed?

'I'm sure it will help no end,' I lied.

'Well, it's worth a try, I suppose.'

He lapsed into silence, and I made a move to leave. The sun was setting, and I wanted to begin making supper for Lucio, like a good housewife or mistress.

'You staying on, then? Or hasn't term started?'

'Yes, and no. It starts in a fortnight, but I'm not going.'

'I'll tell Sylvia. She was asking after you.'

'Was she?' I felt a mixture of hope and unease, hearing this.

'Yup. See you at the *vendemmia*?'

'What?'

'The Dunnetts are having a final vintage, next week if this sun keeps on. Everyone's coming who wants to, including the Guardis and that Oxford bloke you know.'

'Oh.' I felt apprehensive, thinking of seeing Evenlode again and telling him I wouldn't be coming back. He would be angry, I was sure, and yet I wanted to see him. 'Well, see you there, then. Don't forget what I said.'

'No. She'll have to put up with me while I'm trying, though,' he said. 'She's got nowhere else to go.'

'No.'

But we were both wrong. When I got back to Santorno, the whole of Via Garibaldi and the two piazzas were buzzing with scandal, like an overturned beehive. Instead of the usual evening promenade, the ritual of seeing and being seen, people were gathered in excited little knots, laughing and talking. It took some time to work out exactly what had happened, but the gist of it was, Max had left his wife and eloped with Mimi.

22

Afterwards everyone, including myself, wondered how they could have been so stupid. Why else had Max had Mimi's keys, after all? Why else had his car been parked by the rubbish dump when Lucio and J had been making love there? Why had she thought his wife would want to snoop round her flat?

Mimi had concealed the affair by flirting outrageously with everyone; there was not a man over sixteen who had failed to doubt she was doing it with one of their friends, or boasted that he, too, had conquered the Australian blonde. In reality, she had been utterly chaste with everyone but Max, and even him, I realized, she had deliberately worked into a frenzy of jealousy sufficient for him to throw everything else up in order to have her to himself.

Yes, she had been clever. Everyone agreed it, though all condemned it; especially, needless to say, Nastri and the women of Santorno. It was just as well the American students were leaving or they might have been lynched in her place, so high were some of the passions aroused by this coup, or *coup de foudre*.

In the Bar Popolare, Louis rocked with laughter.

'Ah, that Australian, she was like the butterfly with spots like eyes on its wings, you all believed what she showed you! A pretty, painted lady: to pretend to be a whore and live like a good wife, how much wiser than the other way about! No wonder they are all so angry. She has made them see what they are. She had everyone fooled.'

Had she? I remembered that exchange at the party between Mimi and Dave, when the latter had said how keen she was on money. At the time, looking at her clothes, I had thought nothing of it, and then, like everyone else, I had assumed she was being overpaid for her services as an English mistress ... But what if Dave had seen something? Where had that roll of money come from? Izzy would not have paid him to go away, after all, and he wasn't the sort to save up. What if he had been blackmailing Mimi and Max, and been murdered instead? But then, how had his passport and money come into Sylvia's hands? Why would Max kill him, when he could pay him to leave anyway? If the body was Dave's ... There had been nothing more in the newspapers; the whole business was completely cast into the shade by Max's elopement.

My portrait of Tony was hung prominently on display in the front of the Bar Popolare, somewhat to my embarrassment. The carpenter had made a charming frame for it; my decorated cabinets had sold so well (particularly to the Americans, which I found highly amusing) he wanted me to do more, which was just as well, as my two English pupils had informed me they were stopping their private lessons.

'At least it means I can pay the rent,' I told Tony. 'It'll be freezing in winter at the Pistoias', though. I'll have to save up and buy a stove.'

He looked as surprised as his doughy face permitted. 'But Signorina Hemma, now that the Australian *professoressa* has left, why don't you go back to teaching English? You could even rent her flat, if you wanted.'

I thought of the grim oubliette below the piazza, and shuddered; but the idea of teaching children again was not unendurable. With more money, perhaps Lucio would leave his mother's altogether ... I still hadn't written to the Oxford authorities to let them know I wouldn't be taking my place there.

Why should I go? I thought. What could a three-year course in history of art teach me that I couldn't teach myself if I stayed on in Tuscany? Why should I go back to being dependent on my parents, or the state; what would I have in common with a bunch of spotty students, when I could be a grown-up with other grown-ups? Here, I was certain of a place in Santorno society, I had adapted, been accepted: there, the whole damned business of English snobbery would begin all over again.

'That's a good idea, Tony; thank you.'

'And how is the weather in England?'

'I've no idea, I'm afraid.'

He smote his head with a podgy hand. 'Ah, that reminds me. This came for you, the day of the fire, and in the excitement I forgot.'

From between two liqueur bottles, he fished out an air-mail envelope.

I took it, though I was tempted to throw it into the bin, and put it into my bag.

'Aren't you going to read it?' he asked seriously.

'I'm sure it's not important. If it were, she'd have sent a telegram, like the last time.'

I had been dreading something like this. My mother's letters were not so much missives as guided missiles; either that, or like something out of Jennifer's Diary. When I had started at boarding school, I had longed for more than bright chat about cats and charities, something that would reveal a shred of tenderness or imagination. I had imagined a correspondence in which my loneliness would be assuaged, my thoughts guided, my feelings understood, but the only dialogue that had developed over the years was one of acrimony. Instead of revealing ourselves to each other, layer after layer, we tore strips off. The dialogue I had sought had come, however spasmodically, from a total stranger: Sylvia.

I went back, slowly, along the Via Garibaldi and climbed the Vicolo delle Sette Stelle. Pistoia was in the garage on the dark ground floor, tinkering with Lucio's car, for he doubled his wages as a taxi driver with occasional work as a mechanic.

'It's not just the fluid, you need new brakes,' he was saying.

'*Porca Madonna*, this is what happens when I buy an Italian car!' Lucio replied gloomily. 'Nothing but rust and problems. I should have tried the Peugeot. *Ciao, amore mio.*'

He kissed me with enthusiasm, and I him.

'Ah, Luciotto, be careful!' Pistoia called after us as we began to climb the stairs. 'She'll get you into church yet!'

'God, I hate that man,' I muttered.

'He's not so bad, for Santorno.'

'Did you know, Lucio, about Max and Mimi?'

'I suspected, yes, when I saw his car next to mine by the rubbish dump.'

'You don't think he saw us, do you?' I asked, blushing scarlet.

He shrugged. 'Why should you care? They were probably doing the same thing we were. People are all the same when they fuck each other.'

'Yes, but ... I still don't like the thought. Believing and seeing aren't the same thing.'

'Aren't they?' he said, kissing me again.

He was gentle and tender to me these days, taking time when we made love instead of rushing at it. I had learned what gave me pleasure, and him; I was less passive, and he liked that. We spent long, slow siestas on the mattresses, buried in each other, concentrating until everything was reduced or magnified to a few inches of muscle and nerve. I was still dependent on his company for such happiness as I had, outside painting, but I had not allowed him to inflict pain or violence on me since the storm. The delirium of the summer had faded, or perhaps it was I who was becoming more confident, less easy to dominate, in bed or out of it. He told me I was becoming a woman, that I had learned to be decisive, and it was true. Nine months ago, I would never have dared to give Tim Danby advice on his appearance: I would simply have disliked it, and him. Shopkeepers no longer frightened me; neither onions nor insolence made me cry ... Whenever I felt this new assertiveness slipping away, I would repeat to myself what Andrew had told me: I am an ogress, and the descendant of ogresses.

It was in this frame of mind that I opened my mother's letter, while Lucio was dozing during the siesta beside me. It began with five engraved words which never failed to infuriate me with their pomposity:

From The Hon. Mrs. C. Kenward

37 Stanhope Square,
SW7
July 20

Oh, the vulgarity of it! Whom was she trying to impress? Why should I give a damn about her wretched family? Her writing, the debased italic of every conventional, unimaginative rich girl, spiked across the paper like barbed wire.

Dear Emma,
    I have not written to you before because our letters have a history of making relations between us worse rather than better.

This was true enough, but my hackles rose immediately at having it pointed out by her.

However, as you are not on the telephone, and your
father tells me that his meeting with you in May was not
satisfactory, I see no alternative but to write to the address
you left as your poste restante in your 'running away'
note. I suppose the Italian posts are no better than they
were when we lived in Rome, so I must just hope this finds
its way to you in time.

I smiled grimly at this. My mother's letters were not only guided missiles, they were equipped with heat-seeking devices as well. They could be guaranteed to arrive at their destination where all else failed. 'Running away', indeed! I had done it, hadn't I?

I am sure you will agree that matters cannot continue in
this fashion. It is a situation both painful and embarrassing
for the whole family [more the latter than the former, I said to myself; lady magistrates are not supposed to have difficulties with their own children, only other people's] *and one which has to be resolved. You may not like us much as parents, and we find it difficult to like you at present* [so, the old bitch still knew how to flick open old wounds] *but we are stuck with each other for the rest of our lives, and we have to learn some kind of 'modus vivendi'.*

Rubbish, rubbish! I shouted at her. Millions of families quarrel, part, and leave each other in peace. Why should ours be any different? You don't like me and I don't like you, let's leave it at that!

*I know this will be difficult, and perhaps we should have all
tried to mend bridges much earlier. But the awkward age is
so very awkward, not least because you tend to shut us out
so much. We never realized, for instance, how much you
hated school, where you seemed to be perfectly happy and
outstandingly successful academically.*

I was so stunned by this, I read it over several times. I had
not shut them out, they had shut me. How was I supposed to
take the initiative? Why hadn't they realized that people who
became quiet and bookish usually did so because they weren't
happy? My eye continued to travel along the rest.

*If we were wrong, I am sorry. It is a difficult time for
everybody; my own mother always used to say that the eldest
child was the one parents made the most mistakes on. We
tried not to make the mistakes with you that our own parents
made with us, but it seems only discovered new ones instead.*

This I also read with deep indignation. A mistake! Was that
all they thought I was? My examination results had not been a
mistake, nor my place at Oxford.

*However, we may have been somewhat too hard on you. I
don't know whether your father mentioned it, but Justin has
been expelled from Radleigh for having a party on the roof
at which a couple of boys nearly died of alcohol poisoning.*

Justin, expelled? Ha! That slimy little computer creep, caught
out at last. A thrill of triumphant sibling rivalry went through
me. Then I thought, poor little sod. Imagine what it must be like,
bearing the full brunt of Mummy and Daddy's thwarted ambition. I remembered how I had protected him when he was little,

how close we had been in Rome, how close we had all been ...
Oh, what the hell, why should I care about any of them, anyway?

Your father says you are thinking of not coming back to
England to take your place at Oxford. There is nothing we
can do to make you do so, should this be your decision, but
it would be extremely sad for all of us should you cut off
your nose to spite your face, as it were. I should have gone
to university myself, and always regretted not being given
the chance to do so. I do not want you to go in order to
fulfil my own ambitions, but because it is the best chance
you will ever have of making the right sort of friends.

My sympathies, which had been stirring somewhat,
rebounded. I knew exactly what she meant by 'the right sort of
friends': prematurely middle-aged prats in bow ties, men who
would become like my father, men who could be relied on to
provide the Aga, the labrador and the brats that would keep
me chained to domesticity instead of letting me paint.

Please think it over very carefully, and let us know what
you decide. Your father says you have a job as a teacher,
but if you run into any difficulties, medical or financial,
please don't hesitate to get in touch.

I knew what she meant: she meant that if I needed an abortion they'd make sure it was whipped out rather than bring
further disgrace to the family. Bitch, bitch! To offer money
now, when I didn't need it, and not before, when I had been
half starved all summer ... though how could she have known,
really, about Mimi's job only being temporary?

Love from Mummy.

296

It was such a cold letter, I thought; so controlled. She said they were sorry I had been unhappy at school, but I didn't feel she meant it. Why was she so stiff? I remembered the Contessa saying that she had struck her as someone with nowhere to put her energies, but why hadn't she tried loving me a bit more? Why had it always been Justin?

My father had written a short note in his crabbed, tiny script, which always reminded me of crushed beetles:

Dearest Emma,

Sorry our lunch didn't go so well. I enclose a cheque in case you need anything special for the summer. Please come back, we all miss you.

Daddy

I burst into tears.

'I can't understand why you're so upset,' Lucio said. 'Your parents send you a letter and some money, and now we can go out and have dinner at Max's.'

'It won't be open,' I said, blowing my nose. 'He's left, remember? Everyone's leaving Santorno.'

'You don't think his wife would allow it to close when it's still the tourist season? She'll take him for every penny when he gets a divorce.'

'Lucio, I don't feel like eating in a restaurant tonight, I'm sorry.'

Outside my window the swallows gathered and wheeled over the tiled rooftops. The distant clatter from a passing express train floated up the hillside, overlaid by church bells. The rattle of shutters rolling up at the end of the siesta echoed through the narrow streets. The Pistoias' blackbird tried a short trill, and fell silent. A large, shiny dung beetle flew clumsily into the room, across the landing, and out through the kitchen.

'Let's go to celebrate when I've finished my portrait of the Contessa,' I said, making an effort to conceal my depression and kissing the ear with the black star in it. 'When will that be?'

'Soon. By the end of the week, I should think. The English *professore* is leaving then.'

'And then you will paint my mother?'

'Lucio, I don't think I can.'

'Why not? Is it only the aristocracy you paint now?'

'I am not interested in ideas of that kind.'

'Is it that you think a withered old witch like the Contessa more beautiful than Mama? Or the idiot, Lotto? Or that fat barman at the Popolare?'

I took a deep breath. 'Since you ask me, yes.'

'Why? What is it you have against her, my God? Hasn't she helped you find somewhere to live? Hasn't she had you for dinner in her home? Hasn't she shown you every courtesy? How many Italian mothers do you think would have behaved to their only son's woman, and a foreigner?'

'Lucio, I don't want to discuss this, we'll only quarrel.'

'What is it with you? Why are you always so difficult about everything? Why can't you accept things as they are here?'

A weariness began to creep over me. 'Look, *amore*. I'm depressed, I don't want a row.'

'Depressed? Why should you be depressed when everything is going so well? You say your parents don't love you, and now they write to you, sending money. Oh, I give up. I'm going out.'

He got up and flung on his clothes.

'Lucio, where are you going?'

'What does it matter to you? Out.'

'When will you be back?'

'What business is it of yours? What do you think you are, my wife?'.

'Look, I'm sorry, we'll go out to Max's soon.'

'Ciao!'

'Will you be at the Dunnetts' *vendemmia* tomorrow?' I called over the landing as he clattered down the stairs and slammed the door to the Pistoias' quarters.

He made no answer.

Everyone was leaving Santorno: the Dunnetts, the Americans, Andrew Evenlode, even the swallows, I thought, walking along the Via Garibaldi to the palazzo. The shoe shops and boutiques were having sales: SALDI ECCEZIONALI! signs proclaimed in straggling red felt tip, slashing this Armani jacket or that Chloe skirt from three times my rent to twice the amount. I hitched up my ragged jeans, which now bagged around the waist so much that they had to be held on by a belt. Only the other day two of the Virginians had mistaken me for a poverty-stricken Santornese and it was true, I did look poor. I was poor. Apart from my pearl necklace, I had nothing. 'You can use it as pin money,' my mother had said of my legacy, but I had chosen to spend it on something more valuable, something invisible. But now I craved material things again. As soon as Andrew Evenlode paid me, I'd buy some more clothes, something that Lucio and his mother would like, a pair of shoes to replace my worn leather sandals, a new dress. I would not think about the passport in my bag or the dead man from the well. I would not. He could be anyone. Think about the new dress in Via Garibaldi. I would buy a stove for the flat, some new clothes, and accept the commission to paint Signora Ferranti, and Nastri's children.

I walked along the parterre, staring at the dusty gravel. When I lifted my eyes to the sunlit sky, I felt I was falling, endlessly.

23

Lucio did not come back in the evening, nor the morning after. I decided to walk to the *vendemmia* alone. I woke early, and stopped off at the Bar Popolare for breakfast, waiting my turn among labourers and clerks, who were standing up at the stainless-steel counter and bolting down croissants and hot little espressos before they hurried off to Santorno's railway station for work in San Sepolchro, Florence or Arezzo. Tony's plump little wife, rarely seen, was serving: he had already left for the Dunnetts', she told me.

My mood was such that I did not relish the prospect of walking past the burnt house and down the desolate road through the valley, so I was glad when, just outside the main gate, I heard Louis calling from his car to offer me a lift. Evenlode was with him.

Flustered, I accepted. He was perfectly pleasant, but still said nothing about my portrait of the Contessa, which he must surely have seen, and which was so near to completion. I wondered if this was because he disliked it, an idea that depressed me still further. I had been more pleased with it than with anything I had ever done, building up layer after layer of transparent colour, using all the skill I had learned with browns and umbers when confined in Mimi's flat, but the more pointed his silence seemed, the more confidence I lost.

Louis drove the long way round, taking the route down to the industrial zone and across, as Lotto and Tony had done the day of the fire. It looked worse from where the Dunnetts were: half the hillside had been scorched black.

'We were lucky to survive,' Evenlode said quietly.

'It was stupid of us to try and stop it, just the five of us.'

'Was it?'

'No.'

'I don't think so either.'

We lapsed into silence. Louis had a cassette player in his car, and a melancholy tape of Albinoni playing, which Evenlode turned up louder. I could not see his expression, since his back was turned to me. I stared at the nape of his neck, with the dark, ragged hair, and the frayed collar of his shirt. I wondered whether I should tell Tim Danby how erotic or repulsive to women is the way men smell, how vile aftershave and uncleanliness are to us, how Lucio's sweat and clothes were impregnated with mown grass. Evenlode smelled of sun and starch and Pear's soap: happy things, English things, civilization. But people think it's rude to discuss smell, worse luck, and so men (whose senses are patently less acute) never realize. I thought of that day, of his long silhouette, black against the dazzle of river water, of the moment when we both thought we would die, of the shooting stars over the fountain. Say something, I thought, feeling sick, looking out of the window. Say something, I can't bear this.

'The Guardis are coming to the *vendemmia*, did you know?'

'No. I'm glad. How are Izzy and the baby, Louis?'

'Well enough. The baby is just like any other baby, it vomits at one end and shits at the other, and nobody gets any sleep, but they both think it's a miracle,' he replied, shrugging.

'Do you dislike all human beings, Louis?' I asked.

'Not all, but most.'

301

'Don't you dislike any animals, then? What about snakes?'

'Snakes have their place in the world, too. There would be a lot more rats spreading disease in hot countries if it wasn't for them, for instance.'

'Ugh! I hate them.'

'Women nearly always do.'

'They're so disgusting, so evil.'

'Unlike man, they only attack when frightened or hungry. They are not bad in themselves.'

'Nastri the chemist has a sign in his shop of two snakes coiled round a fountain,' said Andrew. 'I always wonder why. It's a little like a caduceus, but why the fountain?'

'Who knows?' said Louis. 'There are signs everywhere in this country. Where else would you find petrol stations advertised with chimeras, like Agip?'

'Nothing in Italy is quite as it seems,' I said. 'I expect that's why it's so good for painting. Even the landscape is so fantastical, it seems more than itself always, like something in a dream.'

'"Yet it creates, transcending these, far other worlds, and other seas;" Yes, it haunts, doesn't it?' Andrew murmured, looking out of his window.

'When are you leaving?' Louis asked.

'Saturday evening at five. I've booked a wagon-lit on the express that goes to Paris. It's one of the disadvantages of being tall, one doesn't fit into normal seats and beds. I wonder if Claudia will ever come to see me in the country, as she promises?'

'Don't you live in the town?' I asked, curious.

'No. I'm not a town person, really, even with a place as pretty as Oxford to stay in. I like academia, but not all the bitching, the bad sherry, and the sordid little affairs with students.'

'I thought the last was one of the advantages of teaching,' Louis teased.

'Not for me,' said Evenlode, coolly.

I stared out of the window. Above the blackened line left by the fire, the olives were strung with vines, like rows of dancers holding up garlands. I could see the silhouette of the Palazzo Felice, as I had done on the night of the party, and the Dunnetts' drive was once again blocked with cars.

There were many more people than there had been that time: all six of the Guardis, Dottor Mantovani and his wife, Tony from the bar, the reclusive English couple I had occasionally seen shopping in town, an English family who were renting part of their farmhouse, Sylvia, the Danbys, Slim, Izzy, the baby. But no Lucio.

I sighed. Everyone was laughing and talking and admiring the baby, who gurgled at the shifting patterns of sunlight and leaves overhead. My heart felt as cold and grey as England.

'Ciao, baby,' said Slim, handing out secateurs and long wicker baskets. 'Where's the Italian stallion, then? Too frightened of snakes?'

'I don't know.'

Something in my tone made him raise his eyebrows. 'Had a barney, then?'

'Sort of.'

I was acutely conscious of Evenlode standing close enough to hear.

'When are you going back to England?' I asked Slim, as we all began to spread out across the hillside and cut off the heavy, sticky bunches.

'End of the month. And you?'

'I won't be going back,' I said, loudly.

Slim gave me a sharp look, quite unlike his usual foxy expression. 'Oh yeah? Well, it's your own business, girlie, but you're making a mistake. First love is very sweet and all that, but there's more to life than a big prick.'

'Don't you think Lucio and I have got anything in common apart from sex?' I asked sarcastically.

'Since you ask, no.'

'Oh, for heaven's sake!'

'Well, do you? What do you care about his sort of music? What does he understand about painting?'

'Painting isn't the only thing in life,' I said.

'Come off it, of course it is – for you. If you're serious about it, that is. You must know it's a vocation, if it's for real. You have to believe in it like nothing else, even if you turn out to be second-rate. Listen, sex is great, but it isn't enough to screw up the whole of your life for. Izzy found that out, Sylvia didn't.'

'It isn't sex, it's love,' I said fiercely. 'What the hell do you know about it, anyway? You married Izzy for her money, didn't you?'

'Did I?' He stopped and looked at me. 'Well, maybe that's what I told myself in the beginning, and what other people thought, including her. But it wasn't.'

I thought of Izzy's spoilt, chinless face, as I had first seen it, and the way she looked now, and thought in astonishment that he was telling the truth.

'People change after they have babies,' I remarked.

'Not that much, believe me. Gabriella just made some things clear that weren't before.'

I remembered Dave's voice saying, mimicking, 'He wants to settle down and start a fambly.' Why had he been so spiteful? Had he ever wanted Izzy even for her money?

My basket was full; I walked back to the Guardis' cart, where their two white oxen were standing patiently, whisking flies, while Louis scratched their heads between their long, curving horns.

'You hardly ever see them these days. All the *contadini* want tractors, even if they're too wide for half the terraces.'

'They're wonderful beasts. So gentle.'

'Castrated,' he said glumly.

'Don't take it so much to heart.'

'I hate what we do to animals. It's so arrogant. They don't belong to us, they belong to themselves, like all living things.'

'Even bad ones?'

'Yes. Even bad ones. Nothing and nobody is ever completely bad, Emma, any more than they are completely good.'

'I thought you believed in absolutes.'

'Yes. But I also believe in judgement.'

'This sounds a very serious conversation,' said Caroline archly, coming up to tip her own basketful. Her hands and knees were stained black with dust and grape juice.

'We were discussing the rights of animals,' Louis answered. 'And also, perhaps, of man.'

'Well, that makes a change from the rights of women,' she remarked, lowering her voice. 'We've had nothing but since Sylvia came to stay. She sits in the kitchen and lectures me about hygiene, drinking cups of coffee and not lifting a finger. It's driving me potty. Timmy's completely under her thumb.'

Louis and I exchanged glances. I knew we were both thinking that Timmy was for ever fated to be under the thumb of one woman or another.

'The rights of women!' said Louis, snorting slightly. 'Men have never been equal to women.'

'Oh, come now!' Caroline breathed through clenched teeth.

'No, only in romantic fiction. That is why so many women dream of ravishment by strong, silent types. As soon as men open their mouths, the women get the upper hand.'

I left them arguing, and walked back to a new stretch of vineyard in the hot, hazy sun. Still no sign of Lucio. The upper hand? I doubted it.

Izzy and Maria had laid on a magnificent lunch under the pergola. There were marbled rings of *coppa,* prosciutto, salami, dotted with glistening great olives, last year's wine, fennel and tomato salad, tureens of Maria's tagliatelle, and a whole roast boar.

'I shot it three days ago,' Guido said. 'It was pulling grapes down off the vines. They are terrible creatures, they destroy half our crops, and for what? So that rich Milanese can come down for the weekend with their friends.'

'Will you go on hunting even without a dog?' Izzy asked, burping the baby.

'Yes, signora. Not birds, apart from pheasants, you understand, but rabbits and vermin, and boars. It is our right, who work the land. It was for this that the laws were made, not for citizens.'

'For myself,' said Dottor Mantovani, breaking off a long discussion in stilted English about Umberto Eco with the elderly couple, 'I had just as soon live and let live. Look at how gentle nature is! Regard this golden air, these tranquil hills all around us.'

'Not in the mountains, it isn't,' Tim Danby remarked.

'*Professore,* nature is never gentle, anywhere,' said Guido. 'Everything is continually struggling for life, plant against plant, insect against bird, animal against man.'

'Most of all, against men,' said Louis, patting the head of the salivating dog at his knee. 'Look at how much is being destroyed in these very hills: fire, neglect, drought, the wrong crops being sown in the plains, animals being shot and plants being poisoned.'

'It's returning to the wild, however,' said Mantovani. 'I remember when all these hillsides were terraced, and now only the middle stretches are maintained. The rest crumbles away, year after year. The *contadini* like Guido here go, and the foreigners like yourselves come.'

'But if we hadn't,' said Sylvia, speaking for the first time, 'the houses and lands would have crumbled away even more. We bring money and work, and have our homes burnt for it.'

The bitterness of her tone took everyone aback, especially Mantovani.

'Alas, signora, I have nothing against foreigners, but before you came in great numbers, there was no theft in these places. You could go out and leave everything unlocked, and nobody would touch what was yours.'

'Are you saying there was no crime before we came? I don't believe it.'

'It's the same all over the world,' Evenlode observed. 'We all have an idea that a golden age existed just before we were born, and we have somehow lost it. Every era, every society in history has lamented its loss: our own age for the Georgians, the Georgians for ancient Rome, tbe Romans for the age of Saturn.'

Maria stirred. 'Ah, yes, they were good times, then.'

'You see?'

'Well,' said Dottor Mantovani, with courtly benevolence, 'Maria's family are more likely to know than most, I can tell you, as an amateur historian. There have been Guardis in Santorno for as long as we have records.'

'Isn't Guardi Guido's name, though?' I asked.

Maria shook her head, and rose to clear the plates.

'No,' said Mantovani. 'In some families here, the woman's line is what counts, as among the Jews.'

'There you are, Sylvia,' said Caroline, 'an example of matriarchy for you.'

Glumly, I thought of Signora Ferranti, and my own mother. If that was matriarchy, I wasn't sure I preferred it.

I lingered, to make sure of being able to walk back to the vineyards with Sylvia after lunch. All around us, the cicadas sang and sang. We walked for some time without speaking; I was too nervous to know how to begin. She was looking better: still plump, but she had hennaed her hair again and lost that yellow, Mongolian look. A row of silver bells hung in each ear, tinkling as she moved, and another in a ring on her long, fine hands.

'Isn't Lucio coming?' she asked, abruptly.

'I don't know. He might do.'

'Still seeing him?'

'Yes.'

'Still screwing him?'

'Yes, if it's any business of yours.'

'Uh-huh. Must be getting pretty close to when you have to go to college.'

'Sylvia, I'm not going.'

We walked on another couple of paces, then stopped and began cutting grapes.

'You're not! You're going to give it all up for him?'

'Giving what up?' I asked, defensive. 'I was never really that keen on going. You always knew that. I told you, right from the start.'

Sylvia blinked rapidly, and her tarnished grey eyes became opaque. 'You seemed pretty darned determined that day that we met.'

'Well, a lot has happened since then, as you know.'

'I know a lot more than you ever will.'

'I don't doubt it,' I said, beginning to feel irritable. 'You're almost twice my age. It would be surprising if you didn't.'

Sylvia looked at me, and I stepped back, afraid she would hit me. She half raised her hand, and then we both heard someone coming up through the groves to join us.

'Emma, you must leave, for your own sake,' she said softly.

'Why? So that you can have him back again?'

308

'I'm telling you this as your friend. You must listen to me. We can't talk here; I'll come round.'

'I'm busy,' I said. 'I've got to finish the Contessa's portrait, and varnish it.'

I raised my voice slightly, for I had seen Evenlode approaching.

'I'll come round in a couple of days,' Sylvia said, and walked away.

Evenlode sat down in the dust beside me, and we both snipped away for a while in the green shadows cast by the vines. I could hear Maria and her mother singing, as they had done nine months ago, a lifetime ago, picking the olives.

'Do you know whether we get to tread them to make wine?' I asked, to make conversation.

'I've no idea. I doubt it,' he said shortly, and went on picking.

Presently I asked in a small voice, 'Don't you like the portrait?'

He turned and looked at me full in the face. I had never seen him so angry; he looked quite white.

'Of course I like it. You must have realized how much you've improved. You might even turn out to be good, if you gave yourself a chance.'

'Oh, not another person telling me I should go back to England, please! What is this, a conspiracy?'

'I haven't the faintest idea what you're talking about. People have plenty of other things to do with their lives apart from discussing yours, I assure you. But if you stay here and vegetate instead of coming back I'll – I'll throttle you, you silly idiot!'

'Why should you care? Why can't you all just leave me alone instead of interfering?'

He turned away and stood up, looking over my head into the setting sun.

'I can't stand waste,' he said, and began to walk down the hill with his basket.

'If you thought that, why did you turn me down in the first place?' I shouted after him.

He stopped and turned. 'I didn't.'

'You *what?*'

'I didn't. You're not supposed to know any of this, but I was for you, all along. It was Piston who voted against. He lied to you if he said otherwise.'

I sat down in the dust, and ground my teeth.

24

My portrait of the Contessa was finished and varnished two days later.

'Almost, I don't want to let Andrew take it,' said the Contessa, in praise.

'I don't much, either.'

'I wonder whether I will live long enough to see it in Lode. It is an enchanting house, though it must have changed since his father's time. Some Bloomsbury man set a novel in it, I believe.'

I didn't want to ask about her godson, his family or his home, wherever that was. I was sick of the whole subject.

I had not seen him since the *vendemmia;* he had left an envelope with my fee in it, in cash, which I hadn't bothered to open.

I was furious at the rudeness of it: paying me off, as though I were a cleaning woman, without so much as a farewell. But what was there to say? He wanted me to come back to England; I was determined to stay in Italy.

'Maria and her family are so excited about the move,' said the Contessa, tactfully changing the subject. 'I wonder whether they'll be as happy as they think in the new house? Her father's family has been born in the old one for generations.'

'Dottor Mantovani says, it's the woman's family that counts, though.'

'Ha! That persistent grubber-up of antiquities,' said the Contessa. 'He wrote that appalling pamphlet the tourist office hands out, did you know?'

'No. It doesn't surprise me, though. He's a dear little man, all the same.'

'Not bad, for Santorno. He will cure you, then bore you to death,' the Contessa acknowledged, with a flash of malice. 'Ah, what shall I do in the evenings when Andrew has gone? I've become accustomed to seeing him, as I have you.'

'I'll still be here.'

'Which reminds me: I had a telephone call from your father last night, asking if I knew about your plans. I gather term starts in a few days.'

'Contessa, I don't want to seem rude, but neither you nor anyone else is going to make me change my mind.'

'No, I quite see that.'

'I'm glad you do. Nobody else does.'

'It's a tiresome business, running away.'

'Well, I've finished with all that.'

'Have you? Really?' She put her head slightly to one side, like an inquisitive bird.

'How is the peacock?' I asked.

She sighed, and smiled. 'Better. I have him and Victoria patrolling the vegetable garden. I think flowers would provide too much of an affront to his dignity, just yet. They make a terrifying noise, those two.'

'Yes, domesticated fowl always seem to have awful voices.' I fell silent, thinking of the Pistoias' wretched blackbird.

The Contessa sighed again, and said to me, gently, 'My dear, if I may give you one piece of advice: don't make up your mind to stay or go until the last moment. If you want to, you can travel back with Andrew, you know. There is no difficulty about that.'

'We'd probably end up strangling each other,' I said, trying to laugh.

'He would never do anything to harm you, you know. I know he can be impatient and difficult, especially in the last few weeks, but he's very fond of you.'

'I must be the best judge of that,' I said, miserably.

The Contessa gave me a sad look. 'The pains of a parent!' she said.

'I'll ring them, I promise. But I'm not going back.'

'I never thought you would do,' Lucio said complacently, when I told him of my decision.

'Didn't you?'

'No. We'll go together, with the band, one day, and you can show me round London.'

'I hardly know it myself.'

'Carnaby Street, Portobello, Golden Square, the 'Ard Rock Café,' he said, dreamily. 'Wembley Stadio . . .'

I could not help giggling.

'Oh, really, Lucio!'

'You don't believe me? I'll buy my house with the white moquettes one day, you wait.'

'Are you still going to make a record, now Max has gone?'

'I have connections,' he said, airily. 'Maybe I'll go to America soon.'

'America?'

'One of the students asked me to come and stay.'

'Oh Lucio, no!'

'Why not? Her father is in the business. She said she liked my songs.'

'I bet she did.'

'She came round a few times, at L'Incantevole.'

'What did you do?' I asked coldly. 'Make love to her?'

He laughed and stretched. 'No, *cara*. She wanted me to, of course.'

'Of course. What did she look like?'

'You don't need to know. Nothing happened. She isn't as beautiful as you.' He unbuckled my belt. 'How I hate jeans, they make everything so much more complicated. I would like you to wear skirts, always, with nothing underneath, I like you with nothing on but your pearls ...'

'You said to me never to underestimate the attraction of novelty for men.'

'Nothing happened,' he said, pinning my wrists with one hand, unlocking my legs with the other. 'You're so funny, to get jealous about nothing. I know that type of woman. They're like an old sack inside, they've had so many men.'

'How do you know what an old sack is like, then?' I asked, prevaricating.

'I suppose I must have tried one, some time. Ah,' Lucio said, with a sly wriggle, thrusting, 'that's better, isn't it?'

I couldn't resist him, ever. When I was angry or cold towards him, it only provoked him the more, for then he would turn all his charm on me like a beacon. I had seen how tom cats in the alleys of Santorno, bored with being ignored, would spring upon females in heat and bite them on the precise point of the neck that made them subdued and acquiescent: they always reminded me of Lucio and myself.

I forgot, sometimes, how beautiful he was. Living with someone, it wears off, that continual squirm of desire that comes from merely looking. He would play games now, muttering in my ear that I was not one woman but three or four: a nun, a nurse, a prisoner, a schoolgirl, all dying for a man, for himself.

For him, I would become a chicken to be plucked, a radio to be tuned, a sow's ear to be turned into a silk purse: anything and everything except myself.

I wondered whether this was what the Contessa had meant by appreciating otherness. What else was there to keep desire alive, once the shock of novelty had worn off? I had overcome my disgust at the fact that my body, and his, sometimes stank, leaked, reeked, could not be compelled by an act of will; but with familiarity, the compulsion of desire had altered, also. One couldn't always be discovering new millimetres of muscle and skin to adore. It was a paradox: the most carnal act two people were capable of had to become a feat of the imagination.

Was it this that kept ugly couples together? I had often wondered how they stood it, the proximity, the intimacy, year after year. Did they become kind, or blind to each other, performing hideous intimacies dispassionately? Or was it something else, some miraculous, hidden lode of the imagination which transformed and redeemed them?

Sometimes, when he was inside me, I would think how lonely it was; and then I would try not to think at all, because this meant I was not giving myself to him, as he demanded.

'You have more muscle than you used to,' he remarked, inspecting me, after, when I was dreaming and vacant.

'Don't you like it? It's only from all those walks up and down to Santorno *inferiore*.'

'Just don't get too thin. You're perfect now.'

'Liar! I know I'm not. Anyway, I thought men liked thin women.'

'Thin ones to look at, and fat ones to lie on.'

'Sylvia has lost weight.'

'Has she?'

'She was at the *vendemmia*. I'm afraid she's still very jealous. She tried to persuade me to go back to England.'

'She's such a neurotic. A compulsive liar, too. I hope you didn't listen to her?'

'No.'

315

'Good.' He yawned and stretched. 'Of course she's upset. She'll never forget me. I'm the best she's ever had.'

I smiled. It always amused me, this Italian self-confidence about sex. He saw it and looked at me thoughtfully. 'Sometimes I wish you had more experience of men, so that you could tell that was true.'

'I don't want anyone else.'

'Perhaps you should try Marcello.'

'Ugh, no!' I hit him with a pillow. 'Go away, I won't have you making jokes like that.' Lucio went out on to the landing, laughing. 'That will teach you!'

'If you're not careful, I'll leave after all, and that will teach you!'

His face changed, and he held me by the shoulders. 'Never, never do that, Emma. Whatever I say, I don't take you for granted. If you leave, I'll kill myself. Or you.'

'Lucio, don't worry, don't say such things,' I said, half frightened. 'I'm not going anywhere without you.'

'Good.' He dropped a kiss on my forehead and grinned. 'Ciao, *amore*, I'm off to practise.'

'When will you be back?'

'I don't know. Probably not tonight, I'll be up too late for the Pistoias to answer the door.'

I bent over the balustrade at the top of the landing and blew him a kiss as he went down the stairs. He stopped, sketched his quirky, self-mocking little bow, and went out through the glass door to the Pistoias' quarters. I did love him, I did. I sighed, and crossed over into the kitchen to wash myself in the basin's cold water with a flannel. Then I sat down to write two letters: one to my mother, and the other to the university authorities, to tell them both that I wouldn't be coming back. I would give them to Andrew Evenlode, I thought, as the posts were so unreliable. He was leaving tomorrow.

The thought of him made me remember that I hadn't counted my fee for the portrait; not that I really doubted it would be less than we had agreed, but it gave me satisfaction to think that he might have got it wrong. I believed him about the interview, somehow. There had been too much spite in the way Dominic Piston, my mother's relation by marriage, had relayed news of my failure.

There had been nothing more about the corpse from the well, though I kept the report on its discovery folded in my bag. The man could be anyone: a wandering shepherd, victim of a private vendetta elsewhere, a casualty from the Mafia or the Red Brigades. Dottor Mantovani had been the only one to see the corpse, besides the Guardis and the police, and had said it was so decomposed as to turn his stomach; something which did not help my nightmares. It had been a three-day wonder, quickly surpassed by the scandal of Max's elopement. People said they had gone to Switzerland, where it turned out Max had been salting money away for years, or possibly to Australia. Nobody was particularly sorry for Max's wife.

'To tell the truth, *figliola*, everybody was surprised he didn't divorce her after the scandal over the orgies a few years ago,' the baker's wife had told me, yawning in the yeasty darkness of her shop. 'Her family may be able to trace their lines back to Roman days, but they've never been popular. Bad blood, bad blood, it always comes out.'

I laughed at this superstitious talk. These feuds that were always flaring up and going round the town, the elephantine memories for imaginary slights and misunderstandings, they were worse than anything that went on in my own family. Santorno was just one big, unhappy family, everyone related to everyone else, hardly anyone marrying out, as Signora Ferranti had done. Lucio had told me, his father had never really been accepted, coming from another town, and he himself was

317

regarded as being, of all things, half foreign. It was this, he said, that had drawn him to Dave and Sylvia in the first place.

I picked up a piece of paper and a Biro, and began to write, 'Dear Mummy and Daddy,' then stopped. The last time I had written those words had been in my running-away letter; expressed in phrases which, in recollection, made me cringe. They had been heavily influenced by my correspondence with Sylvia; I had demanded 'a meaningful relationship, a positive dialogue instead of a negative one'.

We didn't know how to talk, or write, to each other, that was the trouble. I took out my mother's letter and reread it. It was stilted and pompous, but was it really as bad as I believed? Letters are such deceptive things: you think you're getting everything down in black and white, but words twist and buckle according to the underlying mood and needs of the reader, as much as the writer. How could one ever find access to that universal language, that way of arranging thoughts and symbols in such a way that everyone understood what was going on? I thought of the Contessa's gardens and realized that they were indeed a work of art in that they encapsulated all such ambiguities.

Anything, anything, rather than struggle with the phantom presence of my parents and those faceless Oxford authorities. I would count the money the don had bought me off with, salving his conscience and insulting me in one: count it note by note and savour the fact that I had thwarted him.

The notes were all there, wrapped around by a piece of the thick, luxurious palazzo paper I had seen once before, but covered with a different handwriting.

I notice calligraphy; all painters do, I suppose. Evenlode may have sneered at the idea of art being self-expression, but I had no doubt that handwriting is, consciously or not. All writing is chimerical, assembled out of bits and pieces of other people's that we like, admire, or have forced upon us. I would have expected Evenlode's to be sharp and flinty, full of angles and tricksy little italicisms, but it was not. It bounded across the page, small and black, like a series of cogs and springs, or the hairs on his body: energetic, determined, less graceful than idiosyncratic.

Dear Emma,

I feel I must try once more before leaving, however distasteful it is to you, and however fruitless for me. You agreed that it was right that we tried to stop the fire, that day, even if it was foolish, and I feel that this is in some sense similar.

I began to read more attentively.

I don't know what has happened to you here, what you have experienced. I can neither imagine, nor like to imagine, how important Lucio is to you, but, Emma, he isn't more important than you are.

You must believe in yourself, you know. You seem to be so self-confident, your wits are so quick, you have such gifts, such charm, that you get away with pulling the wool over people's eyes. I do not claim to be more perspicacious than the rest, but I have seen you differently. I saw how you were in Florence, and even before. You aren't happy here.

Not happy! I paused. This was nonsense. The man was trying to persuade me the same way cheap horoscopes do: they tell people something about themselves, and people believe them. Not happy! He was blowing a single incident up out of all proportion.

You may not believe me. I can see you scowling and sticking out that formidable Pre-Raphaelite jaw, but it's true. I have told you only one lie, which was that I didn't remember who you were at the spring, with Maria. I remembered everything about that interview, what a bad mood I was in, how I tried to bounce you and how you refused to give in, although I could see you were frightened, like all the rest. You answered back with such ferocious spirit, Piston couldn't forgive you, and I couldn't forget.

Oh, why hadn't he told me all this before?

I've written more than I intended; but, Emma, you must come back. You say, quite rightly, that Italy is a painter's home, and you don't want to go to an art school; yet you do need training. You can't teach yourself everything, no matter how remarkable the progress you've made alone. You need to look more at the past, absorb it, have the luxury of three years as a student to think about it, and not paint rustic furniture in order to pay the rent. You need more stimulus, different people, not closed, provincial minds. (Of course, universities are closed and provincial, too, in their own way, but at least they all have access to other worlds, as Santorno does not.)

Well, he was honest here, though his flattery elsewhere was too blatant for me not to spot it for what it was.

You need this, you must have this, if you are ever to become what you should. I may be wrong – the irony of trying to persuade one stubborn young woman to come to Oxford, when so many long to, does not escape me – but I think not. Believe in yourself, stop running away. Come back.

It was unsigned.

'Bloody hell,' I said.

At first, I put Andrew's letter back in its envelope, resolving not to read it again, and went out on the little balcony to breathe fresh air; but soon the distress and confusion it caused in my mind was such that I had to read it again. I read and reread it, and at every reading my feelings were different.

Sometimes I was irritated by the touches of melodrama in his style; they were unlike him, I thought. Then it would strike me that perhaps he was showing me another side of himself, something that he normally kept hidden, and that his exposure of it was an act of courage. I remembered how he had said that everyone in his family was too polite, that it was difficult for him to show his feelings. What was it about English men that made them so hopeless, so difficult to get on with, so—? Damn, damn, damn.

What could I do? Why did it upset me so much to learn of his good will, his good opinion, now? What business was it of his? What was he to me, or I to him? Running away, indeed!

I went out on the balcony again. The blackbird down below in the Pistoias' gave a faint, melancholy cheep.

Suddenly, all the rage and frustration in me concentrated into a single focus. I had to get that bloody bird out or he would die. I would get him out and take him to the Contessa, and at least something good would come out of this whole stinking mess. They had no right to keep a wild animal in a cage, none at all. I should have screwed my courage up months ago and let it out.

I could hear them watching television in the kitchen – another wildlife film. It was easy, really. All I had to do was climb over the wall, stand on a little ledge, and reach down to open the door of the cage where it stood on a little wooden table.

The bird fluttered so desperately, I thought it would give us both away, but they took no notice. I had to catch it with one hand, which it jabbed at in panic-stricken savagery, but once I had my fingers round its ragged wings, it emptied its bowels and became still. I could feel its heart jumping so hard its whole body shook, and I stroked its head, trying to calm us both.

'Be still, be still,' I whispered, frantically emptying out a box of tissues and putting it inside, with my hand over the hole at the top. The bird hopped twice.

I panicked myself now, running down the stairs on knees that felt like rubber, past the Pistoias' kitchen, down past their bedrooms, down through the garage, out into the little court-yard, where Signora Ferranti was just emerging for the evening *passeggiata*.

'Wait, Hemma!' she called, in her deep, hoarse voice, but I smiled at her, and ran past.

When I got to Via Garibaldi, I slowed. I was afraid that if I ran any more, I'd lose my grip on the box or call attention to what I carried. By the time I got to the main gate, I was almost strolling, though I ran again as soon as I got to the parterre.

It was absurd to feel so much urgency. The guilt of stealing, I supposed, even if I had taken what did not belong to my land-lord. The chestnut trees were starting to yellow at the edges, their vitality retreating back and back along the veins, leaving a skeleton of green. Gravel crunched underfoot; there were cars parked overlooking the plains. Courting couples sat inside or on the marble benches beneath the palazzo walls.

I walked to the end and up the little slope to the archway guarded by the two garlanded caryatids. How silly to have ever thought they were sneering. Full-breasted, enigmatic, graceful, they smiled; and beneath them, wheeling her scooter through the gates, Maria Guardi smiled, too.

'Good evening, *figliola*. Are you coming in?'

I shook my head.

'No. I mustn't. Maria, can you give this to the Contessa? Keep your hand over the top, it's got a blackbird inside. He's been in a cage at the Pistoias' for months and months, and I don't think he can fly any more.'

'Ai-ai!' she said, taking the box and putting her hand in.

'Be careful, he bites when he's frightened.'

'Not this one,' she said, holding it gently. 'This isn't a he, it's a she.'

The ragged little bird looked at her with bright, dark eyes, and let out a long, sweet trill.

I walked back to the town slowly. I knew I was bound to get into trouble for what I had just done. Signor Pistoia had caught me pouring water down into the poor creature's trough, he always closed the cage door with care; Signora Ferranti was inevitably going to complain about how I had rushed past so rudely, carrying something in a box. But what the hell? If I got chucked out, I could always move into Mimi's flat, or find somewhere else. I didn't need to be dependent on them any more.

I was right, I did find trouble waiting for me when I got back to Vicolo delle Sette Stelle, but it wasn't the Pistoias. It was Sylvia.

25

I had forgotten all about Sylvia's promise, or threat, to visit me. I let myself in to the Pistoias' house and went cautiously up the stairs.

'Is that you, Hemma?' Marga Pistoia called.

'Yes,' I said, resignedly.

'There's a lady upstairs in your flat, waiting for you.'

'Oh,' I said, in surprise. 'Is that all?'

'Was there anything you wanted to talk to me about?' She looked at me with a faded eagerness, wiping her hands on her checked apron. 'Any news?'

I knew I should confess about the blackbird, but I realized, suddenly, that she was expecting me to tell her that Lucio and I were properly engaged. I could see the little flush of the worn-out romantic creeping up her cheeks; or perhaps it was the menopause.

'Any news?'

'No – no,' I stammered, edging away. 'Not yet. You'll be the first to know.'

I opened the glass door to my own stair and went on up.

'Hi,' said Sylvia.

'Hallo,' I said, cautiously.

We sat down on either side of the table in the kitchen. I did not offer her anything to drink, with deliberate rudeness.

'Nice place you've got here,' Sylvia said. 'It'll be cold in winter, though.'

'I thought I might rent Mimi's flat, if it's really freezing.'

'That isn't free any longer.'

'Oh?'

'I've taken it over.'

I suppressed a flash of annoyance. 'Really? I thought you were living with Tim and Caroline.'

'Only until something else came up. You'd have to be crazy to go on living there. The place is a shit heap. Neither of them has the faintest idea about making a place homey.'

'Yes, I rather gathered from Caroline that you didn't think too highly of her efforts,' I said dryly.

'Caroline's not so bad, it's that nerd Tim. He's shaved off his beard and goes round reeking of some kinda perfume. Told me he's going to start a launderette in Slim's old shop, and asked me if I wanted a job there. The guy's a nut.'

'He's only trying to please you.'

'Ha! I divide men into bores and bastards: the bores get the hots for me, and I get the hots for bastards. Which brings me to our little talk.'

'Sylvia, if you're trying to interfere between Lucio and me, forget it. He made his decision months ago. I'm really sorry you're still so upset about it, but it was only an affair, for goodness sakes. I mean, it wasn't as though you were married or anything.'

'Do you really think that makes any difference? Some old fart in the town hall saying a few words and signing a piece of paper? I'm just as much married to him as you are – which is to say, not legally, but in the only way that matters, which is screwing.'

Her incised eyes were contracting now; she did indeed look like Salome, with her unbound hair writhing round her shoulders in dark-red snakes.

'I know, everyone now knows, you have peculiar views on what constitutes marriage, Sylvia, whether it was between you and Lucio or you and Dave,' I said, keeping my temper and my pity in check. 'The fact remains that however you describe your relationship with Lucio, it's now over, and has been for quite some time.'

'Oh, really? You think so?' Her mouth stretched as if biting a lemon. 'Where do you think he's been, all the nights he hasn't been with you, huh?'

'Sylvia, this is silly and vulgar. Please leave.'

'Where was he last night, do you think?'

'Don't make things worse by telling lies. You've told quite enough already.'

'I'll tell you where he was, you snotty British bitch. He was with me, in Mimi's old flat.'

'Oh, rot!' I shouted. 'For God's sake, Sylvia, get a grip on yourself! You're becoming completely unbalanced.'

'I'm not lying, you stupid cunt, I'm telling the truth. Did you really think he'd stop screwing us both, just because you wanted him to?'

'Yes, I do.'

'Then you must be even more naive than I thought. Do you think I don't know everything you two do together? About the way he tickles you up with a feather? About the way—'

I felt the blood leaving my head. It was a most peculiar sensation, as though I was being freeze-dried. I recognized it: it was what I had first felt when my parents left me at boarding school, and the sludge of femininity tried to drag me under. I had realized then that I had no weapons except my wits, the particular kind that makes women hate me.

'You could guess that because he's done the same to you,' I said in my cold, calm voice. 'He says people are all the same when they make love.'

326

'And you believed him? Boy, it must be great to screw a virgin! No wonder he's found it such a laugh.'

I felt such hatred for her then that I thought I would faint. I wanted to faint; anything, anything, rather than this horrible pain, but faints don't come for the asking.

'I don't believe you. You're making this up.'

'If you don't believe it, come and stand in Via del Ospedale this evening.'

'You're mad. You're worse than mad, you're a murderess.'

I hadn't meant to say it, I really hadn't, but it was out now. Until that moment, it had still been possible for us to remain friends, but that word shrivelled up whatever sympathy had existed, despite everything.

'What do you mean?'

'You know perfectly well what I mean. Do you think everyone's blind or stupid round here? That body they found in the well, it's Dave, isn't it? You killed him.'

'Now who's the crazy?' she said, softly.

'Don't tell any more lies, Sylvia. I know it's him. I saw his passport in your box, and some money.' A thought struck me. 'That's how you're renting Mimi's flat, isn't it? Tim must have given you the box back, and you found the cash. Where was it from, Sylvia? I'm sure the police could trace it back to you.'

'You little bitch.'

'There's nothing so different between virgins and anyone else, you know. It's a very biblical mistake, to confuse carnal knowledge with any other sort.'

'I didn't kill him.'

'Of course you did. Who else had such a good reason to? Slim? Why, when he was going to get all that alimony? He may say now that he loved her, but he's far too cool to lose his temper over a little infidelity. Louis couldn't hurt a fly. Izzy was in love. Lucio adored him. Tim and Caroline? Mimi? Max?

However duplicitous Dave was in his dealings with them, they only wanted him to leave them alone.'

'Max paid him to go and not come back. It was his money you saw.' She had bent her head. I could see a line of grey at the roots, where the henna had grown out.

'Yes, I guessed as much. So who does that leave? You. You'd do anything to hang on to that house, wouldn't you? It was your obsession, you practically told me so yourself. Your home. You knew that if he decided to marry Izzy, he wouldn't be obliged to do a thing for you because you weren't married. Marriage does have its uses after all, doesn't it?'

Sylvia's long, beautiful hands on the table twisted her rings on and off. I couldn't take my eyes away from them.

'What did you do?'

She mumbled something behind the curtain of her hair.

'What?'

'I didn't kill him,' she said. 'He was already dead when I found him. We'd agreed to meet at the bottom of the valley, by the well, to talk things over, away from the party. Izzy was so jealous, you see; she wouldn't take her eyes off him. He was getting sick of all that possessiveness, I'd never been like that. I think he'd have come back to me, you know, in the end; not that I wanted him any longer. But he was dead when I got there. I thought he'd fallen asleep, and then I touched his head, and it was all pulpy, like a smashed orange.'

She stopped. She had been sinking lower and lower into herself, but now she gave a shiver, or a shake, and her features sharpened.

'It seemed like providence, his being next to the well. I don't know what I'd have done otherwise. All I had to do was break the old lock, take the cover off, and push him in. He made a big splash, falling; it was the only moment I was really scared. I'd taken the passport and the money, of course.

328

Later, I came back and put a new padlock on the well. And that was that.'

I knew, then, that it was all true. The relief was such, I smiled.

'You expect me to believe that? Don't treat me like a fool, Sylvia. Why did you bother to chuck him down the well, if you didn't do it?'

'Why do you think? He was a bastard, and a shit on wheels, but I didn't want him dead. What good was he to me then? I don't believe in all that revenge crap. If people knew he was dead, I'd lose the house all over again, to some cousins in England. It was much better for everyone to think he'd just, like, disappeared. People can disappear for years, going off round the Far East. I had it all worked out, with the postcards. All I had to do was pretend he was still alive, and the house was mine.'

'Then why on earth did you keep his passport, of all the stupid things? You must have known that if anyone found it, things would look bad for you. The money I can understand – particularly after the way you fleeced me – but why the passport?'

Sylvia's pewter eyes brightened, and she leant forward in an almost friendly manner.

'Don't you know how much they're worth on the black market? Particularly the old ones that aren't linked up to a computer. You can get over a thousand dollars for them. I told you, I'm a good cook. I never throw anything away that could be useful or worth money.'

'Like the postcards?' I asked sarcastically. 'That wasn't too bright, was it, sending the Bronzino you had on your wall.'

'I never thought you'd notice.'

'I noticed everything about you, Sylvia, actually, except how you really are. That's the only thing that puzzles me. Why did you bother with me in the first place? I realize now that your invitation to stay must have been sent before you started with Lucio, but why write me letters for a year?'

'I don't know, really,' she said, looking very tired. 'I liked writing to someone outside all this shit, somewhere else. And I enjoyed reading yours. You were so idealistic and intense about art, and all that. I guess you must have reminded me of myself, when I was young.'

She left. We couldn't wait to be rid of each other. I don't think either of us had any idea what to do next. She said that if I tried to tell anyone what she had told me, she would deny it.

'Where's your proof?' she said. 'The fire destroyed everything.'

Tim had evidently not told her it was I who found the box, and I wasn't going to remind her that I might have taken the passport. It was still in my bag; I checked as soon as I heard the door at the bottom of the stairwell close.

What was I to do? It wasn't much evidence, after all: just a passport. I didn't know how murder enquiries went, but I was pretty sure that the police would need a lot more than that to prove the identity of the corpse. The most it might do was prod them into looking up Dave's dental records in England, which presumably someone must have.

But what right had I to stir things up again, anyway? As Louis had said, whose life was worse off because of his death? To whom had it not come as a positive benefit? Oh, but I wanted to get Sylvia now. I had never felt such consuming hatred for anyone, not even my mother or Andrew Evenlode. If they found out the identity of the corpse, she was the natural suspect. Izzy had made no secret of her affair with him, nor Sylvia of her rage. It would be hard on the former, but Sylvia would come out worst.

Was it true what she had told me about her and Lucio?

I couldn't decide. It had always made me feel sick to think of them in bed together, but I had to realize that it had happened in the past, at least. And someone mad enough to conceal, or commit, a murder was certainly crazy enough to keep watch on the Pistoias' house and check Lucio's coming and goings.

There had been so much venom in the way she had talked. I was practically certain she was making it up. If they were still having an affair, why should she suddenly decide to tell me about it now? Because she had expected it to be only a temporary thing? It was plausible, given her peculiar views on sexual fidelity. She had put up with Dave having other women, Lucio had told me as much, as long as she was the chief concubine. On the other hand, if she had simply been waiting for me to leave before trying again, this was her last chance to get rid of me.

I tried to think it all through with that icy detachment that had resumed its grip. So much of being in love is like detection, for a woman. We go over every clue about someone, again and again, until we can read them like a book. A woman never uses one half as much intuition, logic or sheer imagination as she does when in love. What did I know about Lucio? That he was full of contradictions and confusions. He was an anarchist who believed in the family; he was a rebel who would never leave home. He believed people never really changed their natures, whatever happened to them. He was a cynic who was capable of hero-worship. He was conceited and curious about women, yet prone to romantic gestures that would have been comic two hundred years ago. The demon lover, Andrew had called him; but I had seen another picture.

I couldn't believe such a man would be unfaithful to me. He had too much self-respect for that, surely, and too much contempt for bourgeois intrigues. What could be more squalidly provincial, more banal, than two-timing? True artists, like aristocrats, were perfectly open about the whole thing. But

331

what did I know about the former, apart from what I had read? Perhaps the Paris of Balzac and Dumas was pure invention, perhaps great painters had never starved in garrets or fallen in love with seamstresses. I hadn't done too well myself at producing pictures when sustained on boiled eggs and chicory, after all. Perhaps there was no such thing as a freemasonry of creative people, all encouraging and inspiring each other; perhaps that was only the amateurs, the people like those American students, who had to do everything in a group instead of striking out on their own. Lucio himself had said that artists were like birds, singing not for joy, but to keep other artists off their territory.

I couldn't decide, I couldn't decide. I took out Dave's passport and with it my parents' letter, which I reread.

My father's short, affectionate note had already moved me, but now it was my mother's I kept going over. Nothing had changed, and yet I suddenly felt I understood it, and the pride and loneliness in which she had written. She was so stiff-necked: her own worst enemy, just like me.

We were too alike, that was why we kept quarrelling. I laughed, discovering this, amazed that I had never seen it before. We both behaved like ogresses because we were frightened or frustrated by other people. Oh, she was snobbish and pompous and materialistic – 'better to be fenced in that not fitting in' – who would say that except someone who had considered both options, and chickened out? Yet she was brave in a different way. She had let me go. I saw that, now. I hadn't run away, I had been allowed to leave. She had almost thrown me out of the nest, goading me on, working me up to such a pitch of anger that I had forgotten my customary timidity and run off, full of spleen and conceit. It had not been Sylvia who had drawn me half as much as it had been my mother who had pushed me.

It had been under my nose all the time for nine months, and I had never seen it. The pains of a parent, the Contessa had said. They must indeed be unimaginable. Not being able to interfere at the last, putting so much love, effort, money and time into someone who walked away without thanks, and probably with resentment. No wonder Signora Ferranti was so difficult to put up with. Lucio had understood it all along.

How could I not trust him, when he was so wise about love? Because I was curious. Sylvia had said it as a challenge, or a bluff, and I was determined to see which of the two it was.

Mimi's flat overlooked the Via del Ospedale, the street that joined the two piazzas before sloping down past her apartment block to the south gate, and thence to the open hillside and the pilgrims' path to the plains. It was as foul as I remembered: men hawking and urinating against the walls, a little hunchback capering about drunkenly, poor harassed women with the faces of wet hens trying to get their children to sleep in the racket from the giant colour-television sets. Even though the flat was only on the edge of all this, it wasn't a salubrious place to be at night. Nobody from the upper town dreamt of venturing there, which I supposed was why Max had chosen to install Mimi there. Had he climbed up the wall, like the prince in 'Rapunzel', to avoid the notice of the inquisitive old bat living opposite? Nothing would have surprised me now.

I could see straight into the bedroom if I stood on the flight of stairs to the Municipality and looked down. It was brightly lit, the shutters left open. I could see Sylvia moving about inside. She had not bothered to change anything around, as I did, but had clearly cleaned it rather more than the sluttish Mimi. The tawdriness of the furniture was pitiful under that flat overhead light. Of course, I thought, she has nothing else. All her furniture, all her clothes went in the fire. She has lost everything, even the thing for which she committed the worst crime of all.

I was ashamed of myself, spying like this, and afraid someone would see me in the dark. I heard the clock in the Municipality strike half past ten; I could even hear the clockwork that operated the angel and the devil clicking and whirring as they chased each other round, brandishing their theatrical weaponry. It was warm still, and the sound carried on the clear, autumnal air.

Sylvia began to undress, taking off the clothes she had worn at the *vendemmia*. She did so slowly. I wondered whether she knew I was watching, whether she was going to carry on this ridiculous charade, but I was fascinated, all the same, to see the body of my rival.

Nakedness is full of surprises. I had learned that already with Andrew. Sylvia was pale, and her breasts were bigger than I would have thought, with large brown nipples. She was starting to sag a bit. Her waist was good, but her thighs carried the porridgy look of cellulite. She was also remarkably hairy. I was astounded to see a woman with so much hair. I remembered now that she didn't depilate, for feminist reasons, but the stuff on her legs was thick and black, and she had a bush like a beard. I had always thought of her as such a delicate, fastidious woman, all moon and moonshine, and here was this hirsute chimpanzee! No wonder Lucio had left her as soon as someone else came his way, I thought, coarsely; he'd need a machete to hack through that lot.

Poor woman. I began to go down the steps, feeling thoroughly ashamed of myself, and then I saw her go out of the room, still naked. She came back with Lucio.

He had been right: people mostly did do the same things. It was a wonder anyone made such a fuss about it. What an ugly, clumsy ballet it was! Was that really what we had looked like together? All that grunting and rutting and sniffing and licking – how had I ever thought it could be beautiful, an act of grace or feeling? Had my face taken on that doll-like vacancy in orgasm? No wonder men despised us, used us so, arrived at their own with an expression of such snarling ferocity. Those crude, violent words – shafting, stuffing, screwing – they were all the right ones, after all. It was not an act of love in the slightest.

I walked up through the Piazza Venti Settembre and along Via Garibaldi. When I got to the Bar Popolare, I stopped, and went into the sugary, coffee-laden interior.

'Ciao, *nuvola bionda*! And how is the weather in England?'

'Tony, have you got a telephone?'

'But of course. It's next to the toilet, at the back. You dial the number, and then I work out how many *scatti* you've used.'

'Well, if you'll wait a few minutes, I can tell you what you want to know.'

I went to the back of the shop, past the TV set and the table before the arched window, where I had once seen Andrew Evenlode drinking coffee, and into a little, curtained cubicle like a confessional to dial.

'It's me, Mummy,' I said. 'I'm coming home.'

26

I did not go back to the Pistoias' immediately, though I felt very tired. Instead, I scribbled a short note to Andrew, telling him I would meet him at the station, and walked out to the palazzo to post it. I could have telephoned, but it was nearly midnight, and I didn't want to wake everyone up.

I knew that walk so well now. It was strange to think I'd never see any of it again: not the hills, nor the view from Sylvia's, nor the Guardis' funny kitchen, nor the Contessa's miraculous, mysterious garden. I wished that I could see the garden one last time, but it was better not.

I would just have to remember those huge, sombre giants and their children casting shadows in the moon, the Chinese boxes of topiary opening out on to each other in their endless variety of shapes, scents and colours, the streams cascading like threads of silver and pearl, the rose garden with its corkscrew fountain, and the secret I would never find out.

But Sylvia – I was going to make sure she was found out. I couldn't begin to examine what I felt about Lucio, but I had no pity for her any longer. I hadn't known about her affair with him, had been utterly innocent of anything but a naive belief in the holiness of the heart's affections, but she had known about mine. She had shown me what she and Lucio did in bed together, and what he and I had done too, and I would never forgive her.

I went up a side street above Piazza Venti Settembre, where the police station was still lit up, with a couple of bored policemen yawning at the mahogany desk inside. I took Dave's passport out of my bag, wrapped it carefully in the sheet of newspaper about the inquest I had been keeping, and wrote SYLVIA on it. Then I posted it through the brass flap marked *Denunci*.

It made only the slightest of sounds as it fell.

There was more to do when I got back. I washed until my cake of soap was all gone and I had no more shampoo, to try and rid myself of all I had seen and done, of the smell of Lucio and the feel of him.

I packed my old leather suitcase. It surprised me how much I had collected: my Lotto crockery, for instance, which I didn't want to leave behind, though it weighed a ton, and two sketch-books, which, however inept, I still wanted as a reminder of the hills round Santorno. I left my cloak out, though, and the green dress: I would have no further use for such garments.

Then I cleaned the flat and all the furniture, and stacked the two mattresses on top of each other because it was too hateful, seeing them side by side.

Finally, I counted out all the money I had and put it into two envelopes: one for the Pistoias, in lieu of a month's notice, and the other for Lucio, to repay the money he had lent me to buy furniture. I thought of writing a letter, but what was there to say? So I wrote Sylvia, as I had done on the passport wrapping, and put it through the Ferrantis' letter box across the courtyard. When I came back, I put my own passport and what little remained of my various fees into the breast pocket of a clean shirt, for safety.

It was three in the morning by the time I had finished. I

thought I'd never get to sleep, but as soon as I lay down on the double thickness of mattresses, unconsciousness closed over me like water.

Marga Pistoia was shaking my shoulder, her face pinched with anger.

'Signorina Hemma! Wake up! Wake up! My husband wants to see you.'

'Oh.'

'Get dressed, please. He wants to see you now, but I told him you probably didn't have any clothes on.'

'I don't care whether she's dressed or not,' Pistoia roared, bursting into the room, his face puce beneath the strands of his greasy black hair. 'What have you to say for yourself, you little thief?'

'We know it must have been you who took the blackbird, don't try to deny it.'

'We take you in, as a favour, we put up with all your comings and goings and disgraceful behaviour as a favour to Letizia, but this is the end. *Basta!* You get out of this house, you understand?'

'I was leaving anyway,' I said. 'There's an envelope on the kitchen table with a month's rent for you, if you look.'

'Going?' said Pistoia, in a different tone. 'Going where?'

'Elsewhere.'

'Now, wait a moment,' he said. 'I know we have our differences about the disturbances, but there's no need for us to misunderstand one another. If you pay us another 20,000 lire a month, say, we can forget about all this. After all, I dare say I can always catch another.'

'I'm going back to England.'

'But what about Lucio?' Signora Pistoia asked anxiously.

'I'm afraid that's all over,' I said. The town clock struck three.

'Please leave, I have to get dressed. I'm sorry about the bird, but it was never yours to keep in a cage in the first place.'

'Of course it was mine. Who else did it belong to, if not me?' he shouted.

'Itself,' I said. 'Now, please go.'

A little to my surprise, and theirs, they went. I got dressed, slowly.

I was glad I had overslept; it meant I had only an hour to kill before going down to the station. I could have asked Evenlode to give me a lift, with my heavy suitcase, but I had planned to pay Pistoia. Too late now. I could hear shouting from their kitchen, and then he went out, thumping and jingling down the stairs, banging the front door as he went into the street.

I folded the sheets up neatly on top of the mattresses, as we had done at school at the end of term, and went into the kitchen. My envelope with the money had gone, of course; I should have told them they could keep all the bits of furniture I was leaving, too. I dragged my suitcase out onto the landing, across the slippery terracotta tiles. All going, all gone: by this evening the flat would be left to the gecko again.

I went out on the little balcony for a last look at the rooftops and my view of the clockwork figures in the bell tower. They moved again as it became half past three.

'Emma.' I jumped, and turned. He had come in so silently, I thought I was hallucinating. 'What is the meaning of this?'

'You know what it means.'

'Are you mad? Sylvia and I were over months ago.'

'Please Lucio. Don't lie any more. I'm so sick of it all. I saw you with her last night. I saw you both, through the window.'

'*Porca Madonna! Everything?*'

'Yes. So please, just go. I'm leaving.'

'Oh, Emma, my angel, don't go, don't leave me! You don't understand, I don't love her at all.'

'I'm sure you told her the same about me. Please, don't make a scene. I've had enough.'

'Listen to me, listen, and I'll explain everything—'

'Lucio, I don't want to listen any more. I've listened and listened, and all that's happened is that you've made me into a bigger fool than I was to start with. I was just a novelty to you, that's all.'

'No!'

'Yes. Go back to Sylvia, she's going to need you when the police come round.'

'Police?'

'Yes. I should think they'll be coming at any moment. She killed Dave, you see. He didn't leave at all, as we thought.'

'Police? But how do they know?'

'How—?' I had been talking quite calmly, avoiding his eye, but now I looked at him. He had stopped rolling his eyes and running his fingers through his hair, and was now almost ugly with some emotion.

'You knew, didn't you? What was it, did she tell you? She told you and not me? Or – did you help her?'

He stared at me, his face immobile.

'She came to you for help, and you tipped him into the well. That was it, wasn't it? I wondered how she could manage such a big man.'

'I didn't help her,' he said in a low voice. 'She helped me.'

'You did it?'

Lucio nodded.

'Why?'

He was silent.

'I think he wanted to die,' he said at last.

'Wanted? You think someone who's tired of Santorno is tired of life? Don't play games. Why?'

'He killed Gabriella.'

'You told me she died in a car accident. Everyone knows that. I saw the car myself.'

'She killed herself because she was going to have his child.'

'How do you know?'

'He told me, the night of the party.'

Lucio paused and went to the door, shutting it. We sat down at opposite ends of the table.

'The night of the party, Dave and I went for a walk together down the road. I wanted to talk to him. I hadn't seen him since Gabriella died and he'd moved in with Izzy, though I hadn't connected the two things. My parents were being – well, you've seen how they are. They don't talk to each other. It didn't matter so much before, because Gabriella and I had had each other, and then Dave and Sylvia. They were like parents, in a way, as well as friends.

I never thought Dave – it never crossed my mind that there could be anything else.

'I noticed, when I was away on military service, there was a sort of gap, an absence. I told you how it is with twins, they feel each other there. It's different from any other relationship with two people. You're jealous of Sylvia, but it's Gabriella you'd have resented, if she had lived. All my other girlfriends did.'

I looked at him, and he shrugged slightly. 'It's why there wasn't anyone else in Santorno, you know.'

'Apart from me and Sylvia.'

'Yes. The Sylvia thing happened later, just before Christmas. I felt bad about it; it was one of the things I wanted to discuss with him that night. I knew it was all over between them, but I wanted to be sure ...'

'You wanted to ask his blessing?' I said sarcastically. 'Or compare technique?'

He smiled faintly.

'No. I didn't need either of those. I suppose I just wanted to be sure we could still be friends. He was the only person I could talk to here, really talk. Even Gabriella. You're from London, you don't understand what it's like, growing up in a small town. You know everyone, they all know you, and yet none of them really know you ... How can you try to be something more, someone bigger, when people don't believe it? People laugh at the dreams of those they know well.'

I thought of my family. 'I see ... '

'You do, don't you?' he said, his face lighting up. 'You've always seen, that's what's so wonderful. Dave saw, too, but not in the same way. I mean, he understood about people, but he didn't like them, as you do.'

Did I like people, in general? I rather doubted it, even if I had learned to tolerate them better.

The clock struck three quarters past the hour.

'I think he felt that knowledge gave him power over people. He would be so sympathetic, he'd worm all their secrets out of them, and then ... '

'Then what?'

'Use them. Make them do what he wanted, like puppets. Sylvia hated him, really, but she couldn't leave. He had a way of seeing things that was so strong. When he concentrated on you, you forgot everything else, as if his way of seeing the world was the only one. Even that old witch in the palazzo fell under his spell.'

'That can't be why you killed him.'

'In a way. I think it was why Sylvia helped, why neither of us regrets it.

'Once he'd decided he was going to have Gabriella, she didn't stand a chance. She was a virgin, you know, like you; if you'd met her, you'd think now you were older. He told me he felt like a pederast, she was so innocent. It was only now and again, when he felt bored and wanted a different kind of fuck, he said.

'I like to think she was happy while it lasted, but I doubt it. Sylvia told me he liked – unnatural things. No woman consents to that, unless forced. But somehow she became pregnant.'

'She tried to have an abortion. Mimi told me.'

'Did she? I didn't know. I thought she hadn't told anyone except him, and later my parents, that she was pregnant. She knew, you see, that he and Sylvia weren't married. He told her; so to her, there wasn't any reason why he shouldn't marry her. Except that if he was going to marry anyone she had to have money, like Izzy.'

'Did he tell you all this on your walk?'

'Most of it. I started to talk about Gabriella. My parents managed to get the pregnancy hushed up at the inquest. They wouldn't talk about it, not even among ourselves. He told me it was his. It hadn't even crossed my mind that it might be. Sylvia and he hadn't been able to have children; I didn't know then that it was because she had had gonorrhoea, a long time ago. We thought it was him. I think he did too. He was almost boasting of it. Not that he was interested in children, like an Italian man, but he said – he said—'

'What?'

'He said he'd sodomized her so many times, it must have crept in by mistake. That was when I began hitting him.' Lucio fell silent. The clock struck four, but I couldn't move.

'I must have hit him with the torch in my hand. He fell down right away, and the light went out, but I went on. Over and over. I knew I should stop, but I couldn't. I couldn't, Emma. I only stopped when Sylvia came.'

'I remember, when you came back, you said you felt faint.'

'I puked my guts out. She was the one who was quite calm.'

'Did you tell her why?'

He shook his head.

'Why not?'

'She thought I did it for her. So she could have the house.'

'And you didn't tell her, later?'

'No. But she used it to make me keep on with her.'

I sighed, and stood up. I didn't believe him. Oh, she might have threatened him, but there had been no reluctance about what I had witnessed last night, and he knew it.

'Emma, you must believe me. I love you. Sylvia is just a kind of addiction. I hate myself every time I fuck her, whereas with you it's ... I tried to make you become like her, this summer; I thought that if I could make you beg for me, frightened of me, then I would be free of both of you, but I can't. I love you, not her. Last night was the last time. I told her it would be.'

'Lucio, it's no good.'

'What do you mean?'

'I'm sorry about the mess, and the police and everything, but it's no good. It's your problem. I'm leaving in less than an hour.'

He clutched at my arm. I tried not to recoil in loathing. 'You can't leave me, not now. Don't you see, I need you?'

'I'm sure you and Sylvia can work something out to tell the police. Let me go, Lucio. I've got to meet the English *professore* at the station.'

'You're leaving with him?'

'Yes.'

He drew back and looked at me sideways, like a bird. 'You're in love with him, aren't you?'

I began to deny it, automatically, and then I shut my mouth.

Lucio laughed, shortly. 'So that's why you were never quite there with me. There's no need to open and close your mouth like a fish. You've been in love with him for months, haven't you?'

'I didn't know.'

'Come on, women always know such things! You've only got

344

to look at a man to think of love, just as we've only got to look at a woman to think of sex.'

'I didn't know. I thought I hated him.'

'Good. Go on hating, because he's not going to have you.'

'What do you mean?' I asked, frightened, edging round the table.

'I told you before, if you try to leave me, I'll kill you. I told you that. It's your own fault if you didn't believe me. I'll never let you go to another man. I've already killed once, there's nothing to stop me doing it again.'

'Don't be silly,' I said, trying to be reasonable. 'You'd never get away with it this time.'

'Wouldn't I? You're all packed up to leave, just like Dave. It would be weeks before they found out.'

I began to shake.

'That's right,' he whispered, coming closer. 'Feel it, that fear. It goes right through you, like music.'

He put his strong square hands round my neck.

'If you kill me,' I croaked, 'you'll never have me again.'

'No, but he won't either,' Lucio said, smiling.

I could see the yellow rays of his eyes, the black pupil contracting. Shock had paralysed me, but now I began to struggle as he squeezed. It hurt, it hurt like anything. I could feel all the bones in my throat. I was choking. I tried to prise his fingers away, but they were like a vice, so I tried to kick him instead. He moved away, releasing his grip infinitesimally so I caught a whoop of air, then went on. I clawed at his face, but he just smiled. I am strong, but I had never realized before how much stronger a man is, especially a madman.

I had seen him look like this before: the blank, smiling snarl when he had been inside me, and I could feel that he was hard as a bar of iron, pressing against me. If only something would distract him, I thought. I couldn't see anything but black

345

stars, not even his eyes. We were both silent, struggling and gasping. My bladder burst suddenly, soaking my shorts with warm liquid.

Oh, Mummy, I prayed, forgetting everyone, even Andrew.

Then there was a rattling noise. The string of my necklace had broken and the pearls fell on the floor. Lucio jerked his head up, lost balance and slipped on the wet tiles bringing me down on top of him.

I fell heavily on his groin, gasping for air. He gave a high, thin scream, and curled into a foetal shape, releasing me. I dragged myself up and into the doorway, holding the door for support. Something thin and hard got in the way. I dragged the key out as I heard him start to rise and closed the door on him just in time. He pulled and pulled until I thought my arms would crack, while I tried to put the key back in the lock and turn it. My hands shook so much, it took three attempts, but I turned it, before staggering to the stairs.

I could hear him rattling and punching the door, but it wouldn't give. My throat ached, my legs felt boneless with fright, but I knew I had to get out. The suitcase was no good, I had to go right away before he broke the door down. I could hear him now, trying to lift it off its hinges.

I got to the glass door at the bottom as there was a crack and a loud thump. Another key, get it out, quick, lock it the other side. I could see his coloured shadow rushing up the other side of the wavy glass, as though through water.

I thought I was safe for a second, then there was another crack, and the thick glass crazed. He was going to punch his fist through. It came at the door, leaving a blot of blood on the glass, but still it didn't shatter.

I screamed then, and Marga Pistoia rushed out of her kitchen.

'What's happening?' she demanded.

'He's trying to kill me. Oh, God!'

346

Lucio's shape had disappeared back up the stairs. He's going to come down by the kitchen balcony, I thought.

'Don't let him past you,' I said, pushing her out of my way.

'My husband's out,' she bleated. 'What shall I do?'

I was too frightened to stop, or feel sorry for her. Keep going on, keep going down, don't stop concentrating or you'll miss a step. Past the camphorated bedrooms, past the shrouded *salotto* on the first floor. The sound of voices, arguing. Down through the garage, the reek of petrol making me sick again. A shriek from Marga Pistoia, and the sound of something soft, falling. Footsteps on the stairs, like my nightmares, but coming down instead of up. Don't listen. The big, heavy front door within the door. Open, open. A crack of afternoon light, widening. Don't panic, press the latch down, anything to delay him. Footsteps coming faster now. Drag it closed, quickly.

Bang. I was out in the street, on one side of the door, and Lucio was on the other.

27

I ran. Down the Vicolo delle Sette Stelle, across the Via Garibaldi, down the Bocca del Lupo, bypassing the main piazza, and down again. I was too frightened to think of anything except keeping moving. Down, down, twisting and turning like a hare before a dog, to where the alley joined the Via del Ospedale. I didn't know whether he was following, I couldn't hear anything except the sound of my own footsteps and the bang of blood in my ears.

It was an effort to breathe. My throat was parched. My arms and legs chafed with sweat. The town clock struck four fifteen, and I was astonished, in a dim sort of way – that I might have been dead by now.

I thought of Andrew saying that people didn't normally scream and shout and try to kill each other. Oh, but they do in Italy. They do all over the place, if you only look. But most people don't; they don't believe the evidence of their own eyes and ears, and even if they do, they don't want to be involved in someone else's nightmare. They prefer to believe that it doesn't exist.

I passed under the southern gate. The plain below shook before my eyes, but not from heat this time. The tarred road was hard, jarring my spine. I tried to keep my head steady, to breathe evenly. My throat hurt, my heart hurt, my lungs hurt, my feet. One of my leather flip-flops had broken in Via Garibaldi, and I kicked the other away.

A screeching of brakes made me look up for a split second. Lucio's car was coming down Via del Ospedale.

The chink of the path to the lower town was so narrow, I almost ran past it. It was like running on knives. Flints and fragments of gravel rolled underfoot. I didn't dare look behind, in case he was following, but then I heard more revving and squealing as he reversed. He was going to catch me at the intersection, I thought, increasing speed. I had to get past it before he did, to be at the railway station.

My legs were scissoring out of control now, in huge strides. Everything ahead was a blur. In so far as I could think at all, I thought of Andrew, waiting, dragging me like a magnet.

I thought I would die from the pain of running. It was not love or fear that kept me going, it was will. Emotion is the luxury of the amateur. I must go on, I must go on. If I ran fast enough, I could even outstrip fatigue. I ran. Nothing existed except running and breathing, breathing and running. Even the pain in my feet and heart had ceased to matter.

I don't know how I avoided treading on the snake. It was pouring itself across the path like a trickle of brown water, until I came up on it.

We both froze, motionless.

I almost laughed. Of all the times to come across a phobia, this had to be the worst. Its whole body was tensed, corded with muscle like a whip about to fly through the air. I could see its tiny black eye, like a dot of caviar, looking at me. Its pointed head was half lifted, the forked tongue flickering in and out, in and out.

I blinked; and then the snake put its head down and was pouring away, into the ditch and up the stone wall, as a little scooter bumped and snarled down the path.

I couldn't run any more. Heat had caught up with me, and my knees felt like jelly. I doubled over, gasping. My limbs were bright red beneath the brown, and the veins stood out on my hands and feet. To think there were people who actually ran for fun.

The scooter stopped. If it was Lucio, I thought, he could get on with it. I had no more strength to resist.

'You'd better get on,' said Maria, 'or you'll miss the train.'

'Lucio—'

'I know. I came through the town. The whole place is in uproar. Marga Pistoia has telephoned the police.'

'He's trying to catch me,' I said. 'Maria, he may even be there now, at the crossroads.'

'Hold on tight.'

She started the scooter, and I put my arms round her waist, clinging. We began to bump downhill, faster and faster, everything squeaking and rattling. I shut my eyes, too frightened to look. Brambles and vines whipped past, slashing arms and legs. Faster and faster, faster and faster, it felt as though we were flying through the air. Maria's bun came down and streamed across my mouth and nose, soft as smoke.

I didn't see what happened as we shot out across the main road. There was a silence as the stone walls opened out and the flints changed to tar for a split second. Then a screeching, mangling shriek of metal on metal, followed by a muffled cough and a blast of heat. I thought we had crashed, but the motion of the scooter went on. I opened my eyes.

'What happened?'

'There has been an accident,' said Maria. 'The Ferranti boy and Pistoia have collided with each other. They were going too fast in opposite directions when we came out.'

I turned and looked. A wall of flame was shooting up behind us, and the whole of Santorno wavered behind it like a mirage.

'Do you think they're dead?'

'Perhaps.'

'Oh, God.'

Maria pointed ahead, and there, at the edge of the plain, I saw the express train coming.

'It will only stop at Santorno for three minutes,' she said. 'If you hesitate now, you will miss the *professore*. There are others coming. Listen.'

There was a sound of sirens winding down the hill: ambulance, police, or fire brigade. The train below was slowing down, and it was still the size of a toy beneath us.

'It is fate, my daughter. The mother of Ferranti was cursed, long ago. She went with the Germans during the war, and she betrayed the Count, his son, Guido's parents, and my own parents and grandparents. She found a way into the palazzo, and she would go there, with her men; and that was how she discovered that the Count and his son had not left. They organized the Resistance in these parts, the little resistance there was in that shameful time; and she betrayed them all, out of greed and revenge for her own father. She thought she had escaped, she married a foreigner when none here would have her, but now she is punished.'

The train was out of sight now, sunk below trees and buildings as we hurtled towards it. The first houses of the industrial zone flashed past us.

Was it true what Maria had just told me? I did not know what to believe. Had Lucio killed another man, and been killed or maimed for life, simply in order to cause his mother grief? Was retribution so convoluted, so careless of innocents like Gabriella, for that to be justice?

We began to slow, with a screeching of brakes. The supermarkets and factories of Santorno went past, and the pebble-dashed villas with their concrete eagles and little dwarfs

351

on the gate posts and the Christmas tree planted in the front garden. There was rubbish tumbling through the streets, and cars, plastic, and all the detritus of modern life which I had so abhorred. And there, at the end, was the railway station, with the express train waiting.

'Goodbye, my daughter,' said Maria.

I got down stiffly, and for an instant she gave me a quick, fierce hug. The guard whistled, and the heavy doors began to slam, one after another, all the way up the train.

'Run!'

The guard whistled again, and then the train gave a hoot and a hiss of air. Only one door was left open now, directly across the station entrance, and the guard was trying to close it, arguing with Andrew. I gave a sort of croak, and he looked up and saw me. Straight across the tracks I ran, while the stationmaster bellowed, the guard whistled, and the door swung closed.

'Jump,' Andrew shouted, leaning out of the window, as the train began to move. I ran alongside on the platform, not understanding.

'Jump!' he yelled again.

I saw, then, that there was no more platform left, and then I saw nothing except his face.

He caught me, somehow, and dragged me through the window. I collapsed in a heap at his feet.

'You,' he said, 'are really the most terrible nuisance.'

'You've dragged half my hair out,' I said, tears pouring down my face and on to the ridged metal floor.

'I thought you weren't going to come, after all.'

'I very nearly didn't.'

'But now you have.'

'Yes,' I said, looking up. He smiled.

I didn't know what to say to him. I didn't know what he

really thought about me, or how he felt; whether he was bored by me, or irritated, or amused in the wrong way. It's so hard, learning to see yourself as you really are, let alone the way you hope to be. If life were like 'La Bohème', he would have said something, done something, and that would have been that; but all he did was hold out his hand. I did not even shake when I took it, and stood up. I knew now I was a fool; and the least fools can do is try to behave.

The train picked up speed. We went back to his compartment. It had six wide seats upholstered in green plush, with little white linen antimacassars. The evening sun came through the wide plate-glass windows. There was a faint whistle of air conditioning. It was very quiet.

We sat down, facing each other. How will I live with this? I thought. How will I not betray myself by grovelling at his feet? Will he do anything? Will I? What will happen when I get to Oxford and have to sit in this man's presence, once a week, for an hour, for three years? What does he feel?

I looked at his face, rediscovering its planes and curves: the high forehead, the fine nose, the deep, curving eyelids, the long fastidious mouth, and wondered how I could ever have thought Lucio beautiful, how I could ever have loved anyone else. But perhaps one always thinks that, every time.

'Did you sort things out?' he asked.

'Yes,' I said.

'Good.'

'I'm afraid I don't have any money. I don't have anything except my passport.'

'Not even your necklace?'

'Not even that.'

He smiled, and I smiled back, until he looked away. Say that you'll think of some other way for me to repay you, I thought. Do what most men would do. Say it.

353

He reached up into the suitcase overhead. 'Here. Read.' He tossed a paperback at me. It was called *Rasselas, Prince of Abyssinia*.

I took the book, but I did not open it. Not yet, not yet.

I looked out of the window at the landscape drifting back into winter. There were lines of dark cypress, and silver groves with nightingales; there were orchards, and farms, and little white dusty roads, and shining rivers, and white, bare patches up above, which seem artificial in paintings but which do indeed exist. There were vineyards, and poplar trees and forests with wild boar up in the mountains; there were hills, undulating like the bodies of gigantic deities. There were castles and towns, there were windows blinding in the evening sun. All going, going, gone, to be remembered in shadows only, or in uneasy dreams; as they say one cannot remember pain, once it is over.